Lessons
of the
Heart

a novel

Kendra
The greatest lesson to
learn is love

Jodie Larson

JODIE LARSON

Cover Design by Murphy Rae at Indie Solutions by Murphy Rae
www.murphyrae.net

Interior Design by Champagne Formats
www.champagneformats.com

Editor: Melinda Utendorf

ISBN-13: 978-1522810117
ISBN-10: 1522810110

I truly believe that everything that we do and everyone that we meet is put in our path for a purpose. There are no accidents; we're all teachers – if we're willing to pay attention to the lessons we learn, trust our positive instincts and not be afraid to take some risks or wait for some miracle to come knocking at our door.

– *Marla Gibbs*

One

"WHY DO I FEEL LIKE I'M PULLING TEETH TO GET you to go to this party? You should have some fun before we're too old to enjoy it."

I shut my book and sigh. "It's not that I'm opposed to partying. I just don't actively want to participate in the stupidity of our generation. Is it so wrong to sit at home and read a book or study to get good grades in school?"

Penny stops pacing and raises an eyebrow. "*The stupidity of our generation*? Really? What are you, eighty?"

Her comment makes me laugh. "I'm just saying that going out and getting wasted is not my idea of a good time."

"But it's senior year. It's our last chance to be stupid and crazy before we enter the real world."

I rise from my bed and walk over to the window that overlooks our backyard. It's mid-September and the chill of autumn is in full force. A cold gust of wind pushes against the window, making it moan with the sudden assault. Autumn in Connecticut is supposedly the most beautiful time of the year. The trees are beginning to turn, leaving their green hue for a more golden yellow with red and orange scattered in there.

Penny comes up and wraps her arms around me before giving me a supporting squeeze. "Please, Britta? For one night, I want you to forget about getting good grades or preparing to be the world's greatest doctor. Be reckless." She pauses before pulling out the big guns. "You don't want me to celebrate our mutual birthday alone, do you?"

I glance over my shoulder. "You really know how to lay on the guilt, don't you?"

Penny presses a kiss to my cheek. "It's my special talent. Besides, I told everyone to be there for our party so you have to come."

I pat her arm and lean my head against hers. "What would I do without you?"

"Die of boredom?"

I laugh and retake my position on the bed. "Probably."

"Who knows, maybe Chase will be there."

I scrunch my nose. "Ugh, I hope not. That boy will not take a hint."

Penny laughs. "What can I say? The boy loves you."

Chase Woodward and I have been friends since first grade. Sometime around puberty, things started to change and Chase was beginning to act differently around me. It's been a fight to keep him at arm's length, but who wants to be in a relationship with someone who hasn't quite matured past the age of twelve?

"Maybe I'll get lucky and he won't show up."

Penny tosses a pillow in the air next to me. "Or you'll go there and fall madly in love with him and his boyish charms."

I grab the pillow. "Gee, thanks, *friend*."

"I can just see you both at our ten-year reunion, all married with babies everywhere…"

WHACK! A pillow to her face.

We fall all over each other in a fit of laughter.

A knock comes at my door, and my brother, Liam, walks in, grinning a sideways smile toward Penny.

"And just what is going on in here? Shouldn't there be an Enigma song playing and the both of you in your underwear?" He pauses for a moment. "Well, maybe just Penny."

I roll my eyes and launch the pillow at his head. "Get out of my room, perv!"

Liam ignores me and walks into my room. He sits on the chair at my desk and gives Penny a once over.

"So Pen, how's it going?"

She leans back on her arms in a casual yet seductive pose. "It's going well, Liam. How's it hanging in your world?"

"Long and strong, baby. Long and strong."

I make gagging noises. "Could you be any more inappropriate?"

Both of them laugh. Liam has had a crush on Penny for as long as I can remember. He would always try to be in the room with us, even if we were doing something he hated. He used to flick stuff at her or lightly tease her about some silly rumor going around the school. I think the day I knew for sure was in junior high when he beat up Chad Lortimer after making her cry.

"Don't be like that, little sis," he says, giving me his puppy dog eyes.

"Those eyes only work for people who aren't me. Now, is there anything I can help you with, before you can *leave*?"

"I need to get going anyway," Penny says. "My mom said if I'm late coming home again she's going to flip her shit."

Penny stands and stretches her arms above her head. Liam ogles her as his eyes fall upon the flash of skin at her stomach that's now visible. It makes me want to throw another pillow at him.

I stand and hug her, making sure I block Liam's view. "Call me later?"

Penny pulls away and nods. "Definitely. We have plans to make. You won't be sorry! Bye, Britta. Bye, Liam." She waves and lets her long red hair hang over her shoulder. He waves back and watches her walk out. I close the door behind her and glare at him.

He gives me an innocent look "What did I do now?"

I smack him on his shoulder before taking my perch back on my bed. "Stop ogling my best friend. It's creepy, and it's not going to happen."

"Never say never."

"What do you want?"

"You're going out with Penny tomorrow?" he asks, his voice tinged with nerves.

I cock my head to the side and narrow my eyes. "Yeah. Why?"

He looks nervous as he picks at his jeans and flicks off some invisible lint. "Will you call me if you need a ride or anything like that? It's just...I know how these high school parties can go...."

"This isn't the first time we've been out before. Besides, would you willingly let your baby sister and the woman of your obsession go out into the cold, dark night and have unspeakable things happen to them?"

"Fuck no. That's why I'm asking you to call me in case things get out of control. You know I would never let anything happen to you or Penny."

I sigh. "Yeah, I know. But we'll be okay. And if things get uncomfortable or weird, you'll be the first person I call. Deal?"

"Deal."

Liam visibly relaxes and it makes me smile. He may only be sixteen months older than I am, but I swear we're more like twins. And it's sweet that he cares so much about the both of us. I don't know what I'd do without him.

A muffled beep comes from his pocket and he pulls out his phone. He types something across the screen before locking it again. "Gotta go. Douchenozzle is waiting for me."

I roll my eyes. "Why do you hang out with him if he's a douchenozzle?"

He shrugs. "Cause he works at a strip joint and has the connections to, you know…"

I jam my fingers in my ears and squeeze my eyes shut. "Don't want to hear it."

He ruffles my hair on his way out and closes the door behind him. I lie on my stomach, looking at the pictures that line the head of my bed. There's a picture of Penny and me when we camped in the backyard. We couldn't have been more than seven or eight. Several from our combined family vacation to Boston; one after Penny had just caught a foul ball at Fenway. But my favorite one is from the winter formal last year of us looking perfectly elegant and happy.

Penny's right. This is our senior year. It's our last year to enjoy our adolescence, be a little reckless before being thrust into the adult world.

Except I am ready for adulthood. I pick up my book and try to distract myself from wondering just what exactly I'm getting myself into.

Two

"DID YOU HEAR THE NEWS?" Penny asks me, linking her arm through mine.

"Probably not. I get all my gossip from you and since this is the first time I've seen you all morning I'm out of the loop."

She steers us to our lockers before propping herself against it. "Mr. Ward was fired last night."

I shut my locker with slightly more force than I intended to. "Are you kidding me? Why? I loved him."

Penny shrugs. "Word on the street is he was caught having sex with a student."

I turn and my jaw drops. "No way! Who? I mean, not that Mr. Ward isn't handsome, but he's just, I don't know…"

"Old? Unfunny? Flaccid?"

I snort at her last comment. "Gross. I don't know. He always seemed to be so friendly to everyone."

"Obviously a little too friendly."

"Who was it? Do you know?"

She shakes her head. "No one has said who, but I checked the absentee list at the office this morning and Krista Baker was listed."

"Oh my God, she is such a skank. That would totally be right up her alley. He was probably failing her and she needed some extra credit."

"That's my guess too."

Penny slams her locker and checks her watch. "You going to American Lit now?" I ask her.

She groans loudly, making a few heads turn in the process. "Fuck, don't remind me. The witch has it out for me and I'm supposed to give my speech today on F. Scott Fitzgerald."

"Did you read *The Great Gatsby* like you were supposed to?"

"Pfft. Why read the book when there's a movie out?"

I pause outside the door and give her a sideways glance. "Which one?"

"Duh, the one with Leo in it."

"Good luck. That one isn't true to the book. Half of it is way off the mark and the parts that are close aren't even worth it."

Penny steps into the doorway. "I'll be okay. You know me. I can always talk myself out of a situation."

I pat her on the shoulder. "That you can. See you later, crazy."

We wave goodbye and I head to the teacher's lounge for my fourth-period class. Since I didn't want to take two study halls, I volunteered to be a teacher's assistant instead. Mrs. Davis refused my volunteer work because she said it wouldn't show up on my transcript. So for two hours each day I'm her assistant, doing all the stuff that she hates doing. Not that I mind grading papers or creating tests. It's actually quite fun. I love the fact that I get to be away from the prying eyes of the student body and the gossip that always fills the halls, even if it's only for a few hours.

Gossip, like poor Mr. Ward. I highly doubt he would have slept with a student. Because let's face it, Penny's description of him was dead on. He was a middle-aged man with a receding hairline and a mild beer gut. Not exactly someone that I would lay my academic career on the line for. That sort of stigma stays with you forever.

I pull out the chair to my desk and open the grade book, entering in the numbers from the last few assignments over all her classes. Each pile is separated out by period and alphabetized so I can find everything quickly. Yes, I'm kind of a stickler for that, the need to have everything in a place so it can be found. There's a reason why the place exists. Neat and tidy and in order is how I prefer things. Otherwise, it's chaos. And chaos and I do not get along well.

After a half hour, I stretch my neck, getting a small kink in it after hunching over the book without moving. There's murmuring down the hall from a couple teachers who usually take their lunch break at this time.

"Did you hear about Adam? So sad but really it was kind of stupid on his part," someone says.

"I heard he was sleeping with a student."

"No, that's a lie. He wasn't sleeping with a student. He was sleeping with Garrett's wife."

I silently gasp as I eavesdrop on the conversation. Holy shit, Mr. Ward was sleeping with the principal's wife? No wonder he was fired.

"No! With Melissa?"

"Yep. They ran off together when Garrett confronted them. I guess he saw them having dinner and waited until they were done. Followed them to Adam's house and that's where it all went down."

"Wow. Just when you think you know a guy."

"I know. Too bad."

I tune the harpies out, going back to my work until I hear the bell for the end of the fifth period. Gathering up the assignment book, I start walking back toward Mrs. Davis's desk when I run into something. I sprawl on the floor, my ass pounding in discomfort as the papers and book skitter away from me.

"Damn," I mutter to myself.

That's when I start to look up and see it wasn't a something I ran into but a some*one*. A really tall someone. A really *hand-some* someone with green eyes and a head full of disheveled brown hair. My throat tightens and my heart beats just a smidge faster as I look up from my squatted position.

"Are you okay? I'm so sorry. I didn't see you there," he says as he reaches down to grab my hand.

I place my shaking hand in his and am amazed how tightly he grips me. Not painful but strong, sure, almost as if he was meant to always hold my hand. The fit of our hands is perfect with just the right amount of symmetry.

"Yeah I'm fine," I grunt as he pulls me off the floor. I brush the dust off my jeans and sweater.

"It's my fault. I wasn't paying attention to where I was going and then I got turned around back here. It's kind of a maze."

"I hear you there. It took me a while to figure it out my first time back here. Are you new?"

He gives me a smile that has my heart skipping a beat. *Whoa. That's a strange reaction.*

"I will be. I start on Monday, so I was just kind of wandering around trying to find stuff. I guess I got lost."

I laugh, and his smile widens. "I guess you did. Well, what are you looking for? Maybe I can help point you in the right direction."

He pulls out a piece of paper from his pocket and studies it for a second. While he's looking over the paper, I take the moment to examine him further. He's tall but not overly tall, and lean but not skinny. The long-sleeved shirt he's wearing shows off enough to let me know he takes care of himself. Not buff but definitely muscular, judging from the way his body narrows at the waist. And he looks good in jeans. Really good. Damn good. Like the boy-next-door good.

I shake my head, shameful of where my thoughts were going. I have no idea who this guy is or how he ended up back in the teacher's lounge. But if he's a new student starting Monday I need to find out what classes he has. Maybe this school year can be salvaged after all.

"I'm looking for Mr. Herman's office. Someone told me it was back this way."

I shake my head. "No, not back here. He's in the main office, next to Mr. Leonard's office. Mr. Herman is the vice principal."

He rolls his eyes and it makes me smile. It's nice to know I'm not the only person who does that anymore.

"Of course. I should have known that." He looks around for an exit and returns my gaze with wide eyes. "So how do I get out of here?"

"This way," I say trying to suppress my giggle. I place the grade book and papers on Mrs. Davis's desk and show the good-looking stranger the way out of the lounge.

"Why do they make this so confusing?" he asks.

"It's difficult to say. My guess is so students don't go wandering back here without permission. Unless you're back there all the time, you never know whose office is whose or the way to get out without losing your mind."

"I've seen labyrinths that were easier to navigate than this."

I laugh and he smiles again at me. "Supposedly when the school got remodeled they forgot to add the teacher's offices. So it was a last minute thing, throwing together walls behind this study room, hiding it from the students prying eyes."

"So the teachers have an office and a classroom?"

I nod. "Yep. It's better that way really. This way the students can't break into the desks in the classrooms and change their grades and stuff like that."

"Good idea."

He's wearing some sort of cologne and it smells like heaven. And it's not overpowering like some of the other guys around the school. Walking near them is like walking by the Abercrombie store, just makes your head instantly hurt. But his is subtle, blending perfectly into him and whatever pheromones he's giving off, making him that much more appealing.

"So this is the main office. They'll be able to help you out with anything else."

I look down at my boots and scuff them against the floor. For some reason, I don't want to leave. I'm not sure why, though. Maybe because I don't know his name yet.

"Thanks for your help, um. I'm sorry, I guess I never got your name."

I laugh and hold my hand out to him. "Britta."

"James."

He takes my hand again and another round of tingles travels between our fingers. The sudden jolt of electricity surprises me, and I pull my hand back abruptly. James looks down at me with a slight concern on his face, but I force a smile, trying to play off my strange reaction.

The bell rings again and I start backing away. "I better get going to class. Guess I'll see you around."

He nods and flashes one last smile in my direction as I back away. "Guess I will. Nice meeting you."

I quickly turn and half-run down the hall toward my locker to retrieve my books for next period, which I'm already late for. But my sixth-period class I'm supposed to have Mr. Ward and obviously he won't be there today so I think I may have a reprieve from punishment.

As Mrs. Malloy warbles on and on about something that she's reading directly out of the textbook, I can't help but daydream about James. It's been a while since someone has started my heart beating like this again. Okay, so I've never really had that rush of emotions toward a guy, making me all stupid and lovesick. Yeah, I've had a few boyfriends and some of them quasi-serious, one lasting a whole six months. But nothing permanent.

Boys are a distraction I don't need. My only focus this year is passing all my courses and graduating at the top of my class.

"Hey, Britt?" Chase leans over and whispers to me.

"What?"

"You going to the party tonight?"

"Yeah."

"Cool. Want to hang out while we're there?"

I look around trying to find Penny, who is all the way on the other side of the room making goo-goo eyes at Travis Fishman. Gross.

"Why not," I reply, putting as much enthusiasm into it as I can.

"Awesome. You look nice today, by the way," he says, still leaning over.

"Chase?"

"Yeah?"

"I'm trying to figure out what she's saying. I'll talk to you tonight."

He nods and leans back into his chair, leaving me alone again. Thank God. Now I just need to decipher what Mrs. Malloy is talking about because somehow I have a feeling it has nothing to do with the topography of Europe.

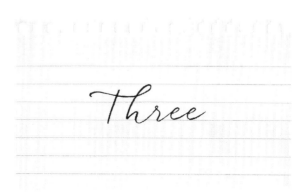

Three

S I WRAP THE FINAL LOCK OF HAIR AROUND MY curling iron, I sigh as I look at my reflection. After watching numerous YouTube videos about how to do the smoky eye and pouty lip, I think I've captured it. My shirt is dressy but casual with the infinity scarf wrapped around me and my skinny jeans are actually behaving themselves for once.

"Damn girl you look hot!" Penny exclaims from the hall behind me.

"Shut up."

"No seriously dude. Smoking hot."

I look over at her as I unplug the iron and lightly spray on my favorite perfume. She's dressed to kill with her destroyed skinny jeans, off the shoulder shirt showing her electric-green bra strap, and messy side ponytail at the nape of her neck. She can pull off stylish better than anyone I know.

"Speak for yourself. Looking good as always. Whose heart are you breaking tonight?"

Penny smirks and leans against the doorjamb. "I was thinking about Travis, but I'm willing to keep my options open."

I head to my room, with Penny following closely behind. "Yeah I saw you making eyes at him in class today. But really, Travis Fishman?"

She shrugs and sits on my bed while I dig out my boots from the closet. "What? He's hot, he's the captain of the football team, and I'm pretty sure he wants me."

I roll my eyes. "Exactly the kind of qualities you should look for in a solid relationship."

"Bitch."

"Love you." I blow an air kiss and she sticks out her tongue.

Liam walks into my room. Of course, his Penny radar is perfect as always.

"Sexy lady...and Britt."

"Munch," I reply, zipping up my boots.

Liam looks over at Penny like she's a shiny new toy. She loves getting attention, and even more so when it's from him.

"Wow Pen, looking hot tonight. You sure you want to go out with her?" he says as he leans against the door.

She raises an eyebrow to him. "Why? You have a better idea?"

He clicks his tongue and nods. "Oh yeah. A way better idea. One that will take you on a ride you'll never forget."

"And now we need to leave," I announce, putting the seduction scene to a halt.

Liam shakes his head and laughs. "God you are such a pill, Britt. I'm just having some fun."

I look over to Penny and don't miss the wince that crosses her face.

"Well, we're off to have some fun of our own. Don't wait up," I sing as we pass him.

He shakes his head and follows us out.

"Britta, remember! Home by one o'clock, please," my mom says from the couch.

My dad puts in his two cents "No taking rides from strangers either. Liam said he'd pick you up."

"Yes, yes I know, but thank you for reminding me." I throw on a light jacket and turn to Penny. "Ready?"

"As I'll ever be," she says. "Goodnight Mr. and Mrs. Fosse."

"Have fun, girls. Be safe," my mom says as I shut the door.

Liam follows us down the driveway and stops at his car. "I've got my phone on me if you need me."

"Don't worry, we won't need you. Where are you headed off to?"

"Douchenozzle's place. We're going to play some poker and the new Call of Duty game Vince just picked up," he says, swinging his keys around his index finger.

"Wow, and you call me a pill? Fun."

"Shut up." He looks over at Penny as she climbs into my car.

"Don't worry. She'll be fine," I whisper.

"Just watch her please? And try not to let her go home with anyone."

"No promises but I'll do my best. Thanks, Liam." I hug him quick and climb into my car.

As we pull up in front of Travis's house, I can see the street is lined with dozens of cars. Thumping music wafts out from the open door.

Immediately I feel on edge. "Wow, this party is huge. What time did it start?" I ask, shutting the car off.

"An hour ago maybe?" She checks her watch and shrugs her shoulders. "Maybe he started early."

"Who knows? It's Travis and his parents are out of town

for the weekend. He probably started the minute he got home from the game. Hell, people probably started partying during the game."

"Probably. But it's our night tonight so let's go party!" Penny loudly exclaims, throwing her arms in the air.

As we get inside, I spot our group of friends. After we push through the throng, we get to Cami and Dez, who are chatting animatedly with Drake and Lyle. They pause to wave us over. Penny rushes toward the girls and flings her arms around them in greeting.

"You made it! Happy birthday, bitches!" Cami yells and hugs me tightly.

"Thanks, Cam." I point at their red Solo cups. "You guys already started?"

"Yep. The punch is in the kitchen and the keg is in the basement."

"Dare I ask?" Penny asks before taking a drink from Drake's glass.

"Coors Light. It's actually decent," he says and then reclaims his cup.

Penny turns to me and shrugs. "What do you want, beer or punch?"

"Neither. How about something diet?"

"Lame!" Dez screams at me. "It's your birthday. Have a shot or seven, in addition to your drink."

I shake my head. "Not big on the shots Dez, you know that."

Lyle drapes his arm around my shoulders. "Come on Britt. You just turned eighteen, right?"

I jab in him the side with my elbow. "Still in high school, still living under my parents' roof. I don't want to be grounded until college."

"Well tough shit, you're drinking tonight," Penny says as

she drags me to the kitchen.

When we get there, she grabs two red plastic cups, fills them with some red concoction, and hands me one.

"Drink and have fun. It's our birthday party. Cheers," she says, clinking her cup to mine.

I take a sip and lean against the center island. "One drink. Remember I'm driving so I can't get drunk."

"We've got Liam to drive us if it gets out of hand. I'm sure he'd be willing to bring us back to pick up your car tomorrow morning."

I take a sip and contemplate my actions. According to Liam, he paved the way for me to be slightly crazy without Mom and Dad going overboard. And it helps that they trust me and my judgment.

I've never actually been drunk before. But this punch tastes like Cherry Kool-Aid, and that's bad.

I whip out my phone and text Liam.

DRINKING THE KOOL-AID. NEED A RIDE.

NO PROB. BE THERE AT 12:45. U OWE ME.

I let Penny know about Liam.

"WOO!" she says, way too loudly. "All right! Time to party!"

She refills our cups before dragging us back to our little group of friends, huddled over on the couch. Justice and Chase have now joined them and I silently groan to myself. *Not Chase. Can I avoid one person all night or would that be rude?*

"Happy birthday, Britta," Chase says, slinging his arm over my shoulder. I wince as his beer breath falls on my cheek.

"Thanks." I try to wiggle out of his hold, but he doesn't take the hint and moves closer to me. I bump into Justice.

"Happy birthday, Britta," she says, taking a sip from her cup.

"Thanks."

"Anything special planned tonight?"

I shake my head. "Nope."

"Other than I'm getting her plastered," Penny chimes in from the couch.

"Yes, apparently turning eighteen is the magical age to get trashed." I pause. "Oh wait, that's twenty-one."

"So who do you think Mr. Ward slept with? My money is still on Krista Baker," Penny says, finishing off her drink.

"Not Krista. She's too smart for that," Cami slurs.

"Besides, isn't she screwing Wes?" Dez asks.

"That's what I heard, but you never know. Maybe she was failing her class and needed the extra credit," Penny says.

"Like anyone would have sex with Mr. Ward," Lyle says, chugging his beer.

"He wasn't sleeping with anyone at school," I say. Everyone's heads turn toward me as if I've sprouted another one.

"How do you know?" Drake asks.

"I overheard a couple of the teachers talking while I was working on Mrs. Davis's papers. They said that he was sleeping with Mr. Leonard's wife, Melissa."

A collective gasp sounds and then everyone scrunches their faces together.

"Dude, that's messed up," Chase says.

"The principal's wife? Holy ballsy. He really must not have wanted his job," Dez mutters.

"Or he was really in love with her," Cami says.

I shrug my shoulders and finish off my cup. "Either way, it wasn't a student."

"Could you imagine what would happen if a teacher slept with a student? I mean, none of the teachers in the school are that good looking," Penny says.

"There's a few though that could be worth it. Mr. Sanchez

isn't bad. He's got that Latino thing going for him," Dez says with a smile.

"What about Mr. Johnston? He could be hot," Justice adds.

"Yeah, if you add more hair and take off ten years," Penny says back.

"All you girls have it wrong. The teacher to sleep with is Ms. Alpine. She's fucking gorgeous," Lyle says.

The other two guys nod their heads in agreement.

"The only reason you say that is because she's got huge boobs," I respond.

"And? Is there any other reason to have sex with a girl?" Drake wiggles his brows suggestively.

We all laugh and I look down at my empty cup.

"I need more alcohol for this conversation. I'll be back."

As I walk away, Chase catches up. "What are you doing?" I say.

"I just want to spend time with you."

Chase could be considered sweet if someone was attracted to him. He's good looking enough, with that classic All-American high school football charm. But he's just not my type.

"You want to come downstairs with me so I can grab more beer?" he asks, leaning close to me.

I contemplate my answer. I don't want to lead him on, but I have a hard time telling him no.

"I, um…"

"Please, Britt. It's just downstairs. Then we'll come back and join everyone else."

I sigh. "Okay, lead the way."

He smiles and grabs my hand, pulling me through the crowd to the basement. I steady myself on the walk down, holding onto the railing before Chase releases me at the bottom. It seems like the entire school is here. A thin film of smoke hovers at the ceiling and the distinct smell of something that isn't cigarettes assaults my nostrils. Even if I didn't know what it smelled like, the bloodshot eyes and zombie stares would have given it away.

We turn into the laundry room where the keg sits in a bucket of ice. Two guys from the football team are manning it, sitting on bar stools and talking with several busty girls.

"Hey, Britt. Happy Birthday," Travis says.

"Thanks, Trav. Nice party. Thanks for the invite."

"You're welcome. Glad you could make it. Penny with you?" he asks.

I nod. "Yep, she's upstairs with the others. You going to head that way?"

A slow smile creeps onto his face. "Oh yeah, I'm heading that way."

"Well, I'm heading up."

"What about Chase?" he asks. I glance over at Chase and he's deep in a conversation about the game today with the two meatheads manning the keg.

"I think he's all right on his own. Come on, let's get upstairs. The smoke is bothering me."

He nods and we walk back up, weaving through the crowd until we find the group. Penny's face brightens instantly when she sees Travis next to me.

"Hey Trav," she says, batting her eyelashes.

Travis looks her up and down and flashes his panty-dropping smile.

"Hey, Pen. You enjoying yourself?"

Penny stands from the couch and moves next to Travis. "Yeah, this is a great party. So much fun."

While Penny and Travis carry on together, I take her seat next to Dez, thankful that maybe Chase will leave me alone.

Travis starts talking about their win tonight against Fairfield with Penny hanging on his every word. Drake and Lyle join in, giving us the rundown of each play and Dez and Cami join in, giving their intake on it since they're both cheerleaders and watched the whole thing.

Another red cup appears before my eyes and I look up into Chase's smiling face.

"Thought you could use another one," he says.

"Thanks."

I take the cup and place it in my empty one. I watch Travis lean down and whisper something into Penny's ear. She nods and wraps her hand into his, allowing him to lead her away from us and toward the staircase, presumably to his bedroom.

"Someone's getting lucky tonight," Drake says.

"I think that was her plan anyway. She was flirting kind of heavy with him during class today," I say, my words getting thicker. *What in the hell was in that punch?*

Chase moves to sit on the armrest next to me and presses his hand lightly against my shoulder. My body feels heavy and I lean into him, looking for stability. Either that or he's pulling me. I can't tell, due to the haziness of my brain.

The conversations around me turn into muffled noise and my eyelids become increasingly heavier.

"You okay?" Chase whispers in my ear.

I turn my head to him and smile. "I feel good. Kind of funny but definitely good," I slur back and lean even more into him.

He runs his hand across my shoulders. I look around and see everyone still engaged in conversation, oblivious to the hand that's wandering around my upper body.

Chase moves and pushes me towards Dez to wedge himself between me and the couch. Dez moves to make room and I sway in my seat.

"You look so beautiful tonight, Britt." He fingers the scarf around my neck, using it to his advantage when I feel his hand slide underneath it, teasing the top of my shirt.

"Chase?"

He turns to me with glassy eyes. "Yeah, beautiful?"

My stomach jerks and the blood drains from my face. "Find me a bathroom. Quick."

"Oh shit, Britt's gonna puke," Lyle says, clearing a path as I bolt from the couch.

I push several people out of the way while Lyle helps me into the bathroom just in time for me to empty the contents of my stomach into the toilet.

"Dude, how much did she have to drink?"

"Not that many, but the couple I gave her I added a little more vodka to it."

Lyle smacks Chase across the head. "You fucker! She doesn't drink very often and you know that. You trying to kill her?"

Lyle crouches down next to me, rubbing my back reassuringly. "You okay, babe?"

I cling to the porcelain with everything I have. A few strands of hair are plastered against my face, but Lyle pushes them away. He tears off some toilet paper, giving it to me so I can wipe my mouth.

"Yeah, I think I'll live."

He laughs but keeps rubbing my back. "Happy birthday to you I guess."

I place my head on my arms still folded over the seat. I don't even want to think about what they could or could not be resting on at this moment. I'm just thankful that Lyle is here helping me.

"Yeah, happy birthday to me."

I can hear Chase behind me and I turn my head. "Britt, I'm sorry about the drinks. Think you can forgive me?"

He hands me the water that someone had brought and I sit

back, eagerly taking it from him.

"Yeah, I forgive you for the drinks," I say, eyeballing him because I'm not sure I forgive his wandering fingers yet.

"Move! Get out of the way! Watch it!" Penny yells from outside the bathroom. She shoves Chase to the side and crouches down next to Lyle. "Hey, girl, you doing okay?"

I lean against the wall and take another sip of water. "Yeah, I'm okay now."

She flushes the toilet, letting the evidence wash down the drain.

"You ready to rally?" Lyle says.

I try to laugh, but it makes my stomach hurt. "I don't think so. Water sounds good right now." I look to Penny. "What time is it?"

She checks her watch with a grimace. "12:40. Liam is going to be here any minute, and he's going to shoot me if he catches you like this."

Penny and Lyle help me up and I only sway for a moment on my feet. Chase is gone, hopefully somewhere feeling sorry for what he did. It'll take me a few days to forgive him, but I know I will. He's Chase after all. He may be hopelessly in love with me, but I've known him since we were kids.

"You weren't overly attached to this scarf were you, honey?" Penny asks as she takes it off my neck.

"Kind of, why?"

She holds it at arm's length and throws it in the garbage. "Because you puked all over it, and it's smelly and red now."

"Shit," I mutter while holding onto her arm. Lyle steadies me on the other side, and they help me back to the couch where my stuff is.

Liam appears at my side with his hands on his hips, and I can't tell if he's amused or disappointed.

"So, enjoy your birthday?" he asks.

"Shut up and get me home, please."

He laughs this time, saying hi and bye to everyone as he and Penny help me out of the house and into his Mustang.

"You puke on my seats, and I'm going to kill you."

"Drive slow, and you won't have that problem, assmunch."

Penny sits in the back behind Liam and holds a conversation with him while I rest my head against the cold glass. *Man, that feels good.*

Before I know it, Liam parks his car in the driveway and helps me out. My stomach has settled, and I feel more stable on my feet.

"You good?" he asks, letting go of my arm.

"Yeah I'm good." I turn to Penny and hug her. "Happy birthday, bitch."

She laughs and hugs me back. "Happy birthday back. Now go inside and shower. You smell like vomit."

She climbs into her car, pulling away and heading toward her house. Liam holds the door open and stays behind me while I make it up the stairs toward our rooms.

"Need help?" he asks.

"Not in the shower, perv," I reply.

"I'll stay out in the hall in case you need me. If you feel dizzy or weak again, just sit down then knock on the glass. I'll come in and get you."

I pause before shutting the door and lean against the wall for balance. "Thanks, Liam."

He smiles back and shrugs. "I'm your big brother. It's what I do."

I close the door and start the water, grateful that I know I can always count on Liam to be there to help me out in any given situation.

Four

I KNOCK SOFTLY ON LIAM'S DOOR, HOPING HE'S AWAKE. There's no noise on the other side and I hesitate before verifying that's he's not in there.

"Liam?" I ask through the door.

There's a rustling now and the door opens with Liam standing before me in his sweatpants and ratty old football t-shirt, scratching his bed head.

"Why are you up? It's like eight o'clock in the morning. Shouldn't you be sleeping off the mother of all hangovers right now?"

I shrug and smile. "Guess I wasn't as drunk as I thought I was."

He walks back to his bed and lies on his back. "Or you got it all out of your system when you puked last night."

I follow him into his room and grab his desk chair, straddling it to face him. "Either way, no head pain, no upset stomach. Just perfectly normal today. And since it's today and I have things to do, I need a ride to go get my car."

He twists his head to the side and scrunches up his face. "Seriously? Can't Penny come get you?"

"You just want Penny to come get me so you can molest her in your mind when you see her."

He smirks. "Don't need her here to do that, Britt."

My head falls back with a loud groan. "You are so impossible, you know that? She's my best friend. Why do you have to obsess about her? Isn't there someone else out there for you to torture and annoy?"

He sits up and shrugs. "Penny will always be my ultimate, the one I compare every single girl with because honestly no one else even comes close. She's the perfect amount of sass and independence all rolled into this beautiful and smart package."

Whoa, that's the first time I've ever heard him talking about her like that. If that's how he really feels, why don't they try to get together?

"So if that's the reason, what's stopping you?"

Liam stands from the bed and walks over to his closet, pulling a hoodie from a hanger. "Because she's your best friend and I know you wouldn't forgive me if something ever happened between us. That's why I'm just waiting, biding my time until we're both ready. I'm going to marry that girl one day."

The thought of Liam and Penny being together twists through my mind and stomach, wondering if I could handle something like that. But the possibility of them getting married excites me because then she'd be my sister and we'd always be together.

"Just promise me you won't go crazy while she figures out that you're the one and only for her as well."

He shoves his hands in the front pocket and sighs. "I'm trying. It's hard, but I know the end reward will be worth it."

I give him a hug, knowing that it's torture for him to watch her go through different guys who treat her like crap. But he's right. She's not ready to make that sort of commitment yet.

"Okay, you're what, almost twenty years old and you're thinking of settling down? Really?"

He laughs and pushes me out the door. "No, I'm not thinking of settling down. And I'm not twenty yet."

"Close enough. You will be in eight months."

"Either way. I know how I feel about her and I know what I want. And she's it. But I promised myself that I wouldn't try until she was older, at least a couple years into college."

"Aw, I'm so proud. Look at you, being all noble and responsible. It almost makes me not want to cut your nuts off for thinking about defiling my best friend with your boy parts."

He laughs as we enter the kitchen. Mom and Dad are in their usual spots, drinking coffee and reading the paper.

"Good morning, kids," my mom chirps.

"Morning, Mom," we say in unison.

"How did last night go?" my dad asks, folding up his paper to give us his full attention.

I chew on my bottom lip and dive into the refrigerator to hide. Liam, of course, has nothing to be ashamed of.

"I ended up picking them up from Travis's, so Britta and I were just leaving to get her car."

My dad looks at me with a raised eyebrow. "Good night then?"

I shrug my shoulders and give a weak smile. "It was fun."

"A little too fun?" my mom questions with a smile on her face.

That makes me relax and laugh a little. "Yeah, a little too much fun."

My dad takes a sip of his coffee. "We were young once and know what goes on at these parties. However, I'm very proud of you for being responsible and not driving. So you two hurry up and get her car. Then you can go about your day."

Wow, that went smoother than I thought it would. I was expecting to get the third degree or something along those lines. Maybe Liam really did pave the way for me.

"Thanks, Dad."

I walk over and hug both my parents.

"I'm going to head out after I get the car so I won't be back right away," I say, grabbing my jacket and purse.

"Sounds good, honey. You have your phone in case we need to get a hold of you?" my mom asks.

I nod. "Yep, it's in my purse."

"Okay then. Have fun today."

"I will." I turn to Liam, who's shoving a piece of peanut butter toast into his mouth. "Ready?"

He brushes the crumbs off his hands and nods. "Yep. Let's go."

After I get my car and Liam leaves, I decide that a dose of caffeine is needed to fully wake me up. I'm still not functioning on all cylinders.

I stop at Perk Me Up, the local coffee house in town and order my usual skinny caramel latte. Once the barista, with a few too many piercings, gives me my drink, I walk to my usual couch and pull out my book. This rare moment of peace is something that I want to enjoy before Penny starts bombarding me with requests to go out and do something.

A half hour passes before I know it and I place the book down in my lap to stretch my arms above my head. I look around at the patrons who've entered and notice it's the usual crowd. Well, except for the guy sitting at the table in front of me, who is hunched over reading something. He takes a sip of his coffee and flinches slightly when it spills on his pants, muttering something I can't hear as he tries to wipe it off. I smile, knowing how that feels because I do it way too often. Grabbing a stack of napkins, I lean forward and tap him lightly on the shoulder.

"Here you go. In case you need some more."

He turns around and I'm greeted by a smiling familiar face.

"Hey you." He takes the stack of napkins from me. "Thanks."

James brushes away what he can of the coffee and turns sideways in his chair to face me.

"No problem," I say, feeling a slight blush creep into my cheeks.

"Apparently I'm having issues drinking my coffee this morning. Hole in my lip or something like that." He points to another stain on his knee, still wet but starting to fade slightly.

I laugh and shake my head. "I guess so. That whole drinking thing always sneaks up on you, being tricky and all."

His smile brightens, making his green eyes dance with delight. He has that 'just rolled out of bed' look going for him, with his disheveled hair and thrown-together clothes.

"Yeah, you'd think I would have learned by now." He nervously fidgets with his cup. "So what brings you here this morning?"

I hold up my coffee and smirk. "What else? Plus I like to come here to read and sneak in some me time."

"Looks like we have the same plan." He picks up his book and shows it to me.

"Oscar Wilde, huh? You like the classics?"

He nods. "I enjoy all kinds of books, but the classics are my favorite. When I need to recharge, I pull one out and get lost within the pages."

"I know the feeling. I read to escape as well. Some days it all just gets to be a bit much, especially on school days. But for those few hours when I'm reading, everything doesn't seem quite as bad."

"I completely understand that. School makes everything harder." He pauses, propping his ankle on his knee. "How early do you usually get there?"

"Around seven or so. I like to be extra early to get my stuff prepped for the day."

"Same here. I'm a planner, that's for sure. My compulsive need to have everything organized and in its place won't let me be anything but that."

"Me too. Wow, I can't believe I've finally met someone else who has a crazy OCD complex like me. Yesterday when I ran into you and all the papers scattered everywhere? I thought my brain was going to explode. I had just organized them after entering them into the grade book and now I have to do it again on Monday."

I can tell that James understands by his knowing smile. "So how long have you lived here in Somerset?" he asks, moving his chair closer.

"My whole life. I just can't seem to get away. It's home, you know. What about you? What brings you here?"

Just then his cell phone rings as he opens his mouth to answer my question. James holds up a finger, pulling the phone out of his pocket and checks the caller ID. He cringes slightly and turns back to me.

"Sorry, I have to take this," he says. He stands and walks out the front door to take the call.

I watch him through the window, admiring his stature and overall appearance. He's good looking. No, scratch that. Great looking. Like no one else I've ever seen before. He's got a model quality to him with a face that is pure symmetry, appealing to my inner perfectionist. But there's something else about him that causes me to smile like an idiot.

He catches me looking and waves with a smile. Then he mocks his call with hand gestures, letting me know that the person on the other line is extremely chatty. I laugh and pull my legs underneath me, getting more comfortable.

I wonder what classes we'll have together. He looks to be about my age so he must be a senior as well. But I'm awful at determining a guy's age. In my opinion, if they're under twenty-five, they all look like they're eighteen.

James's face changes slightly, his smile slipping as his head drops. I chew on my lip and remind myself that I should stop staring at him. But I can't help it. My eyes seem to have a mind of their own, drawing me to him in everything that he does. Every lip twitch, every blink of his eye, every foot shuffle has my body humming. It's an odd feeling for me, one that confuses me slightly.

James walks back inside, his demeanor a little less enthusiastic than before he took the call. His eyes reach mine and there's a hint of regret in them.

"That was my folks. I need to get going." He gathers his stuff from the table.

A shot of disappointment runs through me that he's leaving, just when we were starting to get to know each other.

"Oh, okay," I say while trying to mask the sadness in my voice.

He must notice it because his face softens as his eyes smile at me.

"It was nice running into you again, Britta. We'll see each other on Monday, right?"

I nod. "Definitely."

He pulls his jacket on and the smile he gives sends warmth through my veins. "Good. See you then."

And just like that he walks out the door to the truck that's parked across the street. I sit and watch again, feeling slightly creeper-ish but unable to get him off my mind. In just those few minutes of us talking, I could feel something growing between us. A friendship or kindred spirit of sorts I guess. We have a few things in common, which is a bit surprising. Normally, I don't find guys who enjoy the same things as I do.

I down the rest of my coffee and shove all my stuff into my purse. I dial Penny's number when I get in my car, hoping she's awake by now.

"What's up?" she says in greeting.

"Not much. I'm out and about right now. Want to go shopping? I need to replace that scarf from last night and I have the urge to buy a new book."

"Nerd." I can almost see her rolling her eyes in my head. "Yeah, I'm game for shopping. Give me twenty minutes and I'll meet you at the mall."

"Okay, lazy bones. See you in a few."

I start driving toward the mall with James still on my mind. A bud of hope blossoms in my chest at the thought of seeing him on Monday. He's definitely something to look forward to.

Five

I'M DROWNING IN A SEA OF PAPERS FROM MRS. DAVIS, IN addition to the papers I have to reorganize from Friday after my run-in with James. Even after my attempts at distraction over the weekend, he was still in my brain. There's just something about him that I can't put my finger on. Whatever it is I need to figure it out and soon.

As luck would have it, I haven't seen him in any of my classes or passed him in the halls. At this point I don't know if I'll even see him today. But I'm still hoping.

The bell rings for the end of the fifth period and I head to my locker to grab my stuff for Mr. Ward's class. Well, at least it used to be Mr. Ward's class. I'll find out today who the new teacher is.

Penny comes barreling down the hallway, nearly knocking me over when she grabs my shoulders.

"Holy shit dude!"

I laugh and shake my head. "What? Why do you look like you just ran a marathon?"

She regains her composure, smoothing her hair down from the frazzled mess it once was. "The new teacher they got to replace Mr. Ward? He's hot. Majorly hot. Like ghost pepper, the surface of the sun, you'll-go-blind-from-touching-it-too-much hot."

"You're a nut, you know that? He's a teacher. You make it sound like Chris Hemsworth is here instead." I pause. "And did you seriously just say go blind from touching it too much?"

Penny drags me by the arm to class. "Yes, because he's that hot."

"You know, between you and my brother I don't know who is more inappropriate and lewd."

"Just one more thing we both have in common." She walks to her chair over by Travis, who greets her with open arms and a showy kiss.

I roll my eyes and take my seat, flipping through my notebook to find the next clean page. My pencils are sharpened, my pen is handy, textbook open to the lesson written on the board in rather neat masculine handwriting. After Penny's reaction to the new teacher, I'm kind of interested to see him myself. I wonder if it's true, if he really is the good looking, super hot guy that she depicts.

Chase pulls on my sleeve. He looks sheepish and still carries around regret from Friday night.

"You mad at me?" He chews on his thumbnail, apparently worried about what I'm going to say.

I blow out a quick breath. "No, not really. Not anymore. Neither of us could have known that I couldn't hold my liquor that night. I'm more upset by what you tried on the couch more than anything else."

He looks down and away. "I didn't mean to upset you by

that. You just looked so cute and I thought maybe you felt something toward me since you were leaning against me."

"That was because I was drunk. Chase, you know I like you as a friend," I say. "And because you're my friend I'm going to let this one-time incident slide, never to be brought up again. We'll consider it a lapse in judgment. Deal?"

I stick my hand out and he firmly shakes it. "Deal."

A strange chill runs up my spine as the teacher enters the room. I snatch my hand away from Chase's when I turn my attention to a pair of green eyes staring directly at me. Green eyes that I have seen on two occasions and have recently sparked something to life inside of me. The green eyes of my teacher who really is as hot as the surface of the sun.

"Oh my God," I whisper to myself.

Chase straightens up when he notices that James is staring in our direction.

I can't move.

I can't think.

Shock.

That's what this is. It has to be. I mean, how could he be the new teacher? There's no way he's old enough.

He shakes his head, moving back to his desk in the corner and picks up the seating chart, studying it profusely. I watch his eyes dart up and down, back and forth, reading the paper until locking eyes with me again.

What do I do? I mean, it's not like we've done anything wrong. We've met twice. Both times completely innocent.

The bell rings and James writes his name on the board, using the same masculine script that was previously up there. A mixture of emotions floods me, ranging from dread to happiness to confusion to need. I stare at his back, admiring the way his dress shirt stretches across it, the flex of each muscle as he writes, and the tightness of his ass in those dress pants. I probably shouldn't be looking at that but who can help it. The man is to die for.

"Good afternoon, students. My name is Mr. Dumont. I'm your new teacher, replacing Mr. Ward for the year."

His voice is confident, strong, one of power and authority. And it does something inside me, stirring something up again out of the trenches, bringing it closer to the surface. I shift in my chair, hoping to not draw any attention from the person in front of the class, as well as the person seated next to me.

James picks up the seating chart and leans against the front of his desk, crossing his legs at the ankles. "Since this is my first day and we're going to have all trimester together, I'd like to start with everyone introducing themselves around the room and saying one thing about you, anything at all. We'll start with you," he pauses, looking down at this chart, "Brian."

I map out the route which the name announcing will take, making me the last one to say anything. Damn me and my need to sit in front and pay attention. Why couldn't I have been a slacker and sat in the back row?

Each student states their name and says almost the same thing each time. *I play football, I read books, I play video games and hang out with my friends.* Shit, what am I going to say when it's my turn? *Hi, I run into beautiful strangers and drink coffee with them on occasion.*

A tap comes to my shoulder and I realize that I was too lost in my own head to not know it was my turn to talk. Everyone's looking at me, waiting for me to say something, including James. His eyes stay on mine as I clear my throat and find something witty to say.

"I'm Britta Fosse and I like to be organized."

A few people laugh in the back row and I mentally smack

myself. *I like to be organized?* What kind of an answer is that? Chase snickers to my side and I throw him a look as I hang my head in embarrassment. But James's voice draws my head back up.

"I get it, I like to be organized too. It's kind of my thing," he says with a smile.

My heart melts just a little more as he eases my embarrassment by agreeing with me. But I already knew that he liked to be organized. His neatness borders on crazy like mine. He told me so during our coffee date.

Not a date.

Shit, I'm going to get in trouble if I start thinking things like that.

My eyes linger on him a bit longer before he starts going into teacher mode, picking up the textbook and having us take turns reading parts of the chapter. Of course, all the girls volunteer immediately to talk, each of them pushing their chests out a little more than necessary as they whine and wiggle their hands in the air. I roll my eyes and sit quietly, hoping to blend into the wall next to me. I don't need to draw any attention to myself. This will already be hard for multiple reasons. One, I had an instant attraction to James, one that seemed to be reciprocated both times we've met. Two, he's my teacher and now more than ever I wish it were June so I wasn't in high school anymore.

And three, see problems one and two.

"Ms. Fosse, could you take the next few paragraphs?"

James's voice filters into my scattered brain, making me realize that I have no idea where we are in the book.

"Um," I start, glancing over to Chase for help. He tilts his book to the side, pointing to where I need to be and I nod my head in appreciation. James doesn't miss our exchange when I sneak a peek up at him. The green of his eyes darken slightly and

I swear they even narrow marginally.

Strange.

I read the next few paragraphs, trying to hide my nervousness that could give me away as the girl who is thinking things she shouldn't be. Every once in a while I'll take a natural pause and look up, only to find James looking at me. When our eyes catch he quickly averts them back to the book, making me do the same.

When the bell finally rings, I gather my things as fast as I can to make a hasty escape. Unfortunately, my book was too close to the edge and gets knocked over. I wait until the last person in my row leaves so I can crouch down and pick it up quickly.

A pair of dress shoes appears in front of me and I'm met with the piercing stare of my teacher, who is now down at my level, helping me gather my fallen items.

"Thanks," I say, afraid to say anything else.

"You're welcome." Our fingers brush briefly in the property exchange, sending a shiver to run straight down my spine. Not one of pain or embarrassment, but something else entirely. Something comforting, something that deep down makes me crave his touch just so I can experience it again.

I stand quickly, smacking my head on my desk as I rise.

"Are you okay? Does it hurt?" he asks, reaching out but retracting his hand instantly.

I rub the abused spot and nod. "Yeah, I'll be okay. It's just a bump."

All the other students have left, leaving just the two of us in his classroom.

His classroom. He's my teacher.

I have never wanted something to be less true in my life.

A few seconds of silence pass before he shoves his hands in

his pockets and sighs. "So you're not a teacher."

I shake my head. "And you're not a student."

He shakes his head. "No, I'm not. Why did I find you in the teacher's lounge on Friday if you're a student?"

I press my books into my chest and stare at the knot in his tie, unable to make eye contact with him. "I'm a teacher's assistant for Mrs. Davis. I grade her papers, keep her grade book, create her tests, you know, that sort of stuff."

"Well, then that would explain it. I thought you *were* Mrs. Davis when I saw you back there. You look so much older than you are."

Risking a glance, I meet his eyes and shrug. "I'm not that young either. It was my birthday on Friday, my eighteenth."

Why did I tell him that? What business is it of his to know how old I am? He can figure that out from the class rosters if he really wanted to. I'm turning into one of *those* girls without even trying.

"Happy belated birthday."

"Thanks."

He drags his hand through his hair and suddenly I find myself wanting to do it as well. He's just so unlike any other guy I've met before. And it's not just the fact that he's older and more mature than the guys I hang around with. It's something else, only I have no clue what it could be.

"Well, I better get going. Hope everything was okay on Saturday with your parents, you know, when you rushed off from the coffee shop."

James looks up, meeting my eyes and holding me captive in their bright hue. "Listen, about Saturday. I didn't know, I mean, there was…wow, this was not the conversation I expected to have with you today."

"Yeah, me either." I chew on my bottom lip and look to the

left. "Out of curiosity, what were you going to say?"

He clears his throat, drawing my attention back to him.

"Honestly, I was going to see if you wanted to meet up for dinner. But obviously that can't happen now."

I wish I hadn't asked him that question.

"Oh." My voice is small and quiet.

"What about you? What were you going to ask me?" he says, moving closer.

I drag my eyes to his and debate if I really want to say it out loud.

"If we're both being honest, I was going to ask you the same thing. Maybe not to dinner but coffee after school or meeting up somewhere."

His face falls at the same time as mine. Whatever potential we had together is gone.

"It's a shame really. I had all kinds of plans running through my head," he finally says.

"Yeah, me too." I look over at the clock. "I better go."

I turn to leave, but his voice stops me. "Britta?"

"Yes?"

He saunters over to me, looking nervously out the door. "I wish things could have worked out differently for us. But as it stands I am your teacher so we'll just have to forget everything and pretend we've never met."

"You mean pretend that you didn't plow me over and make me bruise my butt?" I laugh, causing him to laugh with me. The deep sound echoes through my body and I briefly forget that I'm not supposed to like him.

"I'm pretty sure you were the one who ran into me."

My smile falters as he runs his hand through his hair again, a nervous tic I'm beginning to pick up on.

"Either way, it would have been nice to see where this could have gone."

He nods and backs away. "Take care, Britta. I'll see you in class tomorrow."

"Goodbye, Mr. Dumont."

I walk through the door and down the hall toward my locker, my heart beating a mile a minute inside my chest. In a matter of an hour, I experienced a loss without it ever beginning. One thing I know for certain is that sixth-period geography is now my favorite class, even if it slowly kills me.

Six

"M R. DUMONT IS SO HOT. I MEAN, IT'S BEEN A WEEK and he just keeps getting better and better looking. Don't you think?" Penny says through a bite of her sandwich.

Around and around the pencil twirls between my fingers as I'm unable to concentrate on anything, except for the electrical pulse that travels through my system whenever I think about James.

Mr. Dumont.

Fuck my life.

"He's hot all right. Definitely not the standard for a teacher. Maybe he's a mutant or an alien sent from another planet to study our teenage ways."

Penny laughs. "Doubtful. However, if he is an alien he can probe me anytime."

Her comment stirs a sudden jealously within me. This is not a typical reaction for me. This is the response of a jealous girlfriend who sees every girl in a room ogling her boyfriend as a threat. *Retract the claws, Britta. He's not yours.*

"I'm sure you would enjoy something like that. And keep your voice down. Do you want to get me in trouble? Or worse, have one of the teachers overhear you and report us? I'd like to keep my assistant job thank you very much."

"No one is going to hear us. And really, you wouldn't enjoy having Mr. Dumont do something dirty to you? I find that hard to believe."

A throat clears behind us and we turn in slow motion to find said teacher standing in the doorway.

"Ms. Morris, I believe lunch is to be eaten in the cafeteria. You should probably leave Ms. Fosse to do her work since she's technically in class."

James crosses his arms and gives her a look that begs to be challenged. Instead she gathers up her lunch, shoving it back in her bag.

"I'll catch you later, Britt. Sorry, Mr. Dumont, it won't happen again," Penny says, scurrying out the door. I don't miss the wicked smile on her face as she rounds the corner. I'm guessing she brushed up against him on her way out.

"Mr. Dumont, I'm sorry about that. It won't happen again. Please don't let Mrs. Davis know."

James occupies Penny's empty chair and folds his hands in his lap. The past week has been torture for me, seeing him in front of the classroom and not being able to talk to him. Not like I want to, not like we had before we knew of our situation. What I wouldn't give to have spent more time with him that morning at the coffee shop.

James shrugs and smiles at me. "I won't, don't worry."

He leans back and my eyes trace over his features again. As if I don't do it enough when I'm staring at him in class. Everything about him is perfect to me. His eyes are the brightest shade of green I've ever seen in another person. Is it a coincidence that I have a thing for green-eyed guys?

I shift in my chair, wanting to tamp down my thoughts and focus on my papers instead. "So what are you up to? Don't you have class right now?"

He shakes his head and leans forward. The scent of his cologne surrounds me. It's still that subtle hint of manliness which makes my eyelids flutter and my blood run faster through my veins.

"Fourth period is my lunch hour. Today I decided to spend it in my office to catch up on some work. It's been a little hard getting used to everything around here. I try to do as much as I can at home, but I've fallen behind."

I laugh for some reason, finding it funny. "Really? You always seem so put together in class, like you know what you're doing."

"Far from it. I'm absolutely terrified up there, but I can't let you guys see that because you'll walk all over me." He diverts his eyes and I swear I see a hint of pink tinge his cheeks. "Well not you, of course, but others in the class would."

He looks so cute when he's embarrassed like he just admitted something that would get him in trouble, only nothing about his sentence was inappropriate.

"No, not me. I wouldn't do that to you. But you're right. If other kids smelled blood in the water, they would circle you in a heartbeat."

He leans toward me some more and I stop twirling the pencil in my hand, placing it on top of the stack of papers in front of me.

"That's why I came to find you. Could you help me?"

I swallow thickly, my throat tight with nerves. "What do you need help with?"

He points to my computer screen. "That. What program is that? I've been looking for something to help me keep track of scores and create tests. That's what you use for Stacy, right?"

It takes me a minute to figure out that Stacy is Mrs. Davis, only because I hardly ever hear her first name used.

I nod. "It's really easy. I have the disc right here if you want to borrow it."

James looks down at his watch and cringes. "Can't right now. I need to get ready for next period." He looks at me with pleading eyes. "Do you think, I mean, would you be able to download it onto my computer for me so I can start using it after school? You'd be saving my life."

"Well if it's a matter of life and death, how can I refuse?"

His arms lift up slightly, as if he wanted to hug me but thinks better of it and stands instead.

"Thank you. I'll give you extra credit for helping me out." He gives me a sideways smirk. "Not that you need it. I have a feeling you're going to make my job incredibly easy this trimester."

"It's no problem, Mr. Dumont." I look around and frown. "Which one is your office? I don't want to assume you took Mr. Ward's old one and then find myself in the wrong place."

"Sure. Let me show you."

James motions for me to follow him through the maze after I grab the disc out of the drawer of the desk. I stay a safe distance behind him even though I want nothing more than to walk directly by his side.

"You seem to be navigating it better back here now," I say, trying to make light conversation.

His quiet laugh reaches me back here and I close my eyes briefly at the sound. "It took me a few days, but I think I've finally got it down."

"Well, that's good. Glad you stopped getting lost and knocking down poor innocent bystanders."

He stops outside his door to unlock it. "You are never going to let me live that down, are you?" He opens the door and a rush of warm air hits me.

"Never." We walk into the small space and I quickly glance around. There are no personal touches, no picture frames, or anything else that would give me an indication of who he is. Just a few books, his computer, a briefcase, and a coat hanging on a hook. "Wow, you've really spruced it up in here. Going for simplistic?"

He shakes his head with a smile. "Give me a break. It's only been a week."

"Nope. I'm holding you to a higher standard than everyone else," I say, taking a seat in his computer chair. It's soft and I sink right into it. The childish devil in me keeps thinking that my ass is touching the same space his ass has been. The angel in me is gone because she's ogling him standing behind me.

I load the disc as James leans down to hover over my shoulder. I can feel the body heat emanating from him. If I turn my head slightly, my lips will connect with his cheek.

Fuck I need to get him out of here.

"I'll just load it onto your desktop for now. You can put it anywhere after that."

He braces a hand against the desk and turns to face me. We're inches apart; our eyes connecting with each other. I can feel my pulse quicken and my breathing speeds up slightly. My eyes dart to his mouth as it parts, dragging in a silent breath.

"You look really nice again today," he whispers before straightening back up to his full height.

My lips part to say something, but he moves away, putting more distance between us. The breath I was holding releases, deflating my lungs in disappointment.

"Thank you."

He walks toward the door and pauses. "I'm sorry. That was inappropriate of me. Forget I mentioned it."

I swivel in the chair and face him. "It's okay. You look nice today too. I like your sweater. It looks really good on you."

We stare at each other in silence. Nothing is heard except our breaths and the hum of the computer next to me as it downloads the software. My eyes travel across his body, appreciating it for the specimen that it is before finally focusing on his eyes. Something about the way he looks at me has my body on alert. His hand leaves the handle to push the door shut, trapping us in his office.

I've dreamed of being alone with him like this for the past week. Maybe it's the fact that he's my teacher and there's a certain code of conduct that must be held between us. A code that I feel like breaking each time I see him. And there's something about that temptation which makes me crave him even more.

James walks toward me, his eyes flashing with muted desire. Like he's trying to hold something back. He leans forward, resting his hands on the armrest of the chair. Our noses are inches apart, our breaths combining as one in front of our faces.

Can he see my heart beating? Can he see the racing pulse at the side of my neck? Each beat is for him and I don't know why. I've never crushed on a guy this hard before. Never fallen off that cliff without knowing where I'll land. All for someone who I can't even have.

Everything about this is wrong. But my sweaty palms and panting breaths say this has never been more right.

His forehead touches mine, allowing me to feel the warmth of his skin.

"This is a bad idea," he whispers.

"I know," I reply on a breath.

"I need to leave."

"I know."

"You know we can't do this."

I break eye contact and look down. "I know."

James leans back, moving away from me and my idiotic teenage lust. How could I think that something would happen? He's my *teacher*. That's not going to change anytime soon. Any and all thoughts of him in a non-platonic way should be removed immediately.

The loud ping of the computer indicates the software has finished downloading. I swivel back to the desk and eject the disc, placing it back in its case.

"There you go. All set for later."

I stand up, wrapping my arms around my middle while hanging my head down to avoid his stare. He grabs my arm as I try to pass him.

"Wait," he says, making me stop.

"I have to go."

James shakes his head. "Not like this. What I did, what we almost…it shouldn't have happened." He turns my chin to face him, lifting my eyes to meet his conflicted ones. "It's not that I don't want to. Believe me, Britta, if circumstances were different…"

I nod and open the door. "I need to go."

"Okay." He releases my arm and shoves his hands into his pockets, muttering a quick curse before walking away.

The bell rings to indicate the start of the fifth period and I make my way back to Mrs. Davis's office. Shutting the door, I place the disc back in her desk and fold my arms on top of it, crying into my sleeve at the mess I've just created.

Seven

FTER A BRIEF STOP IN THE BATHROOM TO TOUCH up my makeup and wash away any remnants of my breakdown, I walk into James's classroom with my head held high. I won't let that one minor slip affect him or me. It was silly. And nothing happened. I mean, yeah we got close to each other. *Really* close. But we never kissed, even though I wanted to. We never touched each other, outside of him grabbing my arm to stop me from leaving. It was innocent and I'm blowing this completely out of proportion.

Just keep telling yourself that. Maybe you'll believe it.

James looks up from his desk as I take my seat. He looks nervous like he doesn't know how to act around me anymore. He shuffles through several papers, stopping only to look up at me.

"Ms. Fosse, could you come up here for a moment?"

I glance over to Chase, who has a *what did you do* look on his face. I shrug my shoulders and march toward him. My nerves are shot and I'm afraid people can tell by looking at me that I'm a wreck right now.

Standing in front of his desk, making sure not to come to the side next to him, I glance down at the paper he's pointing to. It's not what I was expecting at all. Not a test or piece of homework I turned in, but a handwritten note to me.

> I'm sorry. It was inappropriate of me to invade your personal space. Can you forgive me?

My eyes meet his in silent communication.

"Did you see this?" he asks, knowing that something needs to be said as people are still making their way into the room.

"Yes."

"And you're okay with this?"

I nod. "Yes, I'm okay with what you have there. I'm sorry. It was my mistake to begin with."

Sadness crosses his face again, my icy words hitting like the bitter cold air of January. I don't mean it to sound that way, but I can't let people see anything that they could misinterpret.

"Just make sure you work on it for next time."

Next time? Is he serious? There is no way that I'm getting anywhere near him again. If anything, this little stunt has proven that I can't be trusted to be around him. But there's this magnetism that he gives off and instead of repelling me like the same side of a magnet, I'm drawn to him. We're two opposite poles looking for a connection.

"I will. It won't happen again."

He nods and I walk back to my desk with my head down and arms wrapped loosely around my middle.

"Are you okay? What was that about?" Chase asks when I retake my seat.

"Nothing. I mixed up a few things on my paper from Friday and he wanted to point it out to me so I don't do it again."

Chase's brows furrow. "Mixed something up? But you never get anything wrong. You get straight A's in every class."

I shrug and open my notebook. "I had an off day. It does happen from time to time you know. I'm not perfect."

Chase places his hand on my arm and smiles at me. "You're always perfect to me. I'm pretty sure you can't screw anything up, even if you tried."

Don't bet on it I think to myself. After the stunt I pulled today, you can bet I'm capable of screwing everything up.

A loud thud draws my attention to James as he leans over his desk, his eyes staring directly where Chase is touching me. *What is his problem?* So what if Chase has a hand on me. He's my friend and he's allowed to. And why does James care? He made it perfectly clear that we cannot happen. Ever.

The petty child in me decides to explore this and see what exactly is driving James mad. I move my arm so that Chase's hand is now touching mine. I tilt my head to the side with a reassuring smile.

"You're so sweet. You always see the good in me."

He tucks a lock of hair behind my ear. "That's because you

make it easy to see." He looks over my body and leans closer. "You look really nice again today."

I freeze at his words. The same words were spoken to me by someone else, someone who I desperately wish was the one touching me instead of Chase.

I swallow hard, my throat tightening up again, only this time for a different reason. "Thanks," I whisper.

"Everyone, please take your seats," James says at the front, his tone harsh and scolding. I jerk my body away from Chase at the same time he does. The temperature in the room drops suddenly as I feel the chill run through my body.

He's upset?

"Pop quiz time, people."

The collective groan from everyone can barely be heard through the rushing of blood in my ears. His eyes keep migrating to mine, holding me in an annoyed stare, almost as if he's challenging me to push him.

He walks up and down the aisles, handing each person their paper. I reach to grab the paper and my fingers make contact with his. My head lifts up in confusion when his hand seems to linger slightly near mine. The greens of his eyes spark in the millisecond they make contact before he moves so he doesn't draw any suspicion.

I shake my head and quickly fill out the quiz and flip my paper over. Glancing around the room, I see others holding their heads up with their hands as they scribble furiously with their pencils, obviously annoyed with a test right away on Monday. Not one person is looking up. Everyone is in deep concentration. Everyone, that is, except James. I watch as his lips curl up in the corner while we silently stare at each other. It's a game now, trying to see if we can look at each other without being caught.

But we shouldn't be playing this type of game. We shouldn't even be entertaining the idea of playing anything together. The problem is I don't know how to stop wanting something I can't have.

The curl of his mouth drops slightly as I bite my lip nervously, wondering if anyone can see our private exchange. Time seems to be ticking by slowly as if the world has stopped revolving and we're suspended in limbo, not moving forward and just stuck where we are.

James mouths something to me, but I can't understand what he's saying. Did he just say I'm sorry or was it all in my head? I turn to look out the door instead, needing to get my mind to focus on something other than the gorgeous man in the front of the room. A man who occupies my thoughts more than he should.

"Okay, time's up. Pass your papers to the front," he announces.

James walks over to my desk, accepting the stack from my hands but doesn't make eye contact this time, nor does he try to touch me. It's probably for the best anyway. He's made it clear that we can't happen. Logically I know he's right but my stupid body says otherwise.

The rest of the period I focus on the words in the textbook and what is being written on the board. I ignore James as he walks around and avoid his eye contact whenever he tries. I don't raise my hand to answer questions because I don't know if I can control the strength of my voice. I'm acting irrational and stupid. He's my *teacher*. I'm his *student*. I need to get this out of my head and ignore whatever fantasies live there.

Chase turns to me once the class is over. "So do you want to go grab something to eat and study tonight?"

I shake my head, pulling myself out of the gray clouds of

my mind. Chase is being nice and sweet. He's reliable and such a good friend, even if he tries to push the limits sometimes. And actually I do need to study tonight. We have several large projects coming up, as well as several tests at the end of the week.

I stand and press my books to my chest. "Sure. I'd like that."

"Do you want me to pick you up around six?" he asks, moving toward me.

"No, that's okay. How about I meet you at Sammy's around then?"

"Sounds good to me. I'll see you later." He squeezes my arm before walking out the door with a broad smile.

I turn to follow but I'm held back when I hear James say my name.

I pause, turning slowly to meet his eyes. "Yes, Mr. Dumont?"

He shoves his hands in his pockets and walks toward me. "Listen, I-"

"Please, let's not talk about it again." I cut him off before he can finish his thought. "Let's ignore it and pretend it never happened. For your sake as well as my own. It's better this way."

He shuts the door slightly, blocking us from the view of anyone passing by. With two fingers, he gently lifts my chin to meet his eyes. "As right as that statement is, I can't pretend it didn't happen nor can I forget it either. It may be better this way, but it's hard as hell to stop. Do you know what I'm talking about?"

I nod. "I do, which is why we need to try. You're the teacher, I'm the student, and we will maintain our professional relationship as if today never happened. Everything will go back to normal."

"I'm finding it harder and harder to pretend near you. There's something about you that screams at me to get to know you even though I shouldn't. I mean, being friends outside of school can't happen, right?"

I shrug. "I babysit for several teachers, and I'm friends with some of their kids. It's never been a problem before."

"Well seeing as I don't have any kids both of those situations won't work." He runs his hand through his hair again before meeting my eyes. "But I want to get to know you. I want to get inside your mind and see it for more than an hour a day. Maybe you can help me some other way?"

My lips twist to the side as I think about what he's asking me. "We could meet at Perk Me Up on Saturday mornings and I can help you with the grading program."

He smiles. "I'd like that. And it's a public place with a casual setting so that'd be perfect."

"How about this Saturday then? I'm not busy around ten if it works for you."

"Ten sounds great. I'll bring my lesson books and laptop and you can show me the computer program a little more."

"Make sure you get the VPN and password from the office so you can log into your remote desktop. Otherwise, you'll be running two different programs and they won't sync up together."

"See, this is why I need your help." He laughs and opens the door wider. "Thanks, Britta. I'll see you tomorrow."

"Bye Mr. Dumont," I say as I leave the room.

I'm playing with fire, but I can't help myself. The temptation to see if I'll get burned is too great and I can't pass up an opportunity to spend time with James outside of school. But before any of that happens, I need to get through my study date with Chase. That should be interesting enough as it is.

"So let me get this straight, you're going out on a study date with Chase, whom you actively avoid getting into personal situations with?" Liam asks. He's straddling my desk chair as I sit on my bed and put my shoes on.

"Yep, that about sums it up."

He tilts his head to the side and scrunches up his face. "Why? That's the part I don't get. Chase has been after you for years and you've never gone out on a study date with him, or a *date* date for that matter. Something else is up, I can tell. It's written all over your face."

I sigh and cross my legs. "There is something else behind it, but I can't tell you. You wouldn't understand."

"Try me. You might be surprised."

Liam's looking at me with his puppy dog eyes, begging me to let him in on this huge secret I'm harboring.

"God you look pathetic. Does that face ever work with women?"

"More times than you'd believe," he laughs. "Come on. I'm dying to know what's bugging you. You've been acting weird lately. Is it something I should be concerned with?"

My fingers twist in my lap. "No, I don't think so. It's just... I'm using Chase as a distraction."

"A distraction?"

I nod. "Yeah. I feel like shit for doing it, but my sanity and mental health depend on it."

"What the hell, Britt? What is going on?"

"Promise me you won't say anything to anyone what I'm about to tell you."

"Yeah, sure. You know I won't."

I shake my head and hold his stare. "That's not good enough. Promise me you won't say anything. No one can know. Not Mom or Dad or Danny or Penny."

Liam pauses and lets his mouth fall open. "You're telling me something that not even Penny knows? Whoa, this has to be good."

"Good may not be the right word for it." I clear my throat and fidget some more. "You know Mr. Ward got fired."

"Yeah, everyone knows that."

"Well, the teacher they hired to replace him is hot. Like super hot. Insanely hot."

He shrugs. "Yeah, so?"

"Well, I ran into him, literally, before I knew he was my teacher. Twice. And both times we had this connection, this draw to one another. It was intense and it still is." I chew on my lip, debating on whether or not to continue. Liam just looks at me but nods, letting me know that it's okay to say it. "I almost kissed him today in his office. I was helping him load a program onto his computer and he was leaning over to see what I was doing. Our faces were so close and he smelled so good. But I made a fool of myself, practically begging him with my body signals to kiss me. Luckily he was smart enough to push away and remind me that we can't happen."

Liam exhales slowly and leans back. "Wow. That's not what I was expecting you to say."

"I know. It's stupid of me to think about my teacher that way, but he's constantly in my head and I can't get him out. I mean, James and I, we have this connection that I just can't explain."

"There's your first problem. Don't refer to him as James. You need to stop thinking of him as a regular person. He's your teacher."

"He asked for my help with some school stuff so I suggested we meet at Perk on Saturday. It's in a public setting so it won't look awkward. Plus he'll have his laptop so everyone will see we're working."

Liam's eyes narrow slightly. "I don't know about that. I think you're looking for trouble there."

I focus on my fingers and twist my lips. "I know, but there's a part of me that wants the trouble. I know nothing can happen. I'm not stupid. And I would never do anything to jeopardize his career. Look at Mr. Ward's situation."

"Yeah, but he shot himself in the foot there. I mean, if you don't want to get fired you don't sleep with the boss's wife."

"But the mere fact that people thought it was a student made him an instant antagonist. I would never want that for Ja- Mr. Dumont."

Liam joins me on the bed. "If you are crushing on this teacher you need to make sure it stays that way. A crush. But don't drag Chase around unnecessarily because you feel the need to distract yourself."

I lean my head against his shoulder and close my eyes. "Tell me what to do."

He leans his head against mine. "Just be smart about everything. Don't go looking for trouble. You have a good head on your shoulders and know what's best for you."

"Not helpful. I was looking for something more direct, like stop thinking dirty thoughts about your teacher." I glance at the clock and know I need to get going. "Okay, wish me luck. Tell Mom and Dad I'll be home later."

He nods and smiles. "I'll let them know. Have fun."

I stick my tongue out at him before leaving my room. Fun is not exactly how I would classify my plans for the evening.

Eight

I SPOT CHASE AS SOON AS I WALK THROUGH THE DOOR OF Sammy's. Of course, he would pick something as far away from the public as possible. And a booth no less. So much for wishing for a table to make it less intimate.

"Hey," I say, sitting down opposite of him.

He smiles brightly and gives a small wave. "Hey, glad you could make it."

"Why wouldn't I make it?"

"You've never accepted before so I figured you'd reject me again."

He hands me a menu and I briefly glance at it, even though I already know what I'm going to get.

"So what do you want to work on first?" I ask, trying to keep the conversation about school.

"Let's work on that physics test we have at the end of the week. It's going to be a killer one. What'd she say it was worth?"

I grab my physics notebook and flip through the pages. "Around twenty percent of our grade or something like that. I know it's big enough to make me want to ace it."

He nods his head and finds his own notes. "Yeah, me too." He brings his eyes to mine and gets a funny look across his face. "What was up with Mr. Dumont today? He was acting so weird during class. I just couldn't put my finger on it. Something was off."

I fidget with my pencil. "Don't know. He's new so maybe we still need to get used to his teaching style."

"That could be. I just know he was acting strangely is all. But whatever. All I'm concerned with is passing his class."

"Me too. One trimester with him is probably all I could tolerate." I tilt my head to the side when Chase gives me a funny look. "What?"

"You never have issues with teachers. Why would he be any different?"

Shit. I'm going to give myself away. "That's not what I mean. I don't have issues with him. I'm just saying that I only need geography for one trimester."

Chase seems satisfied with that answer because he doesn't bring it up again.

Once our food arrives, we take a break. I eagerly dive into the chicken parmesan sandwich because it's the best in town. They always make it grilled for me instead of the deep fried breast it's supposed to come with. But that's because Sammy, the owner, loves me. He and my dad have been friends for a long time so he always gives me special treatment when I'm here.

"Do you need more ketchup for your fries?" The ketchup splatters onto his plate as he tries to coax the last of it out.

"Yeah, but I can just grab another bottle from a different table."

I wipe my hands on my napkin and slide out of the booth. "Don't worry about it. I'll just go grab a new bottle from up front."

"You're a doll." The smile he gives me is slightly creepy and it makes me glad I'm moving away from him.

With the empty bottle in my hand, I wander to the front of the restaurant where our waitress is attending another patron. My steps slow when I get a good look at the person, recognizing the messy brown hair anywhere.

"Shit," I mutter to myself.

Ignoring my impulse to walk past him, I quicken my steps to the front counter and lean forward, draping my arms over the top. Propping my right foot up by my toes, I twist my ass from side to side, a wiggle that I always do when I'm leaning against anything. Normally it's an unconscious gesture, but I'm made aware of my actions when I hear a loud cough coming from the person I can't stop thinking about.

With a glance over my shoulder, I see James staring at my ass. His eyes meet mine and he gives me a full megawatt smile. We hold our gaze just until the waitress appears in front of me and I exchange the empty bottle for a new one.

This time I purposely walk past his booth while putting a little extra wiggle in my walk.

"Hi, Mr. Dumont. Enjoying yourself?" I say quickly as I pass. I can hear him half-cough, half-laugh, making my insides surge with excitement. There's a tremendous power in knowing how you can affect someone, even by doing such a little thing like waving. Then again, if the roles were reversed, I would be in the same position.

"Here's the ketchup," I say, putting the bottle in front of Chase while sliding back into my seat.

"Thanks again. I could have gotten it."

I wave a dismissing hand in front of my face. "Don't worry about it." I take a bite of my sandwich and open another notebook. "Let's work on our AP Writing assignment next."

"Sounds good."

We take our time writing our essays and bounce ideas off the other, trying to make sense of what we're doing. I don't usually have issues coming up with stunning essays. But tonight the words aren't flowing. And I know the reason why.

The waitress clears our empty plates and brings me another Diet Coke.

"I'm so full. I shouldn't have eaten that whole thing."

Chase laughs. "You're a trooper, though."

My full bladder is screaming at me and I start to slide out of the booth again. "Need to make a pit stop. I'll be right back."

Chase doesn't look up, just nods his head as he continues to write his thoughts on the paper. I shove my hands in my back pockets and purposefully walk past James's booth again. I know he's watching me. I can feel it, like a slow warmth that crawls over my skin. It's a dangerous thing I'm doing, but I just can't help myself. I need to know that I'm not the only crazy person in this one-sided crush.

I wash my hands and stare at myself in the mirror. After running my finger under my eyes to clean up my makeup, I put on a quick coat of lip gloss, making myself presentable to walk back out there. I don't make it far because James is right outside the bathroom door, hidden in the shadows of the dark hallway.

"You're antagonizing me," he says in a low, hushed tone.

Holy fuck. That voice. I start to tremble. Suddenly my little game doesn't seem like a good idea anymore. I told myself I was going to forget this. But when I see him, I need to have his attention. It's sick and wrong, but it feels more right than anything else I know.

I press my back against the opposite wall and bite my lip. "Yes," I say honestly.

He pushes away from the wall and boxes me in with his arms. "That's dangerous."

"I know."

"Are you trying to push me?"

His face is so close to mine. Those green eyes penetrate through the darkness, almost glowing in the muted light. My chest feels tight as it rises and falls with the shallow breaths I'm taking. God, he smells so good. My head feels light as his face gets closer to my ear.

"What do you want Britta? Do you want me to take you away from here? Or do you want me to leave you alone and continue on with what we agreed upon?" he asks in a raspy voice laced with desire. "Tell me."

A chill runs up my spine as his nose makes contact with the skin just below my ear.

"You smell so good right here. This fragrance stays in my head each time I see you, making it all I can think about. Tell me. What do you want?"

I place my hands on his chest with the intention of pushing him away but finding myself unable to do so.

"I-"

His soft, warm mouth finds mine before I can complete my sentence. My body spirals with need, wanting more than just this one kiss. I'm slowly becoming addicted to him as our lips move against each other, neither of us pushing it any further. Our boundaries are already blurred and anything more will only complicate things.

James leans against me; his forearms now flush against the wall. I feel dizzy with delight and the knowledge that this now confirms what I wanted to know.

He wants me too.

A noise down the hall startles me so I push James away

roughly, breaking our kiss. We're both panting and breathless, our lips swollen and red. The buzzing in my body hasn't decreased any with the distance between us.

Shame and disappointment fill me slowly, making me wish I hadn't been playing my game earlier with him. This was my fault again, leading him on and pressing his buttons to get a reaction. I should know better than this.

"I'm sorry," I whisper, trying to regain control of my body and mind.

James's head snaps up, his eyes narrowing slightly. "Why are you sorry?"

"We shouldn't have done that. It was wrong." I take a calming breath and swallow past the lump in my throat. "You're right. I was trying to push you. I wanted to know if you felt even an iota of what I feel towards you. But I know that's stupid because we can't do anything about it. You made that clear to me in your office and I ignored your wishes."

His eyes darken with something other than anger. "You're right. We can't do anything about it. The attraction we feel is too strong."

I shake my head. "It can't be. We've known each other for a week."

"And a half," he adds.

"Regardless, it's too short a time to even do anything like this. Breaking rules and going against our better judgment? It's not safe. It's reckless and dangerous and-"

He halts my thoughts with a raised hand. "You wondered if I felt the same as you. I'm telling you right now that your feelings are reciprocated in full force. And what I said is also true, that we can't be together. It's dangerous, not only for me but for you too." He looks down at his shoes briefly. "However, you can't deny that there isn't something between us either. Don't sweep this under the rug and pretend it didn't happen. You want it as much as I do."

I nod, still unable to meet his eyes. "So now what? Our previous plan didn't work out so hot for us. Maybe we should just ignore it."

He runs both hands through his hair and blows out a breath. "Ignoring it won't help. It will only drive us mad. What we do is just try to control ourselves. You said before that you have casual relationships with other teachers, right?"

I nod again, wrapping my arms around my middle.

"Look at me," he asks quietly. I bring my eyes to his and see that they've softened now.

"You have such beautiful hazel eyes. It kills me that I've diminished their light tonight."

"You didn't."

"Yes, I did. They were bright before but now they're sad."

"If they were bright before, it was because of you. You brighten my day every time I see you. This crush I have for you is like nothing I've had before," I say quietly. "I don't know if we can attempt a casual friendship."

James props his foot up against the wall. "We need to try. The one hour per day I see you is no longer enough for me. I need to know you, and more than just your knowledge of geography."

"But shouldn't we wait until after the trimester? I mean, with you being my teacher won't it look wrong?"

He contemplates this for a minute and nods in agreement. "You're right. So while you're in my class, we'll just have to contain ourselves. Accidental meetings, staged events, those types of things would be best for now."

"Staged events?"

"Events where we know both of us will be there so we make

it a point to see each other. Sporting events, school functions, things like that. And you shouldn't be afraid to approach me in the hallway just to say hi either. Lots of kids talk to me about random things between classes so you shouldn't be any different."

"I don't know about this James. It seems like we're sneaking around."

"But we're not. We're just two people who want to get to know each other."

"And the attraction?" I ask, biting my lip.

His eyes flash again. "Please stop doing that. It's distracting."

I release my lip from my teeth. "Sorry."

"For now, we're just going to have to push aside the attraction. Do you think we can do that this time?"

I nod. "I just don't want it to be weird between us because I find you very smart and funny and I do enjoy talking to you."

"And I enjoy it too. So we're agreed then." He sticks his hand out to me and I take it while ignoring the shock that flows between us.

"Agreed. Friends."

He pulls me to him and presses his lips against my temple.

"Friends don't do that," I mumble into his shoulder.

I can feel his lips curl into a smile against my head. "Starting now."

He releases me and I instantly miss the contact. I move towards the end of the hallway before holding my hand up to him.

"You better wait a minute before leaving otherwise it'll look like we were doing something back here."

He laughs. "We were."

I roll my eyes at him. "But Chase doesn't need to know that. God, he's the last person who needs to know that."

At the mention of his name, James's stance instantly changes. Tension rolls off him and his jaw twitches with a restrained anger.

"No. We definitely don't need him finding anything out." He closes his eyes and takes a deep breath. "You better go before I forget our agreement again. Are we still on for Saturday?"

I shake my head. "No. Saturday would be a bad idea. But I'll help you during the fourth period if you still need it with the computer program. I'm almost caught up with Mrs. Davis's work so it should be fine."

He nods and moves closer to me. "I'll look for you then." He opens his mouth but then shuts quickly. It takes all my strength to turn around and walk back to the booth, knowing that I'm leaving behind the one person who has made me smile all night.

"Stomach problems? You were gone for quite a while," Chase says, withholding a laugh.

"Funny. There was an issue with the toilet. Had to find someone to fix it. But thanks for thinking the other thing. That doesn't make me feel gross at all."

This time he laughs loudly, causing a few eyes to turn in our direction.

I slam my books shut and gather them together. "I need to get going. We have school tomorrow and it's getting late."

Chase looks at his watch and nods. "Shit. Yeah, I was supposed to call Drake fifteen minutes ago."

We walk toward the door and I can't help myself from looking over my shoulder to James. Chase looks over his shoulder too and waves slightly.

"Hey, Mr. Dumont," he says.

James waves back. "Hi, Mr. Woodward, Ms. Fosse. Have a good evening."

"We will," Chase replies, pressing his palm into the small of my back.

"You okay?" Chase asks in my ear. He must have felt my muscles tense up. I didn't exactly do a very good job at hiding my discomfort.

"Yeah, I'm all right. Just got a chill is all."

We exchange goodbyes at our cars and I let out a sigh of relief. As Chase drives away, I see James out of the corner of my eye walking out the restaurant door. He glances my way. A wry smile plays upon his lips as he climbs into his truck, leaving me standing in my open door dumbstruck and wanton. He pulls out of the spot and heads down the road in a thunderous roar.

Images flash through my head of things we could do in that truck, places he would take me, and secrets we would discover about each other. I shake my head and climb into the seat, gripping the steering wheel tightly.

"Fuck."

I drive home feeling frustrated and confused, yet giddy and euphoric as I remember the feel of his lips against mine. My whole body ignites again with longing for his lips and I wonder just how this new arrangement of ours is going to work. Until then, I'll have to occupy myself somehow.

Tonight sounds like a good night to try to go blind.

Nine

"So, HOMECOMING QUEEN NOMINEE, WHO ARE YOU going to the dance with?" Penny asks me. She's at her usual perch on my bed, flipping through her magazine yet not really paying much attention to it. I think she just needs something to keep her fingers busy. I'm sitting on the floor next to the bed, looking through my phone.

"No one. I'm going solo."

Penny throws down the magazine in a huff. "You can't go by yourself. It's not right, especially when you're going to be royalty."

"Pfft. Whatever. Who says I need a date anyway?"

She stands and walks to my mirror, fluffing her red hair before tucking it behind her ears. "What about Chase?"

I turn to face her. "What about Chase?"

She rolls her eyes and sighs. "You can't avoid him forever. And I know for a fact that he asked you to the dance."

I fall back on the floor and toss my arm over my eyes. "Just because he asked doesn't mean that I need to go with him. Maybe I don't want to lead him on. Maybe I really do just want to go by myself."

Her red lips twist to the side. This is not good. "The only reason why a girl says she doesn't want to lead a boy on is because she's waiting to ask someone else."

I pull my arm up and look at her. "Seriously?"

"So, who is it you're holding out for? Do I know him? Of course I know him. He must be in our school and we know everyone. Is it Lyle? Drake? Matt?"

"No, no, and hell no. It's no one you know."

"Aha! There is someone you're waiting for! I knew it. Who is it? Tell me, tell me, tell me."

"Fuck!" I yell. "It's no one, okay? I'm not holding out for anyone. I just want to be single. Is that so unusual?"

"Yes," she simply says.

"Whatever." I stand and pull her out the door. "Well, if we want to make our hair appointments we need to get going. Stupid dance won't wait forever."

"Come on, lame ass, let's get moving so you can fly solo."

I smooth a hand down the front of my dress, thankful that I remembered to wear a button down shirt on the way to the salon. The emerald green satin dress hugs my curves in all the right places and highlights the flecks of gold in my hazel eyes. My hair is twisted into an elegant updo, soft and curly while accentuating my long neck. An emerald pendant necklace with matching earrings completes my outfit.

"You look incredible," Penny says, entering my room.

"So do you. Don't let Liam see you. He'll probably kidnap you and tie you to his bed."

There's a twinkle in her eyes and she smiles brightly. "You

think?"

I make a gagging gesture. "Gross. Forget I said anything."

And, on cue, Liam walks into my room but stops short in my doorway.

"Holy shit, Penny. Are you trying to kill me?"

"What?" she says innocently, spinning in a slow circle to give him the full view.

She's wearing a short, backless, silver halter dress, coming down to her mid-thigh at most, complete with platform silver strappy heels. Her hair is also swept up with several braids integrated throughout. Gold hoops and a gold necklace she got from her parents are her only pieces of jewelry and really, she doesn't need anything else.

Liam grabs a pillow off my bed and holds it in front of him. "I need to go now." He turns and leaves, making Penny laugh quietly.

"Burn that pillow when you're done with it," I yell at him. "I don't want it after your boner's been rubbing up against it!"

I grab my purse off my dresser and smile. "Ready?"

Penny nods. "Now I am! Mission accomplished."

I roll my eyes and usher us down the stairs. "My poor brother. I don't even want to think about what he's doing in his room right now."

"Maybe I should go in there and find out," Penny says.

I shake my head and keep her on the stairs.

"Don't even think about it. Just walk. We're going to be late."

"Well if you had a date he could have picked you up and we wouldn't have to worry about it."

"I told you I don't need one," I say. We round the corner into the living room where my parents are waiting for us.

"You girls are positively stunning," my mom says, clasping her hands in front of her.

My dad holds up his camera. "Let's take a picture by the fireplace before you go."

We both groan but comply, knowing that it's just easier to give in. After several different shots and nearly going blind from the flash, we climb into Penny's car and head towards the high school.

"Aren't you going to be cold standing out there during the football game?" I ask her.

"Aren't you?"

"I have more dress on than you do," I say. "Besides, there's no way in hell that I'm standing out there the entire time. I'm only going out at halftime to be introduced and then I'm high-tailing it back inside where it's warm."

"And duh, what do you think I'll be doing?" she says with a laugh.

"Good point."

We walk into the warm comforts of the school, noticing how much the homecoming committee has decorated in the few hours we've been gone. Blue and white streamers crisscross above us with several balloons hanging from the endcaps of the lockers. We stash our purses and head to the gym to see if they need any help.

"And now your Somerset High homecoming royalty," the announcer screams through the speakers.

The wind has picked up and I'm desperately trying to keep my dress from flying up Marilyn Monroe-style. I look back at the others around me, ten of us total, as they seem to have the same issue. Well, the guys don't, obviously. The majority of them are on the football team so they're in their sweaty, smelly uniforms.

Unfortunately for me, I end up paired with Chase. I swear someone has it out for me. Either that or Chase bribed someone on the committee to make sure he escorted me onto the field.

"You look beautiful, Britt," he whispers in my ear.

"Thanks."

"Are you sure you don't want to-"

"Chase?" I say, cutting him off.

"Yeah?"

"We're getting ready to walk out there."

His face falls slightly but recovers right away. "Oh, right."

They announce our names and we walk on the red carpet to midfield. When we turn to face the crowd, I give them my best pageant wave. *Elbow, elbow. Wrist, wrist.* With a fake smile plastered on my face, I scan the crowd to look for the familiar faces among them. I find our small group of friends quickly. It's not difficult when Justice is holding a sign with our names on it and whistling the loudest. I laugh and look around more to find my parents, who are sitting right beside Penny's.

But then my eyes find someone else. Someone whose smoldering stare is holding my gaze in place, making me unable to move or focus on anything else.

James.

He stands out plain as day to me, even though he's with the rest of the faculty near the parent section. But he doesn't blink as we look at each other. We haven't had another incident like the one at Sammy's again, and I'm thankful and sad about that. Part of me wants to run to him every time I see him in the halls or pass him in the teacher's lounge. Another part of me wants to keep him at arm's length because I know my treacherous body won't be able to control its desires again.

And even though we've kept it platonic it's been hard ignoring my feelings toward him. The passing jokes in the hallways, the way he keeps his distance when I'm helping him with a problem on his computer, the stolen glances I take in class when he's not looking. All of it just keeps me coming back to him. And the more we talk, the more we discover how much we really do have in common with each other. It's so hard to find someone who loves to watch stupid comedies and really horrible movies from the 80s and 90s. Or will spend hours surfing YouTube because you *need* to watch one more music video. And he's completely right when he says that there's nothing better than listening to a thunderstorm and the relaxing cadence of the rain as it falls. It's like finding the best friend I didn't realize I was missing.

We've had many debates and argued opinions over this past month we've known each other. It's refreshing to have a new opinion; someone who will make you think about how they see the world. Not to change your view, only to broaden it. I guess that's why he's such a great teacher. He's always making you think, even if it's not about school subjects.

"Will you at least save me a dance later?" Chase asks as he leans toward me. I almost forgot where I was and who I was with. I blame it on the man I can't turn away from.

It takes an enormous amount of effort to turn away from James and look into Chase's hopeful eyes. I force a smile and nod. "Yeah, I can do that."

He kisses the back of my hand, causing the crowd to give a collective *aww*. But my smile falters when I see the frown on one face in particular. A guilty feeling passes through me as if I'm doing something wrong, even though I'm not. James should know by now that I want nothing to do with Chase. But I can see how the crowd can think something else. Two homecoming royalty walking together, dressed in fancy clothes, and courting each other with a kiss to the hand. It's all very storybook-ish. Only I want my story to say something else.

We walk off the field and Chase kisses my cheek quickly before grabbing his helmet and running back to the sidelines with his team. I wipe the sweaty kiss from my skin, hoping that no one saw that.

"Again, why aren't you going with him?" Penny says coming up behind me.

"Because I don't like him like that."

She rolls her eyes and hooks her arm through mine. "You confuse and frustrate me. Come on. Let's go inside before we both have a wardrobe malfunction in this wind."

A steady stream of people have been entering the gym for the past hour, raising the temperature from cool and comfortable to humid and sweltering. I'm doing everything I can to avoid becoming a puddle of goo in the middle of the dance floor. Finally someone opens the outside doors, letting in a gust of cool air and we instantly feel the relief.

Over the last four songs, I've watched Penny fling her body all over the floor in a flurry of arms and giggles. Travis hasn't left her side much and I must say that he cleans up well. Then again he kind of has to since he's part of the royal court.

I sit off to the side to save my aching feet. Perhaps my four-inch heels were not the best idea after all, even though they make my legs look fantastic in them. Lyle and Dez are laughing at some joke Drake just told while Cami and Chase dance next to Penny and Travis.

As I watch the crowd around me, I barely register the person standing beside my chair. He shoves his hands into his pockets while he rocks back on his heels.

"This is quite the party. How come you're not out there dancing with everyone else?" James asks just loud enough so I can hear him.

I crane my neck to look at him and almost fall off my chair. Generally I wouldn't react to how he dresses because he's usually very professional, all suit pants and ties. But tonight he looks positively delicious, wearing a dark gray suit with a lighter gray shirt and green tie in the exact same shade of my dress. *How did he know?*

I lift my leg up, showing him my heels and shrug. "Apparently these are not conducive to dancing for extended periods of time."

James's eyes start at my toes and travel slowly up my leg, not missing one inch of exposed skin on his way to meeting my eyes. I shiver at his attention, wanting more of it, wanting to show him more skin so I can have that prickling sensation again. He steals my breath away when his eyes change color in front of me, switching from a bright green to a darker shade filled with heat and desire. The familiar lightheaded feeling comes over me as I attempt to stand next to him. With the addition of my heels, it makes us almost eye level and I take advantage of my new view.

I want to run my hands through his hair, feel his breath on the spot just below my ear as images of that one night come back to my mind. The feel of his soft lips as he kissed me, pressing me into the wall, making my body come undone so easily and without effort.

James starts to speak but is interrupted when the loud system comes on with a squawk of the microphone.

"Good evening, students," Mr. Leonard says, creating a hush around the packed gym.

I move closer to James as the lights dim more. The smell of his cologne, combined with his close proximity, has my eyelids fluttering, stirring that familiar pull to him that I can't seem to shake. Our pinkies touch briefly and I try to control my breathing as I inch closer to him. I've completely tuned out Mr. Leonard at this point. The only thing I can concentrate on is the man standing next to me.

Vaguely I'm aware of people being called onto the stage, each getting a bouquet for being in the royal court. But I don't care about that right now. All I can focus on is the man at my right; close enough to touch but know that I can't, at least not in the way I want to.

"You look beautiful tonight," James says as he leans closer to me.

My heart beats faster as I snake my pinky out to wrap around his.

"Thanks. You look handsome as well," I reply back.

Our moment is interrupted again, this time by the loud roar of the crowd at the announcement of the king and queen.

"And this year's homecoming king and queen are Chase Woodward and Britta Fosse."

I reluctantly drop my contact with James and force a smile on my face as several people turn to congratulate me.

"You better get up there." He takes a step away from me as he claps. "Don't want to keep Chase waiting."

The bitterness of his words doesn't escape me. I want to turn to him and tell him that it's not Chase I want to be up there with. That it's him, only him. But knowing that it's not a possibility, I just nod and walk toward the stage with the fake smile still plastered on my face.

He meets me on stage, his All-American smile intact, and wraps an arm around my waist, pulling me close to his side. My muscles jump in revolt, but Chase doesn't seem to notice as he plays it up to the crowd. We stand together as the crowns are placed on our heads, our friends cheering wildly below us.

"And now we'll have the royal court dance," Mr. Leonard

says.

I turn my head to look at him, unbelieving that I honestly have to dance with Chase. My attention turns back to the crowd, searching for James. Only I can't find him with the lights still dimmed too low.

Chase pulls me toward the dance floor as a slow song begins playing. He wraps his arms around my waist while I rest my hands on top of his shoulders, making sure our upper bodies are not touching. I need to keep this as friendly as possible.

We sway back and forth in silence until Chase decides to speak up.

"You know I had a feeling that we'd be king and queen."

"Oh really? Why is that?" I ask.

He smirks. "Isn't it obvious? We're the perfect couple."

"Look, Chase…"

He sighs. "I know, I know. But I don't understand why. I mean, we've known each other since we were little kids and we run in the same circles, have the same friends. We're always together. Why can't we be *together* together?"

His hands start moving around my hips and rest on the top of my ass. My body goes on alert because the last time he tried this I wasn't able to fight him off. This time, I don't have alcohol running through my system and can at least control the situation.

"Chase? Your hands?"

He just smiles and his fingers graze over the satin of my dress, drawing circles as they make their way further down.

"I like this dress," he says, close to my ear.

I reach around and grab his hands, moving them back to the safe spot of my hips. He gives me a sly smirk and I shake my head.

"Do we need to have another conversation like we did the

last time your hands wandered?"

Chase flinches and looks to the side. "I just can't seem to help myself where you're concerned. You know I like you. I just wish you liked me too."

The song ends and I'm thankful for the chance to get away from him. We pull apart as an upbeat tempo fills the speakers, drawing the rest of the crowd onto the floor.

"Look, I'm going to get something to drink. I'll meet up with you later?"

I don't give him a chance to respond as I quickly exit the dance floor. I feel bad for turning him down, but I just don't feel that connection to him, not in the way that he wants. I can't drag him along when my heart isn't in it.

As I walk through the crowd, I try to find James, hoping he's still where I left him. I turn in circles, but he's nowhere to be seen. My heart drops a little and I let out a sigh. I'm becoming quite pathetic. Is this how Chase feels all the time? Unrequited love really sucks.

"Britta! Hey lazy ass, get over here and dance with us!" Penny screams from the edge of the masses.

I laugh, motioning with my hands that I need to check my phone. She gives me a thumbs up and resumes her organized seizure on the floor.

My heels click loudly against the marble floors as I stride down the hall. I know no one is going to be calling me. I just needed a minute to breathe. I quickly lean against my locker, allowing the metal to cool my heated skin. Things were getting a little intense in there, at least in my mind they were. Standing next to James and sneaking that small contact with him was enough to wake the dormant beast inside me. It makes me crave more of his touch, more of his time, more of his attention. Just knowing he's in the same building as me always gets my heart fluttering like crazy anyway. With him looking the way he does tonight, it's ten times worse.

I don't want to head back just yet, so I decide to wander the halls and take the long way back to the gym. Several students pass by, giggling loudly, or giving each other high fives for our blowout win tonight. I'm so ready to not be in high school anymore.

I should know better than to not pay attention to where I'm going because I find myself walking directly into a brick wall.

A sharply dressed brick wall.

The force of the hit causes me to stumble backward on my high heels and I nearly fall over until a pair of strong arms wraps around me, pulling me close to his chest.

"Oh my gosh, I am so sorry."

He laughs, and it's the laugh that I adore. The one that feels like smooth silk wrapping tightly around me, keeping me safe and warm.

"You have a habit of running into me," James says.

"What can I say? It's a talent of mine. Either that or I'm just drawn to you."

Shit, why did I say that? I cringe slightly, not wanting to give myself away, but James ignores the statement or chooses not to address it. He holds onto me a bit longer than normal before releasing me. I smooth the wrinkles out of my dress and look up into his beautiful green eyes.

"Are you okay?"

I nod while biting my lip. "Yeah, I'm fine. Just distracted I guess."

"Want me to walk you back to the gym?"

"Sure. I'd like that."

We walk side by side down the quiet hall, close enough where I can feel his body heat but far enough away to make it look casual.

"So how's the computer program going? I assume it's going well since you haven't asked me for help in a while," I say, wanting to start some kind of conversation.

He laughs and looks over at me. "Much better now, thanks to you. It was a rough start, but I took your advice and got the remote link on my laptop so now I use it at home to get more practice in."

"Good. I'm glad it's working out for you. I told you it's a relatively easy program to use."

"And as always, you were right."

I smile and bump his shoulder. "Such a smart man. You're learning, Mr. Dumont. Very rarely do I ever get things wrong."

I watch him wince slightly at the use of his formal name. I'm too afraid to say his first name around here because I'm unsure of who could be listening.

"So are you going to keep assisting Mrs. Davis after she goes on maternity leave in a few weeks?"

I shrug. "I don't know. She hasn't actually said anything about it. I can't imagine they'll have me continue on with a substitute. I mean, I guess they could, but I really enjoy working with Mrs. Davis."

"How about working for me instead?" he asks.

I stare back at him. "What? How? I mean, I'm in your class. Pretty sure Mr. Leonard won't let me do that."

"Not this trimester but the next one he would. Unless you plan on taking another class of mine."

"Don't take this personally but there's no way I'm taking another class of yours," I laugh.

"And why not? Am I that bad of a teacher?" he jokes, feigning hurt.

"It's not that at all. I think you're an excellent teacher, especially for one so young. It's just your subject matter isn't exactly what I need to continue on to college. This class was one I needed to graduate to get my required social studies credits for. Plus, another trimester with you would be a bad idea."

"In my classroom I highly agree," he says, surprising me.

I stop and turn to fully face him. I can't help my eyes as they roam over his body again when he leans toward me. My breath hitches in my chest as he nears me, making me look up and down the hall to make sure no one is coming.

"And why is that, Mr. Dumont?"

James smiles and it makes my heart melt. "Because I don't think I can go another trimester of having you in the same room as me without talking to you like this. I like these little conversations we have but let's face it, the quick ones in the hall are just not cutting it anymore. Don't you agree?"

"Yes."

He moves closer again. "So if you don't have any plans for next trimester I'd like you to be my assistant, if that's all right with you?"

His assistant? Work closely with him on projects and assignments and in his office on an everyday basis? I need to pinch myself to make sure this isn't a dream.

"You want me to work for you?" I squeak out.

He shakes his head. "Not especially but circumstances being what they are I think this would be a perfect solution for us."

"Solution to what?" I need to hear him say it so I don't think I'm going crazy.

He leans in close to my ear. The warmth of his breath tickles the side of my face. "The solution for us to be together and to get to know each other."

"Oh."

His hand cups my cheek, making me flush with a mixture

of delight and nerves. I didn't realize how much I crave his touch until I don't have it. And now that I do, I don't want to lose it. His eyes look intense, focused solely on me as they flick back and forth between my mouth and my eyes. His thumb gently rubs across my cheekbone while his fingers play with the lobe of my ear.

"You're so beautiful Britta." His forehead rests on mine. My hands reach up to stroke the side of his face, gliding over the freshly shaved skin. "Can I kiss you?"

"Yes," I breathe.

We lean toward each other, letting our bodies take the lead. The first contact of his lips sends a shock through my system. They're warm and soft, just as I remember from a month ago, yet restrained and cautious. Again we're playing with fire but the heat feels so good that we just can't stop.

A month is too long to go without these lips again, to go without the gentle touch of his hand or look deeply into his eyes and see the secrets he's not telling me.

I risk the chance of taking it further by running my tongue along his lower lip, tasting and teasing until his own tongue greets mine. The minute they touch, I know I'm done for. The taste of peppermint and what can only be James fills my mouth, feeding my addiction even more.

We breathe the same air as our tongues dance together. We hold each other close, not wanting to let the other move away. I can feel his heart beating against my chest. He must feel the same as I do because my heart is matching his rhythm beat for beat, as if they were the same organ.

Laughter filters down the hallway and we pull apart, breathless and dazed. His eyes are still shining, still giving me the warm feeling that I'm addicted to every time I see him.

"I've wanted to do that for a while." He smiles, releasing

my face and backing up several steps so there's a comfortable distance between us.

The frantic beating of my heart is still pounding in my chest. Our eyes stay locked onto each other as I pull myself off the wall on shaky legs.

"I'm glad you did," I say, finally responding to him.

He laughs and we resume walking toward the gym to join the rest of the student body. He stops me before we walk through the doors, lightly touching my elbow.

"Thank you for not apologizing this time."

"There's nothing to apologize for," I say. "We're both adults and there's an obvious attraction between us that I'm refusing to believe is wrong for us to pursue. We just have to be smart about this. Part of me wants to see where this can go, even though I know a relationship is not possible."

James smiles and nods. "You're right. A relationship is not possible. We'll just have to think of something else."

The air stills around us as we remain motionless. How do we move on when going forward isn't an option?

Pushing a smile onto my face, I do the one thing I know will ignite a reaction from him. "So I guess I'll see you Monday afternoon then, Mr. Dumont?"

He grumbles and lowers his head to my ear again. "It drives me wild to listen to you call me Mr. Dumont. When we're not in class, use my first name. Otherwise I cannot promise to behave myself."

I giggle and press a hand to his chest. "Well, right now we're in a public setting in school so unfortunately you're going to have to control yourself, *Mr. Dumont.*"

James rolls his eyes and it makes me giggle again. "God I love that sound. And I wish I could dance with the queen just once out there. But I'll have to take a raincheck."

"Promise?" I ask, my voice filled with hope.

"Promise."

Something passes between us, making both of us take a sharp intake of breath. His hand covers mine on his chest and he squeezes it quickly before releasing me. We smile and move away from each other, going our separate way for the rest of the night. But the smile remains plastered on my face and this time it's not faked.

Ten

"THIS WEEK BLOWS BALLS," PENNY SAYS, SLAMMING her locker shut.

I turn to face her, unable to help the laugh from escaping me. "Why is that?"

She blows some hair off her forehead and pins me with a stare. "Seriously? It's test week since it's the end of the trimester. And I have a test every single day. How in the hell am I supposed to carry on my social life and study for every single class?"

"I guess your social life is going to have to wait until the weekend," I say. "Are we still leaving Friday night?"

She nods. "Yep. I have the tickets in hand and everything." Penny chews on her bottom lip before meeting my eyes again. "Hey, question for you. Would you mind terribly if you stayed in your own room?"

I raise a questioning eyebrow to her. "Why?"

Penny stops and faces me. "Because Travis is going to be there too and, well, you know."

I hold my hand up to stop her from saying anything else.

"No need to elaborate. I'll get my own room. It's no big deal. But I'm making sure it's on a different floor and on the opposite side of the hall from you two. The last thing I want to hear is you two having sex."

She laughs and hugs me tightly. "You're the best, you know that?"

"I know. I'm a goddamned angel."

We stop outside the teacher's lounge and wave goodbye to each other. I make my way to Mrs. Davis's office and boot up her computer before taking out my dish of leftover stir-fry. I decide to heat it up now while I'm waiting for some update to load so I go over to the microwave and set the timer.

Several teachers pass by me, saying hi and asking me how things are going. It's nice and strange at the same time that they don't care if a student is back here. Then again, they're used to seeing me back here all the time so it's not that big of a deal anymore.

The timer dings and I take the bowl out, shuffling it back and forth in my hands in an attempt not to burn myself.

"You know that works better if you use a paper towel or napkin to hold it," a strong masculine voice says behind me.

My lips quirk up into a half-smile at his voice and my heart does that recognizable flutter in my chest.

"Is that so? Well, thank goodness you're around so I don't do something stupid and get a boo-boo."

James laughs and sets down his own plate of food on the counter. "A boo-boo?"

"Yep. But I guess then I'd have to go see the school nurse and I highly doubt she'd kiss it and make it better."

His eyes flash instantly and my body reacts. He leans closer so only I can hear. "If anyone is going to be kissing anything away for you, it'll be me."

My mouth goes dry as I bring a hand up to my throat. That is just about the hottest thing anyone has ever said to me. I blink several times, unsure of how to respond.

"Really?" I whisper. My voice is hoarse with need.

James pins me with a stare and my nipples tighten almost painfully in my bra. Luckily it's padded so he can't see my reaction. The way he's looking at me, devouring me with his eyes makes me want to lock us in a closet somewhere and explore what we're both apparently thinking.

My eyes flick down his body briefly, wondering if there are signs of a similar reaction. That's when I notice his stance is turned toward the counter, hiding the front of his pants. He pretends to look for something in the cupboard and I can see the corners of his lips are turned up with a smile.

"No one will kiss anything away from you but me. That is a promise." He turns his head to look at me and I bite my lip. "Don't do that," he says lowly.

"Why?"

He shuts the door and whispers in my ear. "Because it drives me wild when you do."

My breathing becomes labored, desperate to drag in the precious air I need. "I thought calling you Mr. Dumont drove you wild?"

"Both of those things do. As a matter of fact, there isn't much about you that doesn't drive me wild."

"Friends," I say, swallowing hard. "We're friends, remember?"

James backs away, nodding his head. "Right. Friends."

I take my now cooled bowl of food and grab a fork from the drawer. "I need to get my work done. I'll see you later."

I quickly walk back to Mrs. Davis's office before he can respond. If I stay with him any longer, I think my body would break down and give in to my craving.

Through the jumbled haze of my brain, I remember that I need to book a room for the weekend. I pull up one of the discount booking websites and start entering in my information after selecting a king room in the hotel we're staying at.

I turn my head when someone knocks on the door and come face to face with a guilty-looking James.

"Hey," I say, putting my credit card on the desk.

"Hey." He walks in and sits in the empty chair next to the desk. He folds his hands and rests his elbows on his knees, slumping over slightly. "Look, about what happened out there…"

I hold up my hand to stop him. "Don't say it. We need to stop apologizing to each other for our feelings. We're not doing anything wrong so we have nothing to apologize for."

"But what I said-"

"What you said was the single hottest thing anyone has ever said to me. And I refuse to listen to an apology that will take it back. If you don't like me, fine. Apologize. But then don't say anything like that to me again and we'll stick to safer topics, like the grass or the weather instead of the innocent flirting we've been doing."

The heat I saw before in his eyes flashes again, making my body react in the same way. "This is really not fair."

I shake my head. "No, it's not. But it is what it is so we just need to deal with it."

James straightens up and nods. "You're right. I'm not sorry for what I said, but I'll remember to only say those things when I'm able to make good on the words."

My lips turn up in the corners, giving him a shy smile. "Good."

He turns his head to look at the monitor. "Going out of town?"

I nod. "Penny and I are going to a concert in Boston this weekend. Apparently I need to get my own hotel room, though."

"You're going by yourselves?" he asks, inching his chair closer.

"Originally it was supposed to be just me and Penny, but Travis is coming as well. Which is why I need to get my own hotel room."

"What concert are you going to see?" he asks, leaning his elbow on the desk.

"Foo Fighters. We've been dying to see them for a while and they're finally playing around here."

"That's quite the drive for you both. And your parents are okay with you going?"

I nod. "They trust us and know that we're not going to do anything to put ourselves in danger. Plus we've been to Boston before and have come back alive so it's been tested and proven that we're reliable. That tends to help."

"Sounds like you're going to have an excellent weekend. Are you staying just Saturday night?" he asks.

"No, we're making a whole weekend of it. We're leaving right after school on Friday. It's our reward for the end of the trimester."

"I love the Foo Fighters. They're one of my favorite bands, right next to Collective Soul."

"You like Collective Soul too?" I ask, my eyes wide.

He nods. "Yep. I've loved them since I was younger. I play their Seven Year Itch album nonstop in my car on long drives."

Now it's my turn to lean back in the chair. "No way. That has all the best songs on there. It's my addiction when I need a pick me up."

"That's funny. Let me guess, you also play the Foo Fighters Greatest Hits album as well."

I laugh and nod in agreement. "The CD for my car and the DVD for at home because the videos are so funny. The one where Jack Black and Dave Grohl are in the motel room kills me every time, along with the mock Mentos commercial one."

"Big Me is hands down my favorite video of theirs. Dave Grohl is a genius. And I guess I'm kind of surprised you're that big on those two bands. I figured you'd be more into the pop dance craze."

I roll my eyes. "I like some of the songs from the AT40 charts, but a lot of them are too childish and sound like tweenage crap. I like the older stuff because that's when music was about music and not about making millions of dollars or putting out albums faster than you can process the last one." I pause. "And yes, Dave Grohl is a genius."

"Wow. I think I just fell in love with you." James laughs silently and my breath stills in my lungs for the briefest of seconds. I know he's kidding but oh how I wish those words could be real at some point.

James notices my silence and reaches out to grab my hand, cradling it in his before gently tugging on it, bringing my chair closer to him.

"It's amazing how much we have in common," I murmur. He nods in agreement. "It almost makes me wonder if you're real or just some figment of my imagination." He nods again. "Are you?"

He presses his forehead against mine. "I'm real Britta. And I wonder the same thing as well, if everything is just my imagination or if this truly is a reality."

I resist the urge to close the distance between our lips. "Currently it's a cruel reality."

"It won't be much longer. This is the last week you're going to be my student."

"You're right. But then I'll be working for you and that will just add to a whole new set of complications."

He shakes his head, making mine shake as well. "No complications. This will alleviate them. I'll be able to see you more often like this. It'll be good. I promise."

Several voices can be heard just down the hallway and we push away from each other. I turn back to my screen and resume typing my information in, which I now have to do over again since the session timed out.

James glances down at his watch. "Damn. I'm going to be late again. You are giving me a bad habit of being late to my fifth-period class."

I side-eye him and raise an eyebrow. "Excuse me? I'm not the one holding you back from anything. If you're late, that's all on you, buddy."

The warm laugh that I adore fills the room again and my body heats up at the sound. "You're right. No one is responsible for my actions except me." He turns while shoving his hands in his pockets. "I'll see you in class, Ms. Fosse."

"Goodbye, Mr. Dumont," I chirp, enjoying the quiet groan I hear as he leaves the office.

That man is going to be the death of me. One minute he's too intense and then the next minute it's like we're best friends. But he's my addiction, my craving, and I constantly need my next fix of him to function. Yes, it's wrong to rely on someone else for your happiness, but James is slowly weaving himself into my life, making it so I can't let him go. There's something there between us and I need to figure out what it is. It could be love. It could be lust. It could be all in my head at this point but, no matter what, I need to follow my instincts with this because rarely do they ever let me down.

Eleven

WE PULL INTO THE PARKING LOT OF THE HOTEL AND quickly unload our bags from the trunk. After hours in the car, we all need to just stretch and relax. Being the nice person I am, I let Penny sit up front with Travis. It was worth the potential for motion sickness to hear the happiness in her voice. We quickly check into the hotel and make our way up to Penny and Travis's room first.

"What did you think of Mr. Dumont's test today? That was brutal," Penny says, flopping onto her king-sized bed. Travis pulls their bags further into the room and drops them at the end of the bed, letting them crash together before he jumps on top of her. Her squeals of delight make me want to run to my room as quickly as possible before clothes start flying at my head.

"Travis! Stop! Not while Britta's here."

I roll my eyes. "Yes, please. I don't need to see any naked asses or any other body parts. My virgin eyes won't be able to take it."

Travis laughs. "Are those the only part of you that are virgin?"

Penny smacks him in the chest. "So uncalled for. Plus that's my line."

I laugh at the both of them. "I thought Mr. Dumont's test wasn't bad at all. I finished early and waited patiently for the rest of you."

"Yeah, but you're a brain so that's to be expected. You ace everything you do. It's kind of sick in a way," Travis mutters, nuzzling into Penny's hair.

She moves in between his legs with her back pressed against his chest and his legs crossed over hers.

"I don't know. It was hard, but I don't think it was the worst one I took all week. Mr. Johnston's was worse by far."

I shrug my shoulders and take a seat in one of the empty chairs in the corner. "I only had four tests so it wasn't that bad."

"That's because you're an assistant for two periods. Man did you ever luck out there," Travis says. Penny squeals quietly as he tickles her on her sides.

"You could have the same problem too if you had taken the early morning classes starting in ninth grade," I say.

"Screw that. As if I'm giving up my sleeping in time. Thanks, but no thanks. I'll suffer through falling asleep in my classes and passing because of sports," he responds.

"Well, I'm going to find my room and let you two do… whatever."

"Hey, what's your room number so we can call you and meet up later?" Penny asks.

I pull out the white envelope that houses my key and look at the number scribbled on the flap. "I'm in 820."

"Dude that's like three floors away from here," she says.

"Perfect. Then I'm just far enough away from you two so I won't get hives trying to block out images and noises."

They both laugh and wave to me as I lug my suitcase out the door and toward the elevator. I quietly hum a song that's stuck in my head while I wait patiently for the car to arrive. When I hear the ding, I prepare to enter through the open doors but am momentarily frozen in place.

What I'm not prepared for is to be looking at beautiful green eyes paired with a smile that stops my heart every time I see them.

"Fancy meeting you here," he says.

My mouth slacks open; stuck somewhere between talking and breathing. There's a tightness in my chest and confusion clouds my vision. *Why is he here? How did he get here?*

"What…how…when…"

James laughs and holds the door open until a buzzing noise can be heard. "You getting in or are you going to wait until they send maintenance to figure out what's wrong with the elevator?"

I snap out of my stupor and pull my bag inside, leaving some distance between its only occupant and me.

"Which floor?" he asks with a knowing smirk.

"Why do I have the feeling you already know?" I say, crossing my arms in front of my chest.

His eyes travel over my body, staying a tad longer on my raised breasts due to the placement of my arms. James presses the door close button and I notice that my floor is already illuminated.

"You think you're so smart. Why are you here?"

The air is thick as we travel the three floors up; thick with desire and nervousness and I'm unsure who it's coming from. Maybe it's from him or maybe it's from me or the combination of the both of us. But my heart skips a beat when he moves closer. His warm breath falls upon my cheek, sending a round of tingles to travel through my bones.

"I'm here for the concert. Why else would I be here?"

My hands tremble near my sides, thankful that they're hidden beneath my arms so he can't see them shake.

"And you just happen to be in this hotel?"

"Yes."

We look at each other and start to close the distance between us until the ding of the elevator stops us from moving. The doors open to our floor and the rush of cool air assaults my face. I didn't realize how flushed I was until that moment.

I grab my bag and roll it off the elevator. He places his hand on my lower back as if it's the most natural thing. The fit is perfect, settling right into the curve of my spine. My skin hums as we walk down the hall, only just now registering that he's ushering me right to my room.

"You know which room is mine, don't you," I state as a matter of fact.

He doesn't answer, just gives me that knowing smile again.

"Unbelievable," I mutter. That gets a laugh from him.

"Yes, I know which room is yours. How do you think I was able to get mine right across the hall?"

We pause outside of our doors. I feel like I'm in shock or disbelief at what's happening right now. He's tracked me down to my hotel, making sure that his room is right near mine.

"James, what are you doing?" I breathe, leaning against my closed door.

He runs a nervous hand through his hair. "Honestly, I don't know. I've never done something this impulsive before. But when you said that you'd be going to Boston essentially by yourself, I just had to be there, in case something happened to you. There's just this feeling that's been bugging me since you told me."

"Nothing is going to happen to me. I'm a big girl. I can take care of myself. Besides, Penny and Travis are here. How are you going to explain any of this to them? I mean you have to admit it looks suspicious."

"What's there to explain? It's not like I'm asking to be your date for the whole weekend. We may not even see each other so they'll never know I'm here. It's a big city with millions of people. Surely I can blend in with them."

I laugh at the absurdity of this whole situation. "You blend in about as well as a giant among pygmies. I can always find you in a crowd."

He steps closer, pressing my back further into my door. "As can I. Your long brown hair, your gorgeous hazel eyes, your full pink lips, all of it stands out to me. Everywhere I go, I swear I see you. It's like you're stuck in my head and I can't shake you out. Do you know what I mean?"

Is he saying everything that's always running around my head, reading my thoughts perfectly? I lick my dry lips, his intense stare following my tongue.

"Yes," I breathe. "I do know what you mean. But we can't act on it. We're still in a situation that prevents us from doing anything about it."

"Correction," he says, pushing some hair behind my ear. "I'm no longer your teacher and you're no longer my student."

"But, next trimester-"

"Next trimester," he interrupts, "you're my colleague. You'll be working with me instead of me teaching you."

I shake my head and look to the floor. "That's not entirely accurate. I'll be working *for* you, not with you. You'll still be in a position of authority."

Two fingers are placed under my chin, lifting my hazel eyes to his green. "That's not how I see it. You're my equal, in everything. That's what I see when I look at you. Not a student, not an assistant. An equal, a match. My match."

"James."

Our lips find each other in the short distance, moving slowly at first, savoring the taste of each other. His fingertips brush gently over my cheek, sending another round of chills through my body. My hands slide up his stomach and chest, tracing the hard lines beneath the cotton of his shirt before wrapping around his neck, pulling our bodies closer.

I need him like I need my next breath. My addiction is becoming dangerous and I feel like I'm losing a piece of myself every time I'm near him. And he's picking up each piece and holding onto them, keeping them safe until I can fully give him everything I have.

He breaks away first, his fingers stalling at the hollow dip of my throat. The frantic beating of my heart roars through my ears and a million different sensations make my skin extremely sensitive to his touch.

"You better get into your room," he says huskily. He's as affected as I am, as evidenced by the tightening of his pants.

"You too."

He backs away and my body feels cold without his heat near me. I fumble with the keycard, finally putting it into the slot on the third attempt. His voice stops me before I close my door.

"Britta?"

"Yeah?"

He runs another hand through his hair and looks up at me. "This sounds extremely cheesy but can I get your phone number? I'd like to see you tomorrow if it's possible."

A smile crawls across my face. Jutting the latch for the door out so I don't get locked out, I walk over to him as he holds out his phone to me. Quickly entering my information into it for him, I smile and hand it back.

"Give me a call sometime," I say, walking backward to my propped open door.

James looks down at his phone and smirks. "I like the smiley face after your name."

"Goodnight, James."

"Goodnight, Britta."

I close the door behind me and secure it, just in case he's used his charm and somehow got a key to my room as well. It wouldn't shock me if he did. My fingers trace my lips; his kiss still lingering there makes me smile wider.

As I'm unpacking my suitcase, my phone beeps in my purse. Knowing who it is, I quickly swipe at the screen.

HI.

Hi? I give him my phone number and all he types is hi? What the hell?

Another message comes through, this time making me laugh.

SORRY, THAT WAS LAME.

I settle against the headboard of my bed, barely noticing how comfortable I am in having this conversation with my former teacher. Can I call him a former teacher? *Don't think, just feel* I tell myself.

YOU'RE REALLY BAD AT THIS YOU KNOW.

His response is almost immediate.

I'M NERVOUS.

SERIOUSLY? YOU'RE 22. YOU SHOULD BE OVER THAT.

IT'S NOT MY AGE. IT'S YOU THAT MAKES ME NERVOUS.

ME?

I LIKE YOU.

Whoa. That's probably the first time he's ever directly said anything like that to me. Yes, we've been dancing around it, saying we feel something toward each other but nothing this direct, at least not that I can remember saying out loud. My heart pounds wildly in my chest as I type my reply.

I LIKE YOU TOO.

HOW MUCH?

A LOT.

CAN I KISS YOU AGAIN?

YOU DON'T HAVE TO ASK. YOU CAN JUST KISS ME.

There's a knock on my door and I smirk, knowing who's going to be on the other side. I open the door wide and am greeted by his hands cradling my face. His warm breath beats on my lips followed by the gentle brush of his mouth against mine. He steals my breath on a gasp and I succumb to the kiss, grabbing his biceps to keep him close. His fingers thread through my hair as his tongue explores my mouth, gently probing inside with slow, deep licks.

This kiss consumes me, igniting a fire within that cannot be extinguished. It's everything I want from a kiss and more because it's from him. I can feel his heartbeat against my chest and I fight the urge to drag him into my room.

We slowly pull away, keeping each other in our sight. With a gentle brush of his lips against my nose, he smiles and backs away.

"That is a proper goodnight," he says, swiping his key in the lock.

"Uh huh," is all I can say. He's kissed me speechless, which is quite the feat I must say. I'm always the girl who knows what to say and when to say it. But as this beautiful man stands across the hall, looking at me as if I'm the only person in the world, all my words are gone. Nothing is left. The only thing that remains is him.

"Goodnight, Britta. Get some sleep."

"Uh huh."

I'm left with his quiet laugh as his door shuts and latches, leaving me standing in the doorway in a stupor. He just kissed me to within an inch of my life and then left me to dwell on it. Turning back into my room, my head fuzzy and dazed, I lie on my bed and stare at the white ceiling above me.

He likes me.

I like him.

He kissed me.

He's the best kisser I've ever kissed.

This is bad.

I'm so fucked.

Twelve

STRETCHING FEELS GOOD AFTER A NIGHT OF TOSSING and turning, being unable to get the kiss out of my head long enough to settle my body down. Damn his perfect lips, his perfect face and eyes. Damn him for being a teacher and not meeting him six months from now when we would be able to make a go of it.

My phone beeps next to me and I run a hand down my face, still trying to wake up. I glance at the screen and roll my eyes at Penny's name.

DUDE YOU AWAKE?

BARELY.

YOU HUNGRY?

I look at the clock and register that it's only seven.

NOT NOW BUT IN A BIT.

My phone rings and I'm guessing she has more to say than what she'll be able to type.

"So Trav and I want to get a head start on wandering around today. Can you be ready in an hour?"

I fall back onto my pillow and throw my other arm over my eyes. "Do I have to? I mean, can't I just meet you somewhere later today? I'm exhausted and would like to just veg for a while."

"I don't want to ditch you here in a hotel by yourself. That wasn't my intention when I invited Travis to come along."

"Don't worry about it. I'm a big girl. I can entertain myself just fine." I look over at the door and smile, thinking of how I could pass the time if I had the chance. "How about we meet up for lunch or something later? Let's say around one?"

Rustling and giggling come over the line and I hold the phone away from my ear slightly due to her high-pitched squeal.

"One sounds fine. How about that café down the street?"

"Your favorite one with the kickass panini?" I ask.

"Yep, that's the one."

I nod. "Sold. I'll meet you there at one. This way you guys can have some time alone together. If anything changes or you need more time, just let me know by noon so I can plan accordingly."

"You're the best Britt. Love you lots."

"Love you too. Bye, nut job."

I hit end call and place the phone back on the table next to the bed. Now I'm fully awake when I don't need to be. God this sucks.

Another beep of my phone and I'm half tempted to throw it across the room. I just want to get some sleep but I'm happy to see the newly saved contact name on my screen.

YOU AWAKE?

YOU'RE THE SECOND PERSON TO ASK ME THAT ALREADY THIS MORNING.

LOL. HUNGRY?

YOU'RE TWO FOR TWO SO FAR. ARE YOU GOING TO DITCH ME AS WELL TO HANG OUT WITH YOUR BOYFRIEND?

YOU'RE BY YOURSELF THIS MORNING?

LOOKS THAT WAY.

I wait for his reply while twirling the phone between my fingers. What is taking so long for him to respond?

The knock on my door is the answer to my question. I throw the covers off me and pad barefoot over to the door, holding it open just enough to look at the impeccably handsome man staring back at me.

"Morning," he rasps. Man, his early morning voice is sexy.

"Morning."

"Can I come in?" He shoves his hands in his pockets and rocks back on his heels. How can I say no to that?

I open the door and stand to the side, staying partially hidden behind it. James walks past me and I fluff my hair slightly as I secure the door again. I turn and find him standing in front of my bed, just staring at me.

"Um, I'm going to go in here for a quick second. Be right back," I say, pointing to the bathroom.

He doesn't say anything, just nods his head and smiles. I quickly dash inside and begin to make myself halfway presentable; brushing my teeth and hair and trying to make more of the tank top and sleep shorts that I'm wearing. A futile effort but I have to try. My choices are to have half of my ass hanging out or most of my stomach showing. I opt for the stomach, the lesser of two evils.

When I walk back into the main room, I find him sitting on the edge of my bed, his hands folded neatly in his lap. He's wearing jeans and a sweater, perfect for the early winter weather. I know technically it's still considered fall, but it is positively freezing outside. But his sweater looks nice and warm and soft that I want to just cuddle up next to him and nuzzle my face into his chest.

James clears his throat when I lean against the wall and twist my fingers together in front of me.

"Are you going to get dressed?"

I look down and smirk. "I am dressed. See, clothes?"

He shifts on the bed and looks mildly uncomfortable. "I can see that. There's not a whole lot there, though."

I roll my eyes and walk closer to him. "I'm covering all necessary parts. Nothing is inappropriately showing."

He runs a hand over his face and I sit on the corner of the bed, far enough away from him so he doesn't completely lose his shit. He's uncomfortable, I can tell, but at the same time I can feel the need radiating off him. James looks everywhere except at me.

"Do I make you nervous?" I ask quietly.

He turns his head and smirks. "I think I answered that question last night. But just in case you weren't sure, yes, you make me nervous. Especially when you're barely dressed and looking how you do at this moment."

"And how do I look?"

"Are you kidding me?"

I shake my head, genuinely wanting to know what he's thinking.

"You look radiant, sitting there with your messy bed hair and wild eyes that still have a touch of sleep to them. Like you're just waking up from a dream. Seeing you this way is better than any other time I've looked at you. Even more than homecoming night when you were dressed in your finest. This simple look, this everyday look, is when you're at your most beautiful."

A flush creeps upon my cheeks. His words are so beautiful, so perfect, and they make my heart twinge slightly with a mixture of delight and fear.

"Why do you have to be so sweet?" I whisper.

James inches toward me and tucks some hair behind my ear. "I'm not always sweet. I can be an ass sometimes and also have some possessive qualities that may not be as flattering as they could be. I'm jealous and moody when things don't go my way, but I'm also faithful and understanding and patient. So very patient because when I look at you, I know that I need to take my time to do this right. Screwing this up by going too fast is not something I want to do."

I swallow past the lump in my throat and turn to fully face him, hitching my knee onto the bed. "I don't know what to say to that."

He swallows hard and wipes his hands on his jeans. "You don't have to say anything you don't want to say. I told you last night I like you and today I'm saying it out loud, just in case there was any confusion. I know things are going to get… tricky…with this. And I know you said before that you're not looking for a relationship. And I get it. I do. But I'll wait until you are because the way I feel when I'm around you, it's unlike anything I've ever felt before. I'll be patient for you."

"You're unbelievable, you know that? Not many guys are like you. If there isn't some instant satisfaction or gratification, they bolt without looking back. But you know there's a mountain to climb and you're willing to scale it until you reach the peak." He opens his mouth, but I place my index finger against his lips to silence him. "And I get jealous too, so I understand where that comes from. Such a weird byproduct of emotions between two people. Moody I understand. I am a high school girl.

Drama comes with the territory, even though I like to surround myself with people who live without it.

"And what we're thinking of doing? Of possibly pursuing at some point in the future, be it immediately or later on down the line? It's crazy. But I get it. I understand how you feel because I like you too. So much that I'm addicted to you and it scares me. I worry every day that others can see it written across my face or read into the smiles I give or the tone of my voice. I'm afraid that someone will find out that I enjoy kissing you and everything will be destroyed."

He moves even closer, our knees touching. "No one will find out. Nothing will happen."

"You don't know that," I whisper.

James tilts my chin toward him. "You're right. I don't know that. But I know that I would move heaven and earth to not let it happen. I'll protect you, whatever the cost."

"This is crazy."

"I know."

"You're going to be bad for me."

He smirks. "I know."

"But I like you anyway."

"I know."

Our lips connect in a chaste kiss, letting go of everything else to see where this is going. We cannot fear what isn't there. There are only obstacles if we make them and we're going to try like hell not to let any appear.

I smile against his lips and enjoy the warmth of his minty breath against them. "I think I better get dressed now."

His green eyes connect with mine and a low rumble echoes through his chest. "Please hurry. That tank top is killing me."

Laughing, I get off the bed and grab some clothes out of the dresser. "Funny. I thought it'd be the shorts that did you in."

The heat of his stare burns my skin as he devours every inch of available flesh before him; my feet, my thighs, the tops of my breasts. Every piece is singed by the fire showing in his eyes.

He clears his throat and I laugh. "Those too."

I shake my head and walk into the bathroom to put him out of his misery. Boys are such simple yet crazy creatures.

Ten minutes later I emerge fully dressed with my hair pulled back into a low, messy ponytail draped over my shoulder. "Better?" I ask, giving him a twirl.

"Much," he says, standing from the bed. His soft lips press against my forehead and I smile at the simple gesture.

"Now you can take me out for breakfast," I say.

He laces his fingers with mine. "Is that so? Maybe that wasn't my intention at all when I texted you this morning."

"Pfft. Whatever. Come on, *Mr. Dumont*, we need to eat."

Those green eyes flash again and I giggle as I grab my purse and head toward the door. He stops me by tickling my sides, creating a loud snort to escape. I bang my head against the door while still laughing, enjoying the similar sound of my assailant.

"That was not funny," he says, slowing his ministrations against my body.

I gasp for air and look over my shoulder before opening the door. "I thought it was hilarious."

We walk into the hall with our residual laughter dying away slowly. My stomach hurts but in a good way, and my legs feel shaky but not from the tickling he just gave me. No, it's more from the fact that he had his hands on me. Something so easy as that can mean so much.

Luckily for us, there's a restaurant attached to the hotel so we don't have far to go. The hostess seats us in a booth in the back. We peruse the menus briefly before I set mine down first, resting my elbows on the table while propping my chin up with my folded hands.

"Decided already?"

"Yep. My breakfast staple is on the menu and I'm all for it."

"And what's that?" he asks. His eyes dart from the menu to mine and the makings of a small smile form on the corners of his lips.

"A Denver omelet."

He raises an eyebrow at me once he looks over at my choice. "Three eggs, a heaping pile of vegetables, loaded with cheese on top and served with a side of hash browns. Are you sure you'll be able to eat that much? I mean let's face it, you're tiny and don't exactly look as if you pound down the food very often."

I lean forward slightly and narrow my eyes. "Is that a challenge?"

He nods his head and meets me halfway. "That is most definitely a challenge."

I reach across the table and extend my right hand. "You're on." He shakes my hand with a firm shake but then surprises me by pulling it to his mouth and placing a gentle kiss on top.

"And what are the terms?"

Oh shit. I should have thought of those before I agreed. "Well, I don't know. What do you think they should be?"

James releases my hand and runs a finger across his lips. "If I win, you have to do something fun with me."

"Something more specific or is that it?"

"I can't give everything away. For all I know you'd try to lose on purpose then."

"I never lose on purpose. Have you seen my GPA? Pretty sure that means I win at everything."

He laughs. "Book smarts has nothing to do with this, sweetheart." My heart flutters at his term of endearment. "You'll just have to trust me."

I huff in my seat. "Fine. If I win, though," I start, tapping my finger against my chin. "If I win you have to do something fun with me."

"How original of you," he says with an eye roll.

"You have no idea what I've got planned so don't get too confident there, buddy. For all you know it could be something you absolutely detest."

James crooks a finger at me as I lean forward. "There is nothing you could ask me to do that I would dislike."

That makes me chuckle. "We'll see about that."

The waitress brings our coffees and smiles brightly at James, who doesn't seem to notice her flirting attempts. His eyes never leave mine, making me feel like the only person in the restaurant. She writes down our orders and walks away with a slight frown at her rebuffed attempts.

"So tell me," I start, taking a tentative sip of my coffee, "what was the great James Dumont like in high school? Let me guess, the super jock, popular with the ladies with two or three of them hanging on your arms every day?"

He laughs and takes a sip of his own coffee. "Nothing like that. I was just your typical high school guy. Played sports, sure, but I wasn't the star by any means."

"What'd you play?"

"Football in the fall, basketball in the winter, and baseball in the spring."

"Ooh, the triple threat. I was almost afraid you were going to say track and field for a minute."

His eyes crinkle at the corners with amusement. "That would have made my parents happy. Less money for them to shell out for sure."

"So what positions did you play for each sport?" I ask, enjoying the ease of this conversation.

"Well, in football I was a receiver."

"Damn. I had you pegged for a quarterback."

He shakes his head. "That was Brady Williams. He was the super jock of the team. Made all-state three years in a row and got a full scholarship to Florida State."

"Impressive. But did he have the brains to go with that scholarship?"

"He was smart but not like you. He did well in school. Definitely didn't rely on the teachers to pass him simply because he was in sports, unlike a few students I know."

I sigh and twirl my mug around. "Yeah, I know who you're talking about. They could be so much more if they just applied themselves."

"But Brady and I worked well together on the field. I was his go-to guy and we scored a lot of touchdowns in our high school career."

"Where did you go to school?" I can't believe I've never asked him this before. Somehow we've never talked about where he grew up.

"Hartford."

"I see. A big city guy. This must be quite the culture shock for you, living in our little town."

James shrugs. "I like the smaller towns. They're quiet, peaceful, and generally filled with nicer people than the larger metro areas."

I lean forward and smile. "Really? You're saying you'd rather live there than a large city? I mean there's not exactly a whole lot to do around town other than the bowling alley and the movie theater. Oh, and the mall. Can't forget the mall."

He laughs. "You make it sound like Somerset is this incredibly tiny town. It's actually one of the bigger cities, you know. Just nothing along the lines of Hartford."

"I think I'm just jaded because I've lived there my entire life and I'm used to everything. I need something new, something exciting. Something that will make me love it there again."

"We can fix that."

I raise an eyebrow to him. "Oh yeah?"

"Yeah." James gives me another smile, one that turns me into a puddle in my seat.

"We'll see I guess."

"So do your parents still live in Hartford?" I turn the focus back on him, right where I want it to be.

"Yeah, they still live in the house they bought after I was born. My dad is an engineer and my mom owns a local bakery."

I smile. "That's quite the combination. How'd they meet?"

"They were high school sweethearts. My dad stayed in Hartford to complete his degree because he couldn't leave my mom's side. She didn't have enough money for college so she worked for the family business. Eventually, she took it over from my grandma and has never been happier. She even started recruiting my sister into the business so she can retire with my dad within the next ten years."

"How old is your sister?"

"Twenty-four."

"Wow, you're close together in age."

He nods. "Seventeen months to be exact. And she reminds me of it every time we argue."

Another thing we have in common.

"Did she go to culinary school then?"

He takes a sip of his coffee. "No, she went to school for business, but she's been baking with my mom since she was little. It's second nature to her."

"So three generations will have run the bakery?"

He nods. "Yeah. It's pretty cool."

"I agree. Definitely cool."

Just then the waitress brings us our food, putting an end to the conversation. I look down at my plate and bite the inside of my cheek. Perhaps my eyes were bigger than my stomach when I ordered this.

James laughs and shoves a forkful of hash browns into his mouth. "You better get working if you want to win our bet."

I point my fork at him and smile. "Don't you worry about that bet. I've got this."

Maybe.

I blow out a puff of air and start in on the omelet, knowing that I can always eat the hash browns. They're my favorite. Everything tastes just wonderful. The veggies are crisp and there's just enough cheese covering the top so it's not overpowering.

"So what are your plans for after high school? I guess we've never really discussed it before," James says around a piece of bacon.

My hand hovers in front of my mouth while I chew. "College."

That prompts an immediate eye roll from him. "More specific. Local, far away, community, four-year, Ivy League?"

I swallow the food and laugh. "I've got several applications out right now, some local and some not so much."

"Which local ones?"

I fold my lips over my teeth and think. "Yale, of course, because it's close, Brown because it's also not too far away, and Harvard because I adore Boston."

"With your grades I'm sure you'll probably get accepted to all of them. Which far away ones did you apply to?"

"Stanford and UC-Berkley."

James tilts his head to the side. "California? Why those?"

"Just for a change of scenery I guess. I want to go to med

school and all of these schools have some of the best programs in the country. And with my SAT and ACT scores being what they are, plus my GPA, I should be able to get into whichever college I want."

James is silently staring at me, not really moving except to breathe. "I'm glad you've done your research and know what you're getting into. More importantly that you've created the means for you to go anywhere you want."

I put my fork down and reach across the table to touch his hand. "Do you have a contract with the school? You know, stating how long you have to be there to teach?"

He shakes his head. "I'm on a temporary contract for right now since I was a replacement for Mr. Ward. It's up to them after the school year to offer me one or not."

"What will you do if they don't offer you one? Will you move back to Hartford?" A twinge of panic settles into my chest at the thought of him leaving, even though I won't be staying either.

"I haven't thought that far ahead yet. I mean, I could teach just about anywhere so maybe I'll see where my passion takes me. Whether or not it's Somerset has yet to be seen."

"Did you always want to be a teacher?" I ask, pulling my hand away from his.

He takes another bite of his eggs and nods. "I did. Actually, I'm halfway through my Masters program so once I'm done with that, more opportunities will open up for me. You know, possibly teach at a university or become a Superintendent of a district. Teaching has always been my thing. I love to watch kids learn something new, to see when the light bulb goes off as they finally get a concept."

"Wait, back the train up. You said you're halfway through your Masters program?" I ask, swallowing another bite.

He nods. "Like you, I'm also kind of a brain. I skipped a grade and graduated early from high school at seventeen. Then I spent the next four years in college getting two degrees and went right into my Masters program. I'm doing the majority of it online and rarely have to go to physical classes. If I do, I take those in the summer when I'm off already."

I set my fork down and wipe my mouth with the napkin. "Wow, I've never known anyone who's skipped a grade before. Your super nerd powers must exceed my own."

James laughs. "You basically have skipped a grade. I've seen your transcripts. You could graduate now if you wanted to."

I shrug and dig back into my halfway eaten plate. "I could, but I don't want to. I want to graduate with everyone else in my class." I look down to avoid his eyes. "Plus then I wouldn't get to see you every day if I did."

Our feet tangle together beneath the table and I wrap mine around his ankle. "Hey," he whispers, drawing my gaze back to him. Our fingers entwine together and he gives me a reassuring smile. "I'm glad you're staying until the end."

"Me too."

The waitress stops back, asking how things are going. We both respond at the same time, sending a new round of laughter between us.

James releases my hand and points to my plate. "You better get moving. At this rate, you're going to lose."

I shove another piece of omelet into my mouth and I'm starting to agree with him. "I won't go down without a fight."

"Okay, but we're leaving in fifteen minutes so you better step it up."

My stomach rolls at the thought of eating this too fast and I groan. "You never said there was a time limit."

"I'm not sitting around here all day. You and I are going to go out to do something before you meet up with Penny."

This gives me two options. Leave now and lose or stay here and win. Either way, it means I get to do something with James so I'm a winner no matter what. I shove the plate forward, tossing my napkin on top.

"Screw it. Let's go," I say, starting to get up from the booth.

His eyes grow wide as the smile takes over his face. "Really? You're admitting defeat?"

I shake my head. "Not admitting defeat but I'm done sitting here trying to make myself sick. And trust me, I would not be good company if I'm puking the entire time we're out together. So let's move it, buddy. You're taking me sightseeing."

He bolts upright and tosses his napkin on the table while flagging down our waitress for the check.

"How am I going to take you sightseeing if you love Boston?"

I wrap my arm through his and press myself against his body to whisper in his ear. "I've never seen it with you so it'll be like I'm seeing it for the first time."

That familiar spark is back in his eyes, making my blood heat and run faster through my veins. I love it when he looks at me like that. He presses his lips to mine and I can feel him smile against them.

"You're going to be the death of me, you know that?"

I nod. "Same goes for you. So take me around town for the next few hours before we're both six feet under."

He signs the credit card slip for our food and wraps an arm around my back, escorting me out of the restaurant.

"Jackets first, then tour," he says, walking us back to the elevators.

"I knew I liked you for a reason. You're so smart."

He kisses my temple and I melt into his side. A morning

with James all to myself without worrying about repercussions? Sounds like heaven to me.

Thirteen

"THAT WAS THE BEST CONCERT EVER!" PENNY loudly cries out in the car. I can barely hear her anyway due to the ringing in my ears from the noise inside the venue.

"Babe, it was awesome," Travis says. He reaches over places his hand on her knee. I'm thankful I'm in the backseat so I don't have to see if it moves or not.

"Agreed. Best concert ever."

"So now what do you want to do?" Penny asks, craning her neck to look back at me.

"I don't know. Go to bed? I'm exhausted."

"How can you be exhausted? You didn't even make our lunch date," she says. "What exactly did you do all day?"

The flashing lights of the passing cars draw my attention. I don't want to lie to my best friend, but I know that I can't tell her the truth either. "I lost track of time while I was out and about. I told you that I could entertain myself and I did."

"Who were you with?"

"Huh?"

She turns halfway in her seat to look at me. "You heard me. Who were you with? Travis and I saw your head in the restaurant this morning while you were laughing about something and we saw someone sitting with you. Who was it?"

Oh shit. *Quick, think up a lie.* "It was just someone who wanted to sit with me, you know, out of pity for being alone this morning."

My comment makes her cringe. "Shit, I'm sorry. Really. We should have waited for you instead of rushing off. Can you forgive me?"

I wave a hand in front of me. "Don't worry about it. Plus I don't want to be your third wheel. You know how much I love Boston and can always find something to do."

"How was the shopping?" Travis asks, pulling into our hotel parking lot.

"It was good. Lots of window shopping, though. Clothes weren't working for me today."

"Eat too much with your mysterious stranger?" Penny asks, getting out of the car.

I smirk and laugh to myself. "Something like that."

We walk toward the entrance and make our way to the elevators. "Well was he at least good looking? Tell me more about him."

"What's there to tell? I only had breakfast with the guy. It's not like we were out on a date or something."

Penny wraps her arms around Travis and places her head on his chest. "The mere fact that you even ate with someone is a big deal, Ms. I-Never-Date-Anyone. Seriously, was the guy hot? Ow!" she squeals. I assume Travis pinched her for that one.

We enter the elevator and hit our respective floors. "Yes, okay? He was hot. Majorly hot. Like I could totally date him kind of hot."

"Nice! So did you get his number?" My cheeks flush and she giggles with excitement. "Holy shit. Britta Fosse picked up a stranger in a hotel restaurant. Wait until I tell Cami about this one."

I roll my eyes as the elevator slows to their floor. "Don't tell anyone. It's not a big deal."

"Whatever. What time do you want to meet up tomorrow for breakfast?"

"Nothing too early. How about we plan on ten so we can check out and then leave right after?"

"Sounds good." Travis pulls Penny into the hall. "Come on babe, let's get to our room."

"Text me tomorrow morning," Penny calls out as the doors close.

I wave goodbye to them and sigh against the wall. It sickens me to watch it, especially since I know that it's killing my brother right now. I should call him and check in to see what's going on.

Hitting his number, I walk down the hallway while I wait for him to pick up his phone.

"Yo."

"Yo? What kind of greeting is that?" I ask, opening my door. "What do you want?" he asks gruffly.

I toss my purse on the desk and kick my shoes off. "Nice to hear from you too, big brother. Yes, I miss you too and am glad that I'm still safe in the big city by myself."

The loud voices in the background make it hard to hear, but then they drift off suddenly. I assume he's moving away so we can talk without interruption. "Shit, I'm sorry Britt. It's just, you know."

I sigh and sit on the bed. "Yeah, I know. I'm sorry you're

going through this."

"It's my issue so I'll deal with it the best way I know how." There's a pause and I hear him shuffle something over the phone. "How was the concert?"

"It was great. You know the Foo would never suck. All in all, my whole day was awesome."

"Even being the third wheel?" he slurs.

"I wasn't exactly the third wheel today," I say cautiously.

"What do you mean? She let you wander around Boston by yourself?" he growls.

"Calm down, Liam. Penny didn't leave me by myself, but she thinks she did."

"Okay, I'm a little drunk so you're going to have to dumb that down for me. What do you mean she thinks you were alone?"

I chew on my bottom lip and take a deep breath. "I was with James."

"Who the hell is James?" he asks.

"Shit, you are drunk. How much have you had already?"

A loud thud sounds over the phone. "Damn. Never mind that. Who is James?" There's a pause and I'm assuming it's because recognition has finally set into his inebriated mind. "Wait, your teacher?"

"Ex-teacher," I correct.

"Still a teacher. Britta, are you insane?"

There's a knock on my door and I move to answer it. "Don't worry. I've got this under control."

James is standing in front of me, looking absolutely edible in his flannel pants and a dark gray t-shirt. If I weren't on the phone with my brother, I would be throwing myself at him.

"Liam, I have to go. I'll see you tomorrow when I get back."

"Britt, promise me you're not doing something stupid."

"Come on, it's me. I'm smarter than that."

"Not when it comes to this," he says. "You're playing with fire."

James follows me into the room and sits beside me on the bed. "Maybe I like the burn. Just trust me, please?"

"Okay, I trust you. Have fun and stay safe. I worry about you."

I look at James and smile. "I'll be okay. Thanks, Liam. Love you."

"Love you too, little sis."

I end the call and toss the phone up toward the pillows. "Hi," I say shyly.

James leans over and kisses my lips. "Hi."

"We're kind of lame, you know that?"

"Yeah, but we're our own unique kind of lame." He laughs and links his fingers with mine. "Who were you talking to just now?"

I sigh and move further up the bed. James follows as we prop ourselves against the headboard. "My brother. He has a hard time dealing with the whole Penny situation."

He arches an eyebrow. "Penny situation?"

Leaning my head against his shoulder, I start to explain the tale of Penny and Liam's rather strange relationship.

"So let me get this straight. She likes him, he likes her, but they won't be together?"

"Yep."

"That's stupid."

"Sort of."

"What do you mean sort of?"

I lift my head and look at him. "I'm part of the reason why they're not together. They don't want to hurt me or damage my relationship with either of them so they won't pursue anything.

Yet."

"Yet?"

"Liam told me that he knows Penny is in a different place emotionally than he is. He's not looking for a picket fence and kids right now, but he's looking for something more than a pickup. He's convinced he's going to marry her. And because she's still in high school, he doesn't think she's ready, which I have to agree with. Penny's looking out for Penny right now. She's not thinking of the long-term guy. She's looking for a short-term solution."

"Ah, I see," he says and kisses the back of my hand. "And what about you? What are you looking for?"

A calmness washes over me as I look into his eyes, easing the tension right out of my body. "I don't know what I'm looking for. Do I think I'm mature enough to know when I've found my forever guy? Yeah, I do. Am I thinking about marriage right now? Heck no."

"Do you want to get married someday?"

"Of course. Someday I do. I'd like to wait a few years to even think about it, though. Two years into my undergrad would be nice."

James releases my hand and pulls me close to his side, kissing the top of my head. "I agree. You definitely should wait until then. Those first two years will keep you busy enough."

"Let's find a different topic," I say and lean my head back on his shoulder. "What do you want to do tonight?" My eyes travel up and down his body while my hand rests on his stomach. "Obviously we're not going out."

He laughs. "No, not going out. I thought maybe we could just watch a movie on TV or something. I just don't want to sit alone in my room knowing that you're alone in yours too."

I sit up and smile. "I'd like that." I start to stand, but he tugs lightly on my hand with a questioning look. "Don't worry. I'm just going to change into my pajamas and get out of these concert clothes."

He tugs again and I rest my knee on the mattress for balance. "Not those same ones from this morning? Please tell me you have something else."

Loving his discomfort, I pull my hand away from his and look over my shoulder seductively as I open the dresser drawers. "I guess you'll just have to wait and see." I grab the clothes and hide them behind my back as I walk toward the bathroom.

"You're killing me," he says, throwing his head back.

"You love it," I say before shutting the door. I quickly change into what I grabbed and brush my teeth and hair before stepping back out into the room.

The minute his eyes find mine I know my whole world has shifted with just one look. It's not the same look I've been getting from him – the platonic look of our school relationship. It's something else, something deeper and warmer, familiar and comforting. It's like home or a place of belonging. And I know that whatever happens after this is going to change us. We can't go back to what we were before. We can only go forward as something new from now on. Not just Mr. Dumont and Ms. Fosse. We'll be James and Britta. And I love the way it sounds in my mind.

"Better?" I ask, crawling back into my spot beside him. The way his eyes trace my every movement sends the butterflies fluttering in my stomach again.

"Much." James kisses my temple and links our hands together again.

"Not exactly sexy," I say, looking down at my own flannel bottoms and tank top. James twists my head back to meet his eyes, which are dancing with delight.

"You're always sexy. Remember that."

Our lips touch softly, barely a whisper between them while feeding more into my addiction of James. My growing need for him increases with each kiss, each stroke of his tongue against mine, each breath he steals straight from my mouth.

My free hand reaches around to grasp the back of his neck, pulling him closer to me. His arm snakes around my back, bringing our bodies flush with one another. It's been a while since I've simply made out with a guy and not have it lead to something else, but right now all I want to do is this. I want to make out with James, feel his body pressing against mine as our lips and tongues dance together.

Soon enough James groans and moves away from me. "If we don't stop now we're going to move into a territory we aren't ready for yet."

My short sporadic breaths make speech impossible so I just nod my head in agreement. Calming down more, I tuck some hair behind my ears and swallow hard. "You're right. We're not ready for that yet." I grab the remote once we adjust ourselves, propping up against the headboard again in a slouching position. "What do you want to watch?" I ask, flipping through the channels.

"Stop. This one," he says pointing at the screen.

I laugh as I set the remote down on the table next to my phone. "I love this movie. It's my favorite of his."

I snuggle into his arms and close my eyes when his lips meet the top of my head. "Mine too. I mean who could pass up *The Waterboy*?"

"No one that's sane. So many great one-liners in this movie. I could probably recite the whole thing from memory."

We laugh together at all the funny parts while still holding onto each other. My ear rests against his chest, enjoying the feel of his heart pounding against it. Soon enough it lulls me into a deep sleep, filled with smiles and contentment.

The bright sun shines through my still open curtains and I blink awake with a grumble. Why did I forget to draw the shades last night? I try to move but I'm stuck in my current position. *What the hell?*

"Morning," James says, kissing my forehead.

"Mmm, morning," I say on a stretch. "You stayed here all night? Wait, don't answer that."

He laughs and releases his hold on me. "We both fell asleep watching the movie. Then I woke up in the middle of the night and couldn't bring myself to leave."

I sit up and cross my legs while running my fingers through my hair. "You know technically someone would say that we slept together."

James props himself up on an elbow. "Technically I suppose we did. Actually we *fell* asleep together. There's a big difference when you add that one little word."

I roll my eyes and stand from the bed. "I don't think people would be in a technical kind of mood if anyone got wind of this."

"Probably not. But we won't have to worry about that because no one knows we're here together. So it's a moot point."

"Moot point? And I thought I used old fashioned words a lot," I joke as I enter the bathroom, shutting the door on his soft chuckle.

When I re-enter the room, I find him standing by the window. The bed is already made up and the small coffee pot is brewing the life-giving brown liquid that I know we both need.

"What time are you heading back?" he asks, pouring me a cup. I take it and sit in the chair at the small round table in the corner.

"I'm meeting the two lust birds at ten for breakfast and then we're leaving after that. What about you?" I take a tentative sip of my coffee and wait for the burn to settle in my mouth.

"I'll probably leave before you. I don't think I could handle being here without you again."

I swallow hard and brace myself for my next question. "What are we going to do when we get back home?"

"What do you mean?" James tilts his head to the side, taking a sip from his Styrofoam cup.

"I mean, of course, we won't have days or nights like this again and it's going to be hard to pretend that nothing happened between us."

His fingers play with mine on the tabletop.

"Hey, look at me," he says softly. I raise my eyes to his smiling ones and whatever tension I had leaves me instantly. "We'll figure it out. Everything will be okay. You'll be my assistant this next trimester so we have that at least. For one whole hour, I'll have you to myself."

"At school. Not exactly ideal I would say. Plus we'd have to have the door open the entire time. Do you know how much trouble we'd get into if someone caught us in your office with the door closed? You could get fired."

"Let me worry about that. I told you I won't let anything happen. You believe me, don't you?"

I nod.

"Nothing will happen. We'll find a way to make this work."

He's so optimistic about this whole situation. Maybe we really can make this work, whatever this thing is that we're doing.

I glance at my watch. "Damn, it's nine already. I need to get ready, which means you need to leave."

He nods and moves to leave but braces himself against the

opened door. "Text me when you get home, please? I want to make sure you get there safe."

"I will," I say.

James bends down to kiss my lips while my hand reaches up to cup his cheek, my thumb gently brushing over the crest of the bone.

"Bye, Britta," he says, backing away to his door.

"Bye, James." I blow a kiss to him as he enters his room. He smiles and places it against his heart, making mine beat that much faster.

When his door shuts, I back into my room and sag against my closed door. I'm not sure what happened this weekend between us, but I know that going forward is going to be challenging and yet exciting at the same time. I just hope we can make it work.

Fourteen

"SO HOW WAS YOUR WEEKEND?" CHASE ASKS ME AS WE walk to our first-period class together.

I do my best not to be annoyed by his presence. So I turn a fake smile at him and shrug. "It was all right."

"All right? Dude, you went and saw the Foo Fighters. It had to have been more than all right?"

"Of course that part kicked ass. I mean, it was a concert. You go there to party and rock out. Outside of the concert it was good, though."

"Too bad I couldn't make it. That would have been fun for us to hang out and do things together," he says.

My heart clenches, thinking about how the weekend could have been different had Chase been there. If that had happened, James and I would never have been able to connect as we did, spend our time freely without worry of being found out or judged. Memories flood me instantly, remembering our day of shopping and sightseeing, of him stealing kisses on every street corner and holding me close at every opportunity. A smile crosses my face as I remember his lips on mine while we watched our movie and the feel of his hands as they traveled up and down my arm. All while my ear was pressed against his chest, listening to the calming beat of his heart, beating solely for me.

"Yeah, too bad," I murmur. Chase looks fallen and I realize that I was still smiling when I said that.

"Well don't seem so happy about it." The hurt is evident in his words.

"Shit, Chase, I'm sorry. I didn't mean it like that. I just remembered something that happened on Saturday and I guess I got caught in the moment."

Chase steers us down a hallway and leans into me. My back is pressed firmly against the wall while I clutch my books in front of my chest.

"Go out with me?" He leans his head close to my ear and I want to shove him away. The tiny hairs on the back of my neck stand on end as I fight the urge to do so. I just want to get to class, get through the next few hours so I can see James.

"Chase, I-"

"Is there a problem here?" a strong familiar voice says to my right.

I turn my head and widen my eyes at the sight of James standing there, arms crossed and a less than pleased look upon his face. He almost looks angry. Definitely annoyed with his flashing eyes and lips turned down into an almost sneer. Chase backs away from me, shoving his hands in his pockets.

"No problem, Mr. Dumont. Britta and I were just talking."

James's eyes turn to me, softening slightly around the edges. "Is that true, Ms. Fosse?"

I nod and swallow hard while trying to stay upright. My legs are shaking so hard I'm not sure I'll be able to pull off the wall and walk normal after this.

"Yes," I whisper. "We were just talking before heading to class. Right, Chase?"

He nods and backs farther away from me. James is shooting daggers at his head, challenging him to try to come after me again. This must be the jealousy thing he was talking about before. In a way, it's kind of hot but definitely not something that I want to repeat again in school.

"You two better get to class. The first bell is about to ring," James says. His biceps flex under his dress shirt, making my mouth feel like the Sahara as I watch the muscles bulge and relax. Remembering those arms around me and feeling those muscles flex while holding me gently causes my eyes to close ever so briefly at the memory. My body tingles and slides marginally toward him, needing some sort of contact now that I've seen him. Anything will do. A touch of his finger, a press at my back, even a cordial handshake would suffice. I just need him.

"Come on, Britt. Let's go," Chase says as he turns to walk toward our classroom door.

I start to push myself off the wall, but I'm stopped by a hand at my elbow. My head twists to the side and I look at his troubled face, concern etched across his beautiful features.

"Are you okay?" he asks softly.

"I'm fine."

"What did he want?"

"He asked me to go out with him."

A disapproving noise can be heard and my heart flutters at his jealousy. "And what did you say?"

I tug at my elbow slightly. "I need to get to class."

His fingers tighten around me. "What did you say, Britta?"

"James, not now. We'll talk later, okay?"

He releases my elbow and walks away in a huff. No goodbye or retreating glance. Nothing. I can feel the blistering anger roll off him even though he's already down the hall and out of sight. He wasn't kidding when he said that he gets jealous. And I didn't help matters any by avoiding the question.

"Fuck," I whisper to myself.

I jog down the hall to make it to class on time and find the only available seat left is conveniently right next to Chase. *Double fuck.*

"What took you so long?" Chase whispers.

"Nothing."

"Bullshit. What'd he want?"

"Nothing," I hiss, needing him to drop it.

"Nosy bastard. Besides it's none of his business what we were doing. Who the hell does he think he is?"

"Mr. Woodward?" Mrs. Thompson calls from the front of the class. "Is there an issue?"

Chase's cheeks pink up as he shakes his head. "No ma'am. No issue."

"Good." She resumes writing the various poems and poets on the board that we're to learn this trimester and I take out my notebook to start copying everything down.

My phone vibrates in my pocket and I discretely check the message.

I'M SORRY.

It's from James. I quickly type a response without garnering attention from either side of me.

IT'S OKAY.

His response is almost immediate, as if he was waiting for it.

FORGIVE ME?

As if he needs to ask.

ALWAYS.

I shove the phone back into my pocket and continue my note taking while following along in the book. Chase looks over at me several times throughout class and I do my best to ignore it, even going as far as angling my body away from his even though it hinders my view of the front.

The next few hours crawl by at a snail's pace, even though they're classes that I enjoy. Calculus and physics have always been exciting to me but today they were just okay, not holding a candle to what I know is waiting for me during fourth and fifth periods.

When the bell rings, I bolt out of my chair and practically run to my locker to deposit my unnecessary books and grab my lunch.

"Hey, Speed Racer, what's your hurry?" Penny calls out to me.

I slow my pace, not wanting to seem overly eager to get to my assistant job and throw things off.

"Nothing. I just don't want to waste any time."

"So you're really Mr. Dumont's assistant for the trimester?" she asks, opening her locker after she dragged me back to it.

"I am. It was sheer luck that I got it too since Mrs. Davis is out on leave."

"Isn't that weird, though? I mean, he's new and seems smart enough to not need an assistant. Not that I'm saying you don't do a kickass job or anything."

"Uh huh, sure. Nice backtracking. Love you too."

She laughs and nudges my shoulder. "You know what I mean. But you are one lucky bitch to get to work next to him. I would give my left tit to be in his office for two hours. You think he'll make a move on you?"

My spine stiffens, but I try to brush it off. "Oh, whatever. There's no way he'd be interested in me. I'm nothing special."

"Says the homecoming queen and the more-than-likely prom queen as well."

I roll my eyes and start walking toward the teacher's lounge. "If you say so. Look, I need to get in there because I have no idea what he's going to need me to do. Catch you after sixth period?" I call out to her.

"Definitely."

I give her a thumbs up and step quickly down the hall to the lounge. I don't want to seem eager, but I've been dying to be here all day. To be in the same room as James without the watchful eyes of twenty other students is going to be a relief. We won't have to pretend because we'll have a fair amount of privacy afforded to us. It helps that his office is towards the end of the hall and the surrounding rooms are almost always vacant during the fourth period.

Various smells assault me right as I walk into the commons area from the handful of lunches being eaten by the teachers.

"Hi, Britta," one of the teachers calls out to me.

"Hi, Mrs. Hamilton. How are the girls?"

"Oh, they're good. Say, are you available to babysit in two weeks? Richard and I have theater tickets."

"Sure. I don't have anything planned that weekend. What time would you need me?" I walk closer to the table so we're not shouting across the room at each other.

"Around five, if that's okay? It will probably be a late one as our friends are coming with and they want to have drinks afterward."

"That's no problem. I'll be over at your house by then. Saturday right?"

She nods. "You truly are a lifesaver, Britta. The girls will be so excited. They haven't seen you for a while."

"I'm excited to see them too."

The air changes subtly and I know it's because James has just walked in. My body's recognition of his takes over, sending a delicious chill up my spine at the same time warmth covers my stomach before traveling further south.

"Well, Richard has been out of town so our date nights have been pushed to the side. But I've finally pegged him down so we're able to do this," she says before turning her attention to the man standing behind me. "Ah, James. Nice to see you. How was your weekend?"

The warmth of his body wraps around me, even though we're not touching. It takes all that I have not to lean back into him and feel his hard chest against my body. I can hear his smile as he answers Mrs. Hamilton's question.

"My weekend was excellent, Gail. It definitely turned out better than I could have expected."

"How was your friend?" Mrs. Sanderson asks, stabbing at her salad.

"My friend was great. We spent a lot of time together catching up and I really enjoyed it," he says.

I turn slightly to face him, so I'm not rude and acting like I'm ignoring him. His eyes catch mine out of the corner and his lip curls up slightly, giving me a hint of the boyish charm that has captivated me from the beginning.

"Well, that's good to hear. It's always nice to visit friends," she says, placing her fork to the side in favor of the bottle of water.

"Yes, it is. But I'm afraid I must steal Ms. Fosse from you ladies. We need to figure out our working system for the next two hours."

"Oh yes, I heard that Britta's your assistant. You're a lucky one, James. All of us just adore her and she's such a hard worker. I can say we were all quite jealous of Stacy for that reason," Mrs.

Hamilton says with a smile. She winks at me and I blush with embarrassment.

"I am lucky to have her that's for sure." He looks at me and smiles sweetly. "Shall we?" He extends his arm toward his office and I nod.

"Of course. Bye, Mrs. Hamilton, Mrs. Sanderson."

They wave goodbye and we walk in silence down the hall. My body hums at his close proximity and I wonder what's going to happen when we're inside the small confines of his office. We round the corner and I walk through first, pushing the door open then stand off to the side until James enters. He closes the door halfway so it doesn't draw attention. Then he's on me instantly. His hands cradle my face as my back lightly hits the wall behind the door. I cling to his shirt, careful not to put too many wrinkles in it. The slow seductive dance of our mouths warms my insides again, making me fall further into him with each nip and bite with his teeth. The moment our tongues collide, stars explode behind my lids and I surrender to the feelings inside me that are begging to come out.

My hands slide up to his shoulders, pulling him closer to me, needing to feel the full press of his body against mine. It's been too long since I've felt the hotness of his mouth, the silkiness of his tongue slide against mine. It's been too long since I've fed my addiction and the withdrawal is starting to show, as evidenced by this morning's incident with Chase.

"You have no idea how long I've waited to do that," James says against my mouth. Our movements slow, but the hard evidence of our lust pressing against my stomach makes me want to continue, to push the moment further, and explore the uncharted territory that is James Dumont.

"I think I have a good idea. I would guess since the moment we stopped outside of my door back in Boston."

His lips travel across my cheek to my ear, lightly sucking on the lobe, creating a surge of heat to flood between my legs.

"It's been killing me not to be able to kiss you like this in public as I could in Boston whenever I wanted to."

My short panting breaths beat against his neck and I'm brave enough to lick a small trail from the collar of his shirt to his ear. He groans in pleasure and I savor the sweet taste of his skin against my tongue.

His hips roll into me slightly when I repeat the move and I gasp when his firm thigh hits a rather tender spot between my legs. Our eyes connect and lock onto each other with desire and passion floating between us.

"James," I whisper, feeling his skin pebble as I lick my lips and moan softly. I want to throw caution to the wind. I want to take this man with everything I have. I need to feel everything with him. I just need him.

"Britta, I want you too much. And it killed me this morning to see you with Chase."

"Nothing happened," I say, still clinging to his body for support.

He leans his forehead against mine and reclaims my lips in a sweet, soft kiss. "I know, but the fact that he had you pinned against the wall was enough to drive me crazy." I raise an eyebrow to him and he quietly laughs. "This is different."

"Why? Because you're the one pinning me to a wall?"

"Yes."

And with that one simple response, I'm lost to everything except for James. I press my lips against his once more and sigh at his immediate response. His jealousy, his need for me furthers my need and addiction for him.

"I would never go out with him. He's not the one I want," I say. "He's not the one who lights my eyes up when I see him, who sends heat coursing through my veins with just a smile in my direction. He's not the one I wish was in my bed at night, holding me close, letting me feel the steady beat of his heart."

"Who is?" he huskily asks, cupping my cheeks once more while looking directly into my eyes.

"It's you. It's always been you. Ever since that first day when you knocked me off my feet, it's been you."

"This is going to be difficult," he says.

"I know."

"I'm having a hard time controlling myself around you anymore."

"I know."

"I want to be with you."

I swallow hard. "I know."

"Is this our thing?" he asks. "When we open ourselves up to each other, the automatic response is 'I know'?"

"Everyone needs a thing."

The distant chattering of teachers draws our attention and we reluctantly pull away from each other. I smooth the few wrinkles on his dress shirt and straighten his tie, creating another one of those devilishly handsome smiles to pop up on his face.

"I suppose we better start working," he says. "I don't want to get you in trouble. Your colleague could report you for your poor work habits."

I poke him in the middle of his chest and laugh. "I didn't hear him complain three minutes ago."

James's arms wrap firmly around my waist, pulling me close again. His warm cheek rests upon mine and I cling to his shoulders once more. "Definitely not complaining."

"Good because we have work to do. Come on, let's get to it."

I boot up his computer and he starts going through his papers stacked on his desk, showing me everything that I need to do. For being a smart man, he sure does fall behind easily in his homework grading. Or perhaps he's doing it on purpose as a way to keep me busy to perfect the ruse we're doing. I mean, a man who graduated a year early and is halfway through his Masters program at the age of twenty-two isn't someone who strikes me as a slacker.

James glances down at his watch and sighs loudly. "I need to get something to eat before my class starts in fifteen minutes. Do you need me to heat up your lunch?" he asks, stretching his arms above his head.

"No thanks. I'm okay for right now. Plus I've hit my stride and I'd rather not break it." I barely glance up at him as I correct the papers from his classes this morning. A hand comes down, blocking my view and forcing me to look up at him. I cock an eyebrow in silent question and he smiles.

"Don't work too hard. You'll be running out of stuff to do at that pace and then you'll be bored being in here for the next hour."

I look around the room and smile. "I don't think I'll be bored. Your office may look different though when you return. I tend to nest when I'm left alone too long."

"Nest?" he asks.

I nod. "Nest, as in clean or decorate. I have issues with blank walls."

He rolls his eyes and pauses at the door. "Just don't make it girly if you do."

I salute him with a smirk. "I make no promises."

And with that, he leaves to me to my own devices. Several ideas pop into my head at the same time and I work quickly on the task at hand so I can follow through next hour on my ideas.

Fifteen

"Y OU DID WHAT?" LIAM ASKS ME. HE TOSSES A basketball into the air out of boredom while I'm sitting at my desk working on my homework.

"I redecorated his office," I repeat.

"Why would you do that?"

I shrug and write down my calculus answer quickly. "Because there was nothing in there. It felt like I was trapped in an insane asylum. All white walls and minimal furniture. I mean, who can concentrate in that kind of environment?"

The ball slips from his hands, bouncing several times until it rolls toward my door. "Are you stark raving mad? You can't decorate a teacher's office. Are you trying to get found out?"

I turn in my chair to face my now red-faced brother. "It's not like I did this overnight you twat. I mean, I've been assisting him for the past several weeks. It's been a gradual thing. I didn't bring in a crate of shit one day and start posting flowers and hearts everywhere. Give me some credit, Liam."

"Oh I'll give you something all right," he says.

"Whatever." I throw my pencil down once the last problem is complete. "What are your plans tonight? Last night before winter break must mean big parties around here somewhere."

"Well Douchenozzle is having a party but I really don't want to go to that one."

My nose crinkles at his name. "Thank God for that. I hate it when you go over to his parties. Why don't you come with me to Drake's? You know everyone there so you'll probably have some fun. Besides, we don't hang out much anymore and I'd like to do that."

"Sure. Why not. It could be fun."

"It will be. Promise. Now leave me alone so I can finish my work."

He jumps off my bed and messes up my hair as he walks by. My phone beeps with an incoming message.

YOU'RE STILL GOING TONIGHT?

Penny has been flipping out all week, wondering if I'm actually going to come out or not. She and Travis have been fighting a lot lately. When the situation gets tense, she uses me as her scapegoat. Tonight I'm sure will be another prime example of that.

YEP, GIVE ME A COUPLE HOURS.

GREAT! CAN'T WAIT. IT'LL BE EPIC.

I roll my eyes and focus back on my work. When my phone beeps again, I resist the urge to chuck it across the room just to shut it up. But James's name stops me from following through.

I MISS YOU.

I MISS YOU MORE.

GOING OUT TONIGHT?

YEP.

WITH PENNY?

AND LIAM.

WILL CHASE BE THERE?

PROBABLY.

I WISH I COULD BE THERE WITH YOU.

ME TOO.

CALL ME WHEN YOU GET HOME?

PROMISE.

I wish I could take him with me. I'd give anything to dance with him all night, sit on his lap, and laugh with my friends while his hands run up and down my sides. I'm jealous of all the couples at the parties who are able to do that. Not that James and I are a couple, but we're definitely past the friend thing. Usually when you round first base, it's something a little more serious.

Just thinking about his hands on me has my legs pressing together to quell the deep need for him that's always just below the surface. Even the thought of him makes me hot. I need a cold shower before I head to Drake's otherwise I'll be sending the wrong signals to a certain someone I'm going to actively avoid all night.

We pick up Penny and she grumbles in the back seat the entire way to Drake's house. I guess Travis is going to meet her there. Knowing them, they probably had another fight. They've been having more and more of those lately. Either way, Liam has a satisfied grin on his face, knowing that he's bringing Penny to the party. It's a technicality but who am I to rain on his parade?

The loud music can be heard outside as we pull into the long private driveway. Thick trees surround us, making it the perfect hiding spot for a night of recklessness. I don't plan on a repeat of Travis's party. And with Liam around I know for a fact that it won't happen.

The moment we walk inside, we're assaulted by a booming techno beat.

"What time did this start?" I yell to Penny, who's standing right next to me.

"I thought he said nine."

"Maybe nine this morning." I look around and shake my head. "Everyone is already plastered."

"Wonderful," Penny mutters.

We make our way past the bumping and grinding teens to the kitchen where liquor bottles line every inch of available counter space. Two-liter bottles take residence next to each liquor bottle, making it relatively easy to concoct whatever your heart desires.

"You drinking tonight?" I yell to Liam.

He shakes his head. "You go ahead and drink. I'm driving, remember?"

"I can drive if you want."

"There is no way I'm letting you drive my Mustang. Hell no."

I roll my eyes and turn to Penny. "Drink?"

"God, please. I need something strong and fast."

"Usually girls prefer it slow. Fast does nothing except leave you wanting," Liam says.

"I'm not in the mood for your shit tonight, Liam. If I want it fast, that's how I'm going to get it."

"Anyone who tries anything like that with you will be answering to me," he growls out.

"You know what," I yell at the both of them, garnering their attention. "You two need to fuck and get it over with. I'm not going to sit here and watch you trip all over yourselves when you obviously want to be together. Just stick your dick in her and be done with it!"

Their faces turn from pale white to bright pink at almost the same time. It would be comical if I weren't so frustrated. I mean, I know it's my fault they're not together, or at least I'll accept part of the blame. But my God, if they keep tiptoeing around this forever I'm going to go crazy.

I pour a generous amount of Citron into an ice-filled glass and top it with Diet 7-Up. Penny and Liam are still in a silent standoff and I leave them to it. They need to figure out their shit. Yes, Penny has a boyfriend and yes, my brother can be a giant child sometimes. They're both screwed up and yet are one hundred percent perfect for each other. Or they would be if they could stop hurting the other for more than five minutes.

My face crinkles from the surge of vodka now flooding my mouth. Okay, so maybe I was a little wrist heavy when I poured. *Too late now.*

I push my way through the crowd until I find our little group seated near the fireplace.

"Britta!" Cami yells. She throws her arms in the air while simultaneously spilling her drink all over Lyle.

"What the hell, Cami!" he bellows while wiping away the droplets of alcohol from his navy blue shirt. It clings slightly with each brush of his hands. He's one of my closest friends, but I'm still a girl and can appreciate his hard athletic body.

After Penny and Liam's little display in the kitchen, I've decided to change my plan for the night. Sobriety will not be my friend. I will drink until I forget that I'm unhappy because the one person I want to be with isn't here.

"Sorry baby," she says to him before throwing her arms around my neck. I catch her just in time before she spills my drink all over us.

"Hey, Cam. Hitting it hard already?" I push her upright and

into Lyle's arms.

"Yeah, they make a damn good punch here," she slurs while rubbing his chest. He rolls his eyes and makes a drinking motion with his hands. I laugh and wiggle my way to sit next to Dez and Justice.

"So where's Penny?" Justice asks while taking a sip of her beer.

"She and Liam are either fighting or screwing in the kitchen. I left them to figure it out on their own."

"Is Travis here?" Dez asks.

"I don't know. Penny came with us. I didn't ask her on the car ride over for obvious reasons."

I scan the room, looking for my best friend's boyfriend, but I'm unable to find him anywhere. Unfortunately, Chase locks his sights on me. An uneasy grin plasters on his face as he makes his way toward us, brushing off several girls who throw themselves in his path.

"Fuck me," I mutter before taking another drink. I must be getting used to the taste because the burning has stopped and all that's left is the crisp citrus flavor.

"Hey, Britt. Looking hot tonight," Chase says, not hiding his obvious appraisal of my body. Maybe this body-hugging sweater-dress wasn't the best idea. Although my high-heeled boots could come in handy in case he decides to try anything again.

"Thanks," I reply, turning my head away from him.

"Oh baby, don't be like that. Come on, dance with me."

"I'm good here, thanks."

Justice shoves my side and forces me up. "Go dance with him." She turns to grab Dez and Cami's hands. "Let's all go dance. I love this song."

Like a flock of sheep, we follow Justice to the middle of the makeshift dance floor. The hip-hop beat of "Turn Down For

What" by Lil Wayne fills the speakers as we all scream along while grinding against each other. Chase is pressing against my back and each attempt I make at moving away from him is thwarted by my so-called friends. Justice shakes her head and nods in his direction, apparently wanting me to dance with him.

Chase's hands wrap tightly around my hips, pulling me against him while he grinds us low to the ground. I'm desperate to keep my dress in its proper position and my calves are thankful when we finally straighten up. But then he flips me around, pressing my stomach to his while he dips his head low and licks a trail from my collarbone to my ear.

"God you're fucking hot tonight," he says. "Wanna go somewhere quiet?" The heavy stench of whiskey emanates from his breath and I choke back my disgust.

"No, I just want to dance."

"Where's Penny, your bodyguard?"

"I don't know. I left her in the kitchen."

His hand snakes around to firmly grip my ass and I move it back to its prior position. "Seriously, you have no idea what this dress is doing to me right now."

The poking at my hip is telling me otherwise. "I think I have a good idea. You're not exactly hiding it by any means."

He smirks and grinds his erection into me with a slight groan.

"You feel that baby? That's all for you."

"Chase, you're drunk and I'm not interested. Let me go."

He shakes his head and I realize his eyes are extremely dilated. He's not just drunk, but he's high too.

"Oh, you're interested all right. Everyone is interested in me, but for some messed-up reason you're playing hard to get. I'll let you in on a little secret." He leans lower until our noses touch. "I like the fucking chase. When I catch you, you're going to enjoy every minute of it."

I wiggle in his grasp. My heartbeat kicks up several notches when he won't release me. "Let me go, Chase."

"Hey man, she said to let her go," Lyle says behind me. He crosses his arms and pins Chase with a look.

"Back off. It's none of your business," Chase says.

Bile rises in my throat. My hands tremble and start to sweat. I close my eyes, bracing myself for the worst. But when I open them, Liam is forcibly ripping Chase away from me.

"What do you think you're doing to my sister? She said let go. That means you fucking let her go." He has Chase by the back of the neck. The vein on the side of Liam's throat pulses and is raised more than should be humanly possible.

"Geez, man. All right. I'll back off." He turns and scowls at me. "Sorry, I won't bother you again." Chase shoves Liam off him and stalks off toward the kitchen.

"Are you okay?" Lyle asks me.

I nod and take a shaking sip from a cup he hands me. "Yeah I'm fine. Thanks, guys."

Lyle and Liam look to each other in a silent exchange. "What's up with him tonight? He's never that aggressive toward you."

"I don't know. His eyes were so dilated they were almost black. He must be on something."

Lyle mutters a curse and runs his hands through his hair. "Fucking assbag. I told him not to do anything stupid tonight. He probably scored some X off Nathan. I heard rumors he was dishing it out downstairs. Drake kicked him out soon after, but Chase must have found him before that."

"Wonderful," I sigh.

Liam puts his hand on my shoulder. "Are you sure you're okay?"

I give him a quick hug. "I'm fine. I was two seconds away from kneeing him in the balls before you pulled him away." Not really, but he doesn't need to know that. "Thanks for sticking up for me."

"It's my job."

I look around and get a confused look on my face. "Where's Penny?"

He turns in circles as his eyes dart from person to person. "I don't know. I left her over there and now she's gone."

"You go that way and I'll go upstairs to see if I can find her."

Liam nods and I kiss Lyle on the cheek in thanks. He smiles and leaves me to find my misguided friend.

The crowd has gotten thicker since we arrived. Another dance song plays over the speakers and everyone goes nuts again, grinding on top of each other and spilling their drinks all over the floor. I do not envy Drake for cleaning up this mess tomorrow, although knowing him he's probably already scheduled the cleaning service to come early in the morning.

I climb the stairs and pass several couples making out in the hallway. Heated moans filter from each room I look into and I duck out as soon as I see bodies writhing against one another. Penny had better not be in any of these rooms because that's a visual I really do not want.

I check the next room over. I'm about ready to give up on this floor when a familiar voice calls out from inside.

"Yeah, baby, you like that?"

I freeze, knowing whose voice it is and know that the blonde he's saying it to isn't my best friend.

"Britt, there you are. Look, have you seen Travis? I heard he was here and I really need to tell him I'm sorry."

Do I lie to her and say that I haven't seen him or do I send her inside and watch her as she breaks? I don't want her to get hurt but every scenario I come up with leads to that point.

"Um, Penny, listen…about Travis-" I start, but the loud moan from inside the room makes her head whip in that direction.

"Yes, Travis, do that again!"

Penny's face turns beat red as anger radiates from her body. Her hands ball up into tight fists as she opens the door more and confirms what she heard.

I stand to the side as Penny pushes past me, charging into the dimly lit room with a fire burning in her eyes.

"You no good motherfucking cheater! How dare you do this to me!" she screams at the top of her lungs.

"Penny!"

He tosses the half-naked blonde away from him. She scrambles off the bed and gathers her shirt off the floor before flying past me with her head ducked down.

The poor girl was just a victim in this whole situation, but I have a hard time feeling sorry for her. Everyone in school knows that Penny and Travis are an item. She should have known better.

Yelling ensues and I brace myself for the breaking of objects because I know that's coming next.

"Britt, did you find her?" Liam walks up beside me, still looking worried.

"Oh yeah, I found her."

He breathes a sigh of relief. "Good. Where is she?"

I point to the door. "Possibly castrating Travis right now. We just caught him getting ready to sleep with another girl."

"What?"

He charges into the room. I try to stop him but the sickening sound of bone meeting flesh stops my progress.

"Liam, no!" Penny cries out. More shuffling can be heard.

Another hit, another thud, another sickening groan. I can't do anything but stay rooted to my spot.

"You fucker!" Travis yells. Various items fall off of the dressers and crash to the floor as they shove each other around the room.

"Stop it! Stop it you two!" Penny cries.

I try to get her to come out of the room but she's knocked off her feet when Travis swings and misses Liam, connecting with Penny's side instead.

"Oh my God, Penny. I'm so sorry baby. I wasn't aiming for you," Travis says, backing away while trying to reach for her at the same time.

"Stay the hell away from her, asshole," Liam says. He kneels next to her as she tries to catch the breath that was knocked out of her.

Drake pounds up the stairs. "What is going on up here?"

Travis wipes away a drop of blood from his lip and points to Liam. "He fucking attacked me, bro. Get him the fuck out of here."

Drake looks down to Penny, who's crying into Liam's shoulder while clutching her side. Drake's eyes meet up with Travis's again, but there's no friendly light in them.

"Is that why Sarah just ran out of here like a bat out of hell and half-naked? Because of Liam?"

Travis looks down and shoves his hands in his pockets. "That was before this whole thing started."

If fire could come out of Drake's nose, I'm sure it would right now. He points at Travis. "Get the fuck out of my house. Now!"

Travis picks up his shirt. He stops by Penny to say something but thinks otherwise when he greeted by the hateful stares of those around him.

"Call me tomorrow," he says instead, leaving behind the destruction that he created. We hear the front door slam and a round of cheers follow. Apparently word travels fast regarding dicks that cheat while their girlfriend is at the same party.

"Are you okay?" I say to both of them as they cling to each other on the floor. Liam is rocking her back and forth, pressing his lips against her head in between whispers. Penny is crying into his shoulder and nodding her head to whatever it is he's saying.

I don't want to disrupt this moment between them so I back out and make my way downstairs. Tonight has definitely been an exciting one but for all the wrong reasons.

At the bottom of the stairs, I turn towards the kitchen in search of a fresh drink. This is way too much drama to be sober for.

Just as I was starting to get back into the party mood, someone reaches out and grabs my elbow.

"Hey, baby, look up," Chase slurs with his face close to mine.

The firm grip he has on my arm makes it difficult to pull away. My knees start to shake as his earlier attempts flash through my mind again. He points to the ceiling. That's when I see the mistletoe hanging from the light fixture.

"Pucker up, baby," he says, moving in for the kill.

"Chase, no-"

I don't get the rest of my protest out due to the assault of his lips against mine, slobbering all over my face. He's more intoxicated than I realized.

This is more than I can handle tonight. A burst of energy flows through my veins as I pick my knee up and hit him directly between the legs. He falls to the ground, coughing and sputtering while gasping for air.

"Get off me, Chase. You're drunk and high and I can't be

around you right now. Leave me the hell alone!"

I stomp away, leaving him crying on the floor, as Lyle tries to make his way toward me. I grab my coat from the pile by the door. "I'm leaving. I can't stay here any longer. Tell Liam and Penny that I'll find a ride home."

"Wait, Britt, let me drive you," he says but I hold up my hand to stop him.

"No, you go back to Cami and everyone else. I've got it. Just please let them know I left."

He nods but gives me a sheepish look. "I thought he was gone."

I kiss his cheek. "It's not your fault. Chase is not acting like himself and he's going to regret it tomorrow. For sure with the elephant testicles I just gave him. He'll be lucky if they work at all after that."

He laughs and gives me a returning kiss. "Be safe. Call me if you need anything."

"I will. Thanks, Lyle."

I smile and head outside, needing to get away from the party as fast as I can. This is not the way I wanted to start my winter break.

Sixteen

I STOMP DOWN THE SNOW COVERED DRIVEWAY AND HEAD toward the road. The falling snow feels good against my heated face as I turn it upward and take a deep, calming breath. What the fuck got into everyone tonight? Between Liam, Penny, Travis, and Chase, I'm at my wits end.

Drake lives about five miles from my house and there's no way that I'm trudging home this late at night and in these heeled boots. I dig my cell phone out of my purse.

"Britta?" he asks in a sleepy voice.

Oh God, did he have to answer like that? Now my body is on alert but for an entirely different reason.

"Hi, James, sorry to wake you but I need a huge favor."

I hear the rustling of his sheets. "What's wrong? Where are you?"

I pause at the street corner and lean against the light pole. "I left the party due to...extenuating circumstances. Can you come get me?"

"Where are Penny and Liam?"

I sigh and look up at the sky again. "Look, I really don't want to get into the whole thing on the phone right now. It's kind of cold out here and my feet are starting to freeze. Can you come get me or not?"

Keys jingle, followed by a slamming door. "Yes, of course. Where are you?"

I glance up at the street sign. "I'm on the corner of Maplewood and Divine."

The distinct rumble of his truck engine echoes through my ears. "Don't move. I'll be there in five minutes."

"Okay, just hurry, please. I need to get out of here."

"Look, don't hang up on me. Keep talking so I know you're still going to be all right until I get there."

I smile into the phone, impressed by his need to protect me even when he's not here. "A little overdramatic, don't you think? What could possibly happen to me in this neighborhood?"

He laughs and turns his stereo down. "It's not the neighborhood I'm worried about. It's the drunken idiots you just left that worry me."

"Touché."

I stay quiet for a second; amazed that he's coming to rescue me.

"Keep talking, Britt," he says calmly.

"I'm not dying you know. You don't need to make sure I'm not going to pass out or something like that."

He laughs and I can feel the vibrations through the phone. "I know that, but just humor me, will you?"

"Fine. Fine. But I think you're making a big deal out of-"

"Britta? Britta?" Panic strains his voice.

I silently snicker at my joke. Yes, it's slightly cruel but I find it hilarious. He's being somewhat overprotective and needs to lighten up.

Bright headlights illuminate the darkness as his truck comes barreling down the street. He stops at the corner and climbs out of the cab. The intensity of his eyes breaks my control as I laugh while leaning against the pole. James crosses his arms and stands in front of me.

I hit end call and shove the phone back into my purse. "If you could only see your face right now."

His lip twitches as he tries to hold back his amusement. "You think that's funny?"

"Hilarious."

James moves forward until we're nose to nose with my back firmly against the post. My laughter dies down until nothing can be heard except his idling truck. There's an undertone of fear in his serious eyes. He really was scared something had happened to me.

I reach up to cup his cheek and he leans into the touch. "I'm sorry. You're right. It wasn't funny of me to joke about that, especially since I'm the one who called you for a ride because the party got out of hand."

He twists his head and places a kiss in the middle of my palm before wrapping his arms around me. "You scared me half to death. Please don't ever joke about your safety again."

I lean my head on his shoulder while I cling to his waist. "I promise. No more jokes like that."

"Good." He places a kiss on my temple. We pull away from each other and a shiver runs through me. "Come on, let's get you inside and warm you up."

He opens the passenger door for me and I climb into his truck, turning on the seat warmer as soon as my butt hits the cold leather seat. James climbs in and pulls away from the curb and back toward town.

His eyes flick to mine every once in a while as he navigates the darkened streets. "I really like your hat by the way. You look so cute in it."

I pull it off my head and ruffle my hair a little. "This thing? It's more for fashion than practical use. I think my ears would have frozen off if I would have tried to walk home." I toss the beret on my lap and lean my head back against the headrest.

"So tell me what led to you calling me at midnight."

I look out the window and don't know where we're going or how much time we have. "Where are we going?"

"My house."

I swallow past the lump that just formed in my throat. "Your house?"

He nods. "Yes, my house. Now talk."

"Let's wait until we're inside. This could take a while. And I need to make sure that you won't crash the truck on our way there."

His eyes flash in the dark and I don't know if it's from fear or anger. I know he's going to be upset about what happened at the party. Hell, I'm still a little ticked off. But James's rationality when it comes to me doesn't always mesh up with everyone else's definition.

We make a few more turns until we're parked in the garage of a quiet little two bedroom house, not far from my neighborhood. We enter through a side door into a tiny mudroom. I hang my coat up on the hook, along with my hat and purse, and place my boots next to his. I quickly admire the look of our stuff hanging next to each other. Wouldn't this be a nice sight to come home to every day? Having that blend of his stuff and my stuff, making it ours? The thought makes me smile.

We walk into a small, open-concept kitchen and he points to a bar stool on the other side of the counter.

"Have a seat. Do you want anything to drink?"

I shake my head and run my hands over the black granite countertop instead. "I'm okay for now. Could we sit in the living room instead?"

"Sure," he says, grabbing my hand. "Whatever you want."

He pulls me into his side as we sit on the couch, wrapping his arms tightly around me.

"Better?"

I lay my head over his heart and feel him smile against my hair.

"Much."

His lips touch the crown of my head and I sigh in relief. "Now, tell me what happened."

Well, it's now or never. I take a deep breath and start with the weirdness between Liam and Penny. Then I talk about Chase's dancing attempts and the fight that almost ensued afterward. James stiffens when I tell him about what Chase had insinuated on the floor. I look up at his tortured face and kiss him softly, watching as the lines around his eyes disappear slowly.

"I would never let him do that," I say, kissing him again.

"It's not you that I don't trust. It's him," he says. "There's something about the way he looks at you that sends alarms ringing through my head."

I know exactly what he means. "Which is why I was trying to avoid him, but he found me anyway."

"So obviously there's more to this," he says as he tightens his grip on me.

I nod. James pulls me into his lap and sits quietly as I recount the events of the whole Travis/Sarah/Penny/Liam fiasco. I lower my head and voice as I describe the mistletoe incident.

"I'm going to kill the fucker."

I lean back and cradle his face in my hands. "You can't. You'll get into trouble if you try anything." A slow smile forms on my face. "Besides, I kind of took care of him for you."

He raises an eyebrow. "Oh really?"

"He's probably going to need a bag of peas or two for the next week. I hit him in the balls pretty hard and he doubled over like a little bitch with a skinned knee."

There's a look of pride on his face as he brushes some stray hair away. "My girl, the ball-buster."

My girl. What I wouldn't give to hear him say that again. In fact, I'd record it so every time he'd text me that would be his message alert. *My girl.*

I look down, but he brings my chin back up to meet his eyes. "You are my girl. You know that, right?"

I shrug. "Am I? I mean, is that really what you want?"

He gives me a look that speaks every unspoken word I've ever needed to hear. A look that eases my mind, releasing an endorphin rush that makes me feel as if I can run two marathons and still not be tired. A look that tells me exactly what I already know. That what we have is real.

"More than you know." My lips melt against his briefly. "I want you, each and every single piece of you. And I'm selfish enough to not care about the reasons keeping us apart. There's this need I have to be with you, to see your smile every day, to touch your body in some way, shape, or form. And I want it. I want it all. And it sucks that I've found you at this point in our lives instead of six months from now.

"But at the same time I realize our paths would never have crossed if that were the case. I never would have seen your beautiful face looking up at me after I knocked you to the floor that day. I would never have felt the press of these soft lips against mine in the back of Sammy's Restaurant." His thumb runs along my quivering bottom lip. "I would never have felt this pressure in my chest every day I see you. A pressure that builds and grows with each smile, each laugh, and each stolen glance we take. And I want all of it, all day, and every day. I just want you."

A lone tear slowly rolls down my cheek. It's like he knew everything that was inside of my head and gave voice to it. And he's right. He's absolutely right.

"Say something." His voice catches on the last syllable as he looks deep into my eyes.

"I can't. You took my breath away."

James stares are me as if he's looking straight into my soul. "Will you be mine?"

I shake my head. His face falls slightly, but I kiss the corner of his mouth, making it turn up instead of down. "I'm already yours."

Something stirs inside me the moment our lips meet. It's like I can feel my heart and soul fuse with his to bind us together. I need him like I need the air in my lungs. His mouth moves slowly, seductively against my own, teasing and tasting but not fully engulfing. He's holding back, which makes me pull away to look into his eyes to see why there's restraint.

"What is it?"

A small groan escapes his throat and I smile against his cheek. "You're killing me, you know that, right?"

"One good turn deserves another. You kill me every time I see you and it's a death I would take over and over again."

He runs his hands through my hair again, holding my mouth just out of reach. "What did I ever do to deserve you?"

"Maybe we deserve each other," I say. "Maybe we need to pass this little test to make sure that what we have is real. The things you want most in life aren't supposed to be easy. There's a reason you need to work hard for them because the reward is that much sweeter in the end."

"And I will work hard every day for you," he says. "Every

day that my heart beats, it will be for your happiness. You mean more to me than you will ever know."

I place my hand over his heart, feeling the steady beat of it against my palm. "I have a good idea, though."

Leaning forward, I close the distance between us and seal my mouth over his. Using long, slow licks, I tease him until he opens up and we move to our own tempo. I shift in his lap, causing a grunt to escape him when I make contact with a very pronounced appendage.

"Sorry," I half-whisper, half-giggle. His hands move around to my back, holding me against him as his hips rise off the cushion, repeating my previous motion. This time, it's my turn to gasp and groan at the sensation.

"Don't be. Feels good, doesn't it?"

I throw a leg over his to gain a better position in the off-chance that he should try it again. He does, of course, and the jolt of electricity shoots straight to my aching core.

"So good," I breathe, barely breaking contact with his mouth.

I need him, need his touch, his hands, his fingers, *everything*. And he needs me too. His wandering fingers trail up and down my spine, teasing and touching everywhere that he can.

My hands trail down his chest, teasing the muscles beneath his shirt while lightly scraping my fingernail across his nipple. My tongue twirls with his as we consume each other, swallowing our collective sounds and gasps as we explore each other's clothed body.

James breaks away first. The staccato breaths I'm taking seem to be drawing in less and less air as he traces the pulsing vein on the side of my neck with his nose. Goose bumps follow in its wake, sending hot and cold sensations to run rampant through my system.

"We need to slow down."

"Why?" I ask, tilting my head back to give him more space to roam. The tip of his tongue skims my neck, sending another shock through me. I clutch the waistband of his flannel pants. *Should I or shouldn't I?*

"Because," he says between light licks, "it's late and you're supposed to go home soon."

I finger the drawstring of his pants. My heart beats in double time when I see the lust clouding over his eyes.

"I don't have to. I am an adult and don't need permission to stay out late at night."

"But you're not actually free to be here either, are you?"

I scoot back on his lap and tilt my head. "Do you want me to leave?"

His hands cup my behind again, pulling me back against his body. "God no. I want you here with me forever. But until then, I need to know how this is going to work. I don't want to do booty calls or late night rendezvous like we're two fifteen-year-olds sneaking out of the house. I want so much more than that for us. I want long nights and weekend getaways. I want to wake up with you in my arms every day and your smile being the first thing that I see. You deserve more than a tryst or an affair. You deserve the world."

I chew on my bottom lip. A million thoughts swirl through my head, but I'm afraid to vocalize any one of them because I don't want them to come out wrong.

"James, we are not a tryst. So stop that right there. This, what we have, is so much more than we could have ever known before. And I want the long nights and weekend getaways too. I want to wake up to your beautiful face every day and do everything that normal couples do. I want to walk down the street and proudly proclaim that you are mine. But for now, it just can't be that way. At least we can't here. We could always go on vacations together or tell people we're going out of town and just stay here at your place."

He shakes his head. "I don't want to keep piling up the lies to people. It's hard enough at school to fight what I want most in my heart."

My hand trails down his cheek and rests upon his strong jaw where the muscle ticks slightly in frustration. "We could always leave. I can go to school anywhere. Hell, I'll even do on-line school and get my GED. Or maybe I should talk with Mr. Leonard about an early graduation?"

"No," he says firmly. "You will not do that. I will not have you sacrificing your future just so we can be together. You have one of the best GPA's in school and your acceptance letters will be coming any day now, giving you your options for a bright future."

"But you're my future too," I whimper.

He leans up to kiss the corner of my mouth. "And you are mine. We just need to wait a little longer. I promise it'll be worth the wait."

I frown and cross my arms in front of my chest. "If you're telling me that I have to wait for six months to have *any* kind of contact with you, I can't accept that. Patience is not a virtue that I possess, *Mr. Dumont.*"

A flash of heat crosses his eyes and my insides come to life, knowing how much he loves and hates it when I call him by his last name.

"Say that again." His voice drops to a low, seductive tone.

I sit up straighter on his lap and blink my lashes demurely. "*Mr. Dumont.*"

The movement is so sudden I don't have time to prepare myself, but I let out a loud giggle as he tosses me onto the couch.

When his body presses into mine and elicits a long, slow moan from me, the giggles fade.

"You know it drives me wild when you say that."

There's not enough air in the room as I stare into his eyes. "I know."

James places his forearms near my shoulders, holding most of his weight off of me. His fingers trail lovingly through my hair and the tiny fluttering of butterfly wings goes through my stomach once again.

"You're so beautiful," he whispers, his eyes growing soft around the edges. I reach up and trace his lips with a fingertip, hoping that I'm reflecting the same look back at him.

I reach down and start to pull my dress up my body. He stops me before I can get it over my head. "What are you doing?"

I ignore him and toss the dress onto the floor. "I want you to touch me. I need to feel you against me."

He shakes his head but doesn't hold back his perusal of my body. At least what he can without fully sitting up and taking me all in.

"That's not why I brought you back here. We don't need to-"

"James." I place my index finger on his lips. "I'm not a virgin so please don't think you're stealing my innocence. But I don't sleep around either. I'm careful who I choose to give myself to and right now, I choose you. I will always choose you. There is no one else I will ever give myself to again. Only you."

I grab his hand and guide it to my full and aching breast. He kneads it slowly through the thin lace of my bra, making my nipple harden almost painfully. He shifts his weight to one side, slowly moving between me and the couch so we're facing each other. I rest my head on his outstretched arm, wedging my other arm between us at the perfect point of contact for his growing erection. My fingertips play with him through his flannel pants and he takes a sharp intake of breath.

"Are you sure about this?"

I can't hide my amusement as I bite my lip. "Usually it's the girl who questions the sexual motives, not the guy."

He smirks and kisses the end of my nose. "Funny. But I need you to be sure about this because once we start we can't go back. Everything will change."

I slide my hand against his jaw, the stubble lightly scraping the pads of my fingers. "Everything changed the moment I saw you."

I bring his face closer to mine and kiss him with everything I have. His hand slides down my side, down across my thighs before coming up my back and twisting into the hair at the nape of my neck. I feel like I'm on fire, burning with an intense need for this beautiful man before me.

Grabbing his hair lightly, I twist it between my fingers and bring his lips to my neck, needing to feel the press of his mouth against my skin. He shifts his body lower, dragging his lips with him as I pant out my breaths and give in to the myriad of sensations running wildly through me. He's gentle with his touch, something I've never experienced with another guy before. The others always rushed to the end goal. They never took their time to explore and worship. And that's exactly what James is doing right now. Worshiping me.

When his lips find an aching nipple under my bra, I moan with delight. James pulls the cup down, exposing it to the air, which makes it pucker even more. My hips move of their own accord as his tongue makes contact with the sensitive flesh, flicking it lightly before taking it fully into his eager mouth. The feel of his warm mouth has me panting out his name, begging him to continue.

"You're perfect. So very perfect." He blows on it again and

I arch my back into him. Curling my leg around his, I drag his thigh between my legs and press my needy core against it.

"God, James, that feels so good," I breathe. My fingers gently stroke the outline of his erection through his pants and his hips move in time with mine. I've never felt this level of passion before, from myself or someone else. I need to see how far we can go, how high we can climb.

He bites down on my nipple and I cry out while gripping his shoulder tightly. A desperate need to feel him inside me pulses through me as I attempt to wrap my legs around his waist.

I'm about to roll him on top of me and beg him to do just that when I hear my phone rings somewhere in the distance. A specific ringtone dedicated to the one person who I do not want to think of at this moment.

My hand pauses its movements, as does his tongue against my skin.

"Fuck," I groan, closing my eyes as my head rolls backward.

"Ignore it," he says, letting his lips trail against my skin again.

I wiggle and he pulls back, the haze of lust still lingering in his eyes. We sit up and I adjust my bra back into the correct position. "I can't. It's Liam."

James runs a hand over his face, threading it through his hair before grabbing his neck and pulling down. I kiss his mouth quickly before padding my way to my purse. I remove the phone as it starts up again.

"I'm fine. I'm safe. No need to send out the rescue squad," I say, walking back to James, who is adjusting his rather impressive erection on the couch.

"Where are you?" he asks. The calmness of his voice relaxes me. It's a good indication that he's not annoyed at my sudden departure. But rarely does he ask questions without knowing the answers already, so I keep my guard up slightly and brace for the impact of my reply.

"James picked me up. I'm at his house."

The silence on the line is deafening. I have to look at the phone several times to make sure the call wasn't dropped. James places his hand in mine, giving it a reassuring squeeze.

"Are you mad?" I ask tentatively.

Liam blows out a slow breath. "No, I'm not mad. I was worried about you. You ran off and I didn't know who found you or where you were. Lyle told me you got picked up by a friend after another incident with Chase, who, by the way, is going to lose his balls the next time I see him."

I lay my head against James's shoulder. "No need. I took care of his balls for you. Where are you?"

"I took Penny home, but I'm sitting outside of her house, waiting for her light to turn off."

"Stalker."

"I need to make sure she's okay."

"She's fine. You took care of her. No need to worry about her anymore tonight."

"I'm sorry I couldn't protect you both."

James kisses the top of my head and I know he can hear our conversation. "You don't need to protect me. I already have someone lined up for that job." I can feel his smile against the crown of my head and my heart melts a little more.

"Are you still sure about this?"

I tilt my head to look at James and I know my answer. "With all my heart."

"Okay then. Look, Mom and Dad are expecting us home tonight so I should probably come get you."

Disappointment fills me at knowing I need to leave. James grabs the phone from my hands and brings it to his ear.

"Liam? This is James. If it's okay with you, I'd like to bring her home. I can have her there in ten minutes. I don't live far away."

I wait patiently for Liam to erupt or have some sort of re-action. But it's quiet and muffled and I can only make out what James is saying, which isn't much. A lot of yes's and no's, abso-lutely's and I will's…typical guy talk. But then a smile crosses his face and I know that he just won Liam's approval. He hands the phone back to me and I quickly kiss the corner of his mouth.

"See you in a few."

I end the call and place the phone on the coffee table. "What did Liam say?"

He smiles and runs his hand through my hair. "He asked a lot of questions I would expect a protective older brother to ask. But the main one was if I truly cared for you as more than just a conquest, as someone who I would protect with my life." I bite my lip at the smile that crosses his beautiful face, and I know the answer without him saying it.

"Thank you," I say, kissing him softly. He helps me put my discarded dress back on, taking great care not to touch me again. I'm sure I know the reasons why.

"He's a good brother for wanting to protect you."

I nod and face him. "You're a good man for wanting to pro-tect me too."

"Should we be worried that Liam knows?"

I shake my head. "Liam won't tell anyone. I trust him."

His hands run up and down my arms before leaning for-ward to press a kiss to my forehead.

"Well, then I better stay in his good graces and bring you home. We'll continue this another time."

"Promise?"

When our lips meet, I can feel the answer all the way down

to my toes.

"Promise."

As he drives me back to my house, I can't help but look over at his profile in the muted light from the street lights outside. And for the first time I think I can truly admit to myself that I am falling for James, harder than I ever thought. I just hope that we can make it through the next six months without any bumps along the way.

Seventeen

"**H**AVE YOU TALKED TO HIM YET?" PENNY ASKS AS WE walk to my first-period class. Usually, I'd be walking with Chase since we have class together, but seeing as we're not on speaking terms right now it's Penny who has taken the job instead.

I shake my head and purse my lips. "Nope. And it's probably a good thing too because I'm still pretty pissed off that he ruined my entire winter break that night."

"What a dick. I hope you never forgive him. I mean, it was completely unacceptable the shit that he pulled. I just wish I could have seen you kick him in the balls."

"He had it coming. Twice he had to be told to leave me alone and twice he ignored it. Although he got off easy with me doing it instead of Liam. I had to talk him off the wall and reassure him he did not have to go back and defend my honor."

Penny looks down and scuffs her feet against the marble floor. "Well, that's because he was too busy protecting my honor. God, I feel so stupid right now. I mean, how could I not have seen that coming? And with Sarah? I felt so sorry for her, even though I don't think I should."

We pause in the hall and head to a corner to talk without interruption. "No, you should feel sorry for her too because she was duped by Travis, just like you were. Although the way word gets around no one will be going after him for a while. Once you're branded a cheater and a dirtbag you're pretty much blacklisted as boyfriend material by every girl in school."

"But that won't stop them from sleeping with him just because."

I shrug. "Then those girls are idiots. Just don't give him another thought. You deserve so much better than him. Besides, you've got me."

"And Liam."

My eyebrow rises at the mention of his name. "Yes, and Liam. I've meant to ask you about that. What exactly have you and my brother been up to lately? He hasn't been his usual pervy self when you were over these last two weeks."

A blush appears across her cheeks. Do I really want to know the answer to that question?

"Nothing. He's just been really sweet, calling to check up on me and making sure that Travis is leaving me alone. He took me out to lunch a couple of times but really that's been it."

I smile and jerk my head to indicate we need to start moving again. "You know it's fine, right? If you two want to start something? It doesn't bother me anymore. I just want you both to be happy. And watching you avoid each other like the plague because of me hurts. So if you want to date him, by all means, you have my blessing."

She shrugs and walks next to me. "I'm not really ready to date anyone right now. I mean, Travis is still a pretty fresh wound and I need to spend some time on me, not someone else.

Liam understands and said he just wants to help me however he can."

"Well, I'm glad you've come to this decision on your own and not out of some guilt trip. If you ever decide to further your friendship with him, you have my full support."

I hug her outside of my classroom and she smiles. "Thanks, Britt." Someone clears their throat behind me and Penny's eyes narrow over my shoulder at the source. I can pretty much guess who it is without having to turn around. "I better get to class. Good luck with that," she says out of the corner of her mouth before walking away.

My teeth grind against each other and I can feel the muscle tick in my jaw as I turn around and come face to face with Chase, who isn't really making eye contact with me.

Smart man.

"Hey Britta," he says quietly.

Still feeling childish about the whole thing, I move past him without saying hi and make my way to my seat, even though it's right next to his. He follows and sits down quietly. I can still feel his intense stare on the side of my face. Even with all of winter break to deal with it, I'm still just as mad as I was that night.

My phone vibrates in my pocket and I pull it out, giving a slight smile at James's name appearing on my screen.

LET ME KNOW IF HE GIVES YOU ANY TROUBLE TODAY. I MISS YOU.

Angling my phone away from prying eyes, I quickly type back my response.

MISS YOU TOO. AND DON'T WORRY. HE'S NOT EVEN ON MY RADAR. MY FOCUS WILL BE ELSEWHERE.

I'VE GOT A FEW IDEAS ON WHERE THAT FOCUS COULD GO.

I BET YOU DO. QUIT TEXTING ME AND GET BACK TO CLASS.

SLAVE DRIVER.

FLIRT.

SEE YOU IN A COUPLE HOURS.

CAN'T WAIT.

I lock my phone and slide it back into my pocket as the bell rings. Chase is still focused on me, or at least I think he is from what I can tell out of the corner of my eye. But my suspicions are confirmed when I hear Mrs. Thompson's voice call him out.

"Mr. Woodward, the board is up front."

"Yes ma'am," Chase says, creating a chorus of snickering to be heard. I stay stoic in my chair, not giving him the satisfaction of any kind of reaction because really, he's just not worth my time.

Did this hallway grow in length these past two weeks? I feel like I've been walking forever to get to the teacher's lounge. Maybe my brain is playing a trick on me, but it feels like it's been forever since I've seen him. And I need to see him. Right. Now.

My heart beats faster as I round the corner. We were able to sneak in a few days together over break, with help from Liam. James still isn't comfortable with the lying situation but without another option it's all we have. But James and Liam have formed a mutual understanding over a love of greasy pizza and horror movies. And I wasn't even upset when he crashed our "date". It was the fact he sat between us that upset me more. He paid for it later, courtesy of a bowl of warm water while he slept.

I say hello to several teachers who are enjoying their lunch and the few blissful moments of peace they're allotted during the day. My feet carry me on wings to my destination down the hall, the last office on the right. Only it's empty. No happy greeting, no warm body to hold tightly. Just a desk and chair and quiet.

I guess I shouldn't be too surprised. It's not like I expect to see him in his office every day. That would draw too much suspicion from people. But I had hoped that he'd want to see me right away. Not that I haven't enjoyed our text message banter in the meantime. Thank goodness no one can see those. There are a few that would make even a nun blush.

Settling into the oversized office chair, I start typing away at the grades he left for me this morning, transferring them from the book to the computer. It's sort of redundant, but it's a good backup in case something happens to the system and it crashes. Or worse, someone hacks into it and changes their grades. This way we at least have proof of what is real.

The rustling at the door behind me has my head turning to the side. My smile is instantaneous when James comes into view, all dancing eyes and bright smile.

"Good afternoon, Ms. Fosse," he says, playing his role for whoever may be in earshot.

"Good afternoon, Mr. Dumont," I say, playing along. "I'm just starting to enter the grades you left for me this morning."

He moves toward me, looking over his shoulder one last time before placing a kiss behind my ear.

"I've missed you," he whispers, sending a round of goose bumps to invade my flesh.

"Me too," I reply. My breathing starts to accelerate at his close proximity. James notices the change because when I look at him again, his eyes are dilated and fixed on my mouth. I want nothing more than to kiss those soft full lips right now.

Voices drift down the hall and James straightens back up to his full height while running a hand over his tie to smooth it back down into place.

"Don't look at me like that." He's whispering in a low, passionate voice with his head bent down to look at me.

I bite my lip and feign ignorance. "Like what?"

"You know what. We can't do what is going through your head right now so please don't tempt me."

"And what do you think is going on through my head? Surely it's something completely platonic and nothing at all dirty as you must be thinking."

He laughs quietly and my legs clench at the sound. I love listening to him laugh. Again, I need to make that as a ringtone somehow.

"Liar, liar, pants on fire." He perches himself on the edge of his desk, crossing his arms in front of his broad chest.

"You have no idea," I mumble to myself and turn my attention back to the computer screen. The last thing we need is to get in trouble for being careless.

His brow furrows but then shakes his head to dismiss whatever it was. There's a moment of awkward silence and the temperature in the room spikes about ten degrees. It's hard to sit here and be this close and not touch him. Really touch him, like we started out doing at his house a couple weeks ago. The memory heats my cheeks again and I'm gifted with another quiet laugh.

"Are you going to the basketball game tomorrow night? Heard it's supposed to be a good one against Cottage Grove."

I turn in my chair and nod. "Big rivalry game so it doesn't surprise me that's what everyone is talking about. Last year they creamed us so we're out for revenge, or so I'm told. Why, are you going?"

He nods and crosses his legs at the ankle. "I am. Karen talked me into it. She was on me for never attending anything around the school and said it'd be good for me to go mingle with the student body."

My nostrils flare at the mention of Ms. Hathaway's name. She's young and single and the largest man-eater of the faculty. Rumors of her one-night stands and serial dates have trickled down to the student body, making her every teenage boy's fantasy and every girl's common enemy. She's the one teacher who doesn't feel that business casual is necessary. No, she still believes she's in high school herself with her tiny little skirts and barely-there tops, only furthering my hatred for the woman. If you're going to dress like a stripper, perhaps you should be working somewhere else.

James places two fingers beneath my chin and tilts it up to meet his eyes.

"Don't," he simply says, looking straight into my eyes. I try to look away, but he moves to stay within my line of sight. "Don't worry about Karen. I don't think of her like that and never could. I only have eyes for one woman in my life." I make a scoffing noise, letting my bitter jealousy rule my head, even though I know in my heart that he's not interested in her.

He gets off the desk and braces himself against the armrests of the chair. "Karen? She's nothing to me. A nobody. She doesn't light my soul on fire with a glance or make me want to plow over every person in a crowded hallway just to be near her. That right is reserved solely for one beautiful, amazing, incredibly sexy woman. And that is *my girl*, my ray of sunshine, my beacon in the bleakness of the night." He leans closer until our lips are barely touching. "You, Britta Fosse, are the woman for me. There's no one else that could ever turn my head away from you. No one."

My heart beats faster. Can he see it through my sweater? How every beat imprints his name onto my soul when he says things like that to me?

I don't know how he does it, taking me from a raging green-eyed monster to a lovesick fool in less than a blink of the eye. I swallow hard and quickly close the distance between our lips, needing to have my fix of him before I have to go without for who knows how long.

It's brief, mainly because the door is still wide open, but still feels like an eternity has passed. Every time our lips touch, I lose myself in him; lose myself in the knowledge that he wants it just as bad as I do. And I'll take whatever I can get with him because I need him like I need my next breath.

He cups my cheek and backs away, his eyes still shining with emotions I'm afraid to acknowledge. Lust is definitely there, but there's something else, something more that my mind is subconsciously avoiding. Maybe I'm reading too much into my own emotions. But what we have is more than an infatuation, more than a lustful coupling. There's something there, something real, and it scares me slightly to put a name to it because deep down I want it more than anything. I want to be his, to be claimed by him, and never have to worry about being without him again.

"You better go eat your lunch," I say hoarsely and clear my throat from whatever was lodged in it.

"I'd rather eat it in here with you. Can I heat yours up for you?"

I smile and nod. "I'd like that. Thanks."

He trails his fingertips down my cheek before taking our lunches to the kitchen area. When he's finally out the door, I let out a sigh and sink back into my chair in the most unladylike fashion. My lips still tingle as his residual taste lingers on them. If I close my eyes, I can still smell his subtle cologne wafting in the air. How can I be this turned on without him even here next to me?

My phone vibrates across the desk.

CAN WE TALK?

Oh great. Now he's resorting to text messages because I won't give him the time of day? I roll my eyes and straighten in my chair.

NOT YET. I'M STILL REALLY PISSED OFF AT YOU. I NEED SPACE AND TIME.

I UNDERSTAND. DO YOU THINK YOU CAN EVER FORGIVE ME?

HONESTLY, I DON'T KNOW.

I JUST WANT YOU TO KNOW THAT I'M REALLY, TRULY SORRY. IT WON'T HAPPEN AGAIN.

The hairs on my neck stand on end as I read his last message over and over. He said that the last time he tried putting the moves on me and yet here we are again. Only this time it was worse. Before, it was just a wandering hand. This time, it was a full on assault on my lips and body. Well, maybe assault is too harsh of a word but really there's no other way to describe it. It wasn't welcome and I certainly didn't invite him to do it.

James sets my plate down in front of me and looks at me with concerned eyes.

"What's wrong?" He sees the message on my phone before I have the chance to close the screen. I can actually hear the grinding of his teeth as he reads it. His anger radiates off him in waves, hitting me with a force that I can feel.

"He's got some nerve to be contacting you."

"I can handle him," I say, trying to diffuse the situation. "He's not worth our time. Just ignore him. I know I am."

His long finger points to my phone. "That's not ignoring him. Saying that you need time is encouraging him, making him believe there's a chance you will actually forgive him this time."

I keep my head down as I turn toward him. "He's still my friend and he wasn't exactly in the right frame of mind when all this happened. He was high and drunk so I know he wouldn't normally do something like that."

"And what about the last time? What happened then?"

I look away. I don't want to see the disappointment in his eyes as he sits next to me. "That was my fault for getting too drunk to ward off his advances."

"From what you told me before, *he's* the one who got you drunk and tried to take advantage of you."

I pick up my fork and push my food around the plate. "I'm not encouraging him, but I can't cut him completely out of my life. We've known each other since we were little."

"I'm not saying to cut him out of your life." He stabs angrily at his food. "No, screw that, that's exactly what I'm saying. I know it's irrational and childish but he's trying to hurt you and it's my job to protect you the best way I know how."

"Are you sure you're not just jealous?"

The loud clank of his fork hitting the plate jostles me slightly and I slowly bring my eyes to his.

"This has nothing to do with jealousy. There is nothing about him that is threatening to me, or us, in any way. But his relentless pursuit of you and the carelessness that he exhibits while trying to get to you is dangerous. This is about protecting you because one of these days he's going to try something and there may be no one around to help. As much as I want to, I can't always be with you and there will be times where Liam won't be there either. Just please take my advice and start to sever the line between you two. Do it gradually if you can't cut it now. But he needs to know that his actions are not okay and that what he did is irreparable to your friendship."

I choke back a tear that threatens to fall. Chase has been

my friend for so long that it's going to be hard to not be that way anymore. And as much as it hurts, I know James is right. The damage that Chase has already done cannot be undone and situations will continue to arise if I keep putting myself in them. Actions speak louder than words and so far my words have fallen on deaf ears where Chase is concerned.

"Okay," I say sullenly.

His face softens. Sympathy edges his eyes as he reaches for my hand. "I'm so sorry sweetheart, but it's for the best. And I think you know it too otherwise you wouldn't be feeling this way."

I nod. He's right. He's always right. This just hurts more than I thought it would.

James turns and shuts the door partially to give us privacy. In an instant, I'm engulfed in his arms as he presses my head against his chest. The steady beat of his heart fills my ears as a tear finally breaks loose.

"This is my way of keeping you safe. I'm sorry it hurts, though. I don't like to see you in pain."

I wrap my arms around him, clinging to his muscular back for support.

"I know it's for the best. It's just hard to hear." I press my lips against the pulse along his neck and sigh. "Thank you for taking care of me."

He pulls me back and smooths the hair away from my face. "I will always take care of you. You are the most important thing to me. I will never let anything happen to you."

He seals his words with a kiss. Now we just need to figure out how to make it work.

Eighteen

THE GYM IS A CACOPHONY OF SCREAMS AND bouncing balls, whistles, and loud cheers. The beginnings of a headache form at the bridge of my nose but I do my best to ignore it. I'm not here for the game. I'm here for someone else.

"Look, there's Justice over there," Penny says.

She's sitting with a couple other kids from school, but I don't know them very well. Our usual crowd is already here. Sort of. Drake, Lyle, and Chase all play on the basketball team and Dez and Cami are cheerleaders so that leaves just the three of us to fend for ourselves.

Penny looks at the guys on the court and sneers when she sees Travis passing the ball to Lyle.

"Why did I ever let you talk me into coming here tonight? I don't want to do anything near that loser."

I shake her shoulder and smile. "Because you're not going to let him dictate your life. Show him what he's missing by rubbing it in his face that you're not heartbroken over his inability to keep his dick in his pants."

"That's right. Besides, it's the three amigas tonight so let's have some fun," Justice says. She leans across me and places her hand on top of Penny's knee.

"Thanks, girls. I don't know what I'd do without you."

"Be a loser."

"Sit in a corner sucking your thumb."

"Be a loser."

Penny laughs and smacks my arm. "You already said that one."

I laugh. "Well, it's the truth."

Lyle passes to Drake, who charges down the court after dodging several guys from Cottage Grove to sink the shot. Everyone on our side leaps to their feet, screaming at the top of their lungs. Since we were a little late, it's already halfway through the first period and our team is up 24-18.

"They're looking good tonight," Justice yells.

I roll my eyes when Chase tries to make eye contact with me from the bench. I'm half tempted to give him the finger but restrain myself, remembering that I'm at a school function and shouldn't act like that. Instead, I look around the packed gym, trying to find the one person I'm actually here to see.

And then I see him sitting next to *her*. Ms. Hathaway. My skin crawls as I watch her lean close to him and laugh while placing her hand on his forearm. They're several rows away but close enough to feel as if it's happening right in front of me.

"Hey," Penny says, waving her hand in front of my face. I snap out of it and turn to her. "What are you staring at? The game is down there." She leans over and tries to see where my line of sight was aimed at. Her eyes squint and then widen slightly. "Holy shit. Is that Mr. Dumont and the man-eater herself?"

My stomach rolls and I nod my head. "Looks like it. She is

such a troll."

Penny's eyes flicker between mine and the two of them. I need to look away and not draw attention to the fact that Ms. Hathaway's presence near James is bothering me. I need to stop staring, but I can't. I watch as she rubs her hand up and down his arm while scooting closer to him. She doesn't notice his attempts to move away because she's so focused on staring at his face.

Mine.

Penny continues to stare at me even after I shift my gaze back to the game.

"What?" I ask when I can't take it any longer.

She narrows her eyes at me with a slight frown on her face. "What's going on? You're acting weird."

"I'm not acting weird."

"Yes, you are."

"I am not."

"Why are you so interested in Mr. Dumont and Ms. Hathaway?"

I scoff and focus back on the game. "Who said I was interested?"

"Then why do you keep looking over there?" she asks.

"Maybe I feel sorry for him. I'd hate to see another faculty member be her victim. Do you remember what happened to Mr. Sundberg? He never recovered from it."

That got her attention, only because she had the largest crush on him our freshman year. And then Ms. Hathaway happened and ran him out of the school.

"She better not do that to Mr. Dumont. He's a great teacher and I really don't want him to leave because of her," I say as I fight the urge to look over again.

She sighs and pats my knee. "Yeah, you're right. Plus if she runs out all the hot eye candy teachers what are we going to daydream about during their classes?"

I laugh and bump her shoulder. "Exactly."

We follow the roar of the crowd as Lyle sinks another basket. And because we're still bitter, we boo when Chase and Travis follow with their own lay-ups. They may be part of the team, but asshats shouldn't be rewarded for anything they do.

The halftime buzzer sounds and we get up to stretch our bodies.

"Man, my ass hurts from sitting here. Can't they make these bleachers padded?" Justice says, arching her back.

I rub my ass and laugh. "My butt is so numb that I don't think I'd even feel if anyone pinched it right now."

I should have kept that thought to myself.

"Ow!"

Penny laughs. "That sounded like a challenge to me."

She grabs another handful of my ass, causing me to yelp loudly. Several heads turn in our direction, curious about what's going on with us. I twirl and try to get away from her.

"Knock it off, bitch!" I laugh.

I twirl again but this time I lose my footing. I don't fall far because I land against someone's chest before my ass meets the ground.

"Good evening, ladies. Any problems over here?" he says with a hint of amusement in his voice. Chills run up and down my spine and my nipples pebble in my bra, simply from the sound of his voice. *Please don't let it be noticeable.*

"Hello, Mr. Dumont. Enjoying the game so far?" Penny asks.

I turn around and come face to face with James.

"Actually I am. It's a close game, for sure. I just hope they can maintain the lead."

"James," I hear Ms. Hathaway purr behind him. "I'm heading up to get something to drink. Are you coming?" Her hand trails along his arm and I can feel the anger start to snake through my body. How dare she touch him like that? James looks my way and removes her arm quickly.

"I'm okay for now. Thanks anyway, Karen."

She sticks her bottom lip out slightly and sashays her way up the stairs, making sure everyone is staring at her jean covered ass. I breathe again when she disappears over the top of the bleachers. Unfortunately, the damage is done and I can't erase this feeling going through my head.

James tries to lighten the situation by engaging in conversation with Penny and Justice, only I can barely hear it. I know I shouldn't let her get to me, but that woman irritates me to no end.

"I'll be right back," I say quickly and dart up the stairs, needing to get away and gather my thoughts for half a second.

"Britt, where you going?" I hear Penny call out behind me.

"Outside. I'll be right back."

I walk down the second-floor corridor quickly until I come to a dark staircase next to a large picture window. I slow my feet and stop to look outside before placing my forehead against the cool glass. It's snowing again and the cars are just starting to get a fresh blanket on top of them. This was a bad idea. I should have known better than to come tonight, knowing that *she* would be here with him and that *she* would put every move on him that she has.

I groan and slide down the glass, making it squeak and squeal as I drop to my knees before falling on my ass. It's irrational and unprovoked but I told him that I get jealous too and it's not flattering when it happens.

"Britta?" his soft voice says behind me.

"Yeah?" I whisper, still clutching my knees to my chest with my back to him. He approaches me quietly, squatting down to my right and bracing himself against the wall.

"Sweetheart, please don't do this. You're making a big deal out of nothing."

I nod and feel my chest constrict. My breathing turns shallow and my heart feels like it's slowing in rhythm. "I know it's nothing, but I can't sit there and watch her put her hands all over you as she has been. She has no right to do it."

James reaches over and tucks a lock of hair behind my ear. I turn my head and press my ear against my knee, looking at the beautiful face that I dream of every second of the day.

"You're right. She doesn't. And if you've noticed I've been trying to cut-off her actions the whole time."

"I noticed. It still hurts."

He sits next to me on the floor and pulls me to his side, kissing the crown of my head. "I know. Believe me, I know."

I sniff and snuggle into him. "How do you know?"

He wraps his other arm around me. "Because I feel the same way every time I see one of the boys at school look at you in the same manner."

I tilt my head up to meet his eyes and give a weak smile. "This is pathetic. *I'm* pathetic. We're better than this. We lo… mean so much to each other that we can't let this petty crap get in the way. Just ignore me and my stupidity."

I hope he didn't catch my almost slip-up.

His eyes flash in the muted light as he brings me to my knees next to him. Warm hands cradle my face, pulling it closer to his.

"You were going to say something else."

Shit. I should have known that he wouldn't let it go.

"I…I can't."

"Why not?"

I look down at his shoulder and bite my lip. "It's too soon."

He maneuvers his head until our eyes catch again. "Too soon for what? To admit how we actually feel?"

I lick my dry lips and his gaze follows the path, making his pupils dilate. "Yes," I whisper.

Our lips connect softly with a firm press before molding into each other's movements, allowing the moment to take us over. My hands wind into his hair, keeping him anchored to me as his hands move to my hips to bring me onto his lap.

"Would it help if I said I feel the same way?" he says.

Our foreheads press together as I frame his face with my hands.

"Do you? I mean, this is crazy, isn't it? We haven't even been on a real date yet."

"I know and I hate that I can't do that with you. I want to take you out on an actual date, out of school and away from staged meetings. I want to buy you dinner and take you to the movies where we'll pay a ridiculous amount of money to just sit there and make out in the back row." I giggle and he quickly presses his lips against mine. "Then after we'll go back to my house and snuggle against each other on the couch while I read you one of my favorite books in front of the fireplace. And when we've had enough of the books and we can't keep our hands off each other anymore, I want to take you to my bed. I want to lay you down and make love to you all night long. I want to worship your body, again and again. All of it, I want to do it with you because…I love you."

A tiny gasp escapes me and a tear threatens to fall down my cheek. He said it. He gave voice to what's in my head again as if we're completely in tune with each other.

"Wha-what?" I stutter. He laughs and kisses my nose.

"You heard me. I'm in love with you, Britta Fosse, and I can't hold it back any longer. I need to tell you exactly how I feel because keeping it bottled up is driving me crazy."

He loves me. He's *in* love with me. My heart feels like it's about to beat right out of my chest.

"James," I whisper and brush my lips across his. "I love you too."

His smile brings pure joy to my soul as our lips reconnect and mimic what we'd like to do to each other. Teeth nip, tongues devour, and mouths move to a sensual rhythm that makes every muscle south of my navel constrict with need. He makes me feel beautiful and desirable with little to no effort just by kissing me.

"Take me home," I say between gasping breaths. He leans back and the fire in his eyes says he wants to do the same.

"What about the others? They'll notice we're gone together."

"I don't care. I need you to take me home, to your home."

His hands run through my hair and I lean into the contact. But then I'm lifted off the ground and we're standing against the wall.

"Did you drive here yourself?" he asks. His lips trail down the beating pulse of my neck, causing another round of desire to flood between my legs.

"No," I say while running my hands up his chiseled chest. He groans slightly when I run my nail over his nipple, causing it to harden beneath my hands.

"Fuck. You're making this hard."

"That's the idea." My lips brush his ear as I whisper.

James pulls his head back and grimaces slightly, looking around to make sure that we're still alone. "We need to go back and finish the game because we can't gather suspicion. Not from your friends and certainly not from Karen." A shiver runs through my body at the mention of her name and he kisses my forehead to ease my mind. "You walk back first and join Penny and Justice. Get a ride home with them and I'll come get you after that."

Brain function finally restores itself as I contemplate this plan. "Shit, this won't work. It's Tuesday. I can't stay over tonight and there's too much at risk for us to show up tomorrow morning looking like we had wild, hot, earth-shattering sex all night."

He smirks and presses me into the wall again, this time using only his hips. I groan in response and feel my knees start to get weak.

"You're making me irrational. I want to say screw what everyone else thinks because all I care about, all I'm concerned with is you." His lips cover mine again. "But you're right. Tonight is not the night for this."

"When?"

"Friday? Are you busy this weekend?"

I shake my head and smile. "I am now."

"Pack a bag because I'm not letting you out of my sight until Sunday."

"Three days to get through before I have the best weekend of my life. It seems so far away now that there's something to look forward to."

He backs away, leaving my body feeling cold. "Best of your life so far," he says with a smirk.

"Smart ass."

James quickly crashes his lips onto mine, scorching them one last time before backing up into the darkened hallway. I look at him confused and bite back the laugh that's bubbling up from my throat.

"The gym is the other way," I call out.

He nods and smiles. "I need to walk around for a bit otherwise I'm going to draw some unnecessary attention due to a slight wardrobe issue I'm currently having."

My cheeks heat and flame with a mixture of longing and embarrassment since that wardrobe malfunction was pressed against my hips just a moment ago. "Good idea. I'll see you back inside and I won't get jealous anymore. Promise."

"Good." He stops and looks at me while running a hand through his hair.

"I love you," I whisper.

James brings his hand up to his chest and places the palm over his heart. "I love you too."

He disappears down the darkened hallway, muttering soft curse words with a hint of amusement behind them. My fingers caress my swollen lips as I take a few calming breaths before I head back into the lion's den. Only this time with the knowledge that nothing is going to come between us anymore.

Nineteen

I CAN'T FOCUS. MY MIND IS A COMPLETE PILE OF MUSH AND has been since last night. I should be writing my paper that's due in AP English, only I've been staring at it for the last hour with not one word written.

A knock on my door scares me and I gasp loudly as my mom enters the room.

"Sorry sweetie, did I startle you?"

"A little. I guess I got lost in my thoughts."

She sits on the edge of my bed, and I turn in my chair to face the older version of me. We're practically twins. The only differences are the few wrinkles and laugh lines that give her away as my mom and not my older sister. Same long brown hair, same dazzling hazel eyes and bowed lips. Even our noses are the same, which is a good thing because there's no way that I want my dad's nose. I like my cute little button one.

"Anything I can help you with?" she asks.

"No, nothing like that. Just, you know, flaking out for a second."

She tilts her head as if she doesn't entirely believe me. But I smile brightly back at her, hoping to ease her mind. I don't need her thinking this is about a guy, even though it kind of is.

"Well, I wanted to be the first to let you know that these came for you today."

She hands me three large white envelopes, each with the seal of the different universities I've applied to. My eyes grow wide as I stare and flip them in my hands. Harvard, Yale, and Stanford all stare at me, each of them holding the promise of a future, at least academically.

"Well, go ahead and open them." She can barely contain the excitement in her voice.

"Shouldn't we wait for Dad?"

She deflates slightly. "I suppose we should."

"When is he getting home?"

"He called a little while ago and said he would be home around seven." She looks down at her watch and smiles. "Which is in about twenty minutes."

Instantly I think of James and how I want to share this moment with him because this could affect him as well. I know we really haven't discussed the future, other than agreeing that we both will be in it. But this is something big and I want to share this with him, just like I want to share everything about my life with him.

Mom looks at me funny as I keep twisting the envelopes around in my hand. "Sweetie, is there something the matter? Aren't you excited about this?"

I flick my eyes to hers and chew my lip. "I am. I just-"

"What is it? You know you can tell me anything, right?"

"It's nothing. I'm just acting silly." I need a distraction. "Should we wait for Dad downstairs? Maybe Liam will even be home by then."

I stand from my chair and hug my mom. I want to talk to her about James but I know I can't without getting him or me in trouble. I don't think she would understand.

"That's a wonderful idea. I've got a fresh batch of chocolate chip bars cooling on the rack for you. We'll eat some while we celebrate which college you're getting into."

I shake my head as we walk downstairs. "You know there's still two other colleges I have to hear back from."

We round the corner and I sink into one of the plush seats around the island while my mom goes into full Betty Crocker mode. She cuts each square until they're all uniform and perfectly placed on the three-tier serving dish.

"Don't you worry about those other colleges. You'll get your acceptance letters from them as well and then all you have to do is pick which one is best for you." She offers me a bar and I eagerly take it. "Tell me, have you decided which one you want most?"

"Well, you know I love Boston, so Harvard's my number one choice." She smiles and shakes her head with amusement. "Then Yale because it's close by but I also kind of want UC-Berkeley because it's California and the thought of never having to see snow again is kind of appealing right now."

We laugh as we look out the window. The newly fallen snow glistens on the ground as the moon rises higher in the sky. "You would miss the change of seasons, though. Trust me, I did."

Huh? "What do you mean? I thought you lived here your whole life?"

She shakes her head and runs soapy water in the sink to wash the now empty pan. "Technically I did, but my freshman year of college was spent at UCLA."

"Wow. I didn't know that. I assumed you spent your entire college career at UConn."

Mom smiles and places the clean dish on the drying rack. "No. I started out at UCLA for the same reasons you want to go to Berkeley. But then I came home for winter break and had a life changing experience which made me move back here that next fall."

"Life changing? Like how?"

She wipes her hands on a clean towel and sits next to me. "Let's just say a close call changed my mind."

I narrow my eyes. "Not enough. I want the story."

"Did I ever tell you how your dad and I met?" I shake my head. "I was out doing some last minute shopping, trying to get as many things as I possibly could for my sisters and brother two days before Christmas. We were expected at your great-grand-parent's house the next day so I was a little crazy and distracted. My arms were juggling about seven or so bags as I walked from shop to shop downtown. A gust of wind came by, throwing me slightly off-balance as I crossed the street, which set off a chain reaction of events. My hat flew into traffic so I bent down to pick it up, which caused me to drop a few bags out of my arms. Then when I had everything situated, I got my foot stuck in a pothole, leaving me stranded in the middle of the street.

"I was so busy trying to dislodge my boot that I didn't even see the truck that was heading my way. When I finally heard the noise, I looked up at the headlights of the vehicle and froze. I didn't know what to do. Suddenly a pair of arms wrapped around me and pulled me to the side, leaving my boot still stuck in the middle of the street, just before the truck reached where I was standing.

"We fell onto the sidewalk in a heap with my bags scattered everywhere and me sprawled on top of my savior. That's when I looked down and saw the most handsome man I had ever seen in my life. My whole world stopped when he brushed away the hair from my face and looked at me with such concern in his eyes that I wanted to cry."

She looks wistfully down at her wedding rings and I follow her gaze to the sparkling diamonds that adorn her finger. "The moment he asked my name I knew that was it. I needed to leave California and be here with him because he was the one."

"You knew that all because he said your name?"

She shakes her head and turns to face me. "Well partly. The other part was when I found out he was attending UConn, I knew I had to transfer so I could be with him. I've loved your dad since the first moment we met and I wouldn't change one decision I made to get us to where we are now."

Interesting. "So you're saying that you changed your life because of a guy?"

"No, my life changed because of love."

This is sounding a bit too familiar to me. "How did you know? I mean, you had just met. You couldn't possibly know you were in love just from that."

"You're right. But transferring schools helped our relationship grow even more and later in my sophomore year we got engaged. It wasn't easy because he was a graduate student and a professor's assistant in some of my classes. We had to keep our relationship a secret at times, but it was worth it in the end."

I lean back in my chair and hold my hands up. "Whoa. Back up the train here. Dad was a professor's assistant in some of your classes?"

She nods. "Yes, and back then it was forbidden to date any member of the faculty while attending their class, even if it was an assistant because they were still looked upon as a figure of authority. But I needed those classes to complete my degree so we had to pretend not to know each other. It was hard for those first few months after transferring yet we worked around it somehow. In fact, I think it made us stronger because we knew if we could survive this, we could survive anything."

This is a fascinating turn of events. How did I not know this about my parents? "So you had to hide your relationship from everyone because he was essentially a teacher?"

She nods and smiles. "Yes. It wasn't easy, but we did. And I would do it again if it meant I could have the life I currently have with him and both you and Liam. Things happen for a reason Britta, things you can't explain. And you can't help who you fall in love with. All you need to do is follow your heart because it will never lead you down the wrong path."

I swallow hard and twist my fingers in my lap.

"Mom?"

"Yes, sweetie?"

"What happens if I find myself in a similar situation one day?"

She blinks several times. "Similar how?"

"In love with someone but have to hide it for a period of time."

She tilts her head to the side to get a better read on me. "What are you saying?"

I take a deep breath and open my mouth only nothing comes out because the cheerful voice of my dad rings out from the garage door, announcing his presence.

My mom leaves her chair and rushes over to greet him with a kiss that makes me turn my head away and blush. Apparently our impromptu trip down memory lane has spurred some feelings in her that I'd rather not think about.

"Well that's one way to be greeted after a long day at work," he says, cupping her cheek and pressing his lips to her forehead.

"Britta and I were just talking about colleges."

"And let me guess, you told her about how we met?"

She nods and smiles. "I can't believe we never told her before."

They walk into the kitchen with their arms wrapped around their waists. My dad kisses me on top of my head, just like he did when I was a little girl. "Hi, sweetheart."

I swivel in my chair and hug him tight. "Hi, Dad."

He glances down to the envelopes in front of me and smiles. "I see we've got mail?"

I nod. "We were waiting for you to get home before I opened them."

Dad shrugs his trench coat off and hangs it in the closet. "Well let's open them."

My hands hover over them, still longing to share this moment with James. I look at my parents, who are leaning against the granite countertop with their arms wrapped around each other, and marvel at the love they so obviously share still to this day. I never knew that they had to endure hardships like the one I'm facing with James. My mom said it made them stronger. I hope she's right about that because, for the first time in my life, I want what they have.

I pick each of them up, gently sliding my finger under the flaps. I pull each letter out individually and line them up so I can read them all at once.

"Well? What do they say?" Mom asks.

My eyes grow wide as I look between each letter. I swallow hard and choke back the tears threatening to fall when I look into my parents faces. "I got in. To all of them. Full academic scholarships for all four years."

A tear falls down my cheek and I brush it away, finally letting the emotions of the situation take hold. Mom rushes around and hugs me tightly, repeatedly saying how proud she is of me. Dad joins her on my other side and we laugh as each of us holds a letter in our hands.

"Um, I need to go," I say abruptly. I stand up and wipe my eyes.

"Where do you need to go?" my mom asks. "It's getting kind of late."

"I need to go see someone."

"Can't it wait until tomorrow? It's a school night and you should get some rest," Dad says.

I thread my arms into my jacket and pull on my cream colored beret. "No, I need to see him now."

Both of my parents look at each other before turning back to me as I pull on my gloves and grab my keys.

"Him?"

I kiss them both on the cheek and smile. "Him." I gather up the letters and give them a small wave. "I won't be out long."

Mom leans her head on my dad's shoulder as they watch me run out the garage door. I practically sprint to my car and barely miss Liam as he pulls into the driveway next to me. With an apologetic wave, I back out while sending a quick text to James and ask him to meet me at Brier Park. He responds instantly, of course, and I drive the few blocks to wait for him.

Giant, fluffy white flakes fall from the sky as I trudge through the snow to our favorite secluded spot. The moon casts a soft glow on the trees and surrounding area. Several stars appear like glitter in the sky, each twinkling in the cold night. My breath billows in front of me, curling into the air before disappearing. Only I don't feel the cold, just the warmth. And the source of that warmth is walking toward me right now.

I clutch the letters to my chest and my eyes water at the sight of him. He's just so perfect. Those long legs clad in worn jeans make my heart skip a beat, while his wool pea coat and gray beanie hat make me want to jump him this very instant.

But it's his face that does me in. That gorgeous face, so masculine and strong with those piercing green eyes focused solely on me, that's what makes my fingers twitch and my knees weak. And it's his heart, his need to protect and help those around him that make me fall in love with him more and more every day.

My guy.

"Britta? What's wrong?" he asks as he cups my face.

I shake my head and let out a small laugh. "Nothing's wrong. Look," I say, showing him the papers in my hand. He backs away slightly and flips between each letter with wide eyes. When he's done reading the last one, he gives me the largest smile I've ever seen.

"Sweetheart, this is amazing. Full academic scholarships? Wow, I just can't even put this into words. I'm so proud of you." Our lips touch and a tingle runs through my body.

When we pull back, we're both smiling like idiots. "Sorry to drag you out of the house when it's snowing like this but I needed to tell you in person. I couldn't wait until tomorrow."

James moves his hand to the back of my neck, pulling my body closer to his. Our feet intertwine and I cling to his shoulders, not willing to let him go.

"You know I would do anything for you. Your happiness is my happiness. Your pain is my pain." James kisses me gently and I sigh. He plays with my hair, twirling it around his finger. "You look so beautiful right now with the snowflakes sticking to your hair. An angel sent from above. My angel. My girl."

There is no way I could not have fallen in love with this man. Everything he says, everything he does, is perfect to me. My gloved finger traces his jaw before reaching around and pulling his head forward. The moment our mouths lock it's nothing but a burst of light, dimming the stars and moon with our powerful glow of love.

His tongue touches my lips and I open for him, basking in the joy as he shows me by his actions how much he loves me.

We walk backward slowly until I'm pressed against a tree, never once breaking contact with his lips. Our hands roam over our bodies, separated by layer after layer of clothing. Oh, how I would love to get rid of these layers so I can finally see James.

"Tomorrow we'll celebrate properly," he says. His mouth moves down my throat and I tilt my head to the side, giving him better access to the delicate skin.

"Yes."

"You taste so good right here." The tip of his tongue grazes the hollow dip of my throat and I moan in response.

"James." My voice is breathy, floating in the air like the falling snow around us. He brings his head back up and cradles my face again while his thumbs gently stroke the arch of my cheek.

"I love you," he says, sending me spiraling toward the heavens again.

"I love you too."

"What time can you come over tomorrow?"

My hands run up and down his coat, playing with a few buttons along the way. "After dinner. My parents think I'm going away for the weekend with Penny. Liam has volunteered to keep her busy so no one will question it. Anything in particular you want me to bring?"

"Just you."

I laugh. "Well, are we going out? Are you making me dinner at home? I kind of need more to go on than that."

"Yes, we're going out to dinner. I've made us reservations a couple towns over so I can take you out properly without suspicion."

"Sounds great."

With a final scorching kiss, James backs away and pulls me

toward our parked vehicles. Somehow I was able to still hold onto my acceptance letters, although I'm not entirely sure how.

"Tomorrow," he says, opening my car door for me.

"Tomorrow," I repeat with the smile still plastered on my face.

With a quick peck on my cheek, he closes my door and stands next to his truck, watching me as I drive back toward my house.

"This can work," I mumble to myself. It worked for my parents; it has to work for me.

Twenty

I'M NERVOUS FOR THE FIRST TIME IN WHAT SEEMS LIKE
ages. I double check everything in my overnight bag, just
to make sure that I haven't forgotten anything. Not that it
would be an issue if I did. We could always just go out and buy
whatever it is I need, but that means more sneaking around
and James is still having issues with that. But circumstances
being what they are, our actions are pretty much dictated for
us. Lies, deceit, and covert operations are the beginnings of our
relationship. That's normal, isn't it?

"You ready?" Liam asks from my doorway. I turn to face
him and smile, knowing it doesn't quite reach my eyes.

"I think so." I walk over to hug him tightly. There's so much
gratitude I want to convey with this one simple gesture. "I can't
thank you enough for doing this."

He hugs me back then grabs my bag off the bed. "No need
to thank me. This weekend is for me as well so we're both getting
what we want."

I swallow hard and shift on my feet. "Just please, *please* be careful with Penny. I know how you feel about her and I know how she feels about you. I just don't want you both to rush into something before it's ready to fully blossom. Deep in my heart I know you two could be epic. The timing just needs to be right. You know what I mean?"

Liam smiles and ruffles my hair, making me rush back to my mirror to see the damage. "Relax, I didn't mess it up. And I do know what you mean. I know that we are meant to be together. As painful as it is, I'm going to take it slow because I don't know what's going on through her mind and I don't want to scare her off. We're both still so young, but it's hard to ignore the little voice in my head that says grab her before someone else does."

"You're such a good man. I'm proud to be your sister." We smile and walk out my bedroom door and down the stairs. Our parents are in the living room, cuddled together on the couch with a book between them.

"Stay safe, Britta," my dad says. "We know you think you can take care of yourself but remember, you're still just a young girl."

I walk over and hug them both so they don't have to leave the couch. "I will, promise."

Mom turns her attention to Liam and eyes him carefully. "And what are your plans for the weekend?"

He smirks and kisses her on the cheek. "Shenanigans."

She rolls her eyes and sighs. "Of course. You are your father's son after all."

The look my dad gives her has me snickering to myself. She replies with a kiss on his cheek. "Take it as you will. I've heard the stories of your younger years before we met."

"And where did you hear those from?" he asks.

"Your mother and I do talk to each other, dearest, along

with Tom and David, who were with you when said shenanigans took place."

"You can't believe anything they said."

Mom shakes her head and shoos us out with her hand. "You two have fun and we'll see you on Sunday, preferably by dinnertime?"

"Yes, Mom," we both chime out in unison. We close the front door as my dad's lips falls onto hers. Liam and I both would like to retain whatever contents are in our stomach before we get into his car so we couldn't get out of there fast enough.

He drives the short distance to James's house. We don't really say anything but then again there's nothing left to say. He's spending the weekend with Penny to keep her occupied and I'm spending the weekend with James. We both get what we want in a roundabout way.

"I'm walking you to his door," Liam states with a quasi-authoritative tone. I roll my eyes and follow him to the front door as he carries my bag for me. My nerves are scattered everywhere and I don't think I'm going to have any skin left on my bottom lip as I chew on it incessantly.

"Stop it or I will take you home. You don't have to worry about me beating him up or threatening his livelihood in the event he hurts you. We've been talking quite a bit and have actually become friends. James is a good guy and really cares about you. I know I'm leaving you in good hands."

I turn and hug him again, trying to keep the tears at bay. "Thank you for understanding."

"Just don't go and get pregnant. I can't help you out with that one."

I smack his chest as James opens his front door. He looks positively sexy in just his jeans and cotton shirt. It was hard not seeing him all day today, but he thought it would be difficult to contain himself if we were together at school so he avoided me like the plague. Not that I could blame him. The anticipation of waiting for this moment ate at me the entire day, making it so I could barely focus on anything other than him. I had to be slapped back to reality a couple of times in the form of cold water on my face between classes since a cold shower wasn't really an option.

"Thanks again for this. We really appreciate it." James and Liam shake hands with knowing smiles.

"Just do me a favor and don't give me any details on what you two did over the weekend. As far as I'm concerned I'm dropping her off with a friend and then never looking back."

They laugh and I shift on my feet, half anxious to ditch Liam and half nervous to be left alone with James. He must sense my nervousness because he grabs my hand and pulls me to him. My arms wrap around his back and I bury my nose in his neck, drawn to his masculine smell that captivates me with ease.

Liam clears his throat and my face flushes with embarrassment. I almost forgot he was still here. "Sorry." He responds with an over-exaggerated eye roll.

"I'll be back to pick you up around four on Sunday. Have fun." He pauses. "No, wait, I don't want to know."

The two shake hands again before Liam quickly retreats back to his car. He's anxious for his weekend to start as well. So is Penny because she hasn't stopped chewing my ear off about it since she found out on Wednesday. At least she bought the lie of me wanting to stay home for the weekend to study instead of joining them at the ski lodge.

James shuts the door and removes my coat. He hangs it in his front closet and I place my boots on the rug nearby. I gasp when a pair of strong arms wrap around my waist and pull me into him.

"Hey," he says with a twinkle in his eye.

"Hey," I whisper back.

Our lips meet and whatever fears were present have vanished at the sweet taste of his mouth. My fingers find their way into his hair and glide through the thick silky strands. James's hands have a mind of their own as well, gripping my waist tighter and pulling me flush against him as my back hits the wall with a soft thud. My heart beats a pounding rhythm in my chest, with a matching pulse between my legs, as I feel his hips press into my own.

"I'm so glad you're here." He nuzzles into my hair, breaking the hold he had on my mouth. He gently sucks my earlobe into his mouth. My hands run down his back, feeling each and every muscle flex and move as his hands continue their exploration of my body.

"Me too." Higher brain function does not exist for me. The only thing my scattered mind can focus on is the need to remove the barriers between us until we are connected in every way possible.

A moan escapes me when his mouth latches onto the curve of my neck near my shoulder and samples the skin with his tongue. Goose bumps erupt across my body and I dig my nails into his back. We haven't even left his entryway and I'm ready to throw us both to the ground.

He pulls back and strokes the messy tangles away from my face. I smile at him and blink several times as he draws me in deeper to his spell.

"We should move inside. As much as I enjoy my front entryway, I'm sure there's a more comfortable spot for us to say hello."

I nod as he threads his hand into mine, pulling me gently into his house while carrying my overnight bag in his other hand.

"I'm just going to go ahead and put this in my room. Make yourself comfortable anywhere you'd like. Are you thirsty?" he asks, heading toward the hallway that I assume leads to his bedroom.

A sudden rush of need pulses through my bloodstream. If he's going to his bedroom, I have to follow. I slowly shake my head and take several cautious steps toward him. "Nope. Not thirsty."

James licks his lips and my body reacts with pure carnal instinct. Putting one foot in front of the other, I slowly make my way to him from across the living room. The air changes around us, crackling with a white hot intensity of need and lust. It's been months since I've envisioned this scenario, being alone with him without fear of being caught. Months of longing and wanting from a distance, wondering if he's felt anything remotely close to how I feel about him. Now with the knowledge that he does, I can't wait any longer to be with him, join with him in every way possible.

"You want the five cent tour?" he asks huskily. I nod and give him a lascivious grin. He looks around the living room, gesturing with his hand. "Living room."

I laugh quietly. "I've seen this room before. Take me somewhere I haven't been yet." My soft footfalls close the distance and find myself standing next to him. I place my hand in his. James kisses the corner of my mouth, creating another flurry of emotions to run wild through my system.

With a jerk of his head and a tug of my hand, I follow him down the hallway in silence. It's quiet and clean with several pictures adorning the walls. Black and white stills of various larger cities with the occasional family portrait hung in between.

I stop at a picture of him with his parents and sister when

he was younger. I run a finger along the photo and smile at his cute, cherub face. He stands beside me and watches as I take in the scene captured in time.

"How old were you in this picture?"

"About seven, I think. It was our first trip to New York and I desperately wanted to see the lions at the Central Park Zoo. My mom and dad had initially told me there wasn't much time to sightsee because we were so busy with everything else, but then they surprised us with a whole day at the zoo. We walked around for hours to see each and every animal and they bought me as much junk food as I could possibly stuff in my face." He smiles as the memory flashes in front of his eyes.

"I've never been to New York," I murmur. He squeezes my hand and wistfully smiles at me.

"I'll take you one day. Just you and I, and it will be the best day of your life."

"Promise?" I ask.

He nods. "Promise."

"You know if we keep promising things to each other we should maybe write them down."

James laughs and taps his head. "I've got them written down right here. I'll remember all of our promises and make sure each and every one comes true."

My fingers trace his jaw and he leans into the contact. "You're too good to be true, you know that? Sometimes I have to pinch myself to make sure you're real or that what we have is real. I don't want to wake up one day and have it all vanish without a trace."

"I ask myself those same questions and come up with the same answer every time. You are real. What we have is real and no one is going to take it away."

"Five more months," I breathe. He nods and kisses the corner of my mouth.

"Less than five months until we're free," he corrects. Our foreheads touch and the heat of his breath beats against my lips.

"This weekend, I want you to show me what we're going to be like after this whole mess is done with." I bite my bottom lip and look up at him through my lashes. Heat explodes through my veins when our mouths connect and seal over each other.

My bag drops to the floor and he picks me up with both arms, cradling me against his chest. I throw my arms around his neck as he carries me down the hall and into his bedroom, kicking the door closed behind him.

"We'll finish the tour in the morning. Tonight I want to just focus on you." He sets me down at the edge of his bed. There's moonlight streaming in through his bedroom window, casting a soft, romantic glow into the room. Only I can't focus on anything other than the intensity behind his eyes as he looks at me, peeling away every worry or fear that may lie dormant inside me. No one else will exist this weekend. It will be just the two of us finally getting the chance to be ourselves without judgment or repercussions.

James grabs the hem of my shirt, his knuckles trailing across my heated skin as the material is removed from my body. Every sense is heightened, every nerve on edge as we stand in his room, basking in each other's presence.

Not wanting to be the only one shirtless, I run my hands up his taut stomach, letting the shirt bunch above my wrists as I run up the full length of his torso. He lifts his arms to help me pull it off him altogether. Smooth skin covers his extremely toned body and the hints of a defined six pack tease my fingers as they continue their journey around the newly exposed flesh before me. His biceps and forearms garner my attention, leaving nothing untraced by my curious fingers.

"You like what you see?" he asks. Even in the dark I know his brow is raised and a smirk is gracing his lips.

"Very much," I reply, not feeling the need to elaborate anymore.

His fingers trail between my breasts and down to my fluttering stomach then move around behind me, exploring my back before working the clasp of my bra free. It falls effortlessly to the ground, leaving my full, aching breasts exposed to the cooler air.

"So beautiful," he murmurs before trailing his lips down the column of my throat, licking and sucking a path to the swell of my breasts. My head falls backward, exposing more skin to the ministrations of his lips and tongue as he pays rapt attention to every inch of me. I pull him closer, wanting the skin on skin contact until it feels like we are a single person instead of two individual ones. For he is my match in every way and I was made especially for him.

Once we're fully naked, our eyes travel over the planes of our bodies between deep kisses and soft caresses. James lifts me up onto his bed, guiding me to the middle as he climbs over me, taking his time to admire my body beneath him.

"I've waited a long time for this moment," he says, trailing his lips down the column of my neck again.

"Me too." I run my fingers through his hair. I can't get enough of it and he seems to enjoy it by the soft moans and gasps I hear as I play and pull at the silky strands. But my grip loosens as his fingers run between my legs, finding the warm and wet heat of my aching core. The first contact steals the air from my lungs and with each retreat and entry into my body with his skilled fingers, a new pressure builds inside me. My fists clutch his sheets as the first wave rolls through my body, causing my legs to tense and release as I soar high into the atmosphere then gently fall back down from the clouds.

He leans over to open a side drawer on his nightstand and tears into a new box of condoms. With the foil wrapper in his hand, he leans over me again and runs his nose along my jaw line.

"Can't be too careful," he says before ripping open the wrapper and sheathing the condom over his straining erection.

"Agreed."

James cups my face between his hands while propping himself up on his elbows to keep his weight off me. The greens of his eyes glow in the muted light as shadows dance in the background. I trace his sculpted cheekbones before pulling his lips down to meet mine.

I gasp audibly as he enters me slowly, carefully, lovingly. Our foreheads press together as he pushes himself inside me. The feel of him is exquisite, like nothing I've ever experienced before. Our fit is nothing less than perfect as he slides fully into me. My muscles grip him tightly and adjust to his length.

"God, James, you feel so good."

He doesn't move yet as his eyes search mine. Nothing has made me feel more beautiful than in this moment with him. The way his eyes search my face and lighten when he gives me his special smile causes my heart to skip a beat. I couldn't love him more if I tried.

"You're perfect, you know that? Nothing has ever felt this right before."

He slowly begins to move in a steady rhythm, eliciting a round of soft gasps and moans as he glides in and out of my body, dragging every ounce of pleasure to the surface with ease. My legs wrap around his narrow waist until my heels dig into the small of his back, urging him to go deeper and faster. But he won't have any of it. His pace is still slow and steady, worshipful and reverent as he holds my gaze with each stroke inside me.

"Faster." I pull his upper body onto mine and trace the shell of his ear with my tongue. Another moan escapes him with a sharp thrust of his hips.

"I want to take my time, but you're making this hard."

"That's the idea," I say with a small smirk. Another thrust of his hips has the smirk completely gone from my face, replacing it with one of pure and utter ecstasy.

James moves faster as a thin sheen of sweat appears on his brow. My hands cling to his shoulders as my hips move in tandem with his, lifting and meeting him thrust for thrust.

"Too good," he says through gritted teeth. I try to speak, but nothing comes out except gasps and soft mewling sounds. His lips cover mine, swallowing each sound as we breathe through each other until another orgasm spreads through me like wildfire, stealing all the oxygen from my body with its flames.

"Yes," James cries out against my mouth. His movements become more erratic, thrusting harder and faster until his body jerks and pulses inside me. I cling to him and take in each shudder with the knowledge that it was me who gave him this pleasure, me who extracted this intense orgasm from his body. It's me that he is giving his heart and soul to through the most intimate of acts.

And I know, with one hundred percent certainty that I could never live without him. I will do whatever it takes to keep him by my side for the rest of my life.

James lifts his head up from my shoulder, our chests still heaving while trying to drag the precious air back into our lungs after our intense lovemaking. Because that's what we did. He didn't fuck me and we didn't have something as meaningless as sex. We made love. We transferred a piece of our souls to each other.

He brushes back a damp lock of hair from my face.

"I love you." He kisses me softly.

I melt into his kiss while still clutching him tightly. "I love you too."

"Why did we wait so long to do this? That was incredible."

"I don't know, but we're going to have issues now trying to keep our hands off each other."

With a groan, he rolls away from me and slides the condom off, tying the end of it before tossing it into the wastebasket next to his nightstand. My eyes roam over his body since I wasn't able to fully do so before. Hard muscles beneath soft skin tease my eyes and make my fingers want to roam around just as before. But I don't get the chance because he pulls me to his side and I lay my head against the steady beat of his heart. When the sheets are pulled over our bodies, I sigh into him, teetering on the edge of consciousness. Fingers trail lightly over my cheek, pulling me back to reality.

"I'm so glad you're here with me."

I kiss the corner of his mouth and smile. "There's nowhere I'd rather be than right here in this moment with you."

His lips find my forehead as he wraps his arms around me tighter. "Let's get some sleep. We've got a busy weekend ahead of us."

I hum my agreement before closing my eyes and drifting off into a blissful sleep in the arms of the man I love.

Twenty-One

THE EARLY MORNING SUN SHINES THROUGH THE bottom of the shade, hitting my face at just the right angle to make me squint at the intrusion of brightness into the extremely pleasant dream I was having. Visions of last night play over and over again in my mind as if it's set on a never ending replay. The only thing I can hear is our combined cries of passion as they echo through my brain.

Now, blinking against the light, I force myself to open my eyes, unwilling to leave the shroud of darkness for fear that what I experienced was only a dream. My arm reaches over to where I know James should be but I'm met with an empty space. If it weren't for the dip in the mattress to let me know that he was recently there, I would have convinced myself that I imagined the whole scenario. Except I know it was real because this is not my room and I am most definitely not clothed.

I stretch my arms above my head, feeling the delightful soreness from the strenuous activities of last night and then again early this morning. Waking up to his sinful lips trailing down the valley between my breasts was definitely a surprise. As well as the pressing erection against my hip as he continued to tease my body into consciousness, urging it to wake with a wild hunger that only craves what he can give me.

I smile to myself while rolling over onto my stomach and propping my head on my hands to look around the room for the first time. It's almost exactly as I have pictured it, clean yet masculine with nothing out of place. It's small, but then again his house isn't very large to begin with. There's a chest of drawers on the opposite wall next to a tiny door that I assume is his closet. An armoire is on the wall next to me and I wonder why a guy would need that much dresser space.

Curiosity is getting the better of me as I climb out of bed and pick up his discarded shirt from last night to put on. I walk to the closet to peek inside and find that it's smaller than the closet in his office at school. You could barely fit a handful of clothes inside it, let alone a full season's wardrobe. Now I see the reason behind the multiple dressers.

I shake my head and shut the door. When I turn around, a smirking green-eyed man is standing in the doorway, wearing nothing but a pair of flannel pajama pants that hang deliciously low on his hips. My heart stutters a beat at the sight but quickly regains its normal rhythm when my eyes meet his.

"It's a little early to be snooping, don't you think?" he asks in an amused tone.

"It's never too early to discover things about your lover, especially when he fails to give you the grand tour of his house."

James slowly walks toward me, heat and desire flash in his eyes as they travel up and down the length of my body. Goose bumps erupt across my flesh as he reaches up to gently cup my face.

"Your lover, huh?"

I look down as my cheeks heat up, wishing I wasn't so awkward sometimes when I'm around him. He tilts my chin up toward him as my lower lip disappears between my teeth.

"I'm not sure that word is strong enough for us."

"What term would you use then?" I whisper while twisting the hem of his shirt between my fingers. He gently frees the material from my grasp and pulls my hand to his lips to kiss each of my knuckles.

"My intended? My match? The woman of my dreams whom I can't live without?"

"That's quite the mouthful," I say. "Isn't there something simpler to use? Boyfriend perhaps?"

"Definitely not boyfriend. If I didn't prove to you last night and again this morning that I'm more than a boy, then I need to give you another reminder."

"You're right. Definitely not boyfriend but manfriend sounds rather stupid, don't you think?"

He laughs and picks me up off my feet, gently throwing me onto the bed. I bounce lightly as my hair falls around my head and catches in my mouth. His hand gently sweeps the strands away before lowering his body onto mine, letting me feel each and every hard piece of it.

"The best term I can find to describe what I am to you would be simple. It's one little word, but it takes everything that I feel and rolls it into one tiny package." His nose traces my jawline and my eyelids flutter closed at the sensation.

"And what's that?" I ask, clutching his back as my legs wrap tightly around his waist.

James lifts up onto his elbows, further brushing away any stray hairs that are obstructing our view to each other.

"Yours."

He smiles down at me as I let that word sink into my subconscious. *Yours.* That's how he would describe himself to me. *Yours.*

"I like that," I say. My fingers trail down his back with feather light strokes.

"The same can be said for you. You are mine."

"Always." I lean up to press our lips together, sealing the words and cementing them into our reality. I am his and he is mine. Possession and passion fuel our desires again as his shirt leaves my body and finds its way back into a heap on the floor.

"So where are you taking me?" I ask as I climb into his truck. James climbs in next to me with a slight shiver from the bitter cold wind outside.

"It's a surprise." He cranks the heat up as high as it will go and rubs his hands furiously against one another.

"You know if you wore some gloves you wouldn't be as cold."

He gives me a sideways glance before pulling out of his driveway. It makes me laugh and I utilize this time to take in his profile as he stares out at the road. He opted not to wear that sexy beany hat of his, which disappoints me slightly. He mumbled something about not wanting to mess up his hair, even though it looks as though he just woke up and rolled out of bed. Which, technically, he kind of did but sleeping was definitely not on the agenda.

We pass the city limits and drive in a comfortable silence. The passing streetlights dance shadows across our faces. I'm actually going on a date with him. An honest to goodness, no hiding, out in plain sight, date.

I reach my hand over to rest it on his knee. His hand covers mine and gives it a quick squeeze.

"Are you ready?" He parks the truck in the lot and kills the engine. I glance over at the building and smile. I've never been here before, which is good because it'll be another first for us.

"For an actual date? Yes please."

He kisses the back of my hand before releasing it. I move to open my door but he beats me to it. I didn't even see him get out of the truck. Man, he moves quickly. We hold hands as we enter the building.

"Good evening and welcome to Caravaggio. Do you have a reservation for tonight?"

The hostess greets us with her overly sweet smiling face. She's cute, young, probably in college or just graduated, and according to the name tag placed strategically on her perky breasts, is named Lacey. She's dressed like the rest of the wait staff in a perfectly pressed white shirt and black trousers. The only exception being that the men wear straight black ties while the women wear scarves that peek through the open top button of their shirts. Nervously, I glance down at my own clothing; feeling a little underdressed as I look at everything around us. Somehow I doubt my simple wrap dress is going to make the grade for this establishment.

"We do, under the name Dumont."

There's a soft hum about the room as people speak in hushed tones with each other. An occasional laugh can be heard through the clanking of silverware against the plates. Servers flow steadily into the room, bringing baskets of bread and trays filled with the most delicious smelling food I have ever seen.

The restaurant itself screams class and most definitely high end. Dark, rich wooden floors span the entire eating area with stark white walls in contrast. Each table is adorned with white linen cloths and plush white chairs. I've never been anywhere with cushioned seats, let alone white ones. I'd be too afraid to spill on them. But judging by the clientele, it's probably something that has never happened. Each table is outfitted with several large red candles that stand in the center, bringing a romantic glow to each setting. I couldn't have asked for a more perfect setting for our first date.

"Yes, Mr. Dumont. Right this way," the bubbly hostess says. I don't miss the once-over that she gives James as she picks up two menus from the stack on the side of her podium. The possessive side of me tightens my grip on him as her green eyes roam over his features until they land on our joined hands. *That's right, bitch. He's taken.*

James laughs and places his hand on the small of my back as we follow her. He helps me out of my coat and holds my chair out for me, kissing my ear before I fully sit down.

"Jealous?" he whispers, brushing his lips against my neck before taking his seat across from me. I can't help but notice how sexy he looks in his suit. Again, it's nothing out of the ordinary since he always dresses nicely for school, but to see him get dressed up solely for me has my blood running just a touch faster than normal.

"Not in the least. I just don't like people eyeing up what's mine," I say just loud enough for hostess girl to hear. And obviously she does because her ears heat up as she places our menus in front of us.

"The chef's special tonight is a chicken pasta florentine, served with penne pasta and tossed in a white wine sauce. Your server tonight will be Michael, who will be with you shortly. Enjoy your meal," she says with a weak smile before quickly leaving.

I pick up my menu and attempt to look over everything, but the green-eyed monster is still lurking inside me and it's making me edgy and unreasonable.

"Britta?"

Looking up at James's concerned face, I drop my menu and let out a slow breath.

"I'm sorry. Did you say something?"

"Is everything all right?"

"Everything is fine." I run my hands through my hair before letting them drop into my lap. "I don't know what got into me back there. I mean, women gawk at you all the time and it's never outwardly bothered me like this before. Don't get me wrong, it always bothers me, but this is the first time I've really let it show."

He laughs slightly and folds his hands in front of him on the table. "Sweetheart, you're not really good at hiding your emotions. I always know when you get bit by the jealousy bug. It's written all over your face. Your eyes narrow and the corners of your lips turn down into the most adorable scowl I have ever seen. Not to mention you tug on your earlobe subconsciously while chewing on your bottom lip."

My eyes widen. There's no way that I do all of that. "You're lying."

He makes an X shape over his heart and holds up three fingers in the air. "Scout's honor."

I roll my eyes to the ceiling and then remember just a few moments before that I had, indeed, done all those things in the entryway of the restaurant. Damn him for knowing me too well.

"You think you're so smart, don't you?" I say, taking a rather large drink from my water glass.

"Well, I am working on my Master's degree. I don't think they just hand those out at Wal-Mart."

"Ha-ha. Aren't you the comedian? Well then, Mr.-Smarty-Pants, tell me. How did you first know that I was attracted to you if I seem to wear my emotions on my face?"

James doesn't get the chance to answer because our server decides to show up at that exact moment.

"Good evening. My name is Michael and I'll be your server. How are you both doing tonight?" he asks, looking between the two of us.

Michael is tall, lean, and moderately built. Judging by his youthful appearance, he must be a student at one of the state colleges nearby. He flashes me a white toothy grin as his eyes drop slightly to the modest amount of cleavage showing from the V in my dress. Part of the reason I chose this one when packing my bag is because the wrap accentuates my breasts, making them look fuller than what they really are. My intention was to get James's attention but apparently it's also garnered Michael's as well. I clear my throat and he quickly looks down to take a notepad out of the pocket of his white apron.

"We're doing well, thank you," James says curtly. I giggle to myself as I notice his nostrils flare ever so slightly at his disdain of Michael's roaming eyes. Deciding to put him out of his misery, I reach across the table and link our hands together, giving him a reassuring squeeze. His eyes go from cool to warm in an instant when they connect with mine and a slow sexy smile crawls across his face. Now that is a smile that could probably give me an orgasm if I look at it long enough. I squirm in my chair a little and I can hear James's quiet laugh across from me.

"Is there anything I can start you off with to drink? Perhaps a nice bottle of chardonnay?" Michael asks.

As much as I would love to have a glass of wine, I know that it won't happen. I'm not about to bring any unnecessary attention to who we are or how old I am.

"No, thank you. Do you have any sparkling water?"

Michael nods with a smile. "We do. Would you like a lemon with it?"

"Lemon and lime, please. Thank you."

"I'll have the same," James says, playing with my fingertips. I lick my dry lips with a smile and I'm unable to tear my gaze away from him.

"Excellent. Did you need a few more minutes to look over the menu or did you have any questions?"

I shake my head in response. "I'm ready to order. You?" I ask James.

"Definitely ready."

Every muscle south of my navel constricts at the look that he gives me, filled with a hunger that I haven't seen before. Holy shit. I guess I know what's on the menu for dessert.

I clear my throat and point to my menu, picking the chicken ravioli with the balsamic glaze. James decides on the chef's special and hands Michael both of our menus after he finishes scribbling down our orders on his notepad.

"I'll go ahead and put those in right away for you and be back with your sparkling waters."

Michael quickly turns on his heels, making sure to keep his head down to avoid my eyes. Not that I would have noticed him anyway.

"So are we even now?" I ask, wanting to know if we're really going to act this way every time we're around others. I know we both said that we're jealous people, but this may be a bit ridiculous, considering where we're at in our relationship.

"We're even. No more petty jealousy. We're beyond that, don't you agree?" he says, kissing the back of my hand.

"Agreed. Besides, there's no one I would rather be with than you and nothing or no one in this world could change my mind."

He smiles, lighting up his face and mine in the simple gesture. The white noise of the restaurant fades as we drink in the sight of each other, tracing over each and every feature while burning them into memory. The way his eyes roam over my body makes me feel beautiful in a way that no one has ever made me feel before. Typically when a guy tells you he thinks you're beautiful, you'll second guess his intentions. Is he just trying to get into my pants? Did he lose a bet? Words can mean so little when they're spoken from feelings other than sincerity. But I never get that from James. He can say so much without ever opening his mouth and it's one of the things I cherish about him. We know that we are meant to be together and that nothing can separate our souls, which have been bound by an unseen force. And I can see it every time he looks at me, just as he is right now with nothing but love in his expression.

Michael arrives with our sparkling waters and we each pick up the goblet and hold them out in front of us.

"To the most perfect first date with the woman I love."

I glance to the right, moved by his words but yet feeling shy at the same time. His fingers guide my face back to his and we lean over the table to press our lips together in a soft kiss.

"It may sound a bit funny but just because this is our first official date doesn't make the statement any less true. You are the woman I love, whom I adore and worship and will spend the rest of my life making sure that you have every possible need and want fulfilled."

The smile on my face intensifies. "I feel the exact same way about you. You know I love you more than anything on this planet. I would do anything for you, even if it means making the hard decisions sometimes and sacrificing my needs over yours."

His head tilts to the side and frowns slightly. "You don't have to worry about keeping me safe. That's my job. There is nothing I wouldn't do for you."

"And I you, so let's just agree that we both will protect the other from anything that may or may not happen, foreseeable or not."

We clink our glasses together and take another sip, making sure our eyes stay locked with each other over the rims.

After we've eaten our weight in pasta, we decide to share a tiramisu for dessert. I'm so full that I'm not sure if I can make it back to his truck without exploding. But I keep shoveling the sweet coffee dessert into my mouth, licking my fork clean of any residue after each bite.

"If you keep doing that our drive home will take forever," he says quietly.

I snake my tongue out again and slowly lick each and every tine before dragging it through my red lips. He gives a low grumble and I smile at my seduction attempt. Not that we need it. After last night, I'm positive we're a sure thing wherever and whenever we can be alone.

I place the fork down and pat his hand gently. "Easy tiger. I'm going to head to the bathroom before we go."

"I'll flag down your admirer and pay him so we can hurry home. We still have more things to do tonight for our first date."

I pause as I straighten up to my full height. "We do?"

He nods slowly. "Don't you remember how I described our first date?"

I think back to the night we first talked about it and smile. "Oh yes. You're going to read to me on the couch and then…" I trail off, letting the rest of the sentence hang in the air between us. We both know what's going to happen next. There's no need to put it into words.

"Exactly. So hurry and fix your face or whatever else you're going to do because we have plans, Ms. Fosse."

I press a quick kiss to his cheek as he holds my chair out for me. I walk confidently through the restaurant and quickly head to the restrooms to take care of business and straighten myself up.

As I look at myself in the mirror, I smile at my reflection. There's a glow about my skin and color on my cheeks. My head is held a little higher and there's a smile that is almost permanently plastered on my face. And it's all because of James. It's strange to think that our relationship is considered forbidden solely because of his job. If he was anything other than a teacher no one would even question it. I mean a four year age difference isn't anything. It's probably more common than people realize. And it's not as if he's taking advantage of me. If anything, I probably pushed him more than I should have but no one can deny that what we have is special. The only problem is no one knows what we have except for Liam and us. But for now that's enough.

I exit the restroom and begin to make my way to our table when something catches my attention out of the corner of my eye. I try not to turn my head to stare but a familiar profile can be seen and it quickens my steps back to James.

Closing the payment book and setting it in the middle of the table, James stands when he sees me approaching.

"Is something wrong?" he asks. He runs his hands up and down my arms and places a kiss on my forehead.

I shake my head and shift from foot to foot. "No, not yet. At least I don't think so. But we need to go. Quick."

His brows draw together as he attempts to decrypt my message. I glance over my right shoulder, hoping he'll follow my lead. I can see it in his eyes the minute he understands why I'm acting slightly on edge. He sees who else is in this very same restaurant, who could potentially hurt us if he so wanted to.

He sees Chase.

"Come on. Let's move quickly and walk around the opposite side. Maybe he won't notice us."

I nod and begin to get my coat on, but James helps me

into it before putting on his. We link our arms together and he guides us quietly through the restaurant to the front doors. I glance over my shoulder every once in a while in the hope that Chase will continue to pay attention to his parents and not so much to everything else around him. I don't make a sound or take a breath until we reach his truck, thankful that my small prayer has been answered.

"That was close," I say. James shuts my door and quickly rounds the truck to climb in on his side.

"Not too close but close enough. What are the odds that he would be here tonight?"

I shrug my shoulders and stare out my window as James puts the truck in reverse, taking us out of the parking lot and back toward Somerset and our temporary safe haven.

We stay quiet for the first few miles, probably both contemplating the ramifications of what could have potentially happened if Chase had seen us together. It's something that always sits in the back of my mind but I don't acknowledge it because that means it's the end.

"It was your eyes," he says completely out of the blue.

I turn my head toward him and tilt it slightly in confusion. "Huh?"

He smiles and grabs my hand. "You asked me earlier how I knew you were first attracted to me. It was your eyes. They gave you away the first day we met."

"You mean the day you ran me over and knocked me on my ass?"

He laughs softly and nods. "Yes, that day. I knew the minute you looked up at me that you were attracted to me. There was a hint of anger at first, but then they shifted and softened. The light hit them just perfectly to make them almost appear to sparkle as you blatantly stared at me."

"I wasn't blatantly staring at you," I defend.

"Yes, you were but so was I. You were the most beautiful thing I had ever seen, even when you were sprawled out on your ass. But I knew right then and there that I needed to find out who you were and get to know you. I needed you in my life and I didn't exactly know the reason why other than I just did."

"And here we are now."

He kisses the back of my hand and squeezes it before placing it back onto his thigh. "Here we are, happier than we've ever been and so completely in love with each other, even though we tried to fight it."

"Tried and failed miserably. But you know what?" He shakes his head and glances quickly over at me. "I don't regret one thing about how we got here. Yes, we're unconventional and we have to be a little more cautious than most other couples, but you are worth it. We are worth it because I'm focusing on the full-length novel and not the individual chapter."

I scoot as close to him as I possibly can and lay my head against his shoulder. He brings his arm around me and holds me against him. We don't say anything else on the ride home, both of us eager to finish our date and get to bed, knowing that sleep is not on the agenda for tonight.

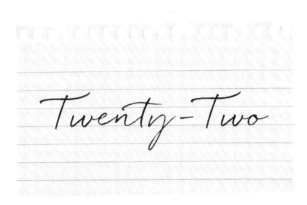

Twenty-Two

"PICK OUT A BOOK FOR US," JAMES SAYS AS HE unknots his tie. He slowly flicks the top few buttons of his shirt open, exposing a small patch of smooth skin at the base of his throat.

I stop and stare. My mouth dries as he slowly drags the tie from around his neck and gently tosses it onto the vacant chair to his right. But when he slowly rolls up the sleeves of his white shirt, the floor falls out from beneath my feet.

Holy. Fuck.

I think my heart just exploded. No, wait, that was my ovaries. Because right now, looking at James in his current state of undress, makes me want to jump him and have each and every one of his babies from now until the end of time.

I stumble slightly, even though I'm not moving or wearing my heels anymore. The sheer force of his gaze upon me, coupled with his undoubtedly male hotness, has damn near blown me over where I stand.

And he's mine.

"I, um, yeah. Book," I mumble, turning toward the bookcase at the far end of the living room. His chuckle at my stuttering makes me smile and hasten my steps, eager to find the perfect book so he can read it to me.

My fingers trail over the spines of his collection, noting that the majority of the books are classics. Not that there's anything wrong with that. On the contrary, I adore the classics. The masters of the written word who have been cherished generation after generation, their works finding new followers at any age and will withstand the tests of time for generations to follow. Those are the books that need to be read, to be loved and adored for this special occasion.

Large hands wrap around my waist and pull me into his chest. He rests his chin against my shoulder while his warm breath tickles my neck. I wrap my arms around his, anchoring our bodies together so there's no chance that he'll let me go.

"Do you need some help?" he asks. The vein he's tracing with his lips pulses wildly as he teases me with the promise of what's to come.

"No," I squeak.

"Hmm," is his only response as he continues to tease my body, stirring it up with so much want and need that I don't know how much longer I'll be able to stand upright.

Focus. I need to focus. On a deep inhale, I reach out and pick a book at random, hoping it's a romantic one and not some sordid tale of misery and woe.

"Excellent choice," James says and takes the book from my hand. I didn't even get a chance to see what I had picked.

He gently pulls me behind him as we make our way to the couch. There's a fire roaring in the fireplace and a few candles set up strategically around the room. *When did he do all this? Was I really that dazed that I never noticed him putting all this together?*

James makes himself comfortable on the couch. He lies on his side and pats the cushions next to him to let me know where he wants me. As if there was anywhere else I'd go.

I stretch my body next to his, easily fitting into his form like a missing puzzle piece. The way our bodies fit together reassures me that this is right, no matter what anyone else says or thinks.

"So what book did I actually pick?"

He laughs quietly and kisses my forehead. "You didn't look?"

I shake my head and bury it in the crook of his neck. "Someone had me distracted and flustered so I grabbed the first book at my fingertips."

"Well, I must say that you chose well then because it's one of my favorites. At least for a female writer."

I raise an eyebrow at him. "Are we a sexist reader, Mr. Dumont?"

James shakes his head and smiles. "Not in the least. But I have my favorite books written by male authors and female authors, classic and newer, fiction and nonfiction. This just happens to be one of them written by a woman."

I narrow my eyes playfully at him. "I don't believe you. I think you're just sexist. I didn't exactly see a whole lot of Austen or Bronte on your shelves."

"You admitted that you weren't really looking so how would you know?"

I laugh and shake my head. "Touché. But just out of curiosity, do you have them on your shelves?"

He rests his head on mine and I can feel him smile against my cheek. "Yes, I have Austen and both Emily and Charlotte Bronte, right next to my Tolkien, Lewis, Wells, Fitzgerald, and Stein."

"Okay, I'll be quiet now. But you never answered my question. Which book did I pick?"

James turns the hardcover over, showing me the first page of the book. *Rebecca* by Daphne du Maurier. The book itself is old and yet seemingly in mint condition. I glance at the date printed on the first page and don't believe my own eyes. *It can't be, can it?*

1938.

"James, this is a first edition," I gasp.

"Yes, it is. I found this little treasure in a used book store back in Hartford. Someone had loved it at one time and either didn't know its value or it was part of an estate and the family was just getting rid of everything. I don't have many first editions, but this is one of them."

"Maybe we should pick something else. I don't want you to ruin the book."

He shifts next to me, bringing us nose to nose. "Nonsense. Books are made to be enjoyed and that's what we're going to do. I'm going to read you this book and you are going to enjoy it."

James gets comfortable again and I lean my head against his shoulder. Part of me wants to turn and see the actual words themselves but the larger part of me wants to stare at his profile.

Unsurprisingly that's the part who wins out in my internal war.

I watch his mouth as he reads, focusing on his lips and the way they curve around each word, making each one my new favorite word just because he's saying them. The quiet timbre of his voice is soothing, giving inflection when necessary and never monotone. He reads with the passion of someone who truly appreciates the literary works of the great ones. There aren't many people in this world who enjoy reading with the technology boom of the last decade. When given the choice between

231

reading the book or watching the movie, most will opt for the movie because, in their opinion, reading is boring. Truly this is one of the downfalls of our society.

And to find someone who shares this same passion, who appreciates it and cherishes it enough to want to share it with me, makes this night the best first date in the history of the world.

James is a quarter of the way through, meaning that we've just been lying here for a couple hours, doing nothing but enjoying each other's company.

He pauses and turns to me. The light from the fire behind me dances in his eyes, making them spark from the glowing embers.

"You still with me?" he asks, placing the open book on his chest to save his place.

"Mmm," I respond and nod my head slowly. My body feels peaceful as my eyelids droop slightly.

Closing the book, he places it on the coffee table next to us while turning his body and pulling me close.

"You look tired, sweetheart. We should go to bed." He gently brushes away some hair from my forehead. I don't think I have the energy to move quite yet. Just listening to his voice has relaxed me so much that I just want to stay here, wrapped up in him and never leave. Forget the outside world and all their judgments that are trying to keep us apart. I just want to be here, in his arms, where I belong.

"I don't want to move. I love being cuddled up next to you."

"Oh really? And why is that?" he asks.

"Because we fit together so perfectly." I scoot closer to him and nuzzle into his neck. "Plus, you smell really good right here." I run my nose over the spot, taking a deep inhale of his scent mixed with the cologne he put on tonight. It's enough to awaken my slumbering libido as it stirs to life.

"What else?" he asks hoarsely. His feet run along mine and then slowly up my calves, pulling my legs between his.

"I love the taste of your skin," I say, taking a slow swipe along the pulsing vein on his neck.

My fingers clutch his shirt; unbuttoning it the rest of the way and pulling it from the confines of his slacks until it's completely open. His breath hitches as I trace each defined muscle I can find before wrapping my arms around his neck.

"Bed," he groans and slowly moves us into an upright position. I straddle his lap with my dress hiked up my thighs.

James's hands follow the path of the newly exposed skin on my legs, climbing higher and higher until he reaches my waist. He stands up in one fluid motion and I instinctively wrap my body around him as we make our way to the bedroom.

"What about the fireplace and candles?" I ask.

He stops and sets me down in the hallway. "Don't move. I'll be right back."

James disappears around the corner. Something rustles, followed by a loud clank and the sound of crumbling wood as it turns into ash. The light dims significantly in the living room, letting me know the fire isn't completely out, but it's not the roar that it once was a few hours ago. And since we never put any more logs on, it shouldn't take long for it to dissipate.

"It'll burn out quickly now that I've spread it around," he says, lifting me from the ground and putting me back into the position we started in. "Now where were we?" he asks.

I grab his face and kiss him with the passion that's slowly building to a boil inside me. White hot heat is pouring out of my every pore, need and lust combining with our underlying love has my body on fire.

He walks us to the bed and gently lays me down. I crawl

into the center as he leans over me, following my movements until he's centered directly above my outstretched body. I run my hands up his naked chest and flick my tongue against his.

"You're wearing too many clothes," I say.

James quickly sheds his shirt, slacks, and socks until he's completely and utterly naked. And nothing has ever looked more glorious in all of humanity than this man completely bared to me. I move to untie the string at my hip which holds my dress together, but his hands cover mine and he shakes his head teasingly.

"Let me. I want to unwrap you as if you're my own special present."

The heat emanating from my skin travels south, igniting every nerve and leaving me aching and panting for him to press his body against mine. James takes his time though, slowly letting the tie unravel and fall apart. The fabric is then slowly lifted up piece by piece as a round of goose bumps appears on the newly exposed flesh.

He sucks in a sharp breath of air when he finds my surprise. "Sweet mercy you're not wearing any underwear."

I give him my best slow seductive smile as the material falls completely away from my body, arching my back off the bed as he tosses it carelessly to the floor.

"Surprise," I say, pulling him back down to me. Our lips crash together, feverishly devouring each other. We roll over one another, moving from one side of the bed to the other. The sheets and comforter get tossed to the floor with our discarded clothes, leaving nothing to get in the way.

"I need you, James. Now," I pant out and blindly reach over to the drawer holding his stash of condoms.

He pulls away from me long enough so I can twist my body to the side to open the drawer with ease. But then all logic and thought are removed from my brain as his tongue makes contact with the sensitive flesh between my legs.

"Oh fuck," I cry out, abandoning my quest. Instead, my hands fly to grip his hair, pulling him closer to me as he sucks on my clit with expert precision.

"God, baby, you taste so sweet. I couldn't wait any longer. I needed a taste of my dessert."

Another slow swipe of his tongue and I can feel the muscles slowly begin to tense in preparation of what's to come. It starts off slow, quiet, then gains intensity as it pulls in energy from all muscles not currently being used in the center of my body. Like creating a tower out of blocks, each one having an exact place as it climbs higher and higher into the sky.

"More. It's so good."

James inserts a finger into my tight opening and begins to rhythmically stroke my front wall, causing my toes to curl and my fingers to grip the sheets beneath me. The carefully constructed building blocks shake and then tumble to the ground, creating a wake of dust and debris as I cry out his name over and over again into the room.

I can barely hear the opening of the drawer through the ringing in my ears. My eyes slowly come into focus as I watch him slip on the condom and brace his body so it's hovering above me.

"You look so beautiful when you come. I need to see it again," he says while guiding himself into my now wet entrance. He slides in with ease, stretching me inch by glorious inch. Our eyes lock when he's fully inside me.

"I love feeling the moment where we become one. There is no greater sensation than this. None."

My hands cup his cheeks again and I pull his mouth to mine with a need to taste him. He stokes the fire deep within me until what's left of the life I knew before is ashes.

"You feel too good to be true," I whisper, barely able to keep my emotions in check.

James slowly starts rocking into me with a leisurely tempo, not rushed or looking for an end. It's as if he's savoring the moment, appreciating it for everything it is, everything it could be and will be. He's making love to me as if I am the only thing that matters to him in the entire world.

Our kisses become less frantic and more in tune with our movements. Slow and sweet, unhurried and reverent. Time stops and stills while we bring our bodies together to match the feeling in our hearts.

"I love you," he whispers against my lips. I wrap my legs around his waist tighter, urging him forward, deeper, needing to chase the release that's looming on the edge of my sanity.

"Faster," I beg while digging my heels into his ass.

He increases his tempo. "I'm not going to last much longer if you keep that up. Are you almost there?" he asks. A thin sheen of sweat appears on his brow and he traps my hands next to my head with his.

"Yes. So close."

James expertly rolls his hips and hits my clit in just the right spot. I explode instantly, pulling him deeper in me as I contract and pulse around him. My eyes want to roll into the back of my head from the intensity. His expression keeps my eyes locked on him as I watch him jerk several times before succumbing to the orgasm while calling out my name. I can feel each pulse as he empties inside me, prolonging my own release. We cling to each other until he falls on top of me, sweaty and breathless.

I run my fingers through his hair as he rests his head on my shoulder. Nothing has felt better than this. Our bodies are a sweaty mess. The sweet smell of sex lingers in the air and James is naked and spent on top of me.

The perfect date.

"Best first date ever," I breathe.

He picks his head up and kisses my collarbone, my neck, my jaw, and then finally my lips.

"Best *last* first date ever," he corrects. We kiss again as he pulls out of me, rolling to the side to remove the condom.

I bend over the bed while he cleans up and tuck the sheets back into place while leaving the comforter still in a heap at the end. James pulls me into his side and covers us with the sheet. Sleep threatens to come fast as we both yawn and press into each other.

"I love you," I sigh, brushing my fingertips against his chest. He grabs my hand and lightly kisses my palm.

"I love you too."

We drift off to sleep, our bodies sated and spent, not worrying about the outside world until we're thrust back into reality tomorrow.

Twenty-Three

"HUNGRY?" JAMES ASKS ME AS HE TAKES OUT SEVERAL pans from the cupboard.

I honestly don't know what I am. I could be hungry if I allowed myself to think of anything other than how much I'm going to miss this free time with him. Instead of giving a verbal cue, I just shrug my shoulders and pray he's looking at me since I can't stop staring at the marble countertop.

"Britta, look at me," he pleads.

My eyes slowly meet his and the same sadness that clouds my thoughts shows in his eyes. He leaves the pan on the stove and rounds the counter to pull me into his arms. James settles in between my knees. I rest my head on his shoulder and cling to his back.

"I don't want to leave. I want to stay here with you. Please don't make me go back."

Tears threaten to fall from my eyes as I burrow my head further into him. This weekend has been the best I've ever had. And I know what will happen the minute I step outside this house. We will go back to secret glances and stolen moments. Things that appease the mind but are never enough for the heart. It's not sufficient anymore to know that he loves me, that he can't stop thinking about me. It's not even close to satisfying just being in the same room as him anymore. He's my match, my soulmate. And I've never been more confident of anything in my life except for this. We belong together. I know it and he knows it.

His hand lightly cups the back of my head and softly strokes my hair as the first tear rolls down my face. He rubs his other hand soothingly up and down my back while pressing his cheek into the crown of my head.

"Sweetheart, this isn't the end. We're not over. We will never be over." He brushes away another tear with his thumb. "This is a minor bump in the road. We won't let this get us down. You are the most important thing to me and it breaks me to see you upset. Please, please don't cry. We'll still see each other," he says, lightly brushing his lips against mine.

"It's not the same. It's not enough anymore. Don't you see? We can't go back to how it used to be. I can't go back to sneaking around and pretending that I don't have feelings for you. Do you know how jealous I get when I watch others who get to talk to you openly? How crazy I feel when I look at the man-eater put her hands on you like it's her right? Part of me wants to run away or transfer schools, but I know it would only raise more suspicion. The other part of me wants to take the GED test now so I can leave school and be done with it. I have my acceptance letters and have already given my intent to Harvard."

He shakes his head and sighs. "You can't do that. I won't let you throw away your future."

"I'm not throwing away my future," I cry as more tears stream down my face. "I'm saving my future, can't you see that?

Say you'll come with me to Boston. I know we've never talked about what's going to happen after I graduate but please, I need you with me when I go to Harvard. You can transfer your graduate work and attend there with me or even BU if necessary."

I feel completely out of control, like I'm grasping at straws and allowing my desperation to show. I don't want to upset James with my insecurities and ramblings, but this has been pent up for far too long. We've been avoiding the subject by brushing it to the side. We need to discuss this, sooner rather than later.

"Please," I beg.

James gives a sad smile and it breaks my heart slightly. "You're working yourself up for no reason. Come here."

We walk into the living room and he pulls me into his lap on the couch. I cry into his shoulder as he rocks me back and forth.

"Even though what you said is true about what we will have to go back to, you know and I know that it's all just an act. We're going to stick with the plan because it will work out."

"And Boston?" I whimper. My lip quivers as I look up into his face. Pushing wet strands away from my cheeks, he cups my face and presses our lips together.

"I will follow you wherever you may go. The beauty of my graduate work is I can do it anywhere. But you are just starting out and need to follow the path you've worked so hard to go down. You don't need me to lead the way. You know your future and how to achieve it. I'm just along for the ride."

I shake my head. "You're not just along for the ride. You're my navigator, my companion, my GPS. All my roads lead to you."

The tears have stopped but I still feel unsettled. I trace his cheek with my index finger and feel his morning stubble beneath before sliding it over his lips. He parts them slightly, kissing the pad of my finger.

"If you need daily reassurances, I will give them to you. But don't ever doubt that we can't do this. Remember, this is our bump in the road. We're stronger than this. Trust in me. Trust in *us*. We will come out on the other side stronger than ever. It's only a few more months and then we're free to have weekends like this all the time."

"Promise," I whisper against his mouth.

I can feel his smile without seeing it. "Promise."

He moves so I'm beneath him, keeping part of his weight on me as he lies on top. I stare into his eyes and whatever sadness that was clouding them before is now gone. Now they burn with a purpose and intensity I can feel throughout my entire body, bringing it to life.

"Britta Rosalind Fosse, I love you, even when you're paranoid and frantic. Let's just enjoy the next few hours before Liam shows up to bring you back."

I giggle at the use of my full name. It never ceases to amaze me at how well he knows me.

"What's your middle name?" I ask. I need this little bit of information to store in the James Dumont section of my brain.

He smirks and ducks his head while he laughs. "You'll think it's silly."

"No, I won't. Tell me."

Warm lips meet mine with a smile. "Xavier."

"Hmm, James Xavier Dumont. I like it. It definitely suits you." I reach up and wrap my hand around the back of his neck, pulling him back down for a passionate kiss. Emotions run high as our hands travel across each other's body and before we know it, there's a knock on the door.

Shit. He's early.

James kisses me one last time before sitting upright between my legs. "Don't move. Just in case it's not Liam."

I nod my head and watch him retreat to his front door. Utilizing this time to think about what's been said, I cross my legs and reason with my subconscious that James is right. Everything will be okay. It's not like we're breaking up. We're still going to see each other every day. And he's right about this just being a bump in the road. We're stronger than everyone else.

A noise draws my attention to the entry as Liam rounds the corner, his face slightly ashen and an apology written in his eyes.

"Britt, I'm so sorry," he starts, but the female voice behind him has my eyes widening with fear. Penny rounds the corner with her arms crossed and looking more upset than I've ever seen her.

I spring from the couch and hit my foot on the coffee table in the process. Hobbling over to where my pissed-off best friend is, I begin to open my mouth to explain the situation but she holds her arms up to stop me.

"Don't even," she says with a frown. Hurt and disappointment are written all over her face and it breaks my heart to see it.

"Pen, please. Let me explain."

She shakes her head and looks over at James as he enters the room with his hands in the front pockets of his jeans. He heads straight for me as I balance on one foot while holding my now throbbing one off the ground.

"Penny, please have a seat and we'll explain everything. That is if you want to hear it," James says. He wraps an arm around my waist and helps me back to the living room.

Penny doesn't say anything as she walks over to one of the chairs adjacent to the couch. James pulls me down next to him but turns me sideways so he can get a look at my foot. I wince slightly as he hits a rather sensitive spot, but he kisses the pain away. Penny's expression hasn't changed as I watch her with careful eyes. Liam is hovering behind her and I don't know if he's in the doghouse with me or not.

Penny clears her throat and looks at me expectantly. "So tell me, how long has this been going on?"

I chew on my bottom lip, not liking the tone that she's taking with me. "Well, officially, we've been together since Boston I guess?" James nods when I look at him, confirming my statement for her.

"And unofficially? How long have you two been sneaking around behind my back?"

James grips my hand and steadies me. Using his strength, I look at Penny and start pouring out the truth.

"I met James the Friday before he started taking over Mr. Ward's class. I ran into him in the teacher's lounge and there was a misunderstanding between us. I thought he was a student because he was looking for the office and he thought I was a teacher because I was in the lounge. It wasn't until his class on Monday that we figured out who each other was. From there it was chance run-ins and brief discussions in the halls or in the lounge during his lunch break."

She doesn't say anything or give anything away by her expression. She just sits there stoically, pondering what I said or thinking of her next question. "So Boston? Was that planned?"

I shake my head and squeeze his hand harder. "Not for me."

Penny turns her attention to James and he nods. "It was planned for me. I already had a ticket for the concert but figured out which hotel you were staying at when she made the reservation for her room and decided to stay there as well. I just wanted to make sure nothing happened to her when I found out she wanted a separate room from yours and Travis's."

She blanches at his name and looks down briefly. "Okay, I can kind of understand that. So let me guess. Saturday morning when you said you had plans, it was with him?" Penny asks, looking back at me.

I nod. "He stayed in the room across the hall. We had breakfast in the restaurant downstairs and then we toured around Boston for a while. It was innocent, for the most part."

James leans forward and looks down briefly before meeting her gaze. "Penny, I just want you to know that we didn't intend for us to happen. It really was a series of events that kept putting us together. And when we started talking more frequently, we discovered that we had a lot in common. Then the growing attraction between us became too much so we stopped fighting it and let it happen."

Penny looks between the two of us. I can see when the light bulb goes off and everything begins to make sense. "The basketball game, when you couldn't tear your eyes away from him and the man-eater. You two were seeing each other, weren't you?"

I nod. "Yes."

She twists her lips to the side in contemplation. "Well, your reaction to them makes sense now. I would have felt the same way if I had seen her anywhere near someone I was seeing." She pauses and leans forward, resting her elbows on her knees. "Are you happy?"

I lift my legs off of his lap and lean forward, matching her stance. "Extremely."

"And he's good to you?"

"The best."

She looks at James and smiles. "You love her, don't you?"

It's not really a question. Not that his loving me would ever be a question. I know it and I'm sure she can see it on his face.

"With all my heart," he replies, grabbing my hand again.

Liam moves forward and places his hand on Penny's shoulder. She reaches up and squeezes it. He's been silent the whole time, but I'm sure he was probably read the riot act on the way over here so he's just letting Penny sort everything out in her head.

Suddenly she stands and nods her head. "Okay then."

We look at each other then back at Penny. "That's it?"

She brushes her hands against her jeans and smiles at us. "Yep, that's it."

I stand slowly and walk around the table, careful not to jam my foot into it again. "So you're not mad?' I ask, standing in front of her.

She shakes her head and I relax for the first time since she walked into the room. "No, I'm not mad. Honestly, I've known about this for a while. You're a terrible liar, Britt. Plus I can read your face. Every time you talk about Mr. Dumont or see him, you light up like the Fourth of July. I've never seen you so happy before and I wasn't about to question it because there are some that would use this information to destroy you."

And we all know exactly who Penny is talking about without having to say his name. "We saw him yesterday at dinner. I don't think he saw us together," I say.

Penny leans over and hugs me close. I wrap my arms around her and sigh in relief, thankful that she understands.

"Hopefully not but we'll handle it if he did." She pulls away and wipes at a tear that has escaped her eyes. "Next time don't keep anything like this from me. You know I hate secrets."

I release her and wrap my arm around James, pulling myself securely into his side. "There won't be a next time. He's coming with me to Boston when I leave in the fall."

Liam raises an eyebrow and smirks. "Oh is he now?"

James laughs and kisses the top of my head. "She's very persuasive."

That earns us both an eye roll from Liam. "Tell me about it."

I shove his shoulder and laugh. "You love me."

"Unfortunately," he replies, roughing up my hair as if I was still a little kid.

"Have you two eaten? I was just about to make some lunch for us. I'd love it if you could stay and eat."

Penny laughs. "Yeah, I'm not interested in your kind of lunch because judging by Britt's swollen lips and disheveled hair when we walked in, I'm guessing it wasn't food she was devouring."

My eyes widen in horror and all the color in Liam's face drains instantly. Penny jabs him in the ribs and laughs loudly. "Oh my gosh, you should see your face!"

James laughs and retreats to the kitchen while I cover my face, trying to hide the redness that I can feel creeping up my neck.

Penny links her arm through mine as she leads us into the kitchen. "Lighten up you two. You should be happy that I know. This way you can stop sneaking around and I can actually help you both get together. Plus now you don't have to push your brother on me again."

Liam playfully pushes her shoulder as she sits on one of the barstools. "I didn't hear you complain this weekend."

I plug my ears and squeeze my eyes shut. "I don't want to hear about it."

Liam ruffles my hair again and I swat his hands away. "Likewise. The fewer details about our weekend, the better."

"Screw that. I want all the deets," Penny says as she leans into her propped up hands.

I look back at James, whose shoulders are shaking with repressed laughter. "Maybe later. But if you think you're getting *all* the deets you're going to be gravely disappointed."

James continues to make the four of us lunch as Penny goes on and on about her weekend with Liam, who decides to help James to get away from the two of us. Seeing them together, talking about sports and getting along so well makes my heart swell inside my chest. There's nothing more I'd love than for one day to have this out in the open. I can't wait to invite James to my parent's house because I know they would love him.

Penny waves her hand in front of my face after zoning out in my daydream. "Earth to Britta. You still with me?"

I turn to face her and smile. "Barely. Listen, I'm really sorry for keeping this from you. We didn't want anyone to know because of the damage it could do to his career and reputation. I mean, if anyone found out he'd be fired and would never get another teaching job. And that's something I couldn't do to him. We just need to be extremely careful for the next few months until graduation. And then everything will be fine."

"Don't worry. I won't say a thing. I've got your back."

Hugging Penny tightly to me, I look over her shoulder and see James looking at us with a smile on his face. He knows this is a huge thing for me, letting Penny into our world and exposing our secret to her. She's trustworthy and would never betray us.

"I love you," I mouth to him.

"Love you too," he mouths back before blowing a kiss and returning to the stove and his conversation with Liam.

What started out as a potentially bad situation has migrated into the best thing that could have happened. Penny knows, Liam knows, and now we have supporters who will help us be together.

Less than five months to go. And I've never wanted time to speed up as much as I do right now.

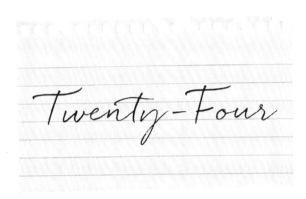

Twenty-Four

THE WEATHER HAS WARMED CONSIDERABLY, GIVING us our first real hope that spring is finally here after what feels like the longest winter in history. The late March weather is welcoming, though, putting me that much closer to graduation and into the arms of the man who is going just as stir crazy as I am through this whole process.

"So what are you doing for spring break?" Penny asks me, shutting her locker door with a loud thud.

"I don't know," I say as I pull out my notebook. "My parents asked if we wanted to go on vacation or something but since Liam's spring break doesn't line up with ours that made it kind of difficult. They don't want to leave him behind. You know how much of a whiner he is," I say, shutting my locker door.

"Tell me about it. He frustrates me like no one else can. Does he practice that at night when I'm not there?"

I pause briefly in my steps and turn to face her. "What do you mean 'when you're not there'? Are you there during the night sometimes?" I raise an eyebrow to her. She blushes a million different shades of red and I contain the cringe that wants to break out from me. "On second thought, never mind. I really don't need to know the answer to that question."

We start walking toward our classroom, briefly saying hello to Lyle and Cami, who are quickly running off to skip their third-period class for a make out session.

When we round the corner, I pause when I see James speaking to Mr. Leonard in the hallway outside of his classroom. My heart rate doubles as I watch Mr. Leonard's face, trying to see what kind of mood he's in. Is he happy? Sad? Angry? Disappointed? Anything outside of the first emotion would spell trouble for us.

"I'm sure it's nothing," Penny whispers into my ear. "After all, James is a teacher and Mr. Leonard is the principal. It's not unusual for them to be talking, right?"

I can barely make out her words. The whooshing blood in my ears has them ringing so loudly that I can't hear anything. Penny places her hand on my arm and I slowly turn my head to face her, willing my body to calm down against the rising panic. Something felt off this morning when I woke up, but I brushed it aside, thinking that it was just residual from the nightmare that woke me up in the early morning hours. But now, seeing James and Mr. Leonard standing in front of me makes me think that I was being issued a warning.

"I don't know," I quietly reply because I honestly don't know. But judging by Mr. Leonard's crossed arms and James's hands shoved into his pockets, it can't be all good.

At that moment, James looks up and eyes me watching them. Something flashes in his eyes and he minutely shakes his head, wanting me to leave the area. Something is definitely not right with this scenario.

"We need to leave," I say and grab Penny's arm but it's too

late.

"Ms. Fosse?" Mr. Leonard calls.

With my back turned to him, I close my eyes tightly and take a deep breath before turning to face him.

"Y-yes, Mr. Leonard?"

He says something to James, who only nods in response, and quickly approaches me with a solemn face.

"Ms. Fosse, would you accompany me to my office, please?"

My eyes grow wide with fear. "I, but, my class," I stutter.

Mr. Leonard just shakes his head and turns his attention to Penny. "Ms. Morris, would you please let your teacher know that Ms. Fosse will be late for class at my request?"

Penny nods her head and swallows hard. "Yes, Mr. Leonard." She brushes her hand against my shoulder before turning to practically run down the hall.

Breathe. It's going to be okay.

But then he gives me a look that contradicts everything that I think I know. It's a look that I've wanted to avoid for the past few months.

He knows. He has to know. Why else would he be talking to James and then want to speak to me in his office during *one of my classes?*

Bile rises in my throat and I swallow it harshly back down. My sweaty palms are barely able to grip my notebook as I follow Mr. Leonard down the halls to his office, taking a seat in the vinyl chair in front of his large desk.

"Ms. Fosse, I appreciate you coming in," he says and takes a seat behind his desk of power.

"Of course. What was it you wanted to see me about, sir?"

He picks up a folder from the top of his desk and begins to read the contents inside. Folding his hands together, he places them on top of the papers and leans forward slightly.

"I was going over your schedule and credit requirements. It appears that you have met and exceeded the credits required to graduate from this school."

I nod my head, wondering where he's going with this.

"However, just because you've met the credit requirement doesn't mean that you've met the subject requirement. According to your transcripts you've been a teacher's aide since last year for two periods during the middle of the day. Is that correct?"

"Yes," I squeak.

"Luckily, those will count toward your elective credit but you still lack one additional graduation credit."

I twist my fingers in my lap nervously, feeling the first cold drop of sweat run down the back of my neck. Is he serious? I know that I've carefully gone over my transcript since freshman year to make sure I had all of my core and elective classes taken care of. What subject could I have possibly skipped?

"Now it's my understanding that you have applied to and have been accepted into the pre-med program at Harvard, correct?"

"Yes," I say again.

He lifts up a piece of paper and trails a finger down the words, studying them briefly before meeting my eyes again.

"Which would explain the heavy emphasis on your math and science courses. Everything looks to be in order except for a missing social studies credit."

Wait, what? A social studies credit? But that's impossible. I know I've taken the correct amount of courses that the school and Harvard require for graduation.

"Are you sure Mr. Leonard? I'm almost positive that I have the appropriate amount of credits for each subject."

He glances down at his sheet again before turning it around to face me. I lean forward in my chair, perched right on the edge so I can get a good look at my transcript.

"Microeconomics, macroeconomics, American history, and geography. That's four credits, isn't it?" I ask, sitting back in my chair.

Mr. Leonard shakes his head at me. "Not entirely. Yes, they are four classes but because you only took one trimester of geography this year, it doesn't count as a full credit."

The color drains from my cheeks at the realization this brings. "So I can't graduate?"

He smiles and shakes his head. "Not necessarily. You still have this next trimester to get the remaining credit needed. I've struck a compromise with Mr. Dumont, who agreed to give you credit for your aide position toward your geography class but you will need to take the rest of the course this next trimester. We've already worked it into your schedule. Unfortunately, that means you will need to give up your teacher's aide position with Mr. Dumont."

I sag into my chair. Relief flows through me that this is the only issue. "I understand. What period has Mr. Dumont put me into for his class?"

Mr. Leonard pulls out another sheet of paper and turns it to me. It's my upcoming schedule for next trimester. I haven't even seen it yet, but I'm not surprised that the majority of my classes have stayed the same.

"Your first- through third-period classes haven't changed. We were able to fit you in so we didn't have to disrupt your schedule too much. Your sixth-period class has changed, now moved to the fifth period," he says, pointing to the paper. "We gave you an open fourth-period since it's the lunch hour. That way you'll be able to do as you please, as long as you don't broadcast that information across the school, that is. Otherwise, we'll have to place you in a study hall."

An open fourth-period? This can't be happening. There's no way he would give me an open hour at the same time as James if he knew we were together. Our secret is still safe, at least for now.

"No, of course. I won't tell anyone about my open period. I'll do something to occupy my time and not draw attention to myself. Perhaps use it to study in the library?"

"The library sounds like an excellent idea. I will let Mrs. Farnsworth know that you will be there during that hour so she won't think you're skipping class or anything of the sort."

I smile and nod, unable to keep the elation from showing too brightly at my new master plan.

"May I keep this?" I ask, picking up my revised schedule.

"Of course. Are you still okay with taking Mr. Dumont's geography class during sixth-period?"

Ending my school day with James? You won't hear me complaining.

"Yes, that's still fine, Mr. Leonard."

He stands from his chair and shakes my hand as I straighten myself up to my full height.

"I'm glad we got that all straightened out. Thank you for coming in, Ms. Fosse." He hands me a pass, excusing me from the time I've already missed from my calculus class.

"Thank you for catching the mistake, Mr. Leonard." I give him a small wave as I exit his office.

My feet carry me swiftly down the hall now that the feeling of dread has left. My mind is still reeling from the fact that we haven't been discovered and that I'm going to be back in class with him again. It'll be a sweet torture, but the alternative isn't something I'd like either. I'd rather sit and look at him than be told that I can't see him at all.

Not looking where I'm going, I run into a hard wall and fall flat on my ass. The notebook and pencil I was carrying scatter across the floor, coming to a stop beside a familiar pair of shoes. Okay, so it wasn't a wall I ran into. It just felt like one.

I look up at him and smile, shaking my head slightly as he extends his hand out to pull me off the floor.

"You really need to pay attention to where you're going," James says with a shake of his head.

"You need to quit knocking me off my feet," I reply, brushing some dirt off the back of my pants.

He leans forward and tucks a strand of hair behind my ear. "Never."

I flush then quickly look around to make sure no one can see us. He does the same before pulling me into a dark alcove underneath the stairs.

"Oh yeah, this won't draw attention at all. What are you doing out here? Shouldn't you be in class right now?"

He pulls my face to his and our lips meet in the most toe-curling kiss he has ever given me outside of his bedroom. Instinctively my arms wrap tightly around his neck, pulling us closer together until I can feel his hard body fully pressing against mine. And when I say hard body I mean *hard* body. With a deft roll of his hips, I feel that same hardness press against my stomach, eliciting a moan to escape my mouth.

"Shh. You can't do things like that and expect me not to react," he says, trailing his lips down my neck.

I try to push him away, but my body doesn't agree with my brain as it presses into him further, making it his turn to hiss out a breath.

"I didn't do anything," I breathe. "I was just walking back to my class, which I'm now extremely late for."

James pulls his head back and looks at me with the utmost love and adoration in his eyes. "You have a pass from Mr. Leonard, who I assume gave you the good news?"

I nod and smile. "Yes. It appears you're stuck with me as your student again, Mr. Dumont."

A low growl can be heard and it makes me giggle again. "You know what it does to me when you call me that."

I brush our lips together before pulling away from him. "I do, however, there's nothing we can do about it right now."

He grabs my elbow slightly before I fully emerge from the alcove. "Meet me tonight?"

I look over my shoulder and grin. "Same time?"

He doesn't say or do anything, just sears me with his hot and intense stare. I love the way he looks at me as if I'm the most important thing in the world to him.

I turn to face him, cradling his cheeks in my hands and rest my forehead against his. "I love you and the way you love me."

Warmth spreads from my lips down to my toes as we seal our goodbye with one last scorching kiss.

"I love you too. Get to class now. I'd hate to have to write you up for being tardy."

Backing away slowly, I keep my eyes locked on his while I attempt to straighten myself out. Pressing a kiss to my fingertips, I blow it to him while wiggling my fingers in the most girlish fashion possible. He catches the kiss and presses it to his heart, which almost makes my legs go out from underneath me again.

I bend to pick up my notebook and pencil, which are still lying on the floor, when I'm met with another set of shoes in front of me. I slowly stand up straight and look into the blue eyes that I never wanted to see again.

"Chase," I say in surprise.

"Hey, Britt. What's going on? How come you're not in class?" he asks, eyeing me skeptically. Unease settles in as I watch his eyes roam over my body before settling in on my lips.

"What happened to your mouth?" he asks. A slight sneer forms on his lips and I bring trembling fingers up to what I know are to be swollen lips; swollen from the kisses James was giving me during school hours.

My chest heaves as I attempt to breathe. A new wave of panic rises inside me, threatening to crumble the stability I just had moments before.

"Um, I don't know. Why? Is there something wrong with them?" It's lame at best because I know he's not buying it.

Chase turns his head toward the alcove, trying to see who might still be in there. *Please let James escape without Chase seeing him* I think to myself. I have to keep Chase away from there because if he sees James there is no way that I'll be able to talk myself out of this one. We'll both be fried.

"Who are you hiding?" he asks, returning his gaze to me.

"N-no one," I say shakily.

He starts to move toward the stairs and my heart beats wildly in my chest. Is it possible to have a heart attack at eighteen? My vision blurs slightly and I start to feel like a weight is pressing down on my shoulders, slowly trying to sink me to the ground.

"Britta?" I hear a voice call out.

I turn and see Penny running down the hall. She quickly runs over to us and her big green eyes are filled with concern as she takes in my appearance. I must look like death because she runs her hands up and down my arms before resting them on my shoulders.

"Britta? Chase, what in the hell did you do to her?" she asks. Penny starts to turn me toward the stairs to sit down, but I furiously shake my head. I glance over my shoulder to give her a clue that we can't go over there.

"I didn't do anything to her. I found her picking her stuff up off the floor and then noticed her lips were bruised so I wanted to know what happened. Then she grew pale and almost fainted."

Slowly my reasoning is starting to sink in and can feel the strength return to my limbs. "I'm fine you two. Quit fussing over me. I just needed a minute to breathe."

I lean against the wall, making sure that Chase's back is facing toward the staircase so James can escape. Only there's no movement coming from under there. I try to squint without making it obvious that I'm looking for something, but he's not there. He must have been able to escape while Chase was distracted by me. *Oh, thank God.*

"Your color is coming back so that's a good thing. Let me take you to the nurse. Maybe you should go home," Penny says.

I shake my head again and push off the wall. "No, I'm okay. Just lightheaded from standing up too fast I guess."

Chase shoves his hands into his pockets and kicks an invisible rock. "You looked fine until I started asking questions," he says suspiciously.

"Well, then you need to keep to yourself. Don't think that we've forgotten what you tried to do to her over winter break," Penny snaps.

Chase flinches at her harsh words. I raise a hand to her to stop a potential tirade. Chase's sullen expression makes me feel horrible for how I've treated him the last few months since the incident.

"Look, I've said I was sorry about a million different ways. It was stupid and foolish and no one is more ashamed of how I acted than me. I know it's not an excuse but the pills I got from one of the guys really messed with my head and the large amounts of alcohol didn't help matters either." He looks back at me with sadness in his eyes. "I'm really, truly, very sorry Britt.

Can we please put this behind us? I just want things to go back to normal. We only have a few more months together and I really would like my friend back."

There's a good chance he's sincere in his apology this time. But a part of me wonders if it's a front because he knows something is going on with me; that I'm keeping some big secret or leading some double life. Which I am. Technically. But at the same time I remember the Chase of the past; the one who gave me his popsicle in the park when we were six because mine fell on the ground. Or the one where he punched Billy Simon in the mouth because he laughed at me when I spilled red Kool-Aid all over my white dress after the choir concert in eighth grade.

I look to Penny, who is shaking her head at me. Letting out a sigh I extend my hand to him and give a half smile. "Friends?" I ask.

He beams brightly as he shakes my hand. "Friends," he says, letting his hand linger over mine just a bit too long. I pull my hand away and hug my notebook to me.

"We better get going. You've missed almost the entire class and I'm supposed to be going to the bathroom," Penny says, pulling on my elbow. I nod and follow her down the hall, leaving Chase standing there with a stupid smile on his face.

"What were you thinking back there?" Penny hisses at me when we turn the corner. We pause at the end of the hall and she turns me sharply to face her.

I shrug. "I don't know. All I know is that I had to do something otherwise he would have found James."

Penny backs away slightly. "Are you shitting me right now? James? What in the hell is wrong with you? It's the middle of the day and you were out in the open. Have you lost your goddamn mind?"

My lower lip trembles slightly. "I know. God, it was stupid

of us, but we honestly weren't thinking. I ran into him after I left Mr. Leonard's office and then one thing led to another…" I trail off because if I continue to talk I'm afraid my voice will betray me. And I don't want to go to class looking like I've just had a meltdown, even though I kind of am.

Penny hugs me tightly and sighs. "You two are going to be the death of me. You're lucky I love you and by proxy him since you love him."

I nod and hold her tight, forcing my emotions back where they belong. We pull away and wipe at the tears threatening to fall from both our eyes.

"Come on, let's get to class before we really get into trouble," she says, pulling me back down the hall.

But I can't focus as I sit in the remainder of the class. My mind keeps wandering to James and how his lips felt on mine and the fear I felt when Chase almost caught us. Again. We were careless and stupid. We need to contain ourselves otherwise this is going to end and not in a good way. So I resolve to talk to him next hour when I'm in his office doing my job. Two more days of alone time with James is all we have left before going back to pretending and then only two more months until we don't have to pretend at all.

Two more months.

Twenty-Five

A KNOCK STARTLES ME FROM WHERE I SIT AT JAMES'S desk. Bringing my head up, I can't help the smile that forms as bright green eyes look me over from where he stands in the doorway.

"Hey," I breathe, unable to speak above a whisper.

"Hey," he says and walks into the room. He looks behind him quickly before shutting the door halfway, giving us some semblance of privacy. I'm pulled quickly from the chair and into his waiting arms, resting my head against his shoulder. Turning into his neck, I take a deep inhale and let his soothing scent calm my fried nerves.

"I was so scared before. I thought Chase was going to find you and then we'd be dead."

James gently holds the back of my head while running his other hand up and down my back, quieting my nerves.

"He didn't see me. I slipped out when you were picking up your stuff and he was preoccupied with you."

He's gritting his teeth and the vein on the side of his neck pulses with anger. It makes me smile as I melt further into him. *He didn't see him. Thank you, God.*

I pull away and force a weak smile. "We can't do this anymore. Not in school. It's too dangerous and we're getting too careless. I mean, can you imagine the ramifications if Chase had seen us? You'd be fired and I'd be…I don't know. Shunned? Kicked out of school?"

He cups my cheek and places a kiss on my forehead. "I agree. We're getting a little careless. I never should have kissed you like that during the school day. But I just couldn't help myself. You looked exactly the same as you did the first day I met you and I guess I wanted to act on my feelings rather than keep them bottled up inside like I did that day."

My head tilts to the side in question. "What do you mean act on your feelings? Are you saying you wanted to kiss me like that when you flattened me out on my ass that day too?"

James smiles and sits me back down in his chair. Pulling up the extra one, he sits across from me and holds my hand in his.

"Yeah, I did. Seeing you looking at me with the same expression on your face as that first time, it did something to me. It took my breath away, just like that first day. You are and will always be the most beautiful woman I have ever seen."

It still amazes me each and every time he's able to take my breath away with the simplest of words.

"You're too good to me. I don't deserve you."

He shakes his head and smiles while his thumb continues drawing circles on the back of my hand. "We're good for each other. Never forget that. You fill a void in me I never knew was there. All it takes is to hear your sweet voice and my heart jumps into my throat. You are, without a doubt, the best thing that has ever happened to me. And I'm going to love you until the day I die and then forever after that."

I bite my lower lip and smile. "Promise?"

He laughs lightly and kisses my lips. "Promise."

We sit and stare at each other for a few more minutes until voices down the hall bring us back to reality.

Right.

Teacher's aide.

Teacher.

School.

Professional.

"Well, Mr. Dumont. In running the risk of getting into trouble, I think you better eat your lunch out in the lounge with the other teachers while I work on my assignments here. I mean, you do only have my services for the next two days so you better make good use of them."

A sparkle in his eye lets me know that what he's thinking has nothing to do with the assignments I'm correcting for him.

"Dirty," I mouth, reading his thoughts before he has a chance to put a voice to them.

He laughs and kisses the crown of my head.

"Later."

"Okay."

Another quick kiss on my lips and then he's out the door with a smirk. *Smartass* I think as I regain my composure and try to focus on the assignments in front of me.

"No, no, no!" I cry, hitting my hands against the steering wheel of my car. Great. The stupid thing is dead. Of course, I hadn't taken Liam's advice and brought it to the auto shop when it wasn't turning over right away yesterday. Ignoring the problem is so much more efficient. Until you're stuck in the parking lot of the school when everyone else is gone.

"Perfect."

I pull out my phone and start to dial Liam's number.

Tap, tap, tap.

I jump in my seat and turn to face the noise, only to be greeted by the most beautiful sight in the world.

"James," I say, opening my door quickly. "Thank God you're here."

"What's wrong?" he asks. He shoves his hands into the pockets of his coat. We're still on school property and who knows if anyone is still lurking around so we're not about to make the same mistake as we did earlier.

"My stupid car won't start. I think the battery is dead."

He places his briefcase on the ground then opens my car door to pull the latch for the hood release.

"Let me see," he says, opening up the hood and sticking his head inside.

I stand and watch as he checks several things out, pushing against the battery cables and double checking my oil levels. There is something so utterly sexy watching him as he tinkers around under the hood of my car, which, of course, makes me think of him tinkering around underneath *my* hood. My thighs squeeze together at the thought and I know I'm blushing because I can feel the heat flash across my cheeks.

"Reminding you of something?" he smirks, catching my eye. My blush increases and I slowly make my way over to where he's standing. His cologne drifts my way on a light breeze, letting it swirl around me. It makes me crave him even more than I already do.

"Shut up. So what's wrong with my car?" I try to play it off and act cool and collected, but it's hard when he's around. And it doesn't help that he knows exactly which buttons to press to send me into a frenzy. Something he's more than capable of doing at any given time.

"For sure your battery is fried. See the corrosion around here?" he says, pointing to the white crusty stuff where the cables connect. I nod and pretend like I know what he's talking about. "That's not good. You'll need a new one. Can you give Liam a call and see if he'll pick one up?"

"I could, I suppose. I'll just have to stay here by myself until then," I say, wondering if he'll take the bait.

"Nonsense. I'm not about to leave a teenage girl in an empty parking lot alone at night."

That stings, whether or not he intended it to hurt doesn't matter. It's the fact that he called me a teenage girl. No one 's listening to us so there isn't any reason why he would have to say it.

He must have caught my flinch because his eyes instantly soften while he frowns. "Oh shit, Britta, I'm sorry. I didn't mean that."

I wrap my arms around my middle and take a step back. "No, it's fine. You're right. I am a teenage girl in a parking lot by myself. You were just telling the truth."

My chest hurts and for the first time it's not from an ache of longing. The pain that is slicing through me is because, for the first time since I've known him, this is where our difference in age and status has really been apparent. He's a teacher and I'm a student. He's twenty-two, almost twenty-three, and I'm eighteen. And as we stand here in the school parking lot, it's smacking me directly in the face.

James is reading my face and gauging my emotions as I'm sure they're written all over my expression. He looks around cautiously, making sure that we truly are alone in the parking lot and hidden from the roadway. I try to take another step back, but he catches my arm and pulls me into his chest.

"God, sweetheart, that's not what I meant. I just had to get out of my professional head for a moment to remember that this is you I'm talking to." He presses his lips against my forehead and sighs. "You are more than just some teenage girl to me and you know it."

"Am I?" My voice sounds weak and I hate it right now. My emotions are getting the best of me because I know what I am to this man. I'm the exact same thing to him as he is to me. We're equals. We're meant to be together. We have to be. Otherwise, all this hardship and struggling would be for nothing. And I know better than that. Nothing good comes free. You have to work for it and James and I are fighting like hell against the outside world to make us work.

When our lips meet, everything vanishes from my mind. All thoughts of students and teachers and anything else keeping us apart drift into nothing as our lips move together, reacquainting themselves as if they haven't seen each other in ages instead of hours. He backs me into my car as my fingers tangle in his hair, loving the feel of the silky strands underneath my touch. He opens the middle three buttons of my coat to slip his hands inside and pull me completely flush against him.

Our tongues tangle together, tasting and licking each and every space they can find. He tastes like coffee and mint and James. A flavor that heightens my taste buds until they tingle and feel almost alive with need. His kiss is my drug and with each swipe of his tongue the addiction grows into something I can't live without.

I pull back breathless and stare into his perfect green eyes. "I'm sorry. I'm acting stupid."

He shakes his head and smiles the gentlest smile I've ever seen on him. "No, you're not. I made the error in my words. Plus we were both on edge today over what happened so it's harder to adjust back into our normalcy." He cups my face in both his hands, letting his thumbs brush lightly over my cheekbone. "I love you. I will always love you. Even if I can't tell you when I want to, even if I don't say the words out loud, I still love you."

"We need a signal or something because these next few weeks are going to be difficult. We're not going to see each other as much and our interactions are going to be scrutinized at every turn."

He smiles at me and nods before pressing his lips to mine again. "I agree. We need a signal. Something easy that we can do if we pass each other in the halls or something not conspicuous that will draw attention during class."

James pulls back and places his index finger on his lips in contemplation. Suddenly he snaps his fingers and a huge grin appears on his face. "I've got it. My signal to you will be this." He holds up his left hand and pretends to twist an invisible ring on his ring finger. I don't miss the significance of it and it sends tiny flutters through my chest.

I nod and think of my own signal, trying to come up with something good. "Okay, I'm kind of lame at secret signals but how about this?" I bring my fist up to my chest and press it hard against my heart, almost making it look like I have heartburn, which would technically be right. My heart does burn when he's not around. It aches with a pain that is sweet and bitter at the same time, making it a real paradox of emotions for that one small organ.

He takes my hand, prying it away from my chest and opens my fingers to press our palms together. "It's perfect." Standing next to my car, our palms pressed together, we just let the world spin around us, caring about nothing more than just this sweet moment where we can be together.

The wind switches and a chill runs up my spine. James

looks at his watch and shuts the hood of my car with a small thud. "Call Liam. Ask him to pick up a new battery for you. But you're not staying here. I'll bring you home or wherever else you want to go."

"But how will I get my car?"

He winks at me and smiles. "We'll figure something out."

"Sounds good to me, Mr. Dumont."

I laugh as I slide into his front seat, listening to him mumble something about frustrating women as he picks up his briefcase and climbs into the truck. It only makes me laugh harder. He's just so easy to goad that I can't help myself. I pull out my phone and call Liam, asking him to pick up a new battery and install it for me so I can get my car later. Hearing Penny laugh in the background is making me think that it'll never happen but he swears he'll get it done.

I rest my head against his shoulder as he brings me to my house. Part of me is anxious to have him come to my house, but the other part of me is jumping up and down to see him in my space for once. Maybe it'll actually feel like we're a real couple with nothing to hide.

As long as my parents don't come home, what could possibly go wrong?

Twenty-Six

$\mathcal{A}$S WE DRIVE TOWARD MY HOUSE, MY PHONE BEEPS in my purse. Pulling it out I check the name that's flashing across the screen. My brows draw together when I realize it's Chase. What could he possibly want right now?

ENJOYING YOUR RIDE WITH MR. DUMONT?

The blood freezes in my veins. We just left the parking lot and I swear it was empty. I don't remember seeing any cars anywhere or noticed anyone who walked by. My breathing spikes as I frantically try to remember if I missed something. No, I couldn't have. There's no way he could have seen us. *Unless he was spying on me.*

WHAT ARE YOU TALKING ABOUT?

I need to play dumb to see what he knows because I can't let on that what he's saying is actually correct.

CAR TROUBLES? I SAW YOU GET INTO MR. DUMONT'S TRUCK AFTER HE WAS LOOKING UNDER YOUR HOOD. WHAT ELSE OF

YOURS HAS HE LOOKED UNDER?

"Oh shit," I whisper and bring my hand to cup my mouth in horror.

"What?" James asks, registering my fear. I turn to face him, my face pale and ghostly white as all the blood has drained from my body. I feel cold, almost numb at the realization that this is it. We're done for.

"Chase. He knows. He saw me get into your truck just now and I think he knew it was you earlier today in the hallway. Oh shit, he knows."

Tears threaten to fall down my cheeks as I start to panic. What are we going to do? How can we keep this a secret for much longer if Chase knows?

"Britta, look at me," James says. We pull into a gas station parking lot. He throws the truck into park and turns to face me. My hands tremble and shake uncontrollably. He reaches out to hold them, trying to calm my nerves, but it's no use. "We don't know that for sure. What did he say?"

I repeat the texts word for word and watch as his face pales like mine. My throat feels dry as I barely make out the last few words.

"What are we going to do?" My lip trembles and James moves his hand to gently press against my cheek, warming it slightly to regain some color.

"We're going to figure out something. We're in this together. Besides, all he has right now is me giving you a ride home. That's innocent enough, especially since your car is broken down at school."

"But what if he saw our kiss?"

An image of the kiss flashes in my mind, remembering how his body felt pressed against me as he explored my mouth with his tongue, how his hands held firmly onto my sides as he anchored our bodies against my car. It was a stolen moment after calling me a teenager, but it didn't lack the passion that we always have. He knows as well as I do that everything we do is passionate. We don't know any other way.

"Then we're going to have some explaining to do." He pauses to think quickly then frowns. "Ask him what he wants."

"I'd rather not. I'd rather tell him to go fuck himself and mind his own business."

"That won't do us any good and you know it," he says, shaking his head.

Dread fills me as I type out my response because I know exactly what he's going to say. I need a game plan, an exit strategy where I can protect James from Chase's wrath.

"Whatever it is, I won't let anything happen to you," I tell him. My phone beeps and the reply is exactly what I thought it would be.

I WANT WHAT'S SUPPOSED TO BE MINE. MEET ME AT MY LOCKER TOMORROW BEFORE SCHOOL AND WE'LL WORK OUT OUR NEW ARRANGEMENT.

My eyes close and I fight to keep the tears from falling down my face. I quickly delete the message because I don't want James to see. He mustn't know what I'm about to do, what I'm about to sacrifice to keep him safe.

"What did he say?"

I swallow hard and clear my throat. "He wants to meet me before school to talk."

"No," he says harshly.

"James," I sigh, knowing he's not going to let me go without a fight.

"No, you're not meeting with him. I'll meet with him and

then it'll be done."

"You can't do that. He'll destroy your career. All your hard work, all your graduate studies will be for nothing if you get fired because of me."

He grabs my face and kisses me hard. I can taste his fear and anger in this kiss. It's not the soft and gentle kiss that I usually get from him. This one is fueled by rage and possibly sadness because his lips slow against mine, changing it again into something more fragile, something that can be broken with the slightest touch. I know that feeling well. It's the same feeling that's in my heart at this very moment. Knowing that everything we've worked towards, everything we've built together in trying to secure our future will be crumbling to the ground, leaving nothing but dust and shattered dreams in its wake.

"You let me worry about my career. I don't trust him. He's unpredictable and will strike however he wants to get the most damage."

I kiss him again, this time with tenderness and understanding. I need him to understand that I'm going to protect him. I won't let this roach infect our lives. I'll squash him like the bug he is. But I need James to know that what I'm doing is for love.

"I will handle this. You stay out of it." I quickly look down before meeting his eyes again. "You're right, though. Chase can do a lot of damage to us if we're not careful. Just please, trust me. I've got this. I can handle Chase. I've done it before and I'll do it again."

His bright green eyes are sad as they seemingly accept what I'm saying. "You don't have to be my protector. I'm pretty sure that's my job for you."

I shake my head and force a smile. "We're supposed to protect each other. That's what love does. It means you fight for the one who you love above all else. And that's you. I love you above all else and I won't see our future taken away from us."

Those sexy lips of his curl up in the corners as he smiles. "Our future. Yes, our future will survive whatever is thrown at us."

"I'll make sure of it. I just need you to trust me."

"I trust you," he says, kissing me once more.

I pull away and straighten back into my seat. "Good. Now take me to your house."

He gives me a puzzled look. "I thought you wanted me to bring you home."

"Change of plans. I have the need to keep you all to myself right now."

His thumb runs over my jaw, sending a round of goose bumps to appear on my body. My nipples tighten in anticipation and my breathing spikes, making the small confines of his truck seem stifling.

"I think we can handle that. We'll be home in five minutes," he says, pulling back into traffic and heading towards his house.

Home. Oh, how I wish it really was my home because that would mean we could be together, permanently. That no one could tear us apart with accusations or destroy our future with exposing us to the outside world. Home is meant to be a safe haven, a place of peace and understanding. A castle to guard you against enemy attacks. But now our home is broken, or at least it will be once tomorrow morning shows. Because what I have to do, what needs to be done to keep James safe is something that will put a crack in our defense. I know he won't understand it. But he can't know. Not yet. Not until I figure this whole thing out.

Soon enough we pull into his garage and walk into the kitchen area. Taking my coat from me, he places it in the closet and ushers me onto a barstool.

"Are you hungry?" He glances at the clock and frowns. "I didn't realize it was this late already." He starts pulling out pans and some cheese out of the refrigerator. "Grilled cheese sound okay?"

"Sounds great," I reply, trying my best to appear normal.

He continues grabbing all his ingredients as I stare off into space, formulating my plan of attack against Chase. I know that I have precious little time with James. Chase will make sure that he takes me away from him.

I'm shaken from my thoughts as James comes into my view mere inches from my face. "Are you still with me?"

"Huh?" I blink at him, hoping that my face hasn't given away too much of my thoughts.

"I was wondering if you wanted some sun-dried tomatoes inside your sandwich."

I force a smile and nod. "Yeah, that sounds good actually."

He turns the burner off, abandoning the sandwich on the stove. Rounding the counter, he pulls me off the stool and into his arms. "Please don't worry about this. We'll take care of it. Chase won't hurt us. Besides, we're stronger than him, right?"

I nod. "Right."

He bends down to brush his lips across mine, but I won't have any of that. I need him to dull the ache that's forming in my chest as I think of our fate. I desperately need to feel the connection between us, to assure myself that my sacrifice will be worth it, even if I die a little each day in the process.

"I need you. Now," I breathe, running my tongue along the seam of his lips until he opens for me. Fire spreads through my veins, mixing with the ever present desire that lies just under the surface whenever James is around.

Picking me up off the ground, I wrap my legs around his waist and cling to him as he carries me to his bedroom and places me in the middle of the bed. He crawls up my body, slowly, like a panther waiting to strike. His eyes have a fierce look to them as if he's devouring me whole. I squirm under his gaze and marvel at my body's reaction to him, even though it's the same reaction that I've had for the past few months.

My shirt is the first to come off, pulling it over my head and tossing it carelessly to the floor. Next I work on his shirt, needing to feel his smooth chest beneath my fingertips.

I start to thread the buttons through the holes when his hands grab mine to halt my progress. "Hey, slow down there. What's the matter?"

I make a small grunt of displeasure as I look into his eyes. "Nothing's the matter. You just have too many clothes on."

He presses into my body further, sending another round of jolts through me. "Slowly, sweetheart. I want to do this slowly."

"We can do slow later. Right now, I want fast and hard. Please don't make me wait." I'm not even ashamed for basically asking him to fuck me now.

James rolls his hips again, hitting me in the right spot. A small gasp escapes my lips. "You want fast and hard?" he asks. I nod, now panting with the need for him to be inside me. "Then that's what it'll be."

I rip his shirt open, letting the buttons fly past my face and scatter across the floor. James reaches down to unbuckle his belt and pants, letting them slide down his legs until he kicks them off. I work my own pants down at the same time. He grabs hold of my hips, dragging me slightly down the bed until I'm directly in the middle of it. With a snap, my panties are torn from my body.

I reach down and slide his boxer briefs off. His cock springs out and glistens with the evidence of his excitement. He wants me as much as I want him. I don't think I can wait much longer.

Needing to feel our connection, I grab his erection and guide it to my soaked entrance. He slowly presses into me but stops abruptly.

"What?" I pant, lifting my hips to complete our connection.

"Condom," he says and leans over to his nightstand. Since we started sleeping together, he always keeps the drawer well stocked. And it's come in handy because we can't seem to keep our hands off each other.

After the condom is rolled on, he takes my wrists in his hands and pins them next to my head.

"Fast and hard?"

I nod. He pushes into me again, only this time he doesn't stop until he's fully sheathed inside me. I cry out from the fullness, trying to let my body adjust to his size.

James briefly looks into my eyes to make sure that I'm okay. Once I give him the nod, he begins a punishing rhythm, making me climb higher and higher into the clouds with each stroke. He moves faster inside me and I lose myself in him. The heavy scent of lust is evident in the air, along with our sweat and passion for each other.

He pulls out suddenly and flips me over, pressing my stomach into the mattress. Lifting my hips until they're the perfect height, he plunges into me again, deeper this time due to my position.

"Ah!" It feels as if he's bottoming out every time he dives further inside me. The twinge of pain is nothing compared to the amount of pleasure I feel at this very moment.

"I need you with me," he says and reaches around to rub my clit. He doesn't need to use the extra stimulation, but I'm not going to say no. He growls in my ear as his chest presses against my back. "Baby, you feel so good. I love being inside you, feeling your muscles squeeze me every time I push into you."

And that's all it takes to have my body release the tension that was building, letting it morph into a powerful orgasm which rips me apart. I scream into the mattress, clawing desperately at the sheets as his fingers and cock continues their assault. Time is irrelevant as I feel like I've been coming for hours with each shake of my muscles and contraction against his cock.

"Britta," he shouts, letting his hips jerk several times before spilling into me. He holds me still as his cock pulses inside me, prolonging my own orgasm even more. We fall onto the bed in a sweaty mess of tangled body parts. He pulls me into him, turning me in his arms until we're face to face with each other.

I kiss his nose and smile, still trying to regain my breath that was stolen from me just moments ago. "Holy shit. That was mind-blowing."

He smirks and brushes some hair from my forehead. "Fast and hard enough for you?"

"Mmhmm," I murmur and relax into his arms.

I must have fallen asleep because the next thing I know James is nuzzling my neck while pressing feather soft kisses against my skin. The sheet is pulled over me and the room is dark with only a faint amount of light coming in through the window.

"Hey, sleepyhead," he says, chuckling into my neck with another kiss.

"What time is it?" I croak. I need to stretch my arms, but I won't because it would mean James has to move from his position and I really, *really* like what he's doing right now.

"It's almost eight. Well past supper and almost bedtime."

I laugh as he props himself up on his elbow. He looks so handsome and carefree. His perfect lips, dreamy eyes, and chiseled face make my heart skip a beat as I burn his image into memory.

"Will you read me a bedtime story then?" I ask. He shakes his head and moves over me. I widen my legs to make room for his body as he settles in between them.

"I've got one for you. Once upon a time, there was a girl who was special in every way. Only she didn't know it at the time. She was also kind of clumsy with a habit of running into people." He smirks and runs his hand down my side. "She was beautiful, enchanting, and the most amazing person anyone has ever seen. One day, a man comes into town and she turns his world upside down with just a single glance. If she had told him that the sky was down and the ground was up, he would have believed her. She enchanted him with her eyes that spoke words to him through some sort of magic. The first time he kissed her, he felt the magic seep into his soul, tearing a piece of it from him and giving it to her. Slowly they formed a bond, one which couldn't be broken because they shared a love so intense it was unlike anything that's been seen before.

"But alas, their love was to be tested time and time again. The outside world didn't believe in their love, told them it wasn't right, that it was forbidden and dangerous. But she didn't give up. She fought with the bravery of thousands and the man felt it with each kiss she gave him, each one a precious gift. And he fought right alongside her, showing their unified front because when they were together, nothing could stop them."

A tear drops down my cheek as I listen to his story. "So what happens to them? Do they succumb to the threats of others?"

He shakes his head and bends low to kiss me. At the same time, I feel him push inside me slowly, gently. My eyes widen as I realize we're acting carelessly at this moment, but his index finger presses into my lips, silencing my fears.

"They stay together and fight because what they have is perfect. Others may be jealous of what they have, but it won't break them apart." He moves further into me and my eyes roll back into my head because this feels different than any other time. I can feel him, all of him, without any barriers stopping us. And it's divine.

"Never," I whisper, raising my hips to meet his thrusts.

He pushes fully into me and stops, looking down at me with the utmost love and adoration in his eyes. "They conquered all and lived a long and happy life together, filled with laughter, love, and a family."

"James," I whisper and pull his mouth down to mine.

"I need to feel you without anything between us because we're in this together. Nothing will ever separate us."

He moves faster now, feeding my craving for his body until it's ready to explode in a fiery ball of heat. Our eyes meet and I can tell he's close because his movements become more frantic and less controlled. And I want that. I want him to lose control over me because that's how I feel whenever I'm with him. All the power that I possess disappears until my reckless thoughts are of him and him alone.

His love, his passion, our life together, all of it sends tears to my eyes as I surrender to him, letting the fiery ball drop and explode around me. I cry out as my body shakes from the orgasm and he follows me, chanting my name as if it's the most beautiful thing he's ever said.

"Promise?" I ask when my rational thoughts return.

His chest presses against mine but smiles as he kisses me lovingly on the mouth. "Promise."

We roll onto our sides, which breaks our contact. I don't panic at the thought of us not using a condom. Feeling him, all of him for the first time was an experience I will never forget.

James pulls me into his chest and professes his love again and again into my ear until his breathing regulates and slows, letting me know that sleep has finally taken him.

I crawl out of his grip, sliding slowly off the bed to retrieve my clothes from the floor. Once I'm fully dressed, I walk into the kitchen and tear off a sheet of paper from the tablet next to the refrigerator. Scribbling down a quick note for him, I bring it back to his bed and place it on my pillow.

"Goodbye, James. I love you." I kiss his cheek gently before leaving the room. I hold my hand over my mouth to control my emotions, hoping it'll keep the sobs from escaping.

I grab my phone from my purse and type a quick text to Liam, asking him to come get me from James's house. He responds right away saying he'll be there in a couple minutes.

I walk around his house one last time, etching everything into memory. After tomorrow, there's a good chance I will never be back. But what I'm about to do is to protect James from Chase and everyone else who thinks they can get between us.

I just hope he understands.

Twenty-Seven

HIS IS IT. THIS MUST BE WHAT IT FEELS LIKE TO BE on death row. The sweaty palms, erratic heartbeat, the fear that every breath could be your last. Okay, maybe not quite that extreme, but I feel like I'm being suffocated. There just isn't enough air to fill my lungs as I walk down the hall to my impending doom.

Chase messaged me again a few minutes ago, making sure that I was going to show up or he was going to expose us to Mr. Leonard and ruin us. That will not happen. Not if I can help it.

"Babe," he says as I approach, but I hold my hands up to stop him from coming any closer.

"Don't start with that bullshit, Chase. Tell me what you want so we can get this over with."

His smirk takes on an almost sneer as his eyes roam over my body. My skin crawls at his perusal and I'm thankful for my preemptive strike of wearing lots of layers today to avoid any further complications.

"You know what I want. I've been dropping not so subtle

hints all year and yet you continually turn me down."

"Has it ever occurred to you that maybe I'm not interested? That maybe I *like* our friendship the way it is, the way it always has been?"

He leans closer and it makes me want to run in the opposite direction. "I've been chasing you for years Britta, but you've been too stupid to notice. I could never get you away from Penny, and now that she's got her own thing going, I figured this could finally be my shot. I could win the prize that I've dreamed about for years. But no, you had to go and fuck it up with *him*."

The way he said that last statement has my panic rising from threat level yellow to orange. He's been chasing me for years? How have I not noticed this?

"Chase, it's not what you think. You're being delusional and are obviously thinking the wrong things."

"I don't believe I misinterpreted his tongue down your throat or him pressing you into your car as he's doing it," he hisses at me in a low tone.

My worst fears come to light as the cold grip of reality sets in. Blood drains from my face, making me feel lightheaded and dizzy. I can't hide that anymore. He knows what he saw and I can't say that he didn't. He knows he has me right where he wants me and I have to play his game or he'll end James.

"What do you want?" I whisper, letting my shoulders sag in defeat.

He runs his hands up and down my arms and I fight the urge to kick him in the balls again. "You and I are going to play nice together for the rest of the school year. *Real nice.* I hope you didn't already make plans for prom because guess who your date is?"

Bile rises in my throat. There's something in his eyes that I've never seen before and it scares me. He's never been this cold before, even when he wasn't acting like himself. I try to swallow past the lump in my throat, but I can't. His eyes narrow, creating another wave of nerves to course through my body.

"I wasn't planning on going to prom."

"Well, now you are." He grabs my hand and pulls me to him with a thud. "You'll be doing all kinds of things with me now. And everyone will know it."

I follow his glance and realize that everyone has stopped moving around us. He's managed to make a spectacle of this, putting us right in the limelight for everyone to see. And I've played right into his hand. Most everyone is either smiling or whispering to each other while they stare. A few less obvious 'it's about time' comments can also be heard, mainly from the guys who are waiting for something to happen.

This is my worst fear come to light. This is the end of my happy high school career. My senior year had so much promise and now it looks as if it'll be tarnished forever. Forced to be someone I'm not just to keep the one I love safe.

But as long as he's safe, it's worth the sacrifice.

"If I do this, if I agree to your demands, you have to promise me that you will leave Mr. Dumont alone," I whisper. "Nothing will happen to him. I don't want a word of what you saw coming out of your mouth to anyone because if something happens to him, you will pay. That I can promise you."

Chase runs his hands down my back before pulling me flush against him. "If you stick with the plan, I'll keep my mouth shut about your boyfriend sleeping with a student."

I want to run, kick, or scream as if I was lit on fire while Chase caresses me. I hate this. I hate what I'm being forced to do, but I don't have any other option. It's the only one left.

"As long as we're clear on that, you have a deal."

He pulls his head back and smiles. I used to think his smile was cute, that he could win over anyone with that smile. But now as I stare at it, I see the evil behind it. It's the smile of a man who doesn't care who he hurts as long as he gets his way.

He grabs my arms and drags them around his neck. "You better start playing the part. Otherwise, this is going to be a long two months for you."

Two months. Here I thought my salvation was almost here. Now I see I'm in purgatory, looking out into paradise as it sits just beyond the horizon while I'm slowly dragged to hell. His lips brush my cheek, causing my stomach to turn.

I need an excuse to get away from here and away from him. My phone beeps in my purse and I pull away quickly. "If that's all, I need to get to my locker before class."

I practically sprint down the hall, leaving Chase standing there with the same stupid expression on his face as when I first saw him. Pulling out my phone, my heart sinks even faster as James's name appears on my screen.

WHY DID YOU LEAVE LAST NIGHT? WHERE ARE YOU?

You can't fall apart right now. This is for James. I lean against my locker, feeling my heart constrict with each passing second.

AT SCHOOL. HAD TO GO SO MY PARENTS WOULDN'T SUSPECT ANYTHING. LIAM PICKED ME UP.

I KNOW. I TALKED TO HIM THIS MORNING ALREADY. HE SAID YOU WERE UPSET. TELL ME YOU HAVEN'T MET WITH CHASE YET.

I press my head against my locker, clutching my phone to my chest. This hurts worse than anything I've ever felt before. It feels like a betrayal even though it's not. It may be my body that Chase has, but he will never have my mind, spirit or heart. Those things already belong to one man and he's keeping them safe while I'm wandering the path to hell.

I HAVE TO DO THIS. PLEASE DON'T HATE ME. I CAN'T DO THIS IF YOU HATE ME. I LOVE YOU.

I power off my phone and shove it back into my purse. I can't read any more texts from him because if I do my resolve will diminish and I'll cave to my need to run to him. Instead, I grab my books for my first-period class as Chase walks up behind me and brings his arms around my waist.

"Ready, babe?" he asks.

I shut my locker and free myself from his hold. "Ready," I say dejectedly. There's no way I'm going to sugar coat this. I can't pretend I have feelings for someone who is using emotional blackmail to get what he wants.

Chase ignores my moodiness and grabs my hand, swinging it back and forth as we walk to our class. Chase yells his usual outbursts to his friends as we pass them in the halls, sometimes stopping briefly for them to give him a pat on the shoulder when they see our hands together. But I ignore it all, shutting my body off so it's numb to everyone around me. That is until we round the corner and I see James standing at the end of the hall. Chase must see him too because he pulls me closer and wraps his arm around my shoulder. But I can't move my eyes from James as I watch the pain register on his face. He knows the plan, or at least has figured it out by now.

I know this is killing him, watching Chase touch me. I know because what happens to him, happens to me. And I'm dying slowly with each passing second.

"Smile pretty for your boyfriend," Chase whispers into my ear before his mouth crashes down on mine.

This is wrong. So, so, so, so wrong. I don't know if I can go through with it because the way James is looking at me, at us, it hurts far worse than anything else. I thought having Chase explain things to me this morning was hard. No. Seeing James standing there, broken, is far, far worse.

"We're going to have a good couple of months together, Britt. You better learn to kiss me better than that." He pulls me into our classroom before I have the chance to give James another glance. But really I'm thankful because I don't think I could bear to see the look on his face again and not break down into tears.

By the time fourth period arrives, I'm no longer surprised by anything Chase does. He's been attached to me every step I've taken today. So when he announced that I was to spend my lunch hour with him in the cafeteria instead of in the teacher's lounge, I just nodded and followed like a beaten puppy.

He knows exactly what he's doing, taking away every opportunity I have to be close to James.

Bastard.

Penny walks past me, slows, and then stops altogether. "Britt? Hey," she says and takes the seat next to me. Chase nods at her before continuing his conversation with some of the guys from the basketball team.

"Hey Pen," I say quietly. I push the food around on my plate. I'm not hungry but wasn't given the choice when Chase bought my lunch.

Penny looks at me in confusion as her eyes float between Chase and me. "So what's going on?"

I set my fork down and force a half smile. "Didn't you hear? Chase and I are together now."

Tears well up in the corners of my eyes and I fight like hell to not let them fall. I didn't consult Penny before I decided to execute this plan. Given the expression on her face, she's completely blindsided at my statement.

"Oh, no, I hadn't heard," she says, grabbing my hand and squeezing it tightly.

"Yeah, Chase made it official this morning."

At the mention of his name, Chase turns and smiles at Penny. "Yep. Finally wore her down enough until she agreed. It was all just a matter of finding her weak spot."

Penny's eyes grow wide. I nod in response. *Yes, he knows and yes he's blackmailing me* I say in a silent communication with her. She squeezes my hand again and I look down, hoping to keep myself together so I can get through this lunch hour.

"So what are you going to do next hour? Aren't you supposed to still be his aide?" she asks quietly.

I shake my head. "I'm skipping that period for the rest of the week. I don't think I can do it, even though I know he won't be there."

Penny stands abruptly. "I need to go to the bathroom. Britt, you need to go?"

I nod and move with her, but Chase pulls me back and kisses me harshly. "Just remember our deal," he says against my lips.

"I will. I'm just going to the bathroom. I'll be back."

Penny practically drags me into the bathroom around the corner. She bends down to look under the stalls before locking the door.

"Are you shitting me right now? Chase? I ought to beat the shit out of you. What were you thinking?"

I lean against the sinks and hang my head, gripping the edge of the counter so tight it turns my knuckles white. "I'm protecting James. This was the only way. I knew what Chase wanted and, unfortunately, that was me. If I didn't agree to this, he was going to tell Mr. Leonard about us and ruin James's career. I couldn't let him do that. I love him too much for him to go down because of Chase Woodward."

One tear slides down my cheek, followed by another, then another. I can't hold them back anymore. They've been building the whole morning and now that the floodgates are open, I'm not sure if they'll stop.

Penny gathers me in her arms and I cry into her shoulder. She holds me tight without saying a word because she knows there's nothing she can say to make me feel better about my situation. A situation that I put myself in because I was too careless and too confident that we were untouchable. How stupid of me as I look back on it all.

"It'll be okay," she says. "How long is he going to blackmail you?"

"Until the end of the school year." I wipe my nose with the paper towel she hands to me.

Her face falls again. "Oh. Look, if you need me to put some pressure on him, kick him around or have someone else do it, I'm more than willing to arrange it."

I shake my head. "No, trust me, I've thought of that already. I just need to do this. It's only two months. Maybe I'll be lucky and it'll fly right by. I mean, the two months that I've been sleeping with James have been nothing. It's like I blinked and they were gone."

Now is not the time to relive those moments. But they come unbidden, flashing quickly through my mind as I remember each and every moment I've spent with him in absolute bliss. We thought that as long as we were together, nothing could hurt us. Our strong, united front was greater than anything the world could throw our way. But we were delusional and reckless, blinding us to what was happening while we were lost in each other.

Deep down I knew we were vulnerable, especially after that

night at Caravaggio's when we saw Chase there. I wonder if that was the turning point. He had to have seen us, which means he's been biding his time until he could strike and do the most damage.

And we walked right into it.

"Is there anything I can do? Pass secret notes to him for you? Arrange a sleepover and have it be at James's place instead?"

I pull away to clean up my smudged makeup and give her reflection a sad smile. "It's too dangerous. We're better off playing by his rules."

She comes closer and puts her hand on my shoulder. "What does James say about all of this?"

I turn away from her. "James wasn't a part of this plan. But his expression when he saw us together this morning almost killed me. He's hurting and it's my fault." I swipe at a tear. "But I'm doing this to save him. I just want him to understand and not give up on me."

"He knows how much you love him. I think it'll take more than this to scare him away. But for your sake, it's probably better to stay away for now."

"Good thing it's spring break next week. That'll give us some time apart before next trimester." Then I smack my head and groan. "Fuck, next trimester. I have a class with him again. This is going to be difficult."

Penny hugs me tight and brushes away the wet hair from my face. "You'll get through it. This is just a bump in the road, but I believe it'll make you two stronger. From what I've seen, you have a love I've only ever dreamed about. You'll be okay."

"You're full of shit, but it's very sweet of you to say that." I nod and wipe my nose again with the paper towel, not caring about the sharp bite of the scratchy material. I welcome the pain because it distracts me from my heart tearing in two. "We better get back."

Sighing, Penny unlocks the door and we head back to the lunch room where Chase is waiting for us. He smiles and kisses my temple, making me flinch only slightly. Penny doesn't miss it and gives me a sad smile. It hurts that I'm causing everyone around me so much pain, but I have to concentrate on the long term goal. This will be better for us because after this trial we're free.

I skip next period as planned, hiding out in the library under the guise of finding books for Mr. Dumont. Mrs. Farnsworth doesn't question it and just lets me go about my business. So I find a quiet corner and sit with my knees pulled up to my chest, staring out the window next to me.

Luckily there's only one more class I have to sit through like a zombie and it's one that I could care less about. When the bell sounds, indicating the school day is over, I walk in a daze back to my locker. Normally I'm talkative with everyone, wondering what their plans are for the rest of the day but I don't feel like speaking to anyone right now, least of all Chase. I've been careful to avoid him since lunch and he hasn't come looking for me, so that's a plus.

A sheet of paper floats to the ground like a feather when I open my locker. I recognize the note instantly and know the words written on it are made of lead. I swallow hard as I pick it up.

My Dearest James,

I know that you won't understand what I'm about to do, but know that it's in our best interest right now. Whatever you hear, whatever you see, just know that it's all pretend. There will only ever be you in my life. No one can ever replace you. Just please ...wait for me.

I love you more and more each day. You are my soulmate, my match, my one true love.

Loving you always,

Britta

Britta,

You don't have to do this. Please stop this nonsense and come back to me. We can work this out. I can't stand by and watch you be the martyr. It's too painful. I don't know if I can bear it.

I love you with all my heart. You are my life, my beloved, my promise that I will keep.

Forever loving you,

James

Tears fall onto the paper, narrowly missing the words he has written underneath my own. I carefully fold it and place it gently in my purse, tucked away where no one will be able to see it. He's in pain and it's my fault. But I need to fix this, need to make this right for us. He called me a martyr. And maybe he's right. Maybe I'm sacrificing myself for our relationship to survive. But it's a sacrifice I'm willing to make because I vowed to protect him and that's what I'm going to do, even if it kills me a little more each day to do it.

Twenty-Eight

I CALLED IN SICK TO SCHOOL ON FRIDAY. I COULDN'T HANDLE being there and pretending to be someone I'm not. Chase called me right away, of course, to make sure I really was sick. So I did my best impression of a dying woman and he bought it, but told me he'd be by later that night to check on me. James was checking on me too but in the only way he could, through text message. Seeing his name appear on my phone had me breaking down in tears again, although that implies I had stopped crying at some point. Ever since last Thursday I haven't stopped crying. He called me his promise. That broke me inside.

I promised to be there for him and look at me now.

I told my parents that I didn't feel like going anywhere this week, not even to Penny's house. They didn't quite understand and have been hovering a bit more than usual. After I had told Mom that it was over a boy, she understood and backed off.

Knock, knock, knock.

I press the book against my chest as I reluctantly lift my eyes to see who it is. Not just any book. It's *Rebecca*, the book that James had read to me a few months ago on our official first date. He gave me his precious first edition even after I protested that I couldn't take it. He said it was a way for us to be together when we're apart. As long as I'm reading it, it'll be like he's reading it to me. And he's right. His voice is all I hear as I read each and every page.

A head pokes through the small opening of the door. "Britt?" my brother asks before fully coming in.

"Yeah, I'm here," I say and pick up my book again.

He takes his usual place on my desk chair, leaning back so he can kick his feet up on the end of my bed. I push them off with my foot. I don't need him here, trying to cheer me up. I'm perfectly content being alone right now. Just me and my book.

"What can I do? I don't like seeing you like this."

I place my bookmark between the pages before shutting my book gently. "There's nothing you can do. Chase has won and I just have to wait it out until the end of the year."

"Assuming that he'll let you go even then."

My shoulders slump more and I grow quiet. "I hadn't even considered that."

Liam is quiet for a moment. I can't believe I never even considered the possibility that Chase would never let me go. Setting my book down on my bed, I press the heels of my hands into my eyes, trying to push the wave of sadness away.

"This hurts Liam. It hurts so damn bad," I somehow manage to choke out.

The bed dips and he slings his arm around my shoulders. He rests his cheek on top of my head and rocks us back and forth like mom used to do when we were kids.

"I have a way to temporarily make it better," he says.

Wiping away the tears so he's not blurry anymore, I raise my head and frown. "How?"

Another knock appears at my door and my heart drops into my stomach. He stands there with his hands tucked into the pockets of his jeans and a ratty old sweatshirt that must have said UConn at some point. His eyes are shadowed with black smudges, looking as if he hasn't slept in days. But even through all of that, he's still the most glorious vision I have ever seen.

"You only have a half hour. I've got confirmation that Chase is with Travis right now in Templeton, but they're leaving soon to come back," Liam says, getting up from my bed and shaking James's hand.

"I-I don't know what to say."

James stands at the edge of my bed, just staring at me with such sadness that my heart breaks all over again. Lifting myself off the bed, I help close the distance, leaving a foot or two of space between us.

"You can thank me by not getting my ass kicked by Penny for this. She said if I didn't do something I was in trouble. So here's my something."

I turn my head to him and chew on my bottom lip. "Mom and dad?"

He smirks and flicks his head to the door. "They're grocery shopping so it's just the three of us. But that still doesn't mean I want to hear anything so keep it to a minimum. Sorry Casanova," he laughs.

James shakes his head and laughs too. "You won't have to worry about that. I just need to see my girl."

My girl. I remember the first time he called me that. It brings a tear to my eye just like it did then. All the trials, all the tribulations, it's all for something. And that something is standing right in front of me, looking at me the same way he always looks at me. *With love.*

"Thank you, Liam," I whisper. He nods and closes the door

behind him, leaving only the two of us standing in the middle of my room.

My heart is beating so hard and so fast that I'm afraid it's going to fly out and land straight into his. He steps closer to me, now with only mere inches between us.

"Hey." His voice is scratchy and laced with pain. As if he hasn't spoken in days and this is the first real breath he's uttered to someone.

"Hey." My voice breaks and I can't take it any longer. I rush into his arms and press my face into his chest, deeply inhaling his scent. He crushes me to him while placing sweet, gentle kisses on the crown of my head. "I've missed you. So much."

Tears soak his sweatshirt as I bury my head further into the safety of his body. I've missed his smell, missed his touch, missed everything about him that makes my insides light up.

He shushes me, but I just cling to him more. I don't want to pull away and find that this is only a dream.

"Sweetheart, please don't cry. I don't want to waste our time together. I only get this half hour with you before losing you for the next two months."

I pull back and hastily wipe at my eyes. He's right, he's always right. His hand cups my cheek and I lean into the touch. Such a simple gesture. You wouldn't think something as simple as a touch could bring peace to a broken mind, but that's exactly what it does. He's easing my mind, calming my fears until they are momentarily forgotten.

"James, I'm so sorry. So, so, so sorry. I didn't want to hurt you, but I needed to protect you and this was the best option to do so. Chase wouldn't have dropped it if I hadn't agreed to his terms."

He tilts my face up and places a whisper soft kiss on my lips. It steals my breath away, leaving me gasping for air at the assault upon my emotions. One minute I'm in agony over hurting James and the next I'm kissing the lips that I dream of every night. My body doesn't know which way to go as it fights pulling him closer to me or stepping back to admire him.

With a few more soft pecks he pulls back and smiles down at me. "Shh, I know you are. And believe me, my brain understands your methods and your need to protect us. But my heart," he starts, his voice catching slightly, "my heart doesn't know what to think. All it knows is that we aren't together. And it hurts. It hurts so much to see you and not touch you, to listen to your voice and not be able to reply, to see your smile and have it not reflected at me."

"If it makes you feel any better, I haven't smiled in days," I sniff.

He leads me to the bed and sits down before pulling me into his lap. "I know. Liam's told me how your week has been and that you haven't left your room except to eat and shower. And it broke me. I told him I needed to see you because it's been killing me to not be able to comfort you myself."

"You talk to Liam?" I ask.

He nods. "Almost every day. We've actually become good friends now. It's nice to have someone to talk to in this town, especially since I'm still considered the new guy."

Who would have thought those two would have become friends? Never, if you would have asked me at the beginning of this all. I guess I don't know everything.

"I'm glad you two have become friends. This makes it easier somehow."

His lips press into the side of my head before resting his cheek there. "You doubt us?"

I turn and move to straddle him, placing my hands on his shoulders to steady myself. "Never. It's just, sometimes I feel like this is all in my imagination or that I'm in some dream where I just can't wake up and I don't want to." I press my forehead to his and sigh. "You're the best thing that's ever happened to me. I can't live without you. You're a part of me now and not being with you is like losing a piece of me."

He pulls me closer and kisses me with all the love and passion that one can possibly pour into a kiss, telling me how much I mean to him without actually saying anything. Because he knows just as well as I do that actions speak louder than words. And right now, he's saying that he loves me.

"I'm going to marry you one day," he says against my lips.

I smile and kiss him again. "And I'll say yes when you ask."

"Promise?" His hands run up my arms before threading into my hair, holding my head so our gazes never leave each other.

"Promise."

That's the easiest promise I've ever made and one I intend to keep.

Not wanting to waste our time, we both lay down on my bed. James picks up the book and opens it to my bookmarked page, cradling me next to him as he reads to me. My head is pressed against his heart and I listen to the rhythmic beat, letting it soothe me until nothing else matters. Just the sound of his voice and the feel of his body next to mine is what I focus on. I'm grateful for this stolen moment with him and make a note to thank Penny and Liam for what they did.

I told myself that it would be easier to go without seeing him secretly but who was I kidding. I realize now that I was barely living before I met him, living a life that didn't have a purpose. Just ideas of how I thought it should be. But lying here, cradled in his arms, listening to his voice, lets me know that our sacrifice is worth it because I now have a purpose. And it's everything I thought I wanted before, only now he's included in the picture to make it complete.

Liam knocks on my door. Our time is up.

"Did you drive here?" I ask, slowly sitting up but still hanging onto James.

He shakes his head. "Liam picked me up. He thought it would be too dangerous in case Chase saw my truck outside your house."

"Smart man," I say.

"I do have my moments," Liam says.

"And modest too," I retort, rolling my eyes at him.

James and I leave the security of my bedroom and walk hand in hand down the stairs. Liam grabs his keys off the hooks by the door and we make our way outside to his car.

"Make it quick," Liam says as he climbs into his Mustang.

James wraps his arms around my waist, pulling me tightly to him. I rest my head on his shoulder, feeling the beat of his heart beneath my ear. At times I swear it's saying my name. I take comfort in that, even if it's only my imagination getting the best of me.

"I don't want you to go," I whisper.

He kisses my forehead and holds me tighter. "I don't want to go either. It's going to be hard to see you and not do this, but we need to think of the end result."

I nuzzle my face into his neck and press my lips against his skin. He sighs. "I know. We just have to pretend like we did at the beginning of the year when we were trying to avoid each other."

James laughs and pulls back slightly to look me in the eyes. "And that worked out so well for us. If I recall, there were a couple of incidents after class that resulted in some close encounters."

I flush as I remember those moments, wanting nothing more than to taste his lips or feel the press of his body against mine. I smile and run my fingers over his cheeks. "We will have to avoid those this time around. But I will play my part and try not to entice you. I'll just be the model student and get perfect grades, do my homework and ace every test."

He laughs and brings his lips to mine, giving me one final kiss goodbye. And it's a kiss that is going to have to tide us over for the remainder of the year because we won't be able to do this again without consequences. As our lips work in sync with each other, tasting and moving in a slow, delicate dance, my love for him grows by the second. I know without a doubt that we'll make it through this and come out stronger in the end. Chase thinks he's won, but he's wrong. We've won because he can't break us apart.

Liam raps his knuckles on the window, pointing at his watch to let us know our time is up. "Time to go, sweetheart," James says.

"I love you," I whisper, taking a step back from him.

He tucks some hair behind my ears and smiles at me. "I love you too."

With a final goodbye, he climbs into Liam's car and they back out of the driveway. I stand and watch them until the tail lights disappear from sight. Turning to go back into the house, I walk back to my room and retake my spot on the bed. The pillow still smells like him and I hang onto it like a lifeline. I close my eyes briefly as a new sense of calm washes over me before opening my book back to the page he left off at. The words blur together and I can't concentrate with his scent still around me. So I close the book and turn to look out my bedroom window before falling into a peaceful sleep for the first time in over a week.

Twenty-Nine

"DID YOU SEE THE NOMINATIONS?" PENNY ASKS ME.

I shrug my shoulders as we walk down the hall. "Yeah, I did."

"And?"

"And what? Ow!" I rub my shoulder. "What the hell was that for?"

"For not being more excited about your prom queen nomination."

I sigh and lean against the wall by the locker bay. "I don't care about any of that crap and you know it. In fact, I hope I don't win because I don't want the attention it created the last time I won some stupid title."

Penny kicks my foot. "Whatever. You know you're going to win."

"I can also guess who's going to be king and I'd rather not think about that."

"True, but you never know. Maybe you'll get lucky. I saw Lyle was nominated too so maybe he'll win."

"Maybe. I wouldn't mind that, just like I'm sure Cami wouldn't mind winning queen too."

Both of our friends have been nominated to the royal court along with me and I'm praying like hell that they win instead of having a repeat of Homecoming where it was Chase and me.

"I'd like to think the student body would be a little more creative this time around, rather than elect the same two people again," I say.

"It's a popularity thing and you know it. And unfortunately for you, you're popular," she says while putting her books into her locker.

"And I still have no idea why. It's not like I'm into sports or any of the clubs. I'm just me, the quiet girl who gets good grades."

She turns to me as I put mine away. "Your good looks and sparkling personality I'm sure have nothing to do with it either."

I smile back at her. "Yeah, maybe that's it."

Our laughter dies when Chase appears next to us. Right on time as usual. Somehow I've managed to tolerate his controlling moods from the short leash that he's put me on. But lately, he's been getting sloppy. His watchful eye isn't always pointed in my direction. But I'm still cautious because I don't trust him. That was broken the minute he decided to blackmail me and ruin my life.

"My two favorite people," he says and lays his arm across my shoulders. I try to shrug it off, but he just holds on tighter.

"Fuck off," Penny says. She clearly doesn't care what he thinks and isn't afraid to tell him so.

"Aww, love you too, Pen," he says, pulling me toward the cafeteria. Despite being forced to eat with him, I've actually enjoyed being in there with the rest of the student population. Perhaps I have been a tad antisocial these last few years at lunchtime, so being able to talk with other people for a good hour isn't all bad.

We enter the line and I grab my usual salad and Diet Coke. Chase pays for my lunch again, even though I repeatedly tell him not to. He says it's his boyfriend duty or some bullshit. I ignore him and just chalk it up to a perk of his blackmail.

I spy my friends sitting at a table near Chase's friends. I turn to him and smile sweetly. "Chase, I'm going to sit with Penny and the group today."

He eyes me cautiously and purses his lips. "That's not part of the deal," he says.

I narrow my eyes at him. "No, you stated that I had to eat in the lunch room. You didn't say explicitly that I had to be chained to your side the entire time. Besides, I'm at the table right next to you. You can still monitor me to make sure I'm not sneaking out, even though I haven't broken any of your stupid rules yet."

Chase thinks about it quickly before giving me a subtle nod. "Fine. But if I see any funny business that'll be the last time you eat with them."

"Why thank you, master. I promise to be a good girl and behave," I say sarcastically. But I quickly dart up the aisle before he has a chance to reply. Penny squeals in delight as I take my seat next to her.

"He let you off your chain?" she asks.

"Yep, the warden let me have a day pass."

"I don't get it," Drake says. "Why do you put up with him if you clearly don't like him? I mean, it's obvious to everyone that you're not into him."

I stab at my salad because I don't know how to respond to him. "It's complicated," is all I can come up with.

"Complicated how? I mean, if you're going out with some-one, shouldn't you actually *like* the person?" Cami asks.

Crap! Think, think. I take a bite and chew it slowly.

"Let's just say it's an experiment that I'm doing. I'm trying to see if I can piss him off enough for him to leave me alone permanently."

Dez dips a French fry in some ketchup and points it at me. "Yeah, but you're the one who looks miserable."

"It'll be fine. I'm keeping an eye out for my girl," Penny says and pulls me into an awkward side hug.

"See. What could possibly go wrong if Penny's looking out for me?"

Everyone laughs and we drop the subject entirely. Justice and Drake both talk about how they're excited to attend UConn this fall. Cami and Lyle talk about the prom nominations and I wisely choose to stay out of that conversation. Instead, I ask Dez how her track season is going and she goes on and on about her improved times in the relay and sprints.

"So, prom," Lyle says, getting the attention of the table again. "Cami and I were thinking of hosting a party. Just a small one so we have somewhere to go afterward. You guys in?"

A collective yes sounds from the table. I cringe because I want to go. But that also means that I'd have to bring Chase with me and he's quickly become *persona non grata* with our little circle. Especially after his last few party appearances. I'm glad I didn't witness his most recent debacle at Travis's house where he puked over the railing into Tammy Johnson's hair. Then he tried to feel up most of the cheerleaders that were there. Yeah, my *boyfriend* is a real winner.

"I think I'll pass since I'll be attending with you know who," I say, jerking my head back toward Chase. "But thanks for the invite."

"That's a shame. We'll miss you Britt, but we totally get it," Justice says.

"That doesn't mean we can't live it up at prom, though," Cami chimes in.

I nod, hoping that she's right. "Yeah, we can totally live it up there. Who knows, maybe that night will actually turn out to be halfway decent."

We go back into a conversation about everyone's summer plans and I kick prom right out of my head, not wanting the reminder of what I'm missing because of what Chase is putting me through.

Even though it's been a month since I've seen James outside of a school setting, the sixth period isn't quite as hard as I thought it would be. Don't get me wrong, it's still tough because Chase is glued to my side during class. And the little vein on the side of James's neck pokes out to the point I'm afraid he's going to have a stroke. But we're trying to make the best of it, acting like we did at the beginning of the year when we were professional and avoided any and all contact with each other.

But that doesn't stop us from silently communicating with each other. He'll write something on the board and then turn around to ask the class a question and my eyes will drift to his hand as he absently plays with a ring that isn't there. To everyone else it appears he has developed a nervous tic. But I know better. I know he's telling me that he loves me, to which I respond by constantly keeping my fist over my heart, making it seem that I have perpetual heartburn. Chase doesn't appear to notice, which makes me happy to have this one thing that we can do without him being any the wiser.

The bell rings for the end of school and everyone jumps out of their seats, but James's voice stops everyone from leaving right away.

"Remember, the chapter test is next Thursday and it's worth one-quarter of your final grade."

Chase waits for me to get out of my desk before grabbing my arm and pulling me to him.

"We're going to Sammy's tonight so you can help me study."

I wrench my arm away from him and narrow my eyes. "Sorry, but I'm busy with my family. My grandparents are in town and we're going out to dinner." I step closer to him and point in his face. "And don't you ever fucking grab me like that. I don't care what kind of blackmail you're holding over me, you will *not* lay your hands on me like that again."

He quickly leads us out of the classroom and presses me up against the wall. "Look here. I don't think you're in any position to give me orders or tell me what to do. If you don't go out with me tonight, then I guess I'll just have to come over to your house. Some alone time in your bedroom might be good for us. You know, spice things up so we're not always in public together." He runs his finger down my arm and my whole body shivers at the contact, and not in a good way.

"That's not going to happen." I swallow hard and turn away from him. "Fine. I'll meet you at Sammy's around six."

"You're sexy when you're feisty." He moves closer and kisses the corner of my mouth. "Don't be late." He tries to kiss me again, but I move my head, making him kiss my cheek instead. He grabs my chin and forces me to look at him. This time he hits his mark. The tang of copper hits my tongue as his teeth clamp down on me. "Don't ever turn away from me again. You'll want to stay on my good side, Britta. Otherwise it's the end for you and your little boyfriend."

He releases my chin and I work my jaw back and forth to try and relieve the stiffness from his assault. Chase walks down the hallway with his head held high, as if he didn't just manhandle me. Tears threaten to fall but I hold myself together because I can't let anyone see how he's affecting me. This is the first time he's ever really been this physical with me. I wonder if he's losing a little bit of the control that he's been carefully wielding to me.

I move from the wall and quickly look up and down the hall, thankful that most of the people are gone or are blissfully unaware of the events taking place around them.

"Britta," a pained voice calls to me just beyond the doorway. I turn to face him and can see the repressed anger in his expression.

"He didn't hurt me. It's okay, I can handle it," I say, trying to keep my voice steady. I quickly dart into his room because I know if I don't he's going to make a scene and we can't have that.

"He put his hands on you," James says. He gently turns my head to examine my sore chin. Marks must be forming because his eyes dilate while his brows turn in sharply. "I'm going to kill the fucker."

I take a step back and brace my hands against his shoulders.

"James, look at me," I plead. His hands bunch up into tight fists at his sides, turning his knuckles white. My hand cups his cheek to guide his eyes to mine. The storm behind his irises finally calms as his face falls slightly. "I'm okay. We can't have you going off and creating problems between Chase and me. I know what I'm doing. Don't worry. I've got this."

"But he grabbed you," James whispers.

I press my forehead against his, breathing in his calming scent. "And I'm okay. Believe me, I have something in the works for dear little Chase. And if he ever touches me again it will all go down. But until then you need to keep a level head and let me handle this."

He backs up and crosses his arms in front of his chest. "What are you planning?"

I smirk and kiss his cheek. "Let's just say that prom is going to be interesting."

Tingles erupt over my skin as his hands rub up and down my arms. "One month to go," he says.

I smile and watch his face light up. "Then we're free."

I turn to leave, letting his fingers slip through mine.

"Britt?" he asks, making me pause in the doorway. I glance over my shoulder and tilt my head to the side. "When this is all said and done, I want to meet your parents and then I want you to meet mine."

Pure and utter happiness warms my heart at this request. "I would love that."

"Good." He smiles and shoves his hands into his pockets. I turn and blow a kiss to him as I disappear through the doorway to head to my locker. After getting everything I need, I sprint to my car and pull down my visor to inspect the red marks on my face.

Penny knocks on my window before climbing into the passenger seat. She frowns when she takes a good look at me. "What in the hell happened?"

I shove my phone into her hands. "Just take a picture," I say and hear the shutter sound as she logs the evidence. She hands it back to me and I smile at the photo.

"Will you mind telling me what this is all about?"

"Chase grabbed my chin after class because he freaked out."

"He did what?" she screams. I wince but talk her down from the ceiling.

"Calm down. Look, this is all going to plan. Remember?"

Her breathing is erratic and heavy, but she slowly calms herself down. "I know but seeing him actually do it is something else."

"Just stick with the plan. Then during prom night we just

need to stage the next step and then we should be golden," I say, putting the car into reverse and backing out of my spot.

Penny slides her hands together conspiratorially. "I can't wait to see the end result," she says as we discuss phase two of Operation Chase Must Pay.

Thirty

"I FEEL LIKE A PIN CUSHION," I GRUMBLE TO PENNY, WHO'S standing beside me in my bedroom as we share the full-length mirror.

Fifty-eight. That's how many bobby pins were used to keep my hair in place when I went to the salon this afternoon. But even with all this hardware in, I must say that Stacy did an excellent job. I know my hair is hard to work with, but she managed to pin the curls so they cascade down my semi-bare back. Only a few tendrils remain loose to frame my face.

The life-sucking monstrosity that is my dress is way too fancy for a person who would rather wear sweats most days of the week. My personal shopper, AKA Penny, told me that it was the most perfect strapless dress on the face of the planet. One suitable for the royal court. I called her a loon and said that there's never a good reason for a strapless dress, especially one that will bring attention to an area that doesn't need any additional attention brought to it.

It killed me to admit that she was right. It really is perfect.

The teal goes fairly well with my skin tone, and the jewel-encrusted bodice seems to match my personality with the intricate floral designs. Layer after layer of chiffon completes the dress, giving me the elegance of a Hollywood movie star at a premiere.

"I still love that diamond cut-out in the back," Penny says.

I turn and bite my lip. "You don't think it's too risqué?"

"Hell no. If the thing would stay up on its own, you wouldn't even need this little piece keeping it together."

"I don't know. I just feel a little too exposed."

"It's fine. You look gorgeous."

"Look who's talking."

Penny's dress is absolutely breathtaking. It's a perfect match for her hair and skin tone. She sort of looks like The Little Mermaid in it, which makes me laugh. The floor length gown is strapless like mine, also with a sweetheart neckline and a green jeweled bodice. A green satin sash separates it from the iridescent blue and green organza with a small train in the back, giving the illusion of a tail.

For fun, I think I'll call her Ariel for the rest of the night.

Liam walks into my room wearing a tux, looking rather dashing. Well, as dashing as my brother is going to look to me. When he sees Penny, his face breaks out into a huge smile.

"Baby, you look edible," he says as he wraps his arms around her.

"Who, Ariel? Yeah, she looks positively enchanted," I snicker.

Penny smacks my arm, which only makes me laugh even harder.

"I do not look like The Little Mermaid," she loudly proclaims. I raise an eyebrow to her and she just huffs back in response.

"Even if you did, I'd still go under your sea," Liam says, nuzzling into the layers of curls around her neck.

"And now I'm going to throw up all over this lovely gown. Excuse me," I say, leaving the room.

Prom is supposed to be a good time for all teens. A rite of passage and all that jazz. For me, it's a means to an end. I'm not excited to go tonight because the person I want to be there with isn't the person whose arm I'll be on. Instead, I'll have to see him from afar, in secret, yearning to touch him but knowing it's forbidden. And isn't there just something about being told you can't do something? Makes you want to do it that much more. And I want to touch, to kiss, to caress, and to hold him so badly I can taste it.

Penny and Liam follow me down the stairs, softly giggling and smacking at each other's hands. I turn to them at the bottom of the stairs and give them a faux glower.

"If you two can't keep your hands to yourselves I'm not riding with you."

Penny plasters on an apologetic pout and can barely contain the smile that wants to break through. "We promise to behave. Besides, we're not about to leave you alone with that twat. God knows what he'd try to do."

"Yeah, safety in numbers. Besides, I promised James that I would be your bodyguard tonight. I'm under explicit instructions that you are to arrive in one piece and unmarked."

Liam is still pissed about the bruises from last week, but once Penny and I explained our plan he was slightly better about it. And by slightly I mean his feelings went from murder to manslaughter; same result just different punishment. But that also gave us a chance to recruit him for the other part of tonight, which should free me from Chase once and for all.

Chase arrives right on time, looking moderately decent in his tux. He's still a good-looking guy, but his appeal is lost on me now after the events that have taken place this past year. The sight of him alone is enough to turn my stomach and sour my mood, which was already down to begin with.

Chase walks up and places his hands on my shoulders to pull me in for a kiss. "Wow, you look beautiful. There's no way you won't be prom queen looking like that."

I pull out of his hold and force a smile. "If only it were based on what everyone was wearing tonight but alas it's based on *votes* that have already been counted." It's hard to hide the sarcasm and contempt in my voice because honestly, how stupid is he?

He misses the meaning behind my words and continues on his train of thoughts. "Yeah, well, it's no contest. You'll be the hottest chick there."

"Thanks," I mutter because I hate being called a chick. Last I checked I didn't have yellow, downy feathers and claws on my feet. Although with the manicure Penny took me to get earlier today I'm fairly close to having claws on my hands.

Chase looks up and finally regards the people standing behind me. "Penny, Liam. Always a pleasure."

Penny mutters something low and Liam laughs, but we can't hear what was said. Probably for the best.

The four of us wave to my parents, after being assaulted by my dad's camera, and climb into the back of the white stretch limo parked out front. Chase climbs in first and I slide next to him, careful not to step on my dress and risk a wardrobe malfunction. I try to put some distance between us, but he pulls me next to him, resting his heavy arm across my shoulders. Penny and Liam sit across from us and we all make small talk, trying to fill the uncomfortable silence in the confined space.

The prom committee went all out this year, making the theme A Night of Romance, which makes me want to hurl in every direction possible. Mainly because of my escort. A red carpet has been run for the approaching limos and various other vehicles, guiding us through a floral archway into the school. Chaperones and teachers line the walkway, greeting each of us and wishing everyone to have a good time. I take that request with an enormous grain of salt.

When we walk into the gym, I scrunch my nose up to what I see. More flowers, helium balloons, and streamers are scattered throughout the space. It looks more like an oversized kids' birthday party than a romantic evening. Curled up with a good book and the one you love, now that's romantic. Throw in a fireplace for good measure and you're guaranteed to be showered with love.

Penny drags Liam over to the table that all are friends are sitting at. Chase, however, sees his jock friends sitting on the other side of the gym and whisks me that way.

"Can I at least say hi to my friends before I'm shackled to your wrist the entire night?" I plead.

Chase narrows his eyes at me. "You get ten minutes with them. But if I see you even talking to you know who, you can kiss your freedom goodbye for the rest of the night."

I bite back the scathing remark I want to throw at him and plaster on a fake smile. "Thank you," I grit out and turn quickly to see my friends.

The DJ is playing some filler music while he continues to set up his system and I hum along to the song as I cross the gym. Everyone is gathered around a small table, talking animatedly and laughing at something that Drake just said.

"Hey guys," I say, wedging myself into the mix.

"Britta!" they all exclaim loudly, making my ears ring while causing a few heads to turn our way. I laugh and hug each one of them, thankful that they're here.

"So where's Chase?" Justice asks.

I point over to the jocks and she nods, scrunching her nose up slightly.

"Even from here he looks like an asshole," Lyle says, pulling Cami in close. She smiles up at him and for a brief second I'm slightly jealous of their relationship.

"I'd say looks can be deceiving but, you know…"

Everyone laughs. I lean in slightly while looking over my shoulder, making sure he's still standing by his friends. "Okay, are we ready to make some trouble?"

"Hell yeah!" Drake exclaims and fist bumps Lyle. Justice, Dez, and Cami all nod their heads with mischievous smiles. Penny and Liam rub their hands together, giving each other an evil look. Their part is slightly larger than the others, but we all need to work together to make this happen.

"Okay, when I give the signal I need you five to keep a look-out for any trouble while Liam, Penny, and I execute the other part of the plan."

Cami claps her hands and squeals in delight. "This is going to be so much fun. He's going to get what he deserves. I'm still pissed off over what he did to you last week."

"Yeah, the only thing keeping me from punching that dick snot in the face is this whole plan. Believe me, I want to break his nose for the marks he left on you," Lyle says while cracking his knuckles.

Luckily for me the marks have cleared up and never became more than slightly red. But the picture Penny took is safe on my phone and printed out just in case our plan doesn't work.

A hand wraps around my waist and I stiffen slightly. Chase stands behind me, smiling like an idiot. Everyone around me plasters on a fake smile and greets him with moderate warmth.

"Sorry guys but I came to steal my date back," he says, leading me away without giving me the chance to say goodbye.

"I wasn't done talking with them," I say as we head over toward Travis and his date.

"Yeah, well, I said you were. It's time to make nice with my friends. You came here with me remember? You're supposed to spend time with me."

"Not by choice," I say under my breath. He doesn't hear me but holds onto my waist tighter as we approach his group.

"Hey, Britt. Looking hot tonight," Travis states, checking me out in a not-so-subtle fashion. My skin crawls as his eyes settle on the top of my strapless gown, ogling the bit of cleavage showing.

"Uh, thanks," I reply, pulling the top of my dress up to try and get more coverage.

"And she's all mine," Chase says and kisses me harshly on my mouth to stake him claim. My lips stay closed and tense and my eyes scrunch together tightly.

Go away, go away.

When he releases me, he has a smug look on his face and it takes all my strength to not smack it off his face.

I zone out as they all start talking about various sports teams and scholarships and programs they got into to begin their college careers. Instead, I let my eyes roam the room, searching for anything that will give me a distraction.

And I find it, leaning against the wall in a perfectly tailored suit with his arms crossed in front of his chest. He looks absolutely radiant, like a bright spotlight calling me to him. In a charcoal gray suit, light blue dress shirt, and black tie, he stands out from the sea of black tuxes worn by almost every other male in the building. Of course, there are the few who are brave enough to wear white tuxes and bright dress shirts. There are even two guys in powder blue and orange tuxes and top hats, channeling their inner Harry and Lloyd from *Dumb and Dumber.*

There's a change in the air, becoming static and electric, charged with an underlying passion and desire as we lock our gazes together. I want to run to him, have him pull me away from this place, but I know that can't happen. Certain events need to take place before the two of us can breathe a little easier at night.

"You want to dance?" Chase asks me, pulling me away from James and back into the present.

"Uh, sure," I say, following him to the dance floor. His group of friends follows us and we all dance in a circle, in typical high school fashion. I laugh to myself as I scan the different groups dancing the same as us. But then again, how do you dance with more than a few people other than in a large circle, outside of conducting a huge mosh pit?

After an hour of dancing, my feet start to ache and the first trickle of sweat threatens to roll down my back. I need to go outside for some fresh air because now the mass of bodies on the floor is so packed that it's almost stifling.

"I'm going to go outside for a moment. I'll be right back," I yell into Chase's ear. He waves me off, keeping his eyes glued to Travis's date as she grinds all over him. Apparently Travis isn't averse to sharing.

I walk toward the outside doors, quickly gesturing for Penny to follow me when I catch her eye. She nods and whispers to Liam where she's going. He nods and leaves to start putting our plan into motion.

The cool breeze feels good against my heated face as Penny pulls me against the wall with a giggle. "This is going to be so much fun."

"Shh! Keep your voice down." She pretends to zip her lips with a smile. "Okay, time to roll. Give me two or three more songs with Chase, let me work him up a bit before Liam brings Ms. Hathaway into the closet. We need to do this just right."

"We're just lucky she decided to be trampy and wear a strapless dress herself," Penny says. It was by some major coincidence that the man-eater also wore a similar dress tonight. She probably found it on the junior's rack at one of the department stores because it is not the right style for someone her age. At least it's a longer dress so it could easily be mistaken as the same in the dark.

"This is good because I wasn't sure how I was going to explain that to him. But he will probably be so lust blind he won't notice anyway. Okay, so I'll work him up without throwing up on myself while Liam works over Ms. Hathaway at the same time. Once they're in the closet together, the others can keep Travis and his group busy while you take the picture of the two of them together. That should give us just enough leverage to make Chase go away for good."

Penny claps her hands again. "I'm ready. Let's do this."

We both walk calmly back into the room. Penny heads over to our group of friends while I look for Liam, who is dancing rather close to Ms. Hathaway. She looks to have a little lust vision herself as she dances with my brother. *I need to buy Liam a gigantic and expensive birthday present next week.*

When I finally find Chase, I run my hand seductively up his back and around his shoulder before I stand in front of him. Judging by his dilated pupils, Travis's date may have done a lot of the legwork for me already.

"Hey," I whisper.

He raises an eyebrow at me. "What are you doing?"

"I saw the way you and little Bambi over there were dancing before I left. And I couldn't help but be jealous." I lean into him more, pressing my breasts against his chest. "I want you to dance with me like that. You know why?" He shakes his head. "Because it made me think of sex." I lean up to his ear, pressing my lips against it and drop my voice low, barely above a whisper. "Hot, sweaty, carnal sex."

How I got that last line out is beyond me. But it was effective because the look he's giving me makes me hope I didn't go a little too far with my seduction tactics. He grabs my waist and grinds his hips into mine, letting me feel his growing erection as he presses into me.

"It's about time you realized that I'm the real thing and not the other fucker. I can give you everything that he can't."

"You are so right," I hum.

He rolls his hips into me again, trying to match the erotic tempo of the song. I numbly let him move my body with his. It's almost indecent what he's attempting to do to me on the floor, but I shamelessly allow his hands to wander freely to keep up the ruse. My stomach rolls with each touch.

For James. This is for James.

Thank God Penny is keeping him occupied so he won't see this little display I'm putting on. With his proprietary tendencies, he would flip out and get arrested if he knew what I was doing.

I turn around and see the hunger in Chase's eyes.

It's now or never.

Over his shoulder, Cami gives me the thumbs up, letting me know that Liam's job is done.

Running my hands up the front of his shirt, I lean in close and whisper in his ear. "I want you. Now."

His grip tightens on my hips. "You tell me where and I'll meet you there."

"The storage closet just down the hall. I checked it out when I went outside and it's unlocked. No one will see or hear us." I roughly grab his face and press my lips to his. When I release him, his blue eyes turn almost black and I know I've got him. "I'll go first. Give me two minutes. Then I want you to knock once before coming inside. Keep the light off and no talking because I want you to do as many kinky things to me as possible."

Chase growls in my ear. "Go. Now."

I back away from him and hold up two fingers. He nods in understanding and I start to walk toward the exit. As soon as I'm out of sight I barrel down the hall, running as fast as my shoes will allow me and hide on the staircase just opposite of the closet that is currently being occupied by the man-eater.

"You ready for this?" Liam asks. He's crouched next to me on the stairs, hidden in the shadows so we can see everything without being caught.

"I'm so ready for this."

Two minutes pass and Chase comes around the corner, right on schedule. He looks both ways before ducking into the dark closet. Perfect. He fell for the bait. I turn to Liam, who gives me a strange look.

"Stop smiling like that. You're creeping me out," Liam says, waiting for the action to start.

"Smiling like what?" I ask.

"You're all sinister looking and shit. It's weird. Just stop."

I laugh quietly and can hear the faint moans and other sex sounds coming from the closet. Apparently Ms. Hathaway isn't a discreet lover.

Penny comes around the corner with her camera in hand and gives the two of us the thumbs up sign. Lyle's next to her and grabs the doorknob, ready to throw it open as Penny silently counts on her fingers. When the door flies open, I'm not shocked by what I see. Ms. Hathaway's dress is completely pulled up around her waist. Chase's pants are around his ankles and he's right in the middle of a thrust when the flash of Penny's camera distracts him. The couple stares in shock and disbelief at being caught and is even more surprised to see who they're with. It's a good thing Chase was never good at paying attention to details.

"What the fuck?" Chase exclaims, pulling away from Ms. Hathaway and quickly trying to pull up his pants. His still hard dick is poking out and I laugh. For as much as he talks, he sure isn't packing too much heat. Ms. Hathaway's face turns ghostly white as she scrambles to fix her dress and flies out of the closet. But by this time, Penny and Lyle are already down the hall, securing the camera into Dez's locker, just in case Chase decides to tear into theirs.

"You ready?" Liam asks, standing up and offering me his hand.

"Yes, let's go."

We descend the stairs calmly, walking without rush over to the closet where Chase is frantically looking around.

"What's the matter, Chase?" I ask sweetly.

"You! What in the hell did you just do?" he barks at me.

I laugh and cross my arms in front of my chest. "Me? I didn't do anything. Imagine my surprise when I walk down the hall and hear the commotion being created as a student is fucking a teacher. My, what will people say?"

Chase sneers at me, but I hold my ground. "As if you should be talking. I can just as easily go to Mr. Leonard with my information and get your little boyfriend fired."

"With what? What proof do you have? Pictures? Letters? Video?" I ask. His face falls slightly. "But yet I have visual evidence of you having an affair with Ms. Hathaway on school property. Now that won't fare well for you, my friend. All your hard work and the full scholarship to Duke won't mean anything. They won't want you for their basketball program if word of this leaks out."

Chase hangs his head while he finishes putting himself back together. "What do you want?"

I take a step forward and poke him in the chest. "For you to leave me alone. No more blackmail, no more forced relationship. I want to finish the rest of my senior year in peace. You are not to come near me or even talk to me ever again. As far as you're concerned, I don't exist. Otherwise, Mr. Leonard will get a copy of that photo and you're history. Is that understood?"

Chase doesn't say anything more. He just nods his head and looks dejectedly between Liam and me.

"I think it's time for prom to be over for you," Liam says. "I'll take care of the limo and even pay for a cab to take you wherever you want as long as it's away from here."

"I can still sink your ship, Britta. Mr. Leonard could find out about you two through some anonymous source," Chase says in a last ditch effort.

Liam hands me my phone and I show Chase the picture of me that Penny took last week. "If any kind of inquiry comes upon Mr. Dumont, the police will get a report from me regarding a domestic assault by my boyfriend. And since you have been so adamant about telling people we're together and they've seen you handling me rather roughly lately, you may end up needing some legal counsel. And I'm pretty sure Duke wouldn't want a convicted abuser in their program either."

Game. Set. Match. Winner.

I walk away from Chase, not giving him the satisfaction of getting in the last word as Liam escorts him out of the building. I damn near bounce in my heels with excitement as I walk to my new destination.

The halls are dark, but I've walked this route so many times over the last two years that I know it by heart. I navigate with ease around the various tables and chairs, following the maze until I reach the office at the end.

Standing with his back to me, I pause before entering the dimly lit room. The soft illumination from his desk lamp is perfect, giving us a warm glow. Something that matches how I feel right at this moment. This is all I want before people realize we're gone. Just some alone time with the man I love.

James turns around and smiles as I step further into his office. "Hey." His voice is hoarse and scratchy, just the perfect mix.

"Hey," I reply, feeling my heart kick up with excitement.

He quickly wraps me up in his arms, letting me relax for the first time tonight. This is where I want to be and now I can be here without fear of reprimand or punishment.

Unless we get careless.

That's not going to happen, though.

Not anymore.

"It's done. We're free. Chase is no longer in the picture and he's going to leave the both of us alone."

Carefully nuzzling into my hair, his warm breath tickles my neck as he lets out a contented sigh. "Are you sure?"

"I'm positive. He was found in a compromising position a few moments ago. It was highly suggested that he leave us alone or else his scholarship to Duke would be in jeopardy."

James pulls back and tilts his head. "Compromising position?"

Biting my lower lip to suppress my smile, I try to keep it together but fail miserably. "Let's just say that I killed two birds with one stone."

"Do I want to know?" he asks, trailing a fingertip down my cheek.

I lean into his touch before turning my head to kiss the

center of his palm. "Probably not. It's best if you're not involved in case this gets out."

"My sneaky little vixen."

I place my phone down on his desk after selecting a song from my playlist. The soft melody of a guitar fills the room and I wrap my arms around his neck.

"Dance with me? I want to make this the best prom ever by dancing with the one person I wish to be here with most."

His lips quirk up in the corners as his arms wrap around my waist. We sway back and forth as Ed Sheeran's "Thinking Out Loud" plays in the background.

The perfect description of our relationship.

I press my cheek against his, thankful for my high heels so we're almost the same height. He quietly sings the words into my ear, making me smile, even though he's slightly off key when he hits the notes.

Partway through the chorus he pulls back to look into my eyes. "I know we're not under the stars, but I was thinking since you're already holding me in your arms that we could…"

He doesn't have to finish the sentence because my lips meet his, pouring my love into this kiss, thankful that our ordeal is over. And soon I can kiss him like this whenever I want without needing to hide. Or invite him over to dinner with my parents because I know they'll love him. This man holds my heart in his hands and I wouldn't trust it to anyone else.

When the song ends, we pull away, knowing that our moment is up. "We should get back. They were about to announce the king and queen before Penny told me it was imperative that I had to go to my office."

"She's a good little helper that one. We'll have to send her a giant thank you note," I say with a wink.

I grab my phone and lead him out of the lounge with our

fingers laced together. We pause just down the hall from the gym doors and James puts his hand on my neck, pulling me in for one final kiss.

"I'll go in first then you follow," he says, trailing his thumb gently over my bottom lip.

Liam appears next to me and holds his hand out to James. "All taken care of man. Don't worry, I've got her from here."

The two men shake and James walks into the gym with a smile on his face. Watching his retreating form has me zoning out again. That is until Liam's fingers snapping in front of me bring me back.

"Ready to actually enjoy your prom now?" he asks, holding out his arm to me.

"Absolutely," I say and thread my arm into his as we walk into the gym.

It doesn't take long for us to find our group of friends, who are all cheering loudly as the first member of the royal court is announced. Penny squeezes me before clinging to Liam, placing a loud smacking kiss on his lips. Cami, Dez, and Justice also give me a giant hug for a job well done while the guys all kiss my cheek, thankful that they've got me back.

When my name gets called for runner-up, I'm elated. I walk across the stage and accept my small tiara with a wave to the crowd. Chase, of course, is nowhere to be seen when his name gets announced. When Cami and Lyle come up for their king and queen crowns, I can't help but cheer as loud as I can. Apparently I can have faith in the student body after all.

Even though the night started horribly, it turned out to be the best night ever. Dancing with my friends, acting like myself without worry of repercussions is the greatest feeling in the world. Well, at least it's one of them. And as James plays with an imaginary ring on his finger, my mysterious heartburn comes back and my right hand comes up to press against my heart, sending my love secretly across the room.

Thirty-One

"TOMORROW'S GRADUATION NIGHT," PENNY SAYS, rummaging through my drawers for something to sleep in. She says she's staying the night with me, but I know better. She's really here to stay the night with Liam.

"I know. It's been a long three weeks, but we're finally at the end."

James and I agreed that since we're almost done with school we would keep up the charade of not being together, just because we don't want to tempt fate. That didn't stop me from sneaking over to his house last weekend, thanks to Liam. A girl can only hold out for so long.

"What are you going to do while I'm next door?" she asks.

I shrug my shoulders. "Probably watch a movie. Or carve my eyes out so I will stop imagining what you two are doing in there. Maybe jam a pencil or two in my ears just in case I hear anything."

She laughs before finally grabbing one of my oversized nightshirts and slides it over her head. She twists her hair into a bun and gives me a quick smile. "Don't wait up," she says, quietly opening my door and slipping down to my brother's room.

I roll my eyes and plop onto my bed, folding my legs underneath. Leaning against the wall, I start to imagine what my life will be like once school is out. No more Somerset, no more high school drama, no more Chase, no more half living my life.

My phone dances across my desk with an incoming message. I don't even have to look to know who it's from because James is the only person who would be texting me this late. Well, Penny would too, but she's…occupied.

WHAT ARE YOU UP TO?

I smile at the text and quickly type out my reply.

NOTHING. JUST SITTING HERE TRYING NOT TO THINK ABOUT ANYTHING.

ARE YOU NERVOUS?

NO. JUST WANT TO SHUT MY BRAIN DOWN FOR A WHILE.

NEED SOME HELP?

WHAT DID YOU HAVE IN MIND?

LOOK OUT YOUR WINDOW.

My window? I bolt to the window and throw it open quickly. James is standing in the middle of my front lawn with his hands shoved into his jeans and wearing one of his ratty old t-shirts and a baseball cap. It throws me for a minute because I don't remember if I've ever seen him wear one before.

"What are you doing here?" I whisper-yell to him.

"Come down and meet me," he replies, heading to my front door.

I quickly throw on a pair of yoga pants and tie my hair up in a ponytail before quietly making my way down the stairs. My parents are heavy sleepers, which is good because I can't remember the last time I've tried sneaking out of the house, even if I'm just going out on the front lawn. I rush through the damp grass, allowing the blades to tickle my feet as I approach him.

"What are you doing here?" I repeat my previous question.

He smiles and closes the distance between us. "I wanted to see you because I have some good news and it didn't feel right to tell you over the phone."

"What news?"

James grabs my shoulders, running his hands smoothly up and down before rounding my back and pulling me in tightly to his chest. "I got a new job today. They called me during my lunch hour for one final phone interview and then when I got home they offered me the position. You are looking at the new geography teacher at Brighton High School."

I leap into his arms and squeeze him tight. This is it. It's finally happening. He's moving to Boston with me.

"That's the school close to Harvard, right?" I ask, pressing my lips to his.

He laughs and sets me back on the ground. "Yes, very close. Since you have to live on campus and I'll be working near you, I can live close by and we can see each other without a major commute for either of us."

"Funny thing you should mention me living on campus." He eyes me suspiciously as I bite my lower lip. "I've been doing some research and yes, most students live on campus and it's highly encouraged for freshmen to stay there. There are a few exceptions to the rules."

"Which are?"

"Well, they say that visiting undergraduate students, those who are attending for only a year, are eligible to live off campus."

"Obviously not you."

"Obviously," I say. "Then there are the commuters, who are

occasionally granted nonresidential status at the time of admission. Their only requirement is that you must participate in activities and social programs of the Yard." He stays silent, waiting for me to say something else. I blink up at him slowly and clear my throat. "And then there are the students who move off campus, typically because they get married."

A twinkle sparks in his eyes as they soften to me. "Sweetheart, I'm glad you've done some research into this, but you and I won't be living together your freshman year."

Not exactly the response what I was expecting. "What? Why not? I mean, this is perfect. We can finally be together, by ourselves."

"Exactly. And we will still be together, just not living in the same house." He walks me over to the front steps and sits me on his lap. "I'm not about to take away your college experience just because we want to be together. Freshman year is filled with so many firsts and new experiences. Living with another person, making new friendships, going to parties, running across campus because you overslept...I want you to experience all those things. Plus, it's Harvard. You're probably going to have a ton of homework and won't want to be too far away from others who are in your program. There will be study sessions, late night cram-fests, projects, all kinds of things you will need to be close for."

"You're really bumming me out right now," I say, laying my head on his shoulder.

He chuckles and kisses my forehead. "I'm not saying that we won't be seeing each other. We still have the weekends. And you need to come with me to look at houses and apartments to rent in the area because eventually you will be moving in with me. Just not the first year. Wait and see how everything goes. Maybe you'll change your mind and want to stay on campus the full four years. Maybe you'll meet someone else and you won't want me anymore," he says quietly.

Lifting up head up, I grab his face and stare into his eyes. "I can guarantee you that won't happen. Why would I want anyone else when I have the most perfect man on the planet right here with me? After everything we've gone through, how could you even say that?"

James kisses me slowly, pulling me closer to him. The gentle brush of his tongue parts my lips, creating a soft hum to escape. I pour myself into this kiss, wanting to erase the thought completely from his mind. I pull back and press my forehead against his.

"Don't ever think that again," I say with finality.

"Okay." He winds his hand around my ponytail, tugging it so it makes my head tilt back. "I like this defensive, possessive little minx you've turned into."

I smile. "You're mine. I protect what's mine." Our lips meet again and he lets go of my hair.

"That we can agree on. Okay, so are we clear about our living arrangements for now?"

"For now. We'll revisit the issue in a year," I say, placing one last kiss on his lips before we stand up.

"You better get back inside," he says, looking back at the door. "I just wanted to come by and tell you the good news. Feel up to a Boston road trip in a couple weeks?"

I smile and nod. "You know I'm always up for a Boston trip."

"Maybe I'll book us in the same hotel as before."

"Two rooms again?" I ask, raising an eyebrow to him.

He laughs, shaking his head. "Now that seems pointless, wouldn't you agree?"

"I suppose but I mean, for nostalgia purposes it'd be fun.

You can woo me all over and make me fall in love with you again."

Heat courses through my veins with the look James is giving me, making me forget that I'm standing on the cold cement steps in front of my house. It makes me want to rip off his hat, grab his hair and throw him down on the ground to get lost in his body.

"Don't give me that look. I know what that look means," he growls quietly in my ear.

I press my thighs together to try and quell the throbbing ache that just formed. "What look? This look?" I mimic the look again and watch as his eyes darken.

"Okay, now it's time for me to go. Be a good girl and go back to bed," he says, kissing my nose.

I stick my lower lip out and pout. "That's the kiss you're going to send me off to bed with? What am I, five?"

He laughs then places his hands on the sides of my neck, letting his thumbs brush over my cheekbones. "When you play games like that, yes. But I'll leave you with this instead."

Fireworks ignite behind my eyelids when our lips meet, sending shivers and goose bumps to run across my skin. My heart pounds harder in my chest as I wrap my arms around his neck while our lips move in sync with each other. It's soft and wet and highly romantic.

My favorite kind.

When he releases his hold on me, I turn around and watch him retreat backward down the sidewalk.

"I'll see you tomorrow at graduation," he says. He climbs into the cab of his truck as I blow a kiss goodnight to him. He presses it to his chest before driving back to his house.

I quietly tiptoe up the stairs back to my room, making sure to avoid Liam's room at all costs. I want to keep my ears from bleeding from the noises that may or may not be coming from there.

Crawling under the covers, I press my head down onto my pillow and close my eyes, dreaming of Boston.

The next evening everyone is milling about in the gymnasium, creating a cacophony of loud voices and clicking heels as they wait to file outside where the graduation ceremony will take place on the football field.

Penny runs up to me, holding onto her cap so it doesn't fly off her head. "This is it," she loudly squeals.

I smile and give her a brief hug. "This is it, the final page of our high school career. It's kind of bittersweet, isn't it?"

Her lips twist to the side before breaking into a smile. "Hell no. I'm excited about the future. Life on our own, no parents, total freedom."

"Bills, homework, buying our own food," I add, bringing her back down to earth.

"Yeah, but it's totally worth it."

"So Liam is okay with you being away from him?" I ask.

Her smile falls slightly, but she recovers it. "No, but we're going to make it work. I mean, NYU isn't that far away."

I shake my head. "You're right, it's not. Just a train ride away. You'll make it work, I know it."

"I hope so. I'm a little afraid of being there by myself. Liam said that he's going to try to come down as often as he can."

"It's a shame you decided not to attend Boston College. We could hang out all the time."

She crinkles her nose. "And be the third wheel between you and James? No thanks. Besides, you need some alone time together now that you'll be able to be in public and all."

"It still doesn't feel real to me, you know?"

She wraps me in another hug and smiles. "Believe me, it's real." She winks at someone over my shoulder.

"Congratulations Ms. Morris, Ms. Fosse."

His voice causes the familiar fluttering of wings to stir up in my stomach as I turn around and come face to face with him.

"Thank you, Mr. Dumont," Penny says. "We sure are going to miss you around here but hey, congrats on the new job."

James smiles brightly and straightens his tie. "Thank you. I'm very excited about my new position and can't wait to start this fall."

"I bet you can't," Penny says suggestively.

I roll my eyes at her and can't help the laugh that escapes. "Yes, thank you, Mr. Dumont. Your new job sounds exciting. And Boston, you know I love Boston."

James winks at me and shoves his hands into his pockets, another nervous gesture of his. "I've heard this a time or two from you."

The need to reach out and touch him is so strong that I'm having difficulty fighting it. But then Cami, Justice, and Dez walk up to us, quashing the feelings like a bucket of cold water to my overly raging libido.

"Hey, Mr. Dumont. I hear congratulations are in order for the new job," Cami says.

"Yeah, Boston. Wow, that's so exciting," Dez exclaims.

Justice turns to me and twists her mouth. "Britt, aren't you going to Harvard?"

My cheeks flush and I nod. "Yes."

The girls look back and forth between James and me. Can they read my thoughts? A knowing smirk comes across Cami's face and her eyes twinkle with amusement. Then Dez and Justice share a look that confirms my suspicions. Let's hope they never get into playing poker when they're on their own.

"Thank you, ladies, for the kind wishes. I'm sad to leave here but I'm excited to open up the next chapter in my life." James avoids looking at me, even though there's no point.

"So you'll be able to keep an eye out for our girl then while she's there in the big city all by herself?" Dez asks.

Now it's James's turn to flush. "I'll see what I can do. There's a chance we may run into each other."

I clear my throat, wanting to change the subject. "Well, I appreciate that very much."

"Mr. Dumont," someone calls from behind him. James turns around and waves to the person while smiling at them.

"Looks like I'm needed elsewhere. If you'll excuse me, ladies."

"Bye, Mr. Dumont," we all chant in unison, making James shake his head while he leaves our little group.

Of course, the onslaught of questions starts immediately when he's out of earshot.

"Whoa, seriously? You and Mr. Dumont?"

"When did this all happen?"

"How long have you been together?"

"Is he great in bed?"

"He looks like a good kisser. Is he?"

"Will you shut up!" I hiss, holding up my hands. "Look, we can't say anything for at least another week because we don't want to rub it in the school's face." I sigh and look around quickly since they're not satisfied with that answer. "Okay, we've been together for a while. It's a long story and I promise to tell you after graduation. We'll get together and have a girls' night out and I'll give you most of the details."

"Only most?" Cami pouts.

I laugh. "I'm not telling you everything. But just to tide you over until then, yes, James is a fantastic kisser. One of the best, if not the best."

Dez sighs and brings her hands up to her chest. "That's so romantic."

"Ladies and gentlemen, may I have your attention, please," Mr. Leonard says as a lull falls across the room. "Thank you. If we could get everyone to line up, we'll start the procession outside. I just wanted to take this moment to say how proud I am of each and every one of you. It has been my greatest privilege to be your principal for the last four years. May you succeed in your endeavors of the future and I can't wait to read about your successes in the newspapers and magazines."

Claps and cheers erupt as we begin to line up in the order that was practiced earlier today. I smooth down my gown, admiring the look of my strappy sandals underneath. My hair falls in gentle waves over my shoulders with my cap secured to my head, courtesy of the bobby pins left over from prom. I wave to Penny, who's standing a few rows behind me, and she gives me a thumbs up.

When the doors open, we walk toward the football field where our parents and loved ones have all gathered to see this moment. So many memories have happened at this school, ranging from my first serious boyfriend to getting straight A's in all my classes to joking around with my friends after a football game. But the most significant memory will be the day that I ran into James. That moment changed my life forever. I experienced love at this school and it's almost bittersweet to be saying goodbye.

As we file into our seats that have been placed on the field, I scan the crowd to look for my family. It doesn't take long, mainly because Liam is standing up and waving his hands around like a fool. Whether or not it's for Penny or me, I don't know. Mom is sitting next to him, crying because her baby is graduating. Dad has his arm wrapped around her, half-smirking and trying to be serious at the same time. She waves him away when he whispers something into her ear and it makes me laugh. Even though I'll be off living my own life, I will miss them.

Then I look at the faculty section and try to find James. That's a little trickier because they're on the stage facing us. Since they're higher and not in stadium seating, I can't see their faces. The one person I do see is the newly reformed Ms. Hathaway. Since her incident with Chase, her wardrobe has changed considerably. Gone are the days of short skirts and skin-tight shirts. She's taken on a more simple style, mostly slacks and blouses. And she stays away from all the students and teachers unless there's a gathering of them around. Apparently she's learned her lesson the hard way.

The band finishes playing the school song and Mr. Leonard gets up to the podium to address the crowd. I sit and listen, taking everything in. This is it, my last day of high school. It just doesn't seem real. From now on I'll be accountable for myself and for my actions. People will treat me differently, as an adult and not a child. Am I ready for that? Am I really prepared to face the world and all that's waiting for me?

I press my lips together and I realize that I am prepared to face the world, to discover new things and experiences. Then I think about what James said last night about me living on campus the first year. As much as it kills me to be away from him, I know that I would lose a piece of myself if I constantly cling to him. He's the love of my life, but he's also right about me needing to live on my own, discover who I am and what I want to be. I could change my mind a million times about where my path will take me, except for one thing. My path will always lead to James, regardless of where we are. We will always find our way back to each other.

After a few more speakers and a performance by the choir, it's finally time to hand out our diplomas. I play with the cord around my neck, making sure that it's even. I wasn't shocked when they said I would be graduating with high honors but when they told me I was graduating third in my class, I couldn't believe it. Luckily it also meant I did not have to give a speech. Thank God for that.

My row stands and we start making our way to the side of the stage. I twist my fingers in front of me, anxious and nervous all at once. Crossing that stage is closing a door in my life. But when one door closes, another opens. And I'm excited to walk through it.

Mr. Leonard calls my name and I can hear the embarrassing sounds my family is making. My cheeks flush with color as I walk across the stage, giving them a small wave. I look to my right and finally I'm able to see James sitting in the second row behind the podium. He gives me a wink and I beam at him. I take my diploma from Mr. Leonard, shaking his hand before walking around him and switching my tassel from one side to the other on my cap.

As I retake my seat, I silently watch my friends and classmates do the same. We're graduates. Adults. Creators of our own destinies.

"Ladies and gentlemen, I present to you the graduating class of 2016."

Hats fly into the air. Loud cheers drown out any noise not coming from the field where we're standing. Confetti and silly string cling to my hair as they fall around me. I join in with the noise makers and hug everyone around me. The crowd erupts in laughter and joins us on the field to partake in the festivities.

Am I going to miss this?

Probably.

Am I looking forward to the future?

I catch James's eye and blow a kiss to him.

With my future directly in front of me, I know it's going to be one crazy, exciting adventure.

Epilogue

One Year Later

"SO WHAT ARE YOU PLANS FOR THE SUMMER?" TRACY asks me. She has been the best roommate ever for my freshman year and I'm sad to see her go back home to Louisiana.

"I'm moving into James's place and getting a really cool summer job."

She laughs and shakes her head. "Starbucks?"

"Probably. There isn't a whole lot to choose from, being a lowly undergrad and all," I say, laughing a little.

"But you're going to write me often, right?" she asks while sitting on her suitcase so she can zip it.

"Definitely. And you're going to send me pictures of your backpacking trip through Europe?"

She smiles and hugs me. "You're number one on my list." We hug for a few more moments before breaking away. "I'm going to miss you."

Tears well in my eyes and I blink them away before they can fall. "I'll miss you too. But hey, we'll see each other in a couple of months. I mean, we're both still in the pre-med program. We're still going to have classes together."

"But it won't be the same if we're not living together. Are you sure you want to move in with James?"

I nod. "Absolutely. He promised me that we'd revisit the issue after my freshman year so I think we're both ready to move on to the next step."

Tracy sinks into her chair and sighs. "You two are so cute together. And the story of how you came to be is just the most romantic in the world."

I sit across from her on my bed with my legs crossed beneath me. "It took a lot of work, but it was totally worth it. James is the best thing that ever happened to me."

"Even if it meant I kept knocking you down on your ass?" I hear a familiar voice call out from the doorway.

James walks in, dressed in his casual jeans and t-shirt, which clings to every inch of lean muscle on his body.

"Is that your way of saying you swept me off my feet?" I ask, patting the bed next to me.

He sits and laughs. "No, that's my way of saying you don't pay attention to your surroundings."

Tracy laughs with him. "I can second that motion. I think I've been to the campus clinic more times with her than I've been to my own doctor my entire life."

I scoff at the both of them. "I am not that clumsy. And it was one time we had to go to the clinic. One time!"

"Yeah, but that one time was because you were running across campus and looking at something over your shoulder and didn't see the *giant* tree in front of you."

"Geez, you get one lump on the head and all of a sudden

you've been labeled a klutz for life."

James smiles and kisses my forehead. "Just promise me that you'll be more careful when there's a scalpel in your hand."

I stand and grab my bags at the end of my bed, wanting to end this conversation. "Well if you two are quite done with the Britta bashing, I think we should head out." I turn to Tracy for one last hug. "Drive safe and call me when you get there."

She squeezes me back and brushes a tear away from her face. "I will. Bye, James. It was nice to see you again."

They shake hands and wave goodbye as James helps me with the last of my things. We've been slowly moving my stuff into his house over the past week, leaving only the basic necessities, which are all packed in these bags now.

"You know, it's a good thing I found a large two bedroom house to rent because with all your stuff, there won't be any room left."

I shove his shoulder as he loads the suitcases into the bed of the truck, shutting the tailgate and fixing the cover on top. Climbing into the passenger's seat, I wait for James to slide in next to me.

Grabbing his neck, I pull him gently toward me, needing to feel his lips on mine.

"Hey," I breathe.

He tucks a strand of hair behind my ears and smiles. "Hey. Did you miss me?"

I sit back and buckle my seatbelt. "Always. But I didn't give you a proper hello up there so I wanted to make sure I did that."

A mischievous smile appears on his face as he reverses out of the parking spot. "I can think of a better way to say hello when we get back to our place."

Our place.

Finally we have a place to be together, and alone. Where

we can be ourselves and worship each other and make dinners together while dancing to the stereo playing in the background. We'll lay on the couch and he'll read to me while stroking my hair or I'll massage his shoulders after a long day at work and take care of his every need.

"What are you thinking about?" James asks as he pulls into the driveway.

"Oh, I'm just daydreaming about what we're going to do tonight."

We drop the suitcases to the floor as we enter the living room. Suddenly I'm scooped up into his arms and he walks us back outside with me clinging to his neck and squealing in surprise.

"What are you doing?"

"I'm going to carry you into our house," he says. We cross the threshold and he gently places me down in the living room.

"You're crazy. I thought only newlyweds did that?"

"We're kind of like newlyweds, just not official yet," he says.

My heart doubles its beats at the thought of being his wife. Yes, we're young but what's the point in waiting when you know what you want?

I walk over to the bookcase and admire the pictures while James goes into the kitchen to start making us dinner. My finger trails over a photo of the two of us at the top of the Empire State Building, fulfilling one of the promises that James and I made. He told me he would take me to New York, just the two of us. And he did. Of course, we visited Penny while we were there but to see the sights with James was absolutely incredible.

My homecoming queen tiara sits on the shelf as well, along with a photo of me that he snagged from my mom in my dress. James comes up behind me and wraps his arms tightly around my waist. He rests his chin on my shoulder and I lean my head against his.

"You looked so beautiful that night," he whispers into my ear. A shiver runs down my spine as his lips make contact with the skin of my neck.

"Remember sneaking our kiss in the hall that night?" I ask, tilting my head to allow him better access. His warm lips continue to trail along my skin, running up and down the pulsing vein, beating in time with my desire for him.

He places a kiss behind my ear and pulls away slightly. Reaching over, he grabs the tiara and puts it on my head. "I believe someone promised me a raincheck for a dance with the queen."

I bite my lip and smile. "I believe I did."

James quickly walks over to the stereo and selects a song from our collective playlist. A guitar plays, soon followed by a piano. It's a familiar song, but I'm having a problem remembering the title.

He holds his hand out to me and smiles. "May I have this dance?"

I nod and fold myself into his arms, melting completely into him until we are one. He guides us across the living room, swaying in time to the song and whispering his love into my ear. My body is so hyped up that I don't even hear the music anymore. All I can hear, all I can feel is James.

I lean my head against his chest and feel his heart beating against my cheek. It's pounding faster than usual, causing me to look up in concern.

"What's wrong? Your heart is racing right now," I say, placing my hand on his cheek.

He wraps his hand around my wrist, slowly bringing it down. "Nothing is the matter. Everything is perfect."

We stop swaying and stand in the middle of the room. He

holds my hands in his and without breaking eye contact looks straight into my soul.

"Remember you had asked me before about all the promises we've made to each other and how we're going to remember what they were?" I nod. "Well, I remember each and every one of them. I remember the promise to dance with the homecoming queen so we can check that one off right now. Then there was the promise to take you to New York. We can cross that one off the list as well. We're also free now to be together and have been for the past year so we can cross that one off too. Then there's the promise to love each other until the end of time."

I squeeze his hand and smile. "That we can cross off because there's no one else I will ever love but you."

He releases a hand to run it down my cheek. "I know, sweetheart. And now that you're moving in here we can keep the promise of never separating because you're never leaving my side."

"So that's all of them, right?" I ask because I honestly don't know how he remembered all those things that we promised in the heat of the moment.

"Almost."

He sinks down on one knee and pulls out a ring from his pocket. A beautiful diamond solitaire sits on a platinum band, surrounded by several smaller diamonds. It must be about one karat in weight at least. My hands fly to my mouth and shake slightly at the sight of it.

"Britta Rosalind Fosse, you are the best thing that has ever happened to me. The day I found you was the happiest day of my life. All the trials we were put through only solidified my feelings for you because if we could survive it all, I knew we were meant to be together. You are my love, my match, my promise to keep, and I will love you until the day I die and then forever after that. So I'm asking you if you'll take my hand in marriage and be my wife. Marry me, Britta."

He slides the ring on my finger and the tears start to fall. His green eyes shine as I nod my head, unable to find the words.

"Yes," I squeak out. "Yes, I'll marry you."

He stands and cradles my face, kissing me with every ounce of his being. I wrap my arms around him and return his love tenfold. The crown falls off my head and rolls across the room as we move to the couch. We fall into a heap with him underneath me, our lips never once breaking our connection.

"I love you," he whispers. His eyes are wet but are smiling at the same time.

"I love you too. I told you I'd say yes if you asked."

His hand travels up my side, touching the skin beneath my shirt as it wanders across my body. "Yes, you did. Now we just have one more thing to cross off our list before we make a new list of promises to each other."

"And what's that?" I ask.

He deftly rolls us over so I'm pinned to the back of the couch. He lifts my shirt off, tossing it carelessly to the floor. "I do believe there was a promise of resuming a particular couch activity a while ago."

Heat crawls across my skin as I vaguely remember the night he's talking about, the night he rescued me from Drake's party. "Oh yes, before we were rudely interrupted by my brother's phone call."

My bra and shorts are the next to come off, leaving me just in my panties. I pull his shirt over his head while he works on the button of his jeans, sliding them down his legs and kicking them off. We work the last remaining pieces of clothing off before adjusting so I'm directly underneath him.

"I can't believe in all the times we've been together we've

never christened this couch," he says, sliding a hand between my legs. I'm wet and ready for him, aching to feel more than his touch, craving that connection that makes us one.

"Such fools we were," I gasp as he hits the spot which drives me wild.

"Not anymore." He guides himself inside me, sliding in inch by inch until he's completely sheathed. I gasp at the fullness and then sigh, clinging to his back as he slowly rocks back and forth into me.

We worship each other's body, moving into several positions, kissing each available inch of skin that our mouths can reach. James brings me to orgasm twice before finding his own release inside me. We lay there with me sprawled on top of him, sweaty and panting while kissing him slowly and reverently.

Life can be complicated and hard at times but with his love, I know we can overcome anything. And we keep proving it over and over again, making sure that nothing ever gets in our way.

Acknowledgements

Words cannot express my proper gratitude to everyone who has helped in making this book. There have been some ups and downs, tears and laughs, excitement and heartache. But each and every emotion I felt was completely worth it in the end because this book turned out beautifully.

To my husband, who gives me the support I need to keep writing these stories. His constant encouragement, letting me know how proud he is of me, lifts me up on the days where I question my sanity. Thank you for being my sounding board when I need to vent and telling me that I can do anything as long as I put my mind to it.

Billie – Again, you've helped me in more ways than I could have ever dreamed of. You've read this book chapter by chapter from day one, giving me feedback, even though it wasn't your favorite type of read. But, when you said that you loved it, that it was perfect and nothing needed to be changed, I knew that you were right. You're my rock and I love you every day for it!

Stacy – Thank you for always being there for me, for reading my drafts and giving me exactly the feedback I'm looking for, whether it's where I've turned wrong or where it's right. I can't thank you enough for it!

Megan – Thank you so much for talking me off the ledge

towards the end. Your support means so much to me and I wouldn't have been able to get to here without you.

Ashley – My book sister! I'm so glad you loved James as much as I did and was willing to be an early reader for me. Thank you for believing in me, for talking me down and picking me back up when I needed it. I love you!

Melinda – Thank you so much for editing my baby for me. Your notes and emails picked me up when I was the most nervous after my confidence was shaken toward the end. I can't thank you enough.

To my girls, my VFFL, your friendship means the world to me. Your constant support keeps me believing in my dreams. I love you all more than you know!

To my fellow Vixen writers, you are all a bunch of amazing, talented writers and I'm thankful every day that we found each other.

Murphy – Once again you have designed a beautiful cover for me. You have such an incredible talent for creating beautiful designs. I'm in awe of your abilities and I'm so glad you've been able to make my book beautiful!

To all my friends and family, thank you for everything that you do for me each and every day, whether it's with a phone call or just a quick message to say hi. Your love and support mean the world to me.

To my readers, thank you so much for taking a chance on my book. Without you, I wouldn't be able to do this. Each and every one of you brightens my day and reminds me of why I do this. From the bottom of my heart, thank you!

About the Author

Jodie Larson is a wife and mother to four beautiful girls, making their home in northern Minnesota along the shore of Lake Superior. When she isn't running around to various activities or working her regular job, you can find her sitting in her favorite spot reading her new favorite book or camped out somewhere quiet trying to write her next manuscript. She's addicted to reading (just ask her kids or husband) and loves talking books even more so with her friends. She's also a lover of all things romance and happily ever afters, whether in movies or in books, as shown in her extensive collection of both.

Other books written by Jodie Larson:
Fated to be Yours
Fated to be Mine

You can find Jodie at:

Facebook: www.facebook.com/jodielarsonauthor
Twitter: www.twitter.com/jlarsonauthor
Instagram: www.instagram.com/jodielarson

25354815R00193

Made in the USA
Columbia, SC
04 September 2018